THE VIPERS' CLUB

John H. Richardson

D0996787

Hodder & Stoughton

British Library Cataloguing in Publication Data

Richardson, John
The vipers' club
1. English fiction – 20th century
I.Title
823.9′14[F]

ISBN 0 340 66684 6

Printed and bound in Great Britain by
Mackays of Chatham PLC., Chatham, Kent.

Hodder and Stoughton
A division of Hodder Headline PLC
338 Euston Road
London NW1 3BH

THE VIPERS' CLUB

For Joel Silver,
who gave me something to write about,
and Susan Lyne,
who gave me a chance to write it.

This book is a work of fiction. Although I put a few real people into brief scenes, the things they do and say are also fiction. The rest of my cast is made up. Really. So please don't blame the actions of Max Fischer or Jennings West or Alan Kramer or Peter James or Barry Rose or Tracy Rose or the rest on any real person. It's not even a roman à clef. Okay?

ACKNOWLEDGEMENTS

Thanks to Laurie Frank for helping so much and so often; Deborah Pines for cheering me through the dark days of serialization; Michael Giltz for factpicking every paragraph; Alan Schechter for teaching me about the chain of pain and suffering (in theory *and* practice); Michael Levy for a critical plot suggestion; Chris Connelly for his baseball expertise; Susanna Sonnenberg for exceptional devotion to English prose; Anne Sterling for telling me what kind of Hollywood novel she *didn't* want to read; Martin Booe and Sarah Towers for listening to the constant whining; Sandy Dijkstra for her astonishingly aggressive salesmanship (who says testosterone is just a male problem?); Liza Dawson for wise and unobtrusive editing . . .

And Kathy and Julia and Rachel for everything else.

'A producer is a guy wandering around
Hollywood with two pieces of bread,
looking for a piece of cheese.'

– Larry Gordon, producer

Part One:

The Whipped-Cream Bikini

Chapter One

'Pastrami.'

Max Fischer never said hello on the phone. He just started in talking, and he usually didn't stop until he'd coasted a few hundred yards onto verbal gravel. 'Pastrami on rye with mustard and a pickle,' he continued. 'I wouldn't have called you so late, but this is a *clinical emergency*. What are you doing? Sitting around feeling sorry for yourself? Wallowing in the *slough of despond*?'

Peter rolled over and turned off the answering machine, picking up the phone and grunting 'Heymax' into the mouthpiece.

'I want Canter's,' he said. 'And don't let 'em forget the pickle. In fact, get an extra pickle. Get a couple of them. Get *five* of them.'

Peter looked at the digital clock – it read 11:03 – and realized that he'd fallen asleep. He seemed to be exhausted all the time lately. And he had a hot date scheduled for that very night, in just fifty-seven minutes. 'You want a pastrami sandwich,' he said calmly.

'Yes,' said Max. 'On rye.'

'I didn't think you wanted it on an egg roll.'

Max chuckled a little. 'I hope it's not *inconvenient* for you.'

Peter had degrees from some of the finest schools in the country. He published his first essay on film when he was still in high school, an eccentric personal meditation that appeared in *Ciné Action!* At twenty-five he became one of the youngest associate professors in the history of Columbia University. Six months later a small press approached him about publishing his collected essays. Which was when Merwin 'Max' Fischer came along and offered to triple his salary overnight. Somehow Fischer had come across an article Peter had written attacking his films – 'classic examples of Hollywood's lurid prurience, sentimentally violent and violently sentimental, antique prayer beads thumbed to a dream of change.' Fischer called him up and started talking sans introduction. 'You're right, I make shitty films, so come *work* with me, help me, *save me from myself*.'

At that point, Peter still didn't know who was talking. 'You don't understand what it's like here,' the voice continued. 'It's a closed ecosystem. I need someone who can think for himself, someone from the outside, someone who's not afraid to say what he thinks. And you – you *slaughtered* me, you *killed* me. I mean, come on, whaddaya want to do – you wanna write these little essays all your life? Or do you want to come to Hollywood and *make movies*?'

Peter flew out for an interview, and for three days Max put him up in a bougainvillea-covered apartment in the hills and took him to parties every night. For Peter it was like being let out of prison – everyone dressed so well, ate so well, lived in such beautiful houses. And they were all so young, so energized. He met the legendary Jeffrey Katzenberg, the bionic executive, and was surprised and touched when Katzenberg made a clever film-history reference for his benefit. He met the formidable Mike Ovitz, called 'the most powerful man in Hollywood' by a fawning press, right up until the day he took the number-two job at Disney. Ovitz shook Peter's hand warmly and looked deep into his eyes. 'Good to meet you,' he said. And he seemed to mean it.

There were women at the parties too, but they weren't the bimbos he expected. They looked about twenty-eight, smart-but-casual dressers, and gave off an air of alarming efficiency. And they also looked into Peter's eyes. 'Welcome to L.A.,' they said, with knowing smiles.

Most of all, there was Max, spitting out theories and gossip and history like a spot-welder throwing off sparks. Peter was amazed that he was only thirty-nine – like the Hollywood moguls of old, already tycoons in their twenties, he combined the energy of a young man with the authority of an old one. Peter had never met anyone like him.

It was February, but Peter quit in the middle of the term, convinced that this was what he'd been looking for all his life. He felt bad about abandoning his students, but the fact was they'd be better off without him: As a scholar, he was a fraud. Looking deep within his heart (on the balcony of his temporary apartment, watching the flirtatious twinkle of the lights in the hills), he had to admit he didn't really care about ideas, at least not that much – he just liked movies. They were the only part of life that moved fast enough. He was born to live in L.A., the designated homeland for America's malcontents? Wasn't L.A. the one city where life moved as fast as the movies? Certainly Max did – he didn't even want to let Peter fly back to pack up – he needed him *yesterday*, for chrissake, *they had work to do*. So Peter ended up paying for a moving company to go to his studio apartment and pack up his dog-eared paperbacks, most of which he threw out the day they arrived. Theory was over. It was time for practice.

Within a week the bitter truth dawned: He was nothing but a flunky, a peon, a slave, his responsibilities no more dignified than placing phone calls and finding exactly which store in town carried the best all-cotton boxer shorts, and heaven help him if he ever said *Yes Max right away Max* a few seconds too late. The lecture would go on for an hour.

It took just one more week and a few eruptions of Mount Fischer ('Think! I thought *at least* you knew how to think!') for Peter to call his department chairman to sniff around his old job, only to be told that his bridge back to academe was burned, finished, over, nothing left but puckered cinders and shanks of smoking metal. *Betrayal* and *sellout* were among the kinder words used. When he hung up the phone Peter checked his bank account: Depleted by his new books, car, apartment and wardrobe, it held exactly $374.52.

'So what you're primarily interested in at this time is a pastrami on rye with mustard and a pickle,' Peter said.

Max answered tersely. 'Yes.'

Peter looked at the clock again. He now had fifty-two minutes before his date, the latest episode in a furtive and dangerous romance he had been working on for weeks, scheduled for consummation this very night. They were going to meet in a room at the famous Château Marmont. She had given him detailed instructions: She would check in first, under a false name, and he was to call her on the house phone, get the room number, then come straight up. She would be waiting, naked . . .

'Then why don't you let me call Greenblatt's and have them deliver,' Peter said. 'That would save me a trip, and since right now I'm tangled in a moist love knot with three lovely Norwegian bodybuilders . . .'

'I want *Canter's*,' Max said. 'Canter's is an institution. If you knew anything about this town you would know that. Now, please, get me the sandwich. And hurry.'

Max took a beat, then added grudgingly: 'Get yourself something too – we got work to do.'

Uh oh. Max was acting almost human. He even said please. Something must really be bothering him. Which made Peter especially nervous, because even in a mere three months Peter had learned that Max was always kindest to those he was about to destroy. With a sigh, he gave in: 'So let me make sure I've got it right – pastrami on white with mayo, right?'

'Fuck you, Peter,' Max said, hanging up the phone.

He never said good-bye either.

It took Peter only twenty-seven minutes to drive to Canter's, pick up the food, and shoot up La Cienega to Max's place in the Hollywood Hills, truly heroic driving. Max took it as his due.

'Hey,' he said, opening the door in his bathrobe and immediately turning back inside. 'Bring it upstairs.'

Even in a glimpse Max was striking – black hair perfectly disheveled, nose like a hunting knife stabbing down his face, black bushy eyebrows like tiny storm clouds that somehow got caught on his nose. After years of obsessive exercise – he sometimes jogged twice a day, morning and night – he was almost as pumped as some of his stars, but he still tied his bathrobe under a little pot belly, like Toshiro Mifune in *Yojimbo*. Goddamn if Max Fischer was going to give up French fries and pâté just to look perfect – he *hired* people to look perfect! Most striking of all were his eyes, which seemed to be wired directly to his brain: One minute they were large and sensitive, flooded by thought, and the next minute they fused into hard bright beads, so impatient they seemed ready to pop out of their sockets and do the job themselves.

Peter followed Max through the dark house, which was full of ladders and scaffolding and drop cloths. Max had bought it six months ago, paying a few million, a modest price by Hollywood standards, but within weeks of moving in he started to see imperfections, little flaws that *upset the harmony of the house*, and started calling in architects, decorators, landscape designers, contractors. Within a month half the rooms were gutted, and now a rising young architect named Yoji was redesigning the entire place in a minimalist

Zen style – Max told everyone he needed simplicity and purity to balance the chaos of his professional life. Meanwhile he lived out of his upstairs bedroom, which was about the size of Versailles, so it wasn't a particular hardship.

When Peter got in the bedroom, Max snatched the Canter's bag out of his hand and looked inside. 'Lot of pickles,' he said.

'I got extra.'

'I asked for *five* pickles and you got *extra*?'

Peter shrugged. 'I didn't want you to go without, should *the urge for still another pickle* take you.'

By his second week on the job, Peter was talking in italics. It took unusual strength of character to be around Max without picking up his habits.

Max was trying to decide whether to take the bait. Then he held up the second sandwich. 'Is this for you?' he asked.

'Unless you want it,' Peter said.

Max grabbed both sandwiches and walked to the bed. He spread out the wax paper, poured out the entire bag of pickles, and took a bite out of one sandwich. Then he picked up a clicker from the bedside table and aimed it at the window curtains. There came a whirring sound and the curtains began to rise, gathering in scallops like the curtains of a movie theater. The windows framed a vast bed of gold lights, the Los Angeles basin pulsing in the darkness, the balmy spring air paradisiacally thick with the sweet smell of night-blooming jasmine. But Max didn't so much enjoy the view as take possession of it and move on – *next*. He picked up the second sandwich, sniffed it, then took a bite. Now both were marked.

'So,' Max said, 'you want to know what's going on?'

'What's going on, Max?'

'Then you admit you don't know what's going on? You admit your *abysmal ignorance*?'

It was his usual teasing, but in an unusually forceful tone. 'It goes without saying,' Peter said.

Max smiled, a sour smile of small triumph. 'Richard Lovett just called.'

Lovett was an agent at the Creative Artists Agency. 'And?'

'Guess whose window just opened.'

Peter tried to think who Lovett's clients were. He drew a blank.

'Hanks.'

Peter tried not to look too surprised. 'Tom Hanks?'

'Lovett said he'd commit to a September start on *Lone Justice* with any one of these,' Max said, tossing Peter a faxed list of ten directors – all action directors, from Dick Donner to Walter Hill.

'What does that say to you?' Max asked.

It could only mean one thing: Hanks was tired of winning Oscars, and wanted to try a stretch in the other direction, to the Great American Testosterone-fueled Epic. Peter reached for the right phrase to express it. Something appropriately Max-like.

'He's ready to carry a gun?'

Max smiled. 'Ride 'em, cowboy,' he said.

Then Peter frowned, teasing out a vague memory. Wasn't there some kind of feud between Max and Hanks? 'But . . . didn't you . . .' He remembered now: Max had been fighting with the producer of *Apollo 13* over some damn thing and had trashed the movie all over town. Hanks, usually not the touchy type, chose to take it personally.

'Ancient history,' Max said. 'In this town *I'll never speak to you again* means *Don't call me for at least two weeks – unless you have a job to offer*. Now don't you have something to *say*? Or do I have to spend the rest of the fucking night teaching you *Hollywood fucking one-oh-one*?'

Max spoke in such a bitter voice that Peter actually felt a chill. He knew from experience that if Max was irritable and decided to fixate on some real or imagined error, it could lead to an avalanche of kvetching and badgering – and in extreme cases a climax in one of the famous Fischer tirades, spit-flecking, arm-waving eruptions of unstoppable rage that Peter compared (after seeing one for the first time) to a TV spot for the World Federation of Wrestling – I'm Mad Max and I'm gonna rip your arms off and *stuff 'em down your throat*! He was still waiting for Peter to catch on. What does he want me to guess, Peter wondered. What am I supposed to say?

A blue light on the telephone pulsed silently: Max's private line. Peter started to reach for it and Max flashed out a hand, traffic cop-style. 'Leave it,' he said.

Peter shrugged. Then he figured it out. 'Let's start making calls,' he said.

If they hurried, maybe he could still make his date.

Max nodded, waiting for more. Peter had to prove himself. No bluffing.

'What's the area code for Cannes?' Peter added.

At last Max smiled. It was breakfast time at the Cannes Film Festival, and almost every player who might end up in the Hanks deal happened to be there. With luck they could catch some of them either starting an early day or ending a late one. 'I was beginning to think you were a moron,' he said.

Then the smile vanished. It took less than a second for clouds to gather and lightning to flash. 'Call Donner first,' Max barked, stuffing his face with pastrami and rye. 'And call Jack and Rick and some of the older guys to make sure they're into a piece of this – I don't want them screwing things up just to mess with the Turks. Fucking place has been a shark pool since Mike and Ronnie left.'

Max paused for a millisecond, which for him was a significant chunk of reflective time. 'And ask 'em if Gwyneth Paltrow is available that month,' he added. 'I love her for the girl.'

Usually the phrase made Peter smile. He'd heard it at least a hundred times in the last ninety days. 'What do you think of so-and-so for the girl?' 'I like so-and-so for the girl.' 'She'd be great for the girl.' It made him smile because it reminded him he was in Hollywood, and in Hollywood there is always a girl. And though few things were lower than a starlet (they called them MAWs – model, actress, whatever), it was still a place dedicated to the spirit of the girl, the iconic girl, the lubricious-life-force-brown-skinned-white-breasted-long-legged-*girl* – and not in the furtive way of academe, where long skirts and tangled hair denied the obvious, but with the most shameless and avid hunger. 'I love her for the girl . . . I love her . . . for . . . *the girl.*'

But tonight there seemed to be something particularly predatory in the phrase, in the way Max leaped so quickly to it. Maybe it was just his impatience to leave, but Peter pictured Max as a wild beast, hunched over a pale body, some slip of a thing, tattered lace drooling from his teeth.

'Better get cranking,' Max said. 'I'm sure that the minute he put down the phone, Lovett called Jerry Bruckheimer and Joel Silver and Brian fucking Grazer and said, "Guess what, *you're the first to know*, Tom's available."'

'How do you know he called *you* first?' asked Peter.

'Fuck you, you piece of shit,' Max said. It was his way of being affectionate.

With that they got to work.

An hour later Max was winding down the last few calls, negotiating for an actor on another movie – might as well, since they were already burning up the international lines. 'Fine. Don't compromise. We've got a lousy two-hundred-and-fifty-grand difference, and the studio is not going to change its mind, and *I'm telling you*, if you want the deal to fall apart over that, fine – it won't hurt the studio, it won't hurt you, it won't hurt your client. *The only person it will hurt is me.* And that's good – I like to be hurt. It makes me *work* harder.'

When Max hung up he ranted for a while about the perfidy of agents – they didn't care about the *business*, they were *parasites*, they were ruining everything, killing the goose, pissing in the champagne. Then he remembered his latest film, *Romulux 147*, a futuristic version of Shakespeare's *Romeo and Juliet*. It was three days from the director's-cut deadline – according to the Directors Guild rules, a movie director gets ten weeks alone at the flatbed editing table before he has to show his cut to anyone – and the ungrateful little ponytailed bastard still wouldn't let Max into the cutting room. 'I gave him his *shot*! I hired him off a *video*, for chrissake!'

Again the blue pulse of the private line. Max shook his head and turned away, walking to the window. Peter looked at his watch. After one. Max wouldn't even go to the bathroom so he could sneak a phone call, the lunatic bastard. Was she still waiting? 'Well,' Peter said, faking a yawn. 'I guess we both better get some sleep.'

Max was standing at the windows looking over the city. After a particularly hard flurry of work, he sometimes allowed himself a pensive moment – not often, though. Usually he just plunged on. Peter waited silently. When Max turned from the window, Peter was startled by his face – dark, drawn, anxious. 'Let's go over the project list,' Max said.

Peter sighed. The project list had exactly one hundred and twelve entries, ranging from raw story ideas to finished scripts, annotated with writers and directors and would-be associate producers and executive producers and relevant studio executives and the dates of various rewrites. Going through it meant discussing at length everything from the validity of the concept to the fitness of the various participants – and even more pertinent issues, such as *Can we bump that fucker off, no way I'm sharing credit*. They'd gone over the damn thing twice this week already. 'Max, it's one in the morning . . .'

Max lingered at the window, looking down at the city lights. 'Millions of people down there,' he said. 'And we're up here.'

But he didn't sound happy about it – he sounded afraid.

'Four: boom,' Peter ventured.

Max curled the corner of his mouth with a tired smile.

'Five: ha-ha,' he said.

The lines were from an old *Road Runner* cartoon. Max described it to Peter on his first day – Wile E. Coyote was looking at a building plan for one of his insane bird-killing contraptions. The first three steps showed the machine, and the fourth and fifth showed the point of it all. Four: boom. Five: ha-ha. It was one of the Maxisms.

Then Max continued, picking up his thread without transition as he crossed the room, heading to his exercise corner. 'I just feel like too many of them are the *same*,' he said, climbing on his stationary bike.

'That's called having a style,' Peter said. He'd avoided Max Angry – now he had to steer the delicate course away from Max Morose.

'Yeah, but you can't sell the same fucking idea all the time,' Max said, switching from the bike to his treadmill. He got bored fast. He also had a StairMaster, a rowing machine, and some free weights, all facing the Max Fischer version of a votive altar: a TV and VCR flanked by inspirational pictures of Arnold Schwarzenegger and Fred Astaire (Max told friends he'd be happy to split the difference). Off to the side was a small framed photo of Fischer *père*, dressed in an expensive suit, with the plump red face of an Eastern European peasant. Peter thought it odd that Max would display the photo, since he'd gotten the impression that Max hated his father – he was hypercritical, ignored his son . . . maybe he drank? And there was no photo of his mother, who defended him against the old man's barbs and took him to all those character-forming Saturday matinees. But then Peter realized the choice made perfect sense: Max fed on hate. That fat red face probably got him out of bed in the morning.

'It's not like selling Coke,' Max continued. 'That's the nightmare of this fucking business – can you imagine if Roberto Goizueta had to come up with a new mixture for Coke for every can he sold? That's what we have to do here – *come up with a new Coke*! Every time! *Plus* mounting a goddamn marketing campaign for *every single can.*'

Peter didn't know what to say. All of Max's films *were* the same – all except the failures. The heroes were usually cyborgs who weren't really living until the love of a good babe (and an explosion of violence) transformed their lives forever, putting them in touch with their repressed human nature. The hero of *Romulux* was a 'haircut' on the theme, as Hollywood screenwriters say, just another all-American kid except for those pesky gills. It was a theme with particular resonance for Max, and he didn't seem to be able to do good work outside it. The irony was that he really preferred romantic comedies and was even known to weep when the boy got the girl.

Again, Peter sneaked a look at his watch. A real girl was waiting, and he was almost two hours late – damn Max for being such a madman. He felt like leaping up and stalking out.

Instead he ventured a small rebellion. 'It does seem like an awful lot of work,' he said, 'considering that the result is usually so trivial.'

Max stared at him as if he were insane.

'I mean, compared to *War and Peace* or something. Feeding the poor.'

'It must be my fault,' Max said. 'Because we know you're not *stupid*.'

'Max—'

'Clearly I haven't taught you anything.'

'Max—'

'Movies *are* trivial. They're *supposed* to be trivial. Triviality is our gift to a grateful world!'

At this point Max jumped off the rowing machine and started pacing around the room, throwing his arms around like a mad scientist explaining the universe. '*Serious quality movies are a historical aberration*,' he shouted. 'Read the first movie reviews in *The New York Times*! They all thought movies were strictly for the *masses*, just bells and whistles for the great unwashed, as far from art as a tits-and-feathers girl down in some Bowery burlesque joint. They *laughed* at the movies.'

The first time Peter had seen him like this, his third or fourth day on the job, he was convinced Max was in the middle of a nervous breakdown. But as he got to know Hollywood better, he realized that all producers were lunatics – or at least all the big ones were, the ones who worked with big stars and huge budgets. Even the most successful of them were always on the battlefield, always juggling razors, always one flop short of *nonexistence*. For them lunacy was practically a job requirement. There was a strange, modern kind of heroism at work in their daily lives – they had to throw all their energy into something that had no reality unless they were able to create it. Neither artists nor businessmen, but some unholy combination of the two, they were the essence of Hollywood, all its astonishing vitality and soul-destroying hunger distilled into a few strong draughts. And since that made them monsters too, all you had to do was add *the girl* and you had a whole fairy tale.

'But then these *artists* got into the mix,' Max continued, so upset now he was almost happy. 'D. W. Griffith started it all – and then movies got more and more complicated. And for a while these incredibly sophisticated European refugees made genius movies for a mass audience – Lubitsch, Wilder, von Stroheim. Fucking *geniuses*. But *then it ended*. The masses *changed*. They didn't want genius anymore – they wanted *shit*. And we changed with them. Because we *have* to change with them. That's our *job*. Do you understand – *that's our job*! So we became shit! And I *like* being shit. I feel I have a *solemn duty to be shit*.'

With that Max broke into a goofy grin, a flash of sunlight through black clouds, and for a moment Peter couldn't imagine why he ever thought of leaving him. He was so *alive*.

And just as quickly he whirled around again, and the grin turned to a frown. 'You think I'm a monster, don't you?' he demanded.

'I don't,' Peter answered, in the most reasonable voice possible. 'Sometimes you *act* like a monster—'

'You don't know what a monster *is*,' Max shouted. 'I'm so easy on you it's *unbelievable*. I *coddle* you. I *baby* you! I pat your bottom with *talcum* powder so you don't get a fucking *rash*!'

'Max—'

'I'll tell you what a monster is,' Max continued. 'One time Barry called me *from New York* and had me call room service – from Los Angeles – to order him breakfast. From *across the fucking country*. The man was *insane*.'

Uh oh. If Max started on Barry Rose, his former boss, his mentor, his show-biz father – and now his most bitter enemy – it would be a long night indeed. 'Max—'

'But I *learned* from him. I learned the concept of *service*. And that's ninety percent of a producer's job. *Service* the stars. *Service* the director. *Service* the production. That's how you *get things done*. And that's what Barry taught me, the hateful self-righteous pain-in-the-ass pathetic old mean-spirited son of a bitch – he *tore me down* and *built me back up again*. If you think I'm such a monster, blame Barry Rose. He *created me*.'

By now Peter had heard this tirade dozens of times. It was one of Max's favorite theories, that all producers were the Frankenstein monsters of their mentors. As Barry begat Max, so Max was creating Peter, passing on the ancient wisdom, putting the victim-prince through his initiation in the most gilded sweat lodge of all time. It was one of the secrets of Hollywood, the reason why the town motto was *Others Must Fail*. He thought again of the girl waiting for him and glanced outside at the black carpet of lawn plunging down the black hill, and beyond that to the flatlands far below where millions of lights shimmered, endless fields of them, or so it seemed, spreading out to the horizon like some magic crop waiting to be harvested.

When he finally got free, Peter raced to the Château, running every stop sign and half the lights. He parked on the hill and cut through the side gate, through the walled garden. The lobby was plastered in faded umber like an Italian monastery, complete with colonnades and arches, which was probably the reason why so many young Hollywood types chose it for their debauches: for the contrast. He found the house phone and asked for Marina Lake, his lover's *nom de boudoir*.

The phone rang six times before she picked it up. 'It's me,' he whispered.

'Mmmm?'

She seemed confused.

'It's me,' he repeated. 'Peter.'

After a moment's hesitation, she murmured the room number and dropped the phone in the general direction of the cradle. He heard it *clack* against hard plastic and then the ocean-in-a-seashell sound of an open phone line.

He hurried up the stairs and found the right door, then knocked and waited, heart pounding. Nothing. He knocked again, harder, looking up and down the hall and feeling unreasonably guilty. He was an adult. He had the right to do this. At last he heard a muffled voice: 'Coming.' Then the door swung open.

Tracy Rose stood there, naked, looking at him through half-mast eyes. She had short white nightclub-goddess hair, like Jean Seberg in *Breathless*, and small private eyes above outsize lips. Normally she looked like a sullen teenage vamp, the kind who paints her nails black and chainsmokes through smeared lipstick, but tonight, with her face puffy and the lips pooched out by sleep, she looked like a dreaming child. 'Gave up on you,' she croaked. Without another word, she turned and slipped back under the covers and rolled her back to him.

Peter still stood in the doorway, frozen by the glimpse of her naked body. It was beautiful, girlish, with white white skin and small breasts and an unexpectedly adult tangle of pubic hair. He had met her in a night club five weeks ago and they had spent every free night since making out in his car or at the movies – she was living with her father and wouldn't let him come home with her. She wouldn't even let him drop her off at the front gate – she would cut through the trees below her father's house and climb the wall into the backyard. Sometimes she let him sit on the wall and watch her open the door to the guest house. Then she would give him a little wave and disappear.

When he pushed it, inviting her to his apartment or begging her to set a date for consummation, she withdrew, accusing him of ugly motives. And she was right. His lust, at least part of it, was inspired by who she was – or rather, who her father was. And what Max would do if he found out. You could even say that Max had drawn them together. They were introduced at a nightclub by people who thought it would be funny, and when Tracy started talking about Max she was so vicious and accurate that Peter couldn't stop laughing. He even began to feel a little jealous.

But it was her too. She was just nineteen, young enough that everything was still urgent and absolute, but at the same time she was alarmingly jaded. Her sexual and drug escapades began at twelve, and by seventeen she had already left home and gone to live in Manhattan, where – while Peter lurked in the stacks of Butler Library like Bartelby the scrivener – she drugged and drank and danced till dawn in downtown nightclubs.

And he loved the bored way she talked about Hollywood, how she realized one day that when they called Hollywood *this town*, it wasn't just an affectation, it really was a town. It had a few local diners (The Grill, The Palm, Morton's), a squabbling city council (the studio heads), and lots and lots of meddling gossips working car phones instead of back fences. It had all the disadvantages of a small town too – everyone knew you, everyone had an opinion, you were watched – but it also had all the advantages, at least for her, because what you do in your hometown matters. You knew everyone, and they talked about you.

Or so she realized after a cocaine bust landed her in Riker's Island for a week. In a sick way, she said, she found herself missing even their disapproval – hell, she *liked* being talked about. There was drama in it, and recognition. What was the point of getting busted if nobody from home knew about it? So she decided to come back and enjoy the notoriety she had earned.

All of which was stimulating and exciting. But it wouldn't have added up to four weeks of hard dating if Tracy hadn't been so damn seductive – more sexual in everything she did than any person he had ever known. They didn't just kiss and cuddle in that car, not by a long shot: Parked at a golf course in Mar Vista three days after they met, she pulled back from a passionate kiss, yanked down his zipper, and leaned right over to take him in her mouth. Ignoring the suburbanites walking their dogs, she drooled, she growled, moved fast and hungry, and when it was finished she smiled and wiped her mouth with the back of her hand. Another time she stroked him to orgasm in a movie theater while watching *The Lover*. People saw; she didn't care.

But she wouldn't let him inside her. She wouldn't let him do anything to her at all. She wanted to be in control of everything, from sex to whatever conversation they were having, always leading him right up to the edge of something and then abruptly changing directions. It was unsettling . . . and exciting. Other girls waited for him to take the lead, to set the pace. Tracy was willful.

He closed the door and moved through the dark room to the phone. He hung it up, then turned to the bed. 'I was working,' he said.

'Kissing Max's ass, you mean,' she murmured, without turning around. Her voice was furry. His eyes went to the empty champagne bottle by the bed. And probably she was stoned on something else too, as usual.

'I was not kissing Max Fischer's ass,' he said, reaching under the covers to caress her. 'I was *polishing* it. With my *tongue*. Because that's my job, and I'm good at it. In fact, I think I have a special gift.'

He was amped up, as he usually was whenever he spent time with Max. But she didn't respond, didn't move at all, lying passive beneath his hands. Her skin was so warm it seemed feverish. He reached between her legs and she squirmed away.

'I'm asleep.'

'Wake up.'

He moved his hands to her back, going into just-a-massage-mode. She seemed to accept that. 'Dad asked who I was seeing,' she said.

'Mmmm?'

'I told him Max.'

'Bet that made him happy.'

'Mmmm.'

'What did he say?'

'Hollered. I told him to fuck off.'

'Are you serious?'

'Yeah.'

'You told him to fuck off?'

'Fuck, yes.'

He could hear her saying it. She was fearless. Which inspired him to tell her what he really felt. 'I was thinking about you,' he said. 'The whole time he was gassing on about your father, I was sitting there thinking: You'll never believe who I'm going to see tonight. You'll never believe who I'm going to be *fucking*.'

He meant it as a kind of joke, to bind them both in their oppression. Though he hadn't yet got the whole story, clearly Tracy and Max had had some kind of twisted relationship when she was a kid. There was no mistaking her glee when Peter told mean stories about his workday; she was avid for details, as if storing up each fact for some future tribunal. But this time she rolled over and stared right at him, as if she'd suddenly seen something in him that she'd missed before.

'Jesus,' she said.

He heard the withdrawal. 'I'm only—'

'You sound just like him.'

Peter forced a laugh. 'God, not that.'

She just kept giving him the suspicious look. He bent over and nuzzled her neck. 'Come on. I was just joking. Let me make it up to you.'

He ran his hands down her toasty belly, feathering over her thighs. 'Mmmm,' he said, nibbling at her ear.

For a moment she responded, grudgingly, arching her neck but turning away her face. Then she got his ear in her teeth and bit down hard.

'Ow! What was that for?'

She pulled back and looked at him, again with that suspicious expression. She seemed to be puzzling something out, and then her face set – she had made up her mind. 'You know what's the matter with you?' she said.

He went back for a kiss. 'Not now,' he said.

She let him kiss her, but started talking again as soon as he stopped. 'You don't know what you *think*,' she said.

'Mmmm.'

He kissed her again, and again she accepted the kiss. But when he paused, she continued, 'You don't know who you *are*.'

'Not now, for chrissake.' He leaned back in – urgent, hungry, letting his eyes fall to slits – but this time she pushed him away. 'You're going to become one of them. Pretty soon I won't recognize you.'

He opened his eyes. 'Can we please talk about this later?'

'No. Let's talk about it now.'

'Tracy—'

'When I met you, I could see right away you were ninety-two percent a good guy,' she said. 'Smart, passionate, earnest, eager to please.' She sounded sad about it.

'What about the other eight percent?'

'Just enough asshole to keep you from being boring,' she said.

He leaned in to kiss her again. 'You bad girl—'

But again she pushed him away.

'What the hell is the *matter*?' he said.

'You're already down to eighty-five percent,' she said. 'Maybe eighty. In just four weeks. Pretty soon you'll be a full-fledged member of the Vipers' Club.'

He sat up, giving her a pitiful look: Please stop torturing me, I've had enough pain tonight already. 'Isn't eighty enough?' he said, his voice a teasing whine. 'You go for bad boys anyway, right?

Motorcycles and leather jackets? Recreational domestic abuse? Come
on—'

He cupped a breast in one hand, bent over to lick the nipple. 'I
mean, eighty percent – isn't that *enough*?'

But Tracy stiffened and rolled away. She rolled off the bed and
stood, naked, beside it. 'That's exactly your problem,' she said,
shaking a finger at him. She was seriously mad, trembling with it.

'What? What?'

'You think you can get away with this.'

'What are you talking about?'

She backed away, leaned up against the closet door. Her arms were
down by her side, palms against the door as if she were pinned to it,
and her breasts rose and fell as she took deep breaths. This must be
some kind of drug reaction, Peter thought. Or a very weird mating
ritual. She stood against the door, her pale little belly quivering above
that black thatch. He got off the bed and went to her, grabbing her
wrists in his hands and raising them above her head. He kissed
her, hard. She twisted her face away and he licked and bit at her
neck, large wet bites. She moaned.

Yes, that's it. Agro-sex. Me Tarzan.

He pulled her back to the bed, pressed down on top of her, kissing, running rough hands up and down her legs, breasts, stomach,
kneading her, pushing her knee aside to open her thighs . . .

'You think you're exempt,' she said.

He put a hand over her mouth. 'Ssssshhhh.' And then he lowered
himself and thrust home, in one sudden move so smooth and quick
it surprised them both. She was so wet, nothing stopped him. He
rocked into her, slowly, and she moved back, almost as if she was
surprised by what she was feeling, as if she were studying it: Is this
real? Peter kissed her lips, her cheek, her neck. He murmured in her
ear, not words but syllables: yugh, lugh, mmgh . . .

Until she twisted her body, trying to get away.

'Whugh?' Peter said.

She pushed at his chest, twisting her hips to buck him off.

'What's wrong?' he asked.

He searched for the answer in her face and was astonished to see
tears in her eyes.

'You've changed,' she said.

'What are you talking about?'

'You changed so fast.'

'I haven't.'

'You have.'

'This is me,' he said. 'I was always like this.'

She shook her head back and forth, refusing his words, and he grabbed her wrists again and pinned them to the bed. It worked before, maybe it would work again. 'I haven't changed,' he said, whispering it hotly in her ear. 'This is me. On top of you. *Fucking* you.' She squirmed and he held her down, riding her writhing body, hurling himself against her, and as he did he kept talking, riding the words too: 'I *want* you, I *take* you, you're *mine*. You're an instrument of my will. A vessel for my pleasure . . .' He'd never spoken this way before, and the words thrilled him, each syllable spurting tiny explosions of excitement. Until he became aware of something flapping against his head – a bird? A bat?

Her fists.

'Stop it! Stop!'

'What? Why? I—'

'*Listen to you*,' she shouted. '*You sound like him*!'

She glared at him, panting. He glared back. He felt savage and incredibly aroused, haunched up on his hands and knees like a wild beast. He dropped his mouth to her neck. She twisted away and he growled, rooting after her white throat. '*No*,' she said.

He missed a beat, then went chasing after it . . .

Almost there. The shiver rushed through him . . .

'*No*!'

There was no doubt that time. Anger in her voice.

He had to stop.

Then everything went white, like a flashbulb going off. She was serious but he was riding her and he couldn't stop, he rode the rush of power like a surfer on a wave, a Mongol on his horse, Slim Pickens on that nuclear bomb.

'Ahhhh!'

Then her body jerked and twisted and her sweaty wrist slipped out of his grip – on the edge of his vision he saw it, coming at his eye, and he flinched just in time. The nails missed the eyeball, sinking into the soft flesh between his eye and the socket. He cried out, whipped his head away, and caught her wrist in his hand, but she slipped loose and went for him again – she was strong, surprisingly strong – and in the struggle he felt his elbow hit bone. This time she screamed. '*Bastard*!'

'I didn't mean—'

She leaped off the bed, tore up the bedside lamp, threw it at him, and if it hadn't got caught short by the cord, which was still plugged in, it might have caused real damage. She hurled an ashtray that hit the bedboard with a thunk. '*You asshole! You shit!*'

'Are you okay?'

Her left eyebrow was gushing red. His elbow had split the skin. The blood went down her chin and wrapped around her throat like a red scarf.

'You're gonna get it,' she said.

It was a schoolyard threat, but whether she intended it or not, it had special power: *Wait till I tell my Daddy.*

'It was an accident. You had your *claw* in my eye . . .'

She took a deep breath and stood straight, displaying the blood, which was beginning to drape her left breast. Peter felt oddly mesmerized by the sight, wanted to just lie there and watch it like TV, but he forced himself up and over to her side. She stood stiff, swaying slightly.

For a moment they faced each other, not speaking. Then, on impulse, he leaned forward and kissed her bloody lips.

She stared at him. He stared back.

He could feel her blood around his mouth, a wet circle like a milk mustache. Slowly, still staring in her eyes, he licked it away. It tasted of copper and smoke. Then she broke the stare and turned into the bathroom, closing the door behind her without another word. After a moment, hearing the water run, Peter went back to the bed. He sat up against the headboard, waiting for her. They would talk it out. But two minutes later the heaviest sleep he had ever known was sucking at his bones, and four hours later, when his wristwatch started buzzing, she was gone.

Chapter Two

Peter took a quick shower, slipped out of the hotel and drove straight to Max's house. He got there sharp on the dot of nine, ready to do his usual morning job dialing the phone and dialing it some more and then dialing it a few more times until Max had talked enough and was ready to take his shower and drive to the studio. Everything seemed perfectly normal: Max in his heaven and all's right with the world.

Until about twenty minutes after he got there, when the doorbell rang. Max was just on his way upstairs to shower, still wearing his bathrobe. 'Get that,' he ordered, curt as ever. Peter would remember later that Max didn't seem especially concerned. He went downstairs, stepping over dropcloths, and opened the door on Joe Dogosta, a private detective who worked for Max's lawyer. He was a big, hairy guy, Brillo tufts poking out around his open collar – one reason everyone called him the Dog. Dogosta had been in Vice and knew all the wrong people, and Max was fascinated by him: Every month or so they went out to dinner and talked for hours and hours about Hollywood scandals both historic and immediate. It was intelligence, always useful.

'Where's Max?' Dogosta said, already pushing through the door.

'Upstairs dressing.'

'Get your ass moving,' he said. 'We've got a situation.'

Dogosta followed Peter up the stairs, then pushed past him and opened the bedroom door himself. He didn't bother saying hello. 'We have about fifteen minutes to clean this place up before the cops get here,' he began, heading straight for Max's bed. He ripped back the blanket and peered at the sheets.

'*What the fuck . . .*' Max said.

'We don't have much time, Max.'

'What are you doing?' Max demanded. 'What cops?'

33

Then Dogosta stopped what he was doing and looked at Peter. 'Can we trust him?' he said.

Despite his confusion, Max stopped and considered the question, looking from Peter to the Dog and back again.

'Yeah,' he said, as if there was no doubt about it and he was even a little insulted – on Peter's behalf – that the question had been asked at all. Peter felt a wave of gratitude and loyalty so strong it surprised him.

Dogosta straightened up and delivered his message: 'Tracy Rose was just raped and beaten – the crap beat out of her.' He still held the sheets in his hands.

'Raped?' Max said.

'She named you,' Dogosta said.

He started pulling the sheets off the bed.

'Wait a fucking minute,' Max shouted, crossing the room and grabbing at the sheets. 'You think I did it?'

'Hey, Max,' Dogosta said, holding up a palm in a gesture that said: Stay cool, let's be professional.

But Max wouldn't stop. 'You think *I* did it?' he repeated, still tugging at the wad of sheets.

Dogosta let the sheets go, throwing Max off balance. 'What do I know? The point right now is, she *said* you did it, and the cops are on their way over. We gotta clean the place up. Any letters, photos, diaries, videotapes – anything that—'

'*Joe,*' Max said, using Dogosta's Christian name for the first time since Peter had known him. 'This is *me*. You've known me for what, ten years? You think *I* raped Tracy?'

Max's voice started out hurt, then bloomed into outrage. Dogosta stared right back. 'Personally, I don't give a fuck. All I know is what the Ripper told me – clean up anything that looks suspicious and keep the police the fuck away from you.'

The Ripper was Max's lawyer. His real name was Jerry Rippert, but he'd been known as Jack the Ripper for so long that sometimes the newspapers slipped and printed his name as Jack Rippert.

'Call him,' Max ordered Peter.

'He's in court,' Dogosta said.

'What's he doing in *court*?'

'I already talked to him, the minute I heard.'

'*Goddamnit,*' Max said.

34

Dogosta jammed a ball of sheets into a pillowcase. 'Like I said, Max, I don't give a fuck,' he said. 'Let's just clean the place up.'

'Really?' Max said. 'You don't give a fuck? What if I killed her? Would you still be helping me clean up?'

Dogosta looked hurt. 'I'm your guy, Max.'

Max stared back at him. After a moment he nodded once, accepting Dogosta's odd tribute. It even seemed to relax him. He slumped down into the chair by the desk.

Dogosta dropped to his knees, searching under the bed. 'I could use some help,' he said, looking at Peter. 'We don't have much more time.'

Peter didn't know what to do. He glanced around the room, looking for things that might be suspicious.

'What did she say?' Max asked. 'I just held her down and *raped* her? For what reason did I do this?'

Dogosta got up, wiping his hands. 'To get even with the old man.' He shrugged, as if it hardly needed to be said.

'The little bitch,' Max said. But he seemed less angry than . . . curious. Curious and deflated. 'When is this supposed to have happened?'

'Four or five in the morning.'

Max considered that.

And so did Peter – that would have been when *he* was with Tracy . . . or shortly after she left the hotel. He felt dizzy, and pictured Tracy again, naked against the bathroom door wearing her scarf of blood. But that was just an eyebrow cut, bloody but not serious, an accident – not 'the crap beat out of her'.

As if he were reading Peter's mind, Dogosta turned to him. 'What time did you get here?'

'This morning?'

'Yeah, this morning.'

'Nine sharp.'

'When did you leave last night?'

Peter thought. 'About three, I guess. Three-fifteen?'

'Where'd you go?'

'What difference does it make?' Peter asked, mixing his fear with indignation.

'The cops are going to ask,' he snapped. 'Where did you go?'

Peter looked at Max. He hesitated for a moment, just a moment, tasting the truth on his tongue. But it was bitter. 'Home,' he said. 'I was fucking exhausted.'

'Anybody see you?'

Peter shook his head.

He pictured Tracy again, bleeding at the bathroom door. *You're gonna get it*.

'You sure?'

'Pretty sure.'

'What happened to your eye?'

'Branch of a tree. Had a couple drinks.'

Dogosta held Peter's eyes for a moment, then glanced at his watch. 'We now have ten minutes, Max.'

'She's like . . . my *sister*,' Max said. 'We practically grew up together.' He seemed to be stuck, as if he was trying to get his mind around something he knew he would never understand.

'Ten minutes,' Dogosta repeated. 'We've got to eliminate every connection between you and Tracy Rose.'

Max looked up. 'How are you going to do that?' he said. 'Everybody in town knows I worked for her father. How you gonna change history?'

Dogosta shoved the wadded sheets into Peter's arms, along with a set of keys. 'The Beamer,' he said. 'In the trunk.'

Peter looked at Max, and Max shrugged. This was the turning point, Peter felt. He would be concealing evidence. He had to think. It was all so crazy. Max *couldn't* have raped Tracy, not unless she rushed to his bed right after the Château. But then why was Dogosta so intent on cleaning the place up, what was all this about pictures and videotapes? There was some guilty secret here, something to do with Max and Tracy – and Peter felt a stab of jealousy, same as he felt when Tracy talked about Max . . . followed immediately by guilt. He had lied. He had cheated. This was his fault.

He turned and headed for the door, carrying the sheets, acutely aware of the two sets of eyes on his back. On the stairs, he heard Dogosta's lowered voice. 'You know what I'm talking about, Max,' he said. 'Pictures. Letters. We got to get them out of here. Get 'em to the Ripper.'

'But they're evidence *against* her,' Max said.

'You know what juries are like,' Dogosta said.

Then Peter was out of hearing distance, crossing the living room floor. He lifted the sheets to his nose, sniffing as Dogosta had sniffed when he first came into the bedroom. They smelled of sex. But was it Tracy's smell?

He sniffed again, but he couldn't tell.

In a daze, he opened the trunk of Dogosta's black BMW and put the sheets inside. He looked around: no one in sight. Then he closed the trunk and stood there, waiting for something to happen.

Okay, suppose that after the Château, Tracy went to Max to tell on him. That would make sense. She was mad, she wanted to punish him. But then Max did something or said something and they got into a fight.

He tried to picture Max hunched on top of Tracy, holding her down . . . tattered lace drooling from his teeth . . .

He shook the thought away. It just didn't make sense. People without power raped, wasn't that the psychiatric cliché? And Max was one of the most powerful producers in Hollywood. Besides, Max was something of a prude – once or twice a week he'd go out 'trolling', as he put it, and several times he'd instructed Peter to create a dossier on some actress he fancied (availability, past boyfriends, sexual preferences, nude photos when possible). But he scorned the more lurid aspects of Hollywood, like high-priced prostitutes and the producers who used them. 'It's bad for the *business*,' he would say, 'especially these days, with all that family values shit. The right-wingers would *love* it – the dirty *liberal Jews* in Hollywood acting like pigs.' And that would send Max off into one of his most morose and obsessive themes: 'It always comes down to that – *the dirty Jews.*'

When he got back upstairs, Dogosta was putting fresh sheets on the bed. He and Max had been arguing about something. 'What about the pictures?' he asked.

Max hesitated. 'Left bottom drawer,' he said. 'Blue folder.'

Tucking in a corner of the sheet, Dogosta looked at Peter and nodded in the direction of the desk. 'Dig 'em out, will you?' Then he started messing up the bed he had just made.

Peter pushed aside the wax deli paper (still littered with sandwich crusts and pickles) and flipped through files until he found the blue folder. Carefully, as if it were something explosive, he pulled it out. Inside he found three letters and three snapshots. In the first picture Tracy and Max grinned at the camera, each with an arm thrown casually over the other's shoulders. Tracy looked about fifteen. She was a strawberry blonde, with a long brown California body. Max looked ten years younger and almost lighthearted, a man standing on the edge of the world. In the second, Tracy was dressed for school in an actual plaid-skirt-black-knee-sock Catholic-schoolgirl outfit. She looked about sixteen. The third picture was a Polaroid, taken recently, judging by the short white hair. In it she was wearing the same schoolgirl clothes, but the skirt was pulled high on her thighs, exposing white panties. And Tracy was looking right into the camera with a knowing and seductive expression.

Peter swallowed, then carefully cleared his throat. 'These are fairly innocent,' he said, looking away from the last picture, from that flash of white.

'She sends them to me,' Max said. 'She's a psycho.'

The letters were written on pink paper. Peter made out a few words – *Dear Max, You bastard, I still hate you* – before Dogosta snapped his fingers. Peter handed him the folder.

'What about the call sheets?' Dogosta said. 'Is she on them?'

Peter waited for Max to answer. He knew that Tracy had called Max about a half dozen times in the last month alone. Peter had put the calls through himself. He figured she was doing it at least partly to tease him. Each time Max said the same thing: 'Listen, Tracy, I'm in the middle of something. I'll call you back.' Polite, but brusque. And he never did call back.

Max didn't answer. He was facing the windows, trying to puzzle something out.

'What about it?' the Dog said, looking at Peter. Peter nodded: Yes.

'Get 'em,' the Dog said.

So Peter dug out the most recently printed copies of Max's daily appointment sheets and gave them to Dogosta. 'Are these on hard disk too?' Dogosta asked.

'Yeah,' Peter said.

'Here or in the office?'

'At the office. But . . .'

Dogosta sat down at the computer, and in seconds the modem was whining and then it clicked in. Dogosta typed the access code, and a few moments later the screen filled with the neat pink and blue bars of Max's Studio System phone-sheet program. 'How is she entered?'

'TR,' Peter said.

'Take over. Search-delete all but . . . two.'

As Peter clicked through the entries, Max turned around. 'Better delete Marina Lake too,' he said.

Peter went still. Marina Lake? That was the name Tracy used at the hotel . . .

Then Peter noticed Dogosta watching him, and as he started typing again, he asked as casual as could be: 'Who's she?'

'Another psycho,' Max said.

'I thought she left,' Dogosta said.

Max shook his head. 'Came back,' he said. To Peter, he explained: 'She grew up with Tracy, lived across the street. Then she turned into some kind of a *hooker*. Cops got involved, there was a scandal, blah blah, and she went to Japan.' He sounded breezy, as if this was just another boring human story. But Dogosta was watching him. Peter saw him give Max a weighted look.

'What's she got to do with this?'

Max tossed his hands, annoyed at all the questions. 'She's just trouble. A wild card. She could say anything.'

Clearly, Dogosta wanted to know more. But he didn't press it, just walked over and put his hand on Peter's shoulder. It was surprisingly fat and warm. 'Do it,' he said. So Peter typed the name into the search box and hit execute. There it was. He hit delete. And again. And again. The Dog watched them fall. 'All of them?'

'She's also under Minoku,' Max said wearily.

Minoku, Peter thought. The voice came back to him: '*Is Max there? Tell him it's his little China girl.*' It was cynical, with a mocking, sexy lilt. She had called three or four times in the last few months, always at night. Max just scowled when Peter gave him the messages, and he never called back. At least not when Peter was around.

He was just deleting the last Minoku when the doorbell rang. Max looked at Dogosta, took a deep breath, then nodded to Peter. 'Go let them in.' Dogosta opened his jacket and started stuffing the blue file into his pants, sliding it around against his back.

Just as the bell rang for the third time, Peter opened the door. The two detectives stood there with expressionless, professional faces, the faces of priests or morticians. The one in front, to Peter's surprise, was a woman, though she barely looked like one – a real

39

potato-eater she was, with the square face and square body of a member of the Albanian Female Weight-Lifting Squad gone to fat. Behind her stood a skinny blond guy wearing a blue windbreaker over a sixty-percent rayon shirt.

'Detective Spinks,' said the woman, sticking out her hand. 'This is Detective Hanson. Are you Max Fischer?'

'Not me,' Peter said. 'I'm just the assistant.'

'Where is Mr Fischer?'

'Upstairs,' Peter said, holding the door open. 'The house is being remodeled.'

Spinks and Hanson took in the construction, then waited. Peter didn't know what else to say, so he just headed for the stairs. They followed without a word. At the landing Peter opened the bedroom door and let the detectives go past him.

'Hey, how's it going?' Max said, crossing the room with his hand out. 'Nice to meet you. Do you want something? I'll ring my housekeeper – she's staying in the guest house because, as you can see, we're a little torn up around here, and she refuses to sleep downstairs. It's good enough for me but not good enough for the housekeeper.' He smiled his warmest smile.

The detectives shook their heads at the offer, saying no thanks, but Max would hear none of it. 'Peter, get them some water or something. Cokes?'

'No, please, no thank you,' Spinks said, without smiling.

Max moved on to Hanson, shaking his hand and trying to force a Coke on him. 'Come on, please, have a Coke. Peter, get him a Coke. Coffee, how about coffee?'

Hanson gave in, partly. 'Water would be fine,' he said.

Max smiled big – Hanson was his new best friend. And he turned back on Spinks. 'Come on, detective. How about some water. I know, no bubbles – you're on duty.'

Hanson gave a chuckle, but Spinks just nodded. 'Thanks,' she said.

Max waved Peter off, and Peter went downstairs and popped the caps off four bottles of Evian – no bubbles – then brought them up on Max's favorite stamped tin tray. As he reached the top of the stairs he saw Hanson standing in front of the poster for *Cyberkill*, Max's first big hit. The adline was a Max Fischer classic: 'This time, they installed revenge at the factory . . .'

'You did *Cyberkill?*' Hanson said. 'I loved that movie. Great special effects.'

'We aim to please,' Max said.

Spinks was looking around the room, not at the posters. Her eyes fell on the bed, and Peter wondered if she could tell the sheets were fresh. 'You work out of your house?' she asked.

'I work everywhere,' Max said. 'Next April I think I'm going to deduct my *toilet*. Last night we were working late trying to get Tom Hanks into my new picture. You like Hanks?' He patted the back of a chair for Spinks – 'Here, sit, sit' – then patted another chair for Hanson. 'Sit, make yourself comfortable.' They shook their heads, but Max just kept talking. 'Anyway, most of the agents and directors and actors are in France for a film festival – they party, I work.' He shrugged, the happy martyr. 'Which means, with the time difference, that we've been keeping some *very* weird hours, dialing across the Atlantic, waiting for calls. Peter was here the whole time, helping me.'

Spinks and Hanson both looked at Peter, who didn't know quite what to say. He gave them a sheepish smile, then instantly wondered if he'd done the wrong thing.

Max plunged on. 'So what can I do for you? I know you're not here to listen to me gas on about the movie business.'

Spinks frowned and hesitated, and scratched absently at her arm, almost as if she were nervous. Peter had seen that reaction before – sometimes it took people a little while to adjust to Max-tempo. But then she looked right into Max's eyes. 'A few hours ago we wcre given a sworn statement by a young woman named Tracy Rose accusing you of rape and battery,' she said, her voice at once stern and polite. 'I'm sorry, but I think we're going to have to take you in for questioning.'

Max looked at Dogosta. 'What does that mean, take me in for questioning?'

Before Dogosta could answer, Spinks continued. 'You don't seem very surprised by our visit,' she said.

Dogosta cleared his throat. 'About a half hour ago I got a tip from a friend about what happened,' he said. 'I came over to prepare Mr Fischer . . . psychologically.'

Hanson spoke up, his tone mild, as if he were merely puzzled. 'Psychologically?'

41

Dogosta smiled, spreading his hands in a helpless, confessional gesture – you caught me lying, you smart cop. 'I was hoping to help him keep it out of the papers,' he admitted.

Spinks nodded. 'And you are . . . ?'

'I know who he is,' Hanson said. 'Joe Dogosta. They call him the Dog. Used to be on the job . . . Vice, right?'

'I still smell Spring Street in my dreams,' Dogosta said. 'The bad ones.' He continued without pause. 'This isn't an arrest, right? No arrest warrant, search warrant, nothing like that?'

Spinks compressed her lips. 'Just an inquiry,' she said. 'At this point.'

'So there's no point in going to the station, is there?' Dogosta said.

Spinks looked at him, her face suddenly going blank, as if she had no idea who he was or what he was doing there. It was an intimidating look, but Dogosta wasn't fazed a bit.

'Mr Fischer's a busy and important man,' Dogosta said. 'And as I recall from my happy days in blue, you don't have a warrant, you don't have shit. We didn't even have to let you in the front door. But because Mr Fischer is a cooperative citizen and because he is completely innocent of any wrongdoing, he'll answer a few questions.'

'Happily,' Max said.

'No point in making life difficult,' Dogosta said. He continued in a gruff but thoughtful voice, one cop to another: 'You should know there's some history here. The alleged victim is the daughter of one of Mr Fischer's . . . former associates. There have been some harsh words.' He let that sink in, then added: 'And the girl – well, I don't want to make any accusations, but—'

'I get the picture,' Spinks said, cutting him off.

Hanson broke in, his voice a touch belligerent. 'It comes to that, we can take a separate statement from you,' he said, giving Dogosta an aggressively friendly smile: We're all colleagues here, asshole.

Dogosta shrugged. 'Just so you know. I wouldn't want you to fuck up, and lose your jobs or something.'

'Thanks for the tip,' Spinks said, her voice neutral.

There was tension in the room now, thrumming away under the ambient hum. But it was enough to drive Max across the room, tossing his hands in the air in a gesture of amiable frustration. 'Listen, officers, this is nothing, all a mistake – we'll answer your questions, go downtown, whatever . . .'

He crossed his hands as if offering them to be bound, then laughed. 'Hell, it's material; I'll use it in my next movie. In fact, I think I already used it – I repeat myself, Peter tells me. Did you see *Blood Hunt?* There was a scene just like this, two cops being very nice . . . only it turned out they had it in for the guy all along.' He stopped walking and gave a nervous laugh. 'But that was just a movie.'

Hanson smiled as the memory dawned. 'I saw that flick,' he said. 'With Richard Gere and what's-his-name. Did you direct that?'

Max gave a pained smile. 'I *produced* it. The director *works* for me.'

He walked back toward the desk, his burst of energy apparently done. He sat down and put on a Cagney voice. 'So go ahead, copper. Grill me.'

When Spinks didn't smile, Max added: 'I think I got one of those goose-neck lamps in the closet, if that will help.'

Spinks took a breath. She looked troubled. 'I'm not sure you appreciate how serious a charge this is,' she said.

Max winced. 'It's just nerves, joking around,' he said. 'I'm sure you must get that a lot.' Then he nodded at Peter. 'You want the real lowdown, ask Peter. He's with me every minute. Isn't that the best way to get info, ask the secretary?'

'Assistant,' Peter said.

'He was here all last night, as a matter of fact. Came right after dinner.'

'So you said,' Spinks replied, then she turned to Peter. 'What time did you leave?'

Max answered. 'We were calling Europe till about, what – two A.M.?'

Peter nodded.

'All you gotta do is get the phone records,' Max said. 'Isn't that what you do? Records searches and stuff like that?' He didn't wait for an answer. 'Then we went over the project list for what, an hour or two?'

Spinks looked puzzled. 'Excuse me?'

'That's what we call our list of films in development – scripts, treatments, ideas, a buncha half-baked shit we paid too fucking much for,' Max said. ' "Projects." Sounds better than "half-baked idea", doesn't it? Makes the writers feel better, like engineers or something. Like they're really working for a living.' He was comfortable now, happy to be talking about the business, almost as if he were lecturing a group of students from USC. 'Some are already assigned to writers, some still need writers, some are written and have actors or directors attached. Others we got to find writers or actors or directors, 'cause nobody makes a deal just because a project has a *producer* attached – I mean, my last six films made more than seventy-five million dollars *each*, and there still isn't a studio in town that will greenlight a picture because *Max Fischer* is attached to it. But you take Eddie Murphy, who these days lays a *turd* more often than a hit, and attach him to the fucking *phone* book, and bang – *instant greenlight*.'

Max stopped, aware that he'd gone on too long. 'So when I get nervous,' he concluded, 'we sit and woodshed – who would be good for this, who would be good for that. That sort of thing.'

'You were nervous last night?' Spinks asked.

Max laughed – you got me, copper.

'What were you nervous about?' Spinks asked.

'Where my next *meal* is coming from,' Max shouted. 'I'm not on *salary* like you guys. I gotta go out there and hustle *every fucking day*!'

He was pacing already, and the hands were shooting up in the mad-scientist gestures. To make it worse, a little of Max's tension broke through on those last few words, so that they came out close to angry: *every fucking day*. Peter thought watching him that if he were a cop, he'd arrest the guy right away and worry later about what crime he had committed.

But Spinks and Hanson just kept watching without much expression. Then Spinks turned to Peter again. 'How long was it exactly, going over this project list?'

Peter looked at Max.

'*Hours*,' Max said. 'I tell you, I'm a lunatic about these things. It's my bread and butter. I drive Peter crazy – don't I?'

Peter nodded, giving the detectives a weak smile. 'It's true,' he said.

But Spinks turned to Max, annoyed now. 'Why don't you let him answer?' she said.

With a big smile, Max held up his hands, a helpless gesture. 'I'm a producer – I'm going to let my *assistant* steal my big scene?'

Spinks nodded, no returning smile, just that ominously blank cop face. For the first time, Max looked nervous. Then Spinks stood up and went over to another one of Max's framed posters. It showed a running man, his body in darkness, looking over his shoulder with a grim, determined expression. In the lower left corner just enough sunlight gleamed to light up the blood dripping off his dangling arm. Spinks read the title, distaste in her voice. '*Blood Hunt.*'

'D'you see it?' Max asked.

Spinks shook her head. 'I don't like that kind of movie.'

Max smiled. 'You don't like action?'

'Not really.'

'What kind of movies do you like? Foreign movies? Merchant–Ivory? *A Room with a View*?'

'Yeah,' Spinks said. 'I liked that one.'

Max smiled some more, as if he were really enjoying himself now. 'Different strokes,' he said. 'But I tell you, you know, Shakespeare's got swords and shit all over the place. Pretty bloody stuff. And what about that ancient Greek shit? Ever see *Medea*? *The Bacchae*? Bloody as hell – I'd be embarrassed to make a movie as bloody as *The Bacchae*. But I'm not trying to compare myself to Shakespeare or Euripides – I make *action* movies. Thrillers. My movies are *basic*, about *basic* feelings and *basic* fears. Afraid of the dark? Afraid of dying? Afraid of being alone? They're like dreams. This one' – he pointed to the poster – 'is the dumb old goofy dream about being chased. *Blood Hunt*. Think about it – what if the same stuff that keeps you alive, that warm stuff squirting down your veins, what if *that* was the same thing that let the bad guys hunt you down? Alien bloodhounds tracking you down by homing in on your personal fucking hemotype! No escape! I thought that was a pretty good gag – I mean, what can you do? You're *fucked*. And so did the public, at least about twenty-one million of them. Maybe it was AIDS, I dunno, but the damn thing *clicked*. Jesus, you should have seen them opening night! They were pissing on the seats!'

Spinks shrugged. 'I didn't like it.'

'You saw it?' Max demanded.

'Almost made me puke,' Spinks said, turning back to Peter. 'Now if you don't mind, can you tell me exactly what time you left?'

'Wait a minute, wait a minute, wait a minute,' Max said. '*Puke* I can live with. But you're telling me you weren't scared? The scene where the bad guy is changing blood with the hero, bleeding him *dry* while the aliens close in – that didn't *work* for you? You needed a box of *No Doz*?'

This time Spinks looked right at him, with an expression so cold it could have frozen sparks. 'I didn't last that long,' she said. 'I walked out in the middle.' Then she turned back to Peter. 'I think this is the third time now,' she said. 'When did you leave the house?'

Max didn't give Peter a chance to answer. He stood in the middle of the room, shaking his hands above his head. 'He was here the whole *fucking* night, I said,' he shouted. 'He stayed *here, working. Working on my crappy movies*!'

Spinks didn't blink an eye. She glanced at the bed, then continued to speak to Peter. 'You slept here?'

'Didn't you *hear* me?' Max shouted. 'He stayed *here*. We *worked*. What, do you think I'm *lying*?'

Max was so outrageous he was convincing. You had to know him before you'd suspect that he was performing, to know that even at full-tilt tantrum, even at his World Wrestling Federation worst, Max never missed a thing – he could repeat other people's muttered asides months later, word for word. Sometimes Peter thought Max was never out of control, that it was all an act, which was the scariest thought of all.

Dogosta stepped in, putting one hand on Max's shoulder and holding the other palm out to the cops. 'I think that's enough. Mr Fischer's been more than cooperative.'

Spinks just kept boring in on Peter. 'You slept here?' she asked again.

'I said, I think that's enough,' Dogosta repeated.

Spinks ignored him. 'On the bed?'

In real time, Peter hesitated for just a second or two, just long enough to think: This is serious, really serious. He was still startled by Max's lie, heart thumping away at the back of his throat. But in a way, he was almost flattered. Max needed him. Max trusted him. And after all, Max only thought he could get away with his lie because of the lie Peter had told him, that he went straight home and nobody saw him. The funny part was that nobody *did* see him, because he didn't go home. So maybe they could get away with it. Peter started to look over at Max, wanting to check his face before he answered, but he knew that was the one thing he couldn't do –

he'd seen that look in a thousand movies, some stupid henchman checking out the boss to see what was the right answer. He had to be casual, matter-of-fact. Unperturbed.

'The sofa,' he said.

In all, his hesitation only lasted a second or two.

Spinks finally acknowledged Dogosta. 'Okay, we're going. Thanks for your cooperation.'

Then she turned to Peter again. 'You must get paid real well,' she said.

'What do you mean?' Peter said, flushing. Was she calling him a liar?

'To work all night,' Spinks said.

Peter laughed with relief. 'Not really,' he said. 'I do it for love.'

Spinks studied him a moment more, just a second, but that was all it took to set Peter's heart pounding loud enough to call one of the larger African tribes to war.

At the door to the bedroom, Spinks paused. 'One more question?'

'Shoot,' Max said.

Spinks looked at Peter again. 'What time did you get started?' She stared at him just long enough to start the drums again, then turned abruptly to Max. 'Or maybe I should just ask you.'

Max gave her a fake smile, then nodded to Peter. 'You answer,' he said.

'He called me around eleven,' Peter said, frowning as if he were trying hard to remember exactly. 'A few minutes after eleven, I think. I stopped off at Canter's for sandwiches.'

Spinks frowned, turning to Max. 'I thought you said you had dinner,' Spinks said.

'*He* had dinner,' Max said. '*I* was starving to death. Suffering acute *food* deprivation.'

'The receipt's probably in the bag,' Peter said, pointing to the desk.

Spinks glanced at the sandwich leavings on the desk. The way Peter had mashed them aside when he was searching the desk for the blue folder, he'd left scattered near the edge at least a dozen carefully wrapped pickles.

'That's a lot of pickles,' Spinks said.

Peter chuckled, releasing his tension. 'Is that relevant?'

Spinks gave him an unfriendly smile. 'It's just unusual,' she said.

This time it was Peter's turn to hold up his hands in a helpless gesture, and even though there was so much more to worry about, he found himself nagged by an incredibly irritating thought: He was imitating Max *again*.

'Welcome to *Hollywood*,' he said.

Peter walked the cops down to the front door. Spinks made social noises on the way down, thanking him for the time, apologizing for interrupting their work. Peter thought it was odd she was saying these things to him instead of to Max. He just wanted to close the door on them and get a moment to breathe. But at the door Spinks turned and said, 'How about walking us down to the car? Just take a minute.'

Peter looked up at the bedroom door. What could he say? Max wouldn't like it? Too suspicious. Besides, he didn't want Spinks to think he was some kind of castrato, acting only at the whim of his master, especially after the scene they'd just been through. Maybe he could even help, put Max in context a little. 'I guess,' he said, with a shrug.

They walked down the steps. With heightened senses, Peter noticed the tufts of exotic grass poking between colored Spanish tiles, the koi pond bubbling away. So peaceful, especially on a cool California morning like this, disturbed only by the white noise of distant cars. Spinks chatted on, her voice friendly and casual. 'I just thought we might make a little more progress without your boss watching you,' she said. 'You know what I mean, just get a few details down to save time.'

'Yeah,' Peter said.

'It must be hard working for a guy like that.'

'Sometimes,' Peter said.

They got to the car, a boxy blue Ford so institutional it could have had Government Issue stamped on its side. Hanson got into the driver's seat, leaving Spinks to cross to the passenger side, where she stopped and leaned on the roof, resting her chin on the back of one hand and giving Peter a look of sleepy wisdom, as if she understood everything and was ready to absolve it all. It was seductive, almost motherly – until Peter noticed a faint but unmistakable tinge of contempt. He spoke first, to let her know he wasn't fooled. 'It didn't happen, you know,' he said.

'What didn't happen?'

'Max and Tracy.'

Spinks raised her eyebrows: oh?

'It's just not possible,' Peter continued.

'Why not?'

Peter had to think for a second. Why indeed, aside from the logistical issues only he and Tracy knew about.

'She hates him. The whole family hates him.'

'Sounds like a motive to me.'

'Buy why would they even be in the same room together? Why would she come over to his house?'

Spinks gave him a curious look, as if he'd said something peculiar and interesting. 'Well, it's a moot point, isn't it? I mean, if you were here the whole time like you said.'

Peter flushed. This was a mistake. He should have gone straight back upstairs. 'I meant theoretically,' he said.

'Oh,' Spinks said. 'Theoretically.'

The amusement and disdain in her voice spurred Peter on. 'I'm just saying the whole thing doesn't make any sense,' he said. 'It's not plausible. I mean, maybe her father beat her up – maybe she did something to piss him off and he smacked her around, then turned around and blamed it on Max.'

'That's more plausible?' Spinks asked.

Peter pictured the scene: Tracy with her arms up, dodging big fists, swearing and crying. He saw a bruise on her cheek. 'Is she really hurt?' he asked.

'How well do you know her?' Spinks asked.

Peter thought of the times he and Tracy had been seen in public: not many, but enough. 'Not real well,' he said. 'I've seen her in clubs a couple of times.'

Then Spinks smiled. 'You're lying,' she said. Peter tried not to react, waiting for more. 'I'm not sure exactly what you're lying about, but you're lying about something. Lying for your rich boss. And there's a nineteen-year-old girl a few miles away all beat up and degraded.'

Peter shook his head. 'It didn't happen,' he said.

Spinks made a disgusted sound, horse-flapping her lips. She seemed to enjoy thinking the worst about him. 'You're so far up Max Fischer's ass, all I can see are your shoes dangling in the crack.'

Peter actually blushed. It was such a startling, crude remark, completely out of character with her previous demeanor. It was disconcerting as hell. Which was probably just the effect she wanted. Speechless, he took a shuffling step backward, making good-bye noises.

Spinks kept staring at him with that malicious smile. 'You know, if I find out you're lying, I can charge you with obstruction of justice,' she said. 'If you lie to a grand jury, that's perjury.'

She opened the car door, then added over the roof of the car, as if it were an afterthought. 'Unless you want to change your story.' It was a last, casual offer of clemency, the offhand tone implying that it would be every bit as easy to take back as it was to give. She held out a business card.

Peter met Spinks's eyes. She despised him, he could tell. All his life, a certain kind of person had despised him, almost on sight. They were always the same, the righteous, God's-in-his-heaven, I'm OK-you're Satan types. Somehow they knew that Peter was ready at any moment to change his entire philosophy of life, and hated him for it. And he hated himself for it too, but he couldn't help it. He'd get a crush on a person or a style or an idea and overnight begin acting like a different person. Sometimes he thought it came from all the years he'd spent in movie theaters, each night entering a completely different world: Today I'm epic, tomorrow noir. His first year at college, his entire freshman philosophy class tried to convince him he had faith, and he kept insisting he was an atheist, trying to keep the courage of his lack of convictions, and they kept insisting that he had to have faith in *something* – you have faith this building will be here when you come to class, don't you? Peter said that he had a reasonable expectation the building would be there, that was all. They got annoyed with him, and one beefy football player gave him that look of disgust, the same look Spinks gave him now. Finally one girl asked him, tenderly, what about faith in yourself? And he had to admit the truth: myself least of all. She was so disappointed she looked away, ashamed for him. And he was ashamed too. He blushed, stared longingly at the clock, willing time to hurry. But what could he do about it? Change? Ha! His only hope was that his habit of entering other worlds was really a kind of strength, a flexibility that would eventually make him wise. But the shame wouldn't go away, and every now and then he would try to make a stand.

So he shook his head: No, I'm not changing my story.

She put the card back in her pocket. 'How does it feel?' she said. 'To be a rich man's boy?'

Ah . . . the bitch. She seemed to know just where to jab, where it would hurt the most. Of all the people Peter had dreamed himself into, Max was the most compelling. Peter wanted what he had, that imperial self-absorption and unstoppable drive, as if nothing existed in the world but what he desired and what he created to satisfy that desire. It was the arrogance of power, and it gave off a ruddy glow. That was what made his relationship with Max so exciting . . . and degrading . . . and dangerous. With Max, there was a chance Peter might lose, that he wouldn't just be trying someone on but losing himself in him. Instead of taking what he needed and moving on, he'd become nothing but a flunky, a pallid imitation . . . a rich man's boy. He'd felt this shame and anger before, when Max ordered him around, especially when he did it in front of others, but now, with Spinks grinning at him, Peter felt it as strong as a slap in the face. He saw a future full of the same grinning contempt, and a light popped on in his head: No wonder Max hated Barry Rose so much. No wonder he could never forgive him. Rose made him feel like *this*.

Chapter Three

'Come on come on come on come on – we got *work* to do.'

Peter chased the furious little cyclone that was Max down the driveway, but by the time he opened the door of his little red Fiat – a convertible, bought the same day as his new wardrobe, back when he still thought a declaration of joy appropriate to his new environment – Max had already hopped into the shotgun side and was beating feverishly on the little dashboard. Before Peter got into second gear Max snapped: 'Try him again.'

But the Ripper was still in court, and Max fell to brooding. 'I hate this fucking car,' he muttered. 'Only a schmuck would buy a Fiat.' Peter kept his mouth shut. Finally Max snapped his head up and jabbed a finger at the phone. 'Kramer,' he croaked.

Alan Kramer was the chairman of the studio, a somewhat misleading title since the studio had at least three chairmen heading up various divisions, and they reported to still more chairmen-*sans* back in Japan. But Kramer was the point guy, and Max called him every morning on the way to work.

'He's not there,' Peter said.

Max said 'Fuck' and looked at his watch and said 'Fuck' again.

Peter couldn't stand it anymore. Even if Max was in a historically foul mood, he had to talk about what had happened. 'Interesting morning,' he said, hedging concern with irony.

Max grunted. 'The Ripper will handle it,' he said.

Fifteen minutes later, Max charged through the studio lot like General George S. Patton on a tear, Peter flapping along behind him like a human shirttail. This wasn't unusual – Max always charged around the studio like Patton on a tear, and Peter always flapped along behind him. Peter couldn't decide if Max was trying to impress people or if being on the lot just pumped him up. But this time he charged with extra urgency, if only because it was so

53

late in the day – almost noon! Moving so fast they almost tilted forward, they wound through the twisted alleys, past soundstages and editing rooms and the ubiquitous rolling golf carts, down the alley called Myrna Loy until they got to Max's 'bungalow' – an imposing adobe structure with a red-tile roof, the last old-style movie-star bungalow on the crowded Columbia lot. Inside it looked like a Santa Fe ranch, with floors of red Talavera tiles, adobe walls, and thick oak beams. Passing his receptionist and first secretary without stopping, Max tossed out the first command of the day: 'Get me Kit Bradley! *Now*!'

'You have Flip Mosely in ten,' said Sarah, the first secretary. Behind her, six desks flanked six offices, which housed Max's creative executives (glorified script readers) and vice presidents (glorified gofers). At the six desks sat five attractive young assistants with Ivy League degrees and up-to-the-minute haircuts. The empty sixth desk was Peter's.

'He'll have to wait,' Max snapped.

'He's here already,' Sarah said, pointing around the corner to the bathroom. Then she gave him a big, cheerful smile. 'Happy birthday,' she said.

Max scowled.

'Happy birthday,' the five assistants echoed in unison.

Until that moment, Peter had completely forgotten – it was Max's 40th birthday. They'd been planning the party for weeks, to be held that very night at Morton's, a massive affair involving tents, valets, and multiple celebrity testimonials. Everyone in Hollywood had RSVPd.

'And happy birthday from me too,' said a young man in a wheelchair just then rolling around the corner. It was Flip Mosely, last year's hot film school grad. He'd been prepping his first movie when a random bullet hit him in the back, and now he was physically challenged for life. Max shook his hand eagerly, grateful that work had rolled right up to interrupt this awkward personal moment. 'You're looking good, Flip. Feeling all right? I'll be with you in just a minute – I got fires to put out.' He smiled sheepishly to emphasize just how sorry he was.

'No problem,' Mosely said.

Peter followed Max into the office, immediately settling on the sofa as Max slipped behind his desk and hit the button that released the automatic door, rapping out an impatient drumbeat on his desk as it swung closed: the usual routine. Seconds later the Amtel toned, making the lambent computer release-of-sound that heralds an airport announcement, and the green digital strip glowed: KIT BRADLEY. Max hit the speaker button.

'*Maaax*,' a woman's voice crooned. 'I was just going to call you.' She sounded cocky, very pleased with herself.

Max kicked back in his chair. 'I got so much to *tell* you,' Max said. 'Hanks said he'll commit to *Lone Justice* if the studio will make his new deal. We're working on it right now. I got the rewrite coming in on *Desperado* – that's my Kristin Dunst project, great story, she's a hacker who gets mistaken for a computer terrorist and ends up outsmarting the entire CIA. It's *Wargames* meets *Three Days of the Condor*. So much is *going on*.'

Bradley was a staff writer for *Hollywood, Inc.* magazine, a publication with the perverse mission of taking Hollywood seriously. (The rest of the media world saw it only as a comic sideshow, a source of cover photos, or – at the really out-of-it publications like *The New York Times* – an art form.) She always knew everything first.

Today was no exception: 'And in your quiet moments you have your Tracy Rose problem to keep you entertained,' she said.

Peter and Max both mimed the same dropped-jaw astonishment. How could it have gotten out so fast? Someone was spreading the word for sure, stoking the fire and hoping Max would burn in it. 'What did you hear?' Max barked, snatching up the phone. '*Tell me.*'

Peter felt his face burning, as if he'd been snubbed at a party. Why did Max take her off the speaker? On general principle, to control the information flow? Or were his antennae picking up hints of Peter's guilt?

Max was listening hard, biting his lip. He picked up the letter opener from his desk – purely an ornament, since he had a vice president for opening mail – and stabbed at the desk with it. 'It's just not *true*,' he said when she finished. 'I've never even gotten a *speeding* ticket.'

There was a brief pause, and he covered the phone. 'She's fishing,' he told Peter. 'Thinks we got arrested, not sure exactly what for, knows it's something to do with Tracy.'

Max turned back to the phone. 'Kit, it really hurts me to hear you talk like that. I mean, this is *me*, Max *Fischer*. I always help you –

remember when you were on deadline with the Matsushita thing? You have to tell me *everything*.'

He listened, then his face contorted in horror. '*What*?'

He covered the phone again giving Peter a stricken look. 'She says Barry Rose is after Hanks, airlifted some script to him in Montana.' The look turned accusing. 'What do you know about this?'

It was funny – with all his troubles, Max seemed more upset about this than anything else. And Peter felt a responding panic: Hanks in Montana? In a place so remote a script had to be airlifted to him? When did this happen? How would he reach him when Max ordered him to place the call? Without waiting for the order he picked up the phone and dialed Clavius Bass, Hanks's company – a number he had no trouble remembering. It was almost a relief to transfer his terror to something ordinary. 'Hey, Terry, this is Peter James,' he said. 'Is Tom really in Montana? How can I reach him? It's a matter of life and death – *mine*.'

On his line, Max continued: 'You can't say I got arrested, Kit. It's not *true*. It would be *libel*.' Without a pause he pushed on: 'So you're talking to Barry. What else did he tell you?'

'What do you *mean*, he can't be reached?' Peter said.

'*Obviously* you're talking to Barry,' Max continued. 'I'm not a *moron*. Come on, Kit – didn't I introduce you to Geffen? He talks to you now, right? Didn't I come through for you?'

'I can't believe you're telling me this,' Peter said. 'How can you *do* this to me?'

Max stabbed his finger at Peter's phone, meaning he should pick up and listen in. 'I'll call back,' Peter said, clicking off one line and onto the other. He heard Bradley laugh. 'Don't bullshit me, Max,' she said. 'If you helped me before, it was for sick reasons of your own. You're the king of the hidden agenda.'

Somehow Bradley was flirtatious and belligerent at the same time. She was thirty-five and single, almost pretty by Hollywood standards, with a well-toned body and a romantic tangle of dark hair. But the real secret of her success was that she was just as psychotically aggressive as the people she covered, so they tended to forget she was a reporter.

'Listen to you,' Max said. 'You're so mean to me. I think you must enjoy it.'

'I'm kind to you, believe me,' Bradley answered.

'Then just be logical for a second – you heard this vicious rumor from Barry Rose . . . ?'

'Max . . .'

'Ergo, Barry is trying to *fuck* me. What this is all about is Tom Hanks. *That's* what it's about. He needs Hanks, I have Hanks, and suddenly you're hearing these rumors. Can you believe someone sinking that low just to make a deal? It's *pathetic*.'

Midway through his speech, Max's voice began to carry a furious conviction, and Bradley started to weaken. 'Max, stop trying to worm my source out of me,' she whined. 'Just answer the question – are you going to be arrested? Have you ever been arrested? Do you ever *plan* to be arrested in the future under *any* conceivable auspices, be they federal, state or Bureau of Alcohol, Tobacco and Firearms?'

The Amtel beeped, and Max leaned back to read it: Jack Rippert.

'Kit, can you hold for a minute?' Max said. 'I want to answer that question.'

Then jabbed at the phone buttons. '*Jack*,' he barked.

'Maaax,' Rippert brayed. 'You left so many messages my secretary is putting in for haaadship pay.'

Rippert's accent was a peculiar mixture of Brooklyn and Boston, and came out sounding like a Kennedy pulling on a leash.

'Well, excuse me if my life is in a fucking meltdown,' Max brayed back. 'Where the fuck were you, anyway?'

'In cawwwt – it's something lawyers do once in a while. What's the matter with you anyway, lying to the fuggin' cops? Why'd you tell him your kid was with you the whole night?'

'You talked to the Dog?'

'Fuggin' A I talked to the Dog. Whadda ya think I sent him ooover faa? To keep ya from shooting your fuggin' mouth off. And whadda ya do? Ya shoot ya fuggin' mouth off!'

Rippert always acted this way, as if his honor depended on giving new meaning to the word '*abrasive*'. He'd gotten his start in Hollywood as a protégé of the gun-toting wing of the Directors Guild, the Peckinpah–Milius annex, who took him up because his Harvard degree hadn't completely ruined him as a human being – or so they liked to joke. By now surliness was his calling card, his claim to fame. A call from his office could inspire a cuticle-chewing orgy in the toughest minimoguls.

'I thought you sent him over to steal my sheets,' Max snapped, with such bitterness that Rippert stopped short. Even Peter was surprised – Max hadn't mentioned the sheet incident since it happened.

'Maaaax, settle down. We're just trying to cover all the bases. I already talked to the DA. From what it sounds like they got no case.'

'Meanwhile everybody in fucking town knows about it. It's hurting my *business*.'

'Maaax, Maaax, Maaax. Slow down. Let's play this out step by step. I got the Dog working the cops, checking everything out. Because of your big mouth he's going to have to trace your kid, make sure nobody saw him, take care of 'em if they did. Then he goes to work on the girl. Don't woorrry, everything's gonna be all right.'

'The girl?' said Max. 'What's the Dog going to do to her?'

'Investi*gaaate*,' Rippert said. 'That's what he does, right?'

Max didn't respond. Peter looked up and saw him frowning.

'Whatsamatta?' Rippert said. 'You gotta problem with that?'

'She's a kid,' Max said.

'Awww, Christ, I got work to do. I'll call you when I get something new.'

Max glared at the dead phone, then stabbed his finger at the pulsing hold button. 'Kit, you still there?' he said, continuing without pause. 'I've decided you *do* enjoy it. You're consumed with bitterness.'

'Max, be serious,' Bradley said, using her patient-with-a-mental-patient voice again.

'I *am* serious,' he continued. 'That's your *problem*. You're consumed with bitterness because you really want to be in the business and you can't admit it to yourself because you have this insane fixed idea about the romance of journalism. I mean, it's like you watched *His Girl Friday* a few dozen times too many when you were a kid. You're not hiding innocent men in rolltop desks! You're *hurting* people.'

'Enough with the cruel-media sermon, Max,' Bradley said. 'I've heard it about a dozen times already. *Today*.'

Max ignored her. 'I mean, for God's sake, Kit, we're not *politicians*. We're making *movies*, bringing smiles to the faces of innocent children. Go bother the politicians!'

There was a rhythm to these conversations. You had to allow the other person to let off enough ego-steam before interrupting. Bradley let Max go on for another minute or two before interrupting. 'Max,' she said finally, her voice stern. 'Don't try to change the subject. I have been very kind to you over the years, given the fact that you're just about the biggest moving target in Hollywood. I even like you, which scares me.'

'How can you say these—' Max began.

Bradley cut him off. 'But if you *don't* tell me the truth about Barry and his lovely daughter Tracy, I will feel that you are holding out on me and I will be . . . less kind. I will put my affection for you in a little airtight box and treat you like *any other producer*.'

Bradley was starting to sound like Max. You almost had to just to stay in the conversation, like speeding up on the freeway so you can enter a faster lane of traffic.

'You're so *mean* to me.'

'Come on, Max. I'm just a hard-working newsgal trying to do her job.'

Max looked around his office – a lot of mahogany, paintings by Ed Ruscha and David Salle, a few brassy awards, all for technical categories – and then he heaved a theatrical sigh and asked her to hold for just a sec. He hit the hold button and glared at Peter. 'What have you got?'

'Called Clavius – he's in Montana.'

'I know he's in Montana, for chrissake.'

'He's on some river. He's fishing.'

Max slammed the phone down and shot up, coming around his desk as if he were preparing for a physical attack. 'Call CAA! Call his wife! Call his kids at school!' He opened the door and held it, waiting for Peter to go.

As Peter slinked to his desk, Max stood at the door and shouted after him: 'I want him on the phone! I don't care if you have to rent a parachute and a cellular phone and jump out of a *fucking plane*!'

He stood there for a moment, glaring down the row of desks. The assistants quickly turned their eyes back down to their work. Then he went back to his desk and snatched up the phone again, punching at the pulsing hold button to resume his conversation with Bradley. Wasting no more time, he did what he'd probably been planning to do from the moment he put in the call: co-opt her with kindness. 'Okay, this is the whole story,' he began. 'But I'm telling you this as a friend, *off the record*.'

From his desk, Peter could still hear Max gassing on: how he befriended Tracy as a girl and how her father resented it and Kit, you have to remember that everything in Hollywood is personal, it's like high school with money . . . Peter shut the voice out and called CAA. We'll get back to you, they said. He called Hanks's house. No luck. Only then did he permit himself to dial his own answering machine. There were messages from Bradley and a few professional semi-friends he'd met on the assistant circuit, all sniffing after fresh Max-rumor, and a mysterious call from the director John Sayles . . . but nothing from Tracy.

His fingers stroked the telephone keys. Should he call her? Could he risk it, with all these people listening? But then Max would probably march down the hall just as they were getting started and start bossing him around again. Tracy would love that. If only he could figure a way to get a minute to himself . . .

Then Max hung up and stalked to the door again. 'Send Mosely in!' he barked. Then he glared down the hall at Peter. '*Well*?'

'Still no luck.'

'*Fuck*! What *good* are you?'

Peter shrugged.

'Work from here,' Max said, hooking a finger toward the office. 'I want you here in case I want you.'

Peter almost laughed. It was a classic Maxism: I want you in case I want you. Without looking at the other assistants, he slouched back down the hall and plopped into Max's sofa, snatching up the phone again. Who to try next? Who were Hanks's friends?

While Peter strategized, Sarah ushered Mosely back from the reception area. Max was just launching into the obligatory small-talk when a man poked his head in the door. 'Excuse me,' he said. 'Sorry to interrupt.'

Their eyes went to his briefcase. To Peter it seemed ominous, formal, a rude truth in the murmur of sweaters and sneakers. He remembered meeting the man in the commissary in a group of studio lawyers.

'We have to talk,' the lawyer said.

'Now?' Max said. 'I'm in a meeting.'

Ten minutes?'

Max apologized to Mosely and waited while he wheeled himself out the door. The lawyer glanced at Peter. 'I'd prefer one on one,' he said.

'Is it about . . . ?'

The lawyer nodded. 'Alan sent me over.'

Max aimed a finger at Peter. 'Call him,' he said. To the studio lawyer he said, 'Just give me a minute.'

Peter speed-dialed. 'He's in a meeting,' Kramer's secretary said. Peter told her again that it was Max Fischer calling, but the secretary said Kramer could not be disturbed. Peter hung up the phone.

'In a meeting,' he said.

Max didn't seem at all perturbed. 'Get me the Ripper,' he said, almost sweetly.

The studio lawyer shifted in his chair as Peter put in the call, but otherwise showed no expression. Max snatched up a magazine and flurried through the pages.

'Back in court,' Peter said.

This time Max looked incredulous – but only for a second.

'What about *Hanks*?' he said.

Peter took a deep breath. Three strikes, you're . . .

'Camping,' he said.

'What, in a *tent*?'

'Sleeping bag, Sterno lamp, the whole thing,' Peter said, hoping to amuse. 'Possibly even a Davy Crockett hat.'

But Max wasn't amused. 'And you accept this as an answer?' he said, glancing at the lawyer as if for support. 'Barry Rose can get a script to him, and I can't get him on the fucking *telephone*? This is acceptable? This is how you do your job?'

'Well—'

'Maybe that's how they did things back at Columbia University, but this is Columbia *Pictures*.'

'I'll find him,' Peter said.

'Maybe we should get you a map – ass, elbow, *Hanks*.'

The lawyer tried not to look.

'I'll do my best,' Peter said, trying for dignity. This was the part he hated most, the ritual public abuse. They had been heading toward this moment ever since they left the house, and once Max got to the office and threw himself into that manic work pattern, the whole office could see it coming. It followed such an invariable pattern they had a name for it: the Max Attack. Drive drive drive drive drive . . . *kabloom*! But this time Max started in over drive, so all morning the staff had been wondering just how big the *kabloom* would be when it came. Peter had felt the eyes on him, sensed the heads poised inside the doors along the hall: Curiosity has its own specific density, like iron or steel. The lawyer met his eyes and looked away, embarrassed for him.

But Max just shook his head in disgust. 'You're *pathetic*.'

Through the open door, Peter met Sarah's eyes. She made a sad face: Poor Peter.

The lawyer put his briefcase on his knees and took out a yellow pad and a microcassette player.

'Is that an Olympus?' Max said.

Nodding, the lawyer held up the tiny silver cassette player.

'Beautiful. How's the sound quality?'

'Great,' the lawyer said.

'Can I?'

The lawyer handed him the tiny machine, and Max studied it. Then he looked up at Peter, who was sitting on the couch trying to be invisible. 'Get me one of these,' he said. 'Since you can't even find a fucking phone number, we'll demote you to *personal shopper*.'

Then he turned back to business.

The lawyer held his hand out for the cassette player. 'I'd like to turn that on – do you mind?'

Max nodded his permission.

'This is the situation,' the lawyer began. 'We've got a source in the LAPD says the chances are very good you'll be charged. Therefore we have to conduct our own investigation . . .'

Max stared at the lawyer, unblinking, until the lawyer stopped talking. For a moment they just looked at each other, and Peter got an eerie sense that Max was trying to communicate telepathically: *I'm Max Fischer, for chrissake . . . I've made millions for this studio . . . How can this be happening? . . . How can you talk to me this way?*

Then the lawyer shrugged. 'We have to protect the studio,' he said.

Max shot his eyes back at Peter. 'What are you *waiting* for? Get out of here. I don't want to see your face till you have the number *and* the tape recorder. Get out! Get out! *Get out*!' Max hit the button under his desk, releasing the door. As it swung closed, Peter saw the lawyer look up from his pad with a smile, as if he'd just remembered something nice. 'By the way,' he said. 'Happy birthday.'

The minute he got to his car, Peter dialed Tracy's home number. No answer. It kept ringing. Where the hell was she! And why didn't she ever turn on her answering machine?

Peter pointed his Fiat north, toward Beverly Hills. He'd park near the Sharper Image and work his way out. After all, every fancy new toy in existence could be found somewhere in that golden radius. And it was on the way to Tracy's house.

He wanted to see her. He wanted to talk to her. Was she okay? Was she hurt? Where did she go after he fell asleep?

As he drove, he opened his glove compartment and turned on his scanner. He did this automatically now. Two weeks ago he'd heard at a party that the smarter assistants were now using police scanners to listen in on cellular phone calls – you could actually hear people making deals! Gain valuable intelligence! And sometimes listen in when guys talked dirty to their girlfriends, which they did with surprising frequency. He went out and bought one the next day, and had rapidly become a police-band addict.

'. . . And call Margie, tell her to pick up the lawnmower . . .'

But most of the time, it was just guys talking to their secretaries. Peter fiddled with the knob.

'. . . No, the motion *has* to be filed by Wednesday . . .'

When he got to Wilshire he switched it off. Too many agents stalking these particular sidewalks, and he didn't want his snooping overheard.

Ah, Beverly Hills. It was always a kick, so surreal, an all-American small town stuffed to its capped teeth with money, a reverse-Potemkin village where everyone tried to pretend things were just as normal and homey as could be – we're jes' folks, honey. Jes' rich folks. But Peter liked it. In fact, he liked it a lot. He knew that a Casio told time as well as a Rolex, but if he'd learned one thing in the last three months it was this: Power was the ultimate drug, the high you wanted over and over. And power wasn't just fat men smoking cigars, a cliché art snobs had foisted on the public. It was also the artist capturing the perfect image and the composer making music and the beautiful woman flaunting her string bikini at the beach . . .

and the producer bossing his assistant. Each a dictator in his little domain. And what the stores along Rodeo and Camden sold was nothing but a vast collection of different signs flashing the same neon message: I have power. And Peter had to admit (because honesty was another form of power, and insight was another) that he wanted to wear the clothes and drive the car and escort the woman. He didn't want anyone to mistake him for a loser. Least of all himself.

He parked in the underground lot and set off in search of the Olympus. The Sharper Image had a statue of the Alien alien in its window, all veins and insecty metal carapaces. Tourists browsed, and Peter marched past them: I have *work* to do.

'Nah, try over on Camden,' the clerk said.

Peter found a pay phone and tried Tracy again. Still no answer.

He ambled to Camden, wondering: What do I look like to people, in my Gap khakis and button-down white shirt? No tie, so I'm not an office wonk. Sneakers instead of loafers, so probably not rich. Hair too messy to be an actor. Clothes too neat to fit into the category of video-store clerk/film student/aspiring director. Probably they figured he was between identities.

That was funny. What he meant to say was between *careers* – thanks and a tip of the hat to Dr Sigmund Freud and his collection of ladies' underwear . . .

He found the right store, put the tape recorder on plastic. Gene Wilder walked by, looking very tall and much older. What had happened to him?

Peter went looking for another pay phone, suddenly aware that his palms were sweating. He wiped them on the khakis and watched the brown marks appear, hoping it was just wet, not grime. It occurred to him that he should talk to a lawyer, instead of putting himself completely in Max's hands. Then it hit him, a quick little electroshock of clarity: He was trying to act normal, and things weren't normal anymore. He put the quarter in the slot, dialed the number for the last time. It rang once, twice, three times . . .

Dammit! Still no answer. His chest felt tight. It was hard to breathe. He started running.

*   *   *

64

When Peter got to the car he was sweating. He fumbled with his keys, then just jumped over the door into the seat, jamming the ignition key into the keyhole and pushing in the clutch all at once. Seconds later he was pulling out of the parking lot, through a red light, slamming the Fiat back into low to roar around a pokey Saab. 'Don't you have anywhere to *go*!' he yelled, aiming for Coldwater Canyon and glancing at his watch: 1:50 P.M. He could probably get away with another hour, say he had trouble finding the cassette player.

He pulled into the upper parking lot of the Bel-Air Hotel, stuffed the tape recorder under the seat and jumped out without opening the door. He walked in the wrong direction, away from the hotel, scrambling through bushes into the trees. He climbed up the hill until he reached a tree next to a high white wall, then scrambled over it, slinging himself down into the backyard of a large estate. He waited in a crouch for a moment, until he was sure nobody heard hi.n. Then he cut through the bushes to the guest house. Tossing a nervous glance up the driveway, he knocked. After a moment, he knocked again. Finally he heard footsteps.

Tracy opened the door. She was wearing a blue silk robe and looked as if she'd been crying, with smudged-mascara eyes and white bangs stuck to her forehead. She gave Peter a smirk. 'It's the assistant,' she said.

Peter was sweating from his climb, his breath coming fast. For a moment all he could think of was: What am I doing here? What made me think I could trust her? Then he looked closer – she had a black eye, almost perfectly covered with makeup, and under the makeup she looked tired. 'Are you okay?' he asked.

'Fabulous.'

Peter shot a glance at the big house. 'Can I come in?'

'I'm not receiving.'

Was she high again? She seemed so arch and fragile.

'What's going on, Tracy? What is all this?'

'Whatever do you mean?' she said, a parody of girlish innocence. It was annoying. Peter reached out and grabbed her by the arm. '*Tracy*,' he said, trying to cut through.

Her eyes narrowed. 'You're hurting me . . . again,' she said. But she didn't try to pull her arm away.

Peter let go, surprised by himself. He hadn't been aware of squeezing. 'Can we go somewhere or something?' he pleaded. 'I have to talk to you.'

Tracy started to close the door.

'I never wanted to hurt you,' Peter said, putting all the feeling he had for her into his voice. Tracy hesitated, studying his face. 'Please?' he said.

Tracy shrugged and stepped aside. Carefully wiping his feet, Peter walked into a big rec room with a pool table in the middle and skis mounted on one wall. There was a rustic bar against the back wall, complete with an ice-maker and three full tiers of liquor bottles. Drawn by motion, his eyes went to the staircase at the back of the room.

A woman stood on the stairs. All Peter could absorb of her at first was dark hair and an impression of extreme beauty – she was one of those women who are so gorgeous they are hard to look at directly, as if they throw off a glare. She studied him without saying anything. Evidently she had been listening to their conversation.

Peter turned and saw Tracy closing the door and coming around to face him, her hands pulling together the lapels of her robe as if she were gathering her attitude about her – Elvis curl in her smile, challenge and contempt in her eyes. 'Have you met Marina?' she said.

'Hello,' he said. Was this the big secret? The reason she had never let him in before? Was Marina her lover? Was that why she had used her name?

Then Marina Lake said one word, *hello*, and he recognized the voice immediately: *Tell him it's Minoku, his little China girl* . . .

'I think we've spoken on the phone,' Peter said. He took in high cheekbones, Slavic eyes, a mysterious feline poise, as if she were deciding to turn into a statue or pounce. Then he forced himself to look away and concentrate on Tracy. 'Why don't you answer your phone?' he asked.

'Why'd you lie to the cops?'

Peter gave a pointed look toward Marina. 'Could we go somewhere to talk about this?'

Tracy shrugged, retying her robe belt and heading for the stairs. 'I talked to my father,' she said over her shoulder, her voice teasing. 'He said he'd love to sit down with you.' He hadn't even asked. She was throwing it at him, as if that were all he

66

really wanted. When in fact, even in this horrible situation, he still couldn't help watching her climb the stairs and noting – *studying* – the absence of a panty line . . .

Down boy.

Passing Marina, Peter thought of an exhibit in a museum, treasures under glass. Her skin was very pale and fine, and short black hair curled at her temples and neck, framing the perfect face like a jewel in a bed of velvet. As he passed she smiled and wet her lips with her tongue, a carnal and suggestive gesture that instantly jellied his knees. As he climbed to the second floor, he was relieved to be out of her presence.

There was a studio apartment up there. Tracy crossed to a coffee table – blue-washed pine, left over from the Southwest craze – and snagged a cigarette out of a Hopi pot. 'Tracy,' Peter said, pleading. 'Be straight with me. For *once*. God, you drive me crazy. You must like it.' It was a Maxism, but he kept on. 'What happened, anyway? Won't you just tell me?'

She lit her cigarette, back to him. 'Answer me first,' she said.

'What was I supposed to say?' he whispered, coming up behind her. ' "Sorry, Max, I can't be your alibi because six hours ago I was *fucking* the victim"?'

Tracy turned back. The way she looked at him then, amused and almost tender, Peter thought she was going to be sane about this. She understood that things had gone too far. She would explain, and everything would turn out okay . . .

Then her smile turned mean. 'Couldn't do that,' she said. 'Definitely a bad career move.' Before he could respond, the smile went on automatic. 'So how is Max, anyway? Taking this well?'

'What do you think? You charged him with rape. The *police* came.'

Tracy blew out a stream of smoke, considering that. 'How did he react?'

'He was a tad upset.'

She nodded, taking it in.

'Well?'

'What?'

'Did he or didn't he?'

'Only his hairdresser knows for sure,' she said, airily quoting the old commercial.

'Did he or didn't he?'

'Or his valet. That would be you, I guess.'

'Come on, Tracy, cut the bullshit. Did Max rape you?'

'Does it really matter?'

She looked at him.

'Yes,' Peter said. 'It matters.'

'You gonna avenge my honor?'

There was so much cynicism and bitterness in her voice that Peter felt an abrupt internal lurch: elevator belly. And then she made it worse by laughing. 'That would be a good trick,' she said, starting to hiccup.

Tracy bit her lip and looked at the floor. He had hurt her. She seemed on the verge of tears. Was it all just an act, then, trying to be tough? She was still just nineteen, after all. Peter reached a hand toward her shoulder. 'Tracy,' he said, in his kindest voice. 'What's up?'

'You should – *hic* – know.'

Guilt raised a hot tingle on his scalp. 'Me?'

'You shouldn't have slugged me,' she said, touching her cheek near the black eye.

The tingle went away, washed by relief. 'That was an accident,' Peter said. 'You were totally wasted.'

She shrugged.

'You had your claws in my face. Practically blinded me.'

From the way she frowned, he could tell she didn't remember. 'I guess Percodan's just not my drug,' she said, softening.

Peter wanted to comfort her . . . but knowing how changeable she was, he decided to keep after the answers first. 'So why'd you blame it on Max?' he asked again.

She gave him a look like he should know, and Peter remembered the smell in Max's sheets.

'I mean, I know you hate him, but—'

She interrupted, cocking her head. 'Maybe I was trying to protect you. Did you ever think of that?'

She was kidding, right? She could be cruel that way, when she really meant she didn't care for him at all.

'What I don't understand is why you went up there in the first place,' he finished.

Tracy returned a look of genuine astonishment. 'You think *I* went over to see *him*?'

'Didn't you?'

She flicked her cigarette at him. 'Asshole,' she said. The cigarette bounced off his chest and landed on the carpet, scattering tiny red coals. 'You want to know how it happened? The old man made the report. He has property rights, after all – I'm his "girl". One of them, anyway.' While she was talking, Peter patted out the coals and picked up the cigarette butt. As he leaned forward to drop it in the ashtray, Tracy flashed him a rotten smile, like she knew the world's dirty secret. 'Remember I told him I was going out with Max?' she said. 'Just to piss him off? Well, when I got home I guess I hadn't cleaned up the blood too good and he catches me in the driveway and chases me around the house asking, "Did *Max* do this to you? Was it *Max*?" Here I am bleeding and all he fucking – *hic* – cares about is having one more reason to hate Max. So I just laugh, and I go and take a shower and twenty minutes later the cops are at the door, asking me for a statement.'

'Why didn't you just tell them the truth?'

She didn't answer.

'Tracy?'

She didn't answer.

It was just an act, Peter decided. She was really just a kid, putting on attitude and hoping it would make a colorful fit, maybe even redeem some of the anger and fear inside. He should have started with a hug, but the moment for that had passed. Instead he put it in his voice. 'I'm sorry if . . .' He let it trail off.

She lit another cigarette, keeping her eyes on the floor. 'I told you to stop,' she said.

And there it was. He had pushed it out of his mind almost completely. 'We were *naked*,' he said, with a nervous laugh.

'I said no.'

'I was *inside* you.'

'I changed my mind.'

'But we planned it. You—'

'You *hit* me.'

69

That made him mad. He'd explained already that it was an accident. So he said the most horrible thing he could, knowing that it was a horrible thing but also feeling that there was some truth to it: 'You asked for it.'

'Fuck you,' she snapped.

'Come on, Tracy, be reasonable,' he pleaded. 'You're acting like one of *them*.'

Then Tracy started laughing, as if the ironies had overwhelmed her. She continued laughing as she let herself fall back across the sofa . . . and maybe she didn't even realize that her robe had fallen open. Peter knew he should look away but couldn't. The wild black bush was like a taunt: Tracy had something he would never have, this ability to just throw herself away, this talent for oblivion, an aristocrat's disregard for the material consequences of her actions. She threw the cigarette, he picked it up. Then Tracy followed his eyes down to her own body, and smiled. 'Detective Spinks feels very sorry for me,' she said. 'She thinks you're all a "nest of vipers".' And finally she smoothed the robe down over her thighs, her gestures as formal as Kabuki, conjuring leather jackets and bruised lips, motorcycles flying through the wind. There was something humid and unreal about it all. These people, he thought, in what may actually have been a mild form of clinical shock, *seemed perfectly willing to destroy each other* – in fact, *eager*.

'I don't think you're seeing this very clearly,' Peter said, licking dry lips. 'You accused Max of a terrible crime.'

Tracy took a drag of her cigarette and exhaled – '*hic*' – tapping it theatrically in the general direction of the ashtray. 'I'm sure he's committed lots of terrible crimes,' she said.

Peter started to splutter a protest, but Tracy cut him off with one of the coldest looks he'd ever seen. 'Max sent you to use me and you used me,' she said. 'I can accept it. Why can't you?'

'That's so unfai—'

'You're an *errand boy*, Peter,' she said.

Peter stopped and just stared at her, scrambling to rise above the situation, which seemed to be whirlpooling into madness.

'I'll tell you one thing,' Tracy continued. 'If Max had raped me, he wouldn't have lied about it. Max knows what he is. He knows what he wants.'

'Can we not say the name Max for *five fucking minutes*?'

'You think being ninety-two percent good gives you immunity,' she said. 'Like the eight percent that made you betray him with me doesn't count.'

This is really getting annoying, Peter thought. Here she is, a fucking basket case, and she comes off like Marian fucking Williamson. 'That's crazy,' he said.

'You better watch out, because that eight percent is going to grow like a tumor,' she said. 'Boys like you come here, you *fall* for these bastards, pretty soon you can't change fast enough. And you're changing fast, Peter.'

She wasn't kidding with this, he could hear it in her voice. The expression on her face was angry and disappointed. Even her hiccups were gone. Maybe she was really talking about herself, maybe she was the one who was changing and it scared her, so she was getting mad at him the way you get mad at a friend who drinks too much if you drink too much yourself.

Or maybe she was right.

'It must be a burden to be so smart,' Peter said.

She turned her face to profile, dismissing him. Peter didn't know what else to say.

At the top of the stairway, he turned and blurted out the first thing that came to mind: 'Hey, you don't happen to have Tom Hanks's phone number in Montana, do you?'

She laughed, nicely this time, shaking her head at the craziness of Hollywood. Before answering she picked another cigarette out of the pot. 'No,' she said. 'But my daddy might.'

'I bet he does,' Peter said.

Tracy lit her cigarette, and then Peter tried one last time. 'You've got to tell the truth about all this, you know,' he said. 'Sooner or later you're going to have to.'

She sucked at the cigarette, then blew out the smoke. 'Why don't you?'

Chapter Four

When he reached the bottom of the stairs Peter saw Marina sitting in a leather club chair by the window, sipping an espresso. Even seated, her body had that same aloof poise, between withdrawal and attack. Peter hesitated, nodded awkwardly, and headed for the door.

'I didn't hear you drive up,' she said.

'I came, uh . . .'

'Through the woods?'

'Yeah.'

'Parked at the Bel-Air?'

'Yeah.'

She nodded, confirming a memory. 'I used to do that when we were kids,' she said. 'When me and the Trace Element were in getting-high school.'

Peter glanced back at the staircase, and when his eyes came around again Marina was getting up. 'I'll give you a ride,' she said. She put her coffee cup down on the pool table and called up the stairs: 'I'm giving Peter a ride to his car.'

She knew his name.

'Of course you are,' Tracy answered. Peter could tell from her voice that she was still in the same position, lying back on the sofa.

Grabbing her bag, Marina opened the door and held it, waiting for Peter to pass through. He gave a last look up the stairs.

Marina took his arm and led him up the driveway. 'If the EPA was doing its job, the whole family would be sealed in lead and buried in the New Mexico desert,' she said. 'They have a half-life of ten generations before they turn normal again.'

Peter glanced at Marina, wondering how to take this remark. Were she and Tracy friends, or what? 'You grew up around here?' he asked.

Marina pointed over the wall toward a very large red-tiled roof.

'Your folks still live there?'

73

'Probably,' she said, with a shrug, opening the door of a ratty little Volkswagen. Peter got in, pushing aside cassettes and old newspapers to make way. Marina didn't make any apology for the mess, the way most people would. 'So you're pretty well fucked, aren't you?' she said. She seemed pleased by it, or at least amused.

'How much do you know?'

'Everything,' she said. The way she said it, so world-weary and annoyed, she seemed to be talking not just about this incident, but about all the conditions of life that led up to it.

'Then I wish you'd explain it to me,' Peter said, going for boyish confusion. To which she didn't respond at all – the perfect face went perfectly blank, and when she reached the end of the street she took the turn hard enough to push Peter against the door. 'So what are you going to do?' she asked.

'I haven't got the faintest idea.'

She smiled.

There was something cold about her, Peter thought. He remembered that she had been a hooker. Isn't that what Max said? Something about being a hooker in Japan?

'What do you think Max is going to do when he finds out?'

Peter shrugged.

'What about Tracy?' she asked. 'Are you in love with her?'

That was an odd question. What was she after? 'In love? I don't know. Involved. I'm in volve with her.'

'How in volve?'

'I don't know. She's got me pretty confused.'

She pursed her lips, breaking up the classic planes. 'But you find her attractive?'

'Yeah.'

'Because of who her father is,' she said, stating a fact. 'And because of Max.'

She made another sharp left turn, pushing Peter against the door even harder this time. Evidently that was just the way she drove.

'No, that's not it,' Peter said, starting to get angry. Why did this woman assume she knew him? 'Maybe at first. But now, no. I wish she wasn't.'

Then the Bel-Air came in sight, huddled down amidst the spreading trees, and Peter thought about walking through the cloisters of the Château, remembered Tracy at the door – her bleary, disarmed face, her sleep-warm body. He felt a wave of tenderness and remorse. How did he let things get so fucked up? He should have soothed her. He should have held her in his arms.

'So how's Max taking it?' Marina asked.

'Yelling a lot,' Peter said.

She grinned. For a moment she looked like a real teenager. Peter pointed to his car and Marina pulled up behind it, but as he started to get out she stopped him with a hand on his arm. 'What if I could give you a way out?' she asked.

'What do you mean?'

'I could make it happen,' she said. 'One phone call. Tell the cops everything Tracy told me. Max had nothing to do with it. Would you like that?'

Peter didn't know what to say. It seemed like just a game to her, but she was watching him closely, as if his answer really mattered. 'I guess I would.'

'But you wouldn't want Max to know, right?'

'No,' he said.

'That wouldn't help at all, would it? Max would fire you, and then you wouldn't become a big shot in Hollywood.'

'Right now I'm just hoping to stay employed.'

'But maybe Max would never have to know,' she said, still watching him. 'I could tell them on the QT, just tell 'em the facts and say I'll testify for you if it ever goes to court. For you and Max. They'd just drop it, I promise you. I even know a couple of other people who might testify.'

'Really?' Peter said. This was starting to sound good. But why did she keep watching him like that?

'So what would you do for me? Would you make it happen for me?'

'What do you mean?' he asked.

'Would you make it happen for me?' she repeated.

It seemed to be a phrase with some kind of significance, but Peter wasn't getting it. Make *what* happen?

'I don't know,' he said. 'What do you want?'

She laughed in his face. Then she patted her mouth, tamping the laugh back down, as if she knew it was rude but just couldn't help it. 'I'll have to think about that,' she said, patting him on the leg. 'I'll give you a call.'

75

'You want my number?'
'Oh, I've got your number, Peter.'

Back at the studio, Peter parked in his marked spot in the Washington Boulevard executive lot – driving Max around had its privileges – then cut down the Thalberg Building alley and through the studio gate. As he passed, he glanced up at the Sony sign, a modest black-and-white job that seemed to defer to the grand old MGM lion it had replaced. Once again he wished he hadn't come so late, that he'd gotten a chance to enter under the lion, but Kerkorian had sold that along with everything else. He slowed down to savor the ersatz small-town streets, once again feeling that ripple of pleasure at the artifice: Behind the hat-shop window was a brick wall, behind the bank facade just another studio office. If they had been a real bank or a real hat shop he wouldn't have looked twice or felt anything at all. He could explain it a dozen different ways but it was still a mystery: Why did the illusion give such pleasure?

He hooked past the little row of cutting rooms and made a sharp left, passing through a block of Olde Manhattan, complete with gas lamps and a burlesque joint. A production assistant wearing headphones waved him around a horse-drawn carriage. A painted lady stood on a street corner, with ruffled skirts and old-fashioned décolletage – as Peter passed, she winked.

And up ahead, an alien with a large, gunmetal head stood by a soundstage door, putting a cigarette deep into his mouth, past rows and rows of ragged teeth. Peter couldn't help smiling. He glanced in at the stage door and saw a set: below, a utilitarian scramble of pine planks and struts, and above, the flight deck of a starship. I don't want to lose this, he thought. I don't want to *lose*—

A voice murmured in his ear: 'If it isn't Peter James.'

Startled, Peter twitched.

'What's the matter? Guilty conscience?'

It was Marlon Spurlock, his immediate predecessor in the job of Max's 24-hour-a-day slave, a strange-looking creature with a pasty white face and a pouf of hair that levitated above his head like something floating underwater. Peter had met him a couple of times before, at restaurants and clubs, introduced by people who thought it would be amusing to put the two of them together. Max's abuse of Spurlock was legendary, the tales told at assistants' parties from

Laurel Canyon to Tribeca – did you hear about the time Fischer sent Spurlock fifty miles through the jungle for a diet soda? When he sent him location hunting in Death Valley? When a reporter from *Vanity Fair* came to do a profile on Max, and he made Spurlock catch grapes with his mouth? Spurlock had survived four years of this, rising at least nominally to the job of president of Fischer Pictures before Max portioned him off with a screenplay deal.

'What are you doing on the lot?' Peter asked, making conversation.

Spurlock ignored the question. 'Heard you guys had a little excitement this morning.'

Peter pretended he didn't know what Spurlock was talking about. 'Well, you know how it is,' he said, thinking: Does he mean what I think he means? How did he find out so fast?

'Let's go in here,' Spurlock said, taking him by the arm, an unexpectedly intimate gesture. With the other arm he pushed open one of the heavy soundstage doors, leading Peter through a little decompression chamber to another door. A sign said DO NOT ENTER WHEN LIGHT IS RED, but the light was not red and Spurlock pushed through the second door.

Inside the soundstage, pitch black. Peter couldn't see five feet, but he felt the vast empty space around him. Spurlock skittered off toward the wall, then there was a clack and the lights came on.

The soundstage was a huge empty space, like a vast padded cell, an asylum for giants. The entire back wall was covered by the biggest bluescreen Peter had ever seen. It looked unreal, as if some dizzy god had stuck the ocean up sideways, or decided to jam the sky itself into this particular corner.

'Biggest bluescreen in history,' Spurlock said. 'They're shooting Dick Donner's new movie in here next week.'

For a moment they both stared. There was something very pleasing about it, something almost magical. Which was appropriate, because bluescreens were one of the most basic elements of movie magic, the effect that made Luke Skywalker skywalk and let E.T. ride that bike across the moon. With a bluescreen you could put an actor in Rome, fly him to a mountaintop, or hang him off the edge of a skyscraper. You could get something out of nothing, transubstantiate dull matter. From the first, Peter was fascinated by the process and kept badgering Max with questions, until finally Max called a friend at Universal and had him comped to the studio tour so he could see for himself. On the tour Peter learned that filmmakers also used pinkscreens and greenscreens, but blue was the favorite because it was literally inhuman – it had no trace of blood, the better to contrast with human flesh.

'Personally, I hate 'em,' Spurlock said. 'Everything's special effects now. Realism, drama, ordinary human life – *over*.' But then his eyes went darting around the space again. To the side near the door there was a small office, and next to it a carpenter's table littered with scraps of plywood. The only sign of modern times was a large phone among the scraps. Spurlock sat back against the edge of the table and crossed his arms, smiling at Peter. 'So?'

'I should get back,' Peter said.

'Come on, you can tell me.'

'Tell you what?'

'I heard a rumor. Something about Barry Rose calling the cops on Max.'

He was smiling. This was a joke to him. But he was also very interested.

'I don't know anything about it,' Peter said. He didn't like the way Spurlock was acting, and he had a vague sense that despite the screenplay deal, things were not that good between Spurlock and Max.

'Don't be that way.'

'Honest,' Peter said. He looked longingly at the door, but decided that tact required another exchange or two. Meanwhile Spurlock pursed his lips, considering another approach.

'I guess you know about Max and Barry,' he asked.

Peter nodded. Oh yes, he did.

'When I started with Max, they were still a team,' Spurlock said. 'I'm the only person who saw them together day in, day out . . . except for Tracy, of course.'

Again Peter asked himself: How much does he know? What is he after?

'The things I saw were *brutal*,' Spurlock continued, with a sigh that seemed genuinely sad. 'Barry treated Max worse than anything I've ever seen – one time he threw one of those big heavy metal Rolodexes at him because Max opened a soda while he was on the phone. The *fizz* distracted him.'

'I really got to go,' Peter said.

Then Spurlock smiled, as if something brilliant had just occurred to him. 'Wait, wait, I want to show you something.' He grabbed the phone and pulled it to the end of the table, then he went into the office and came out with an identical phone, shaking out the long thick cord behind it. Both phones were the big, clunky old office phones, with lots of buttons for different lines. 'Someone showed me this when I first started working for Max,' he said. He handed one phone to Peter and picked up the other one himself. 'This seminar is called *Hollywood 101: The Business of Relationships*. First you dial . . .' He thought for a second. 'Mike Ovitz,' he said, with satisfaction. 'Then I will call Mr David Geffen. Then we patch them together.'

Peter hesitated – was this smart? Ovitz and Geffen were two of the most powerful guys in the business, and they had a legendary (if obscure) loathing for each other.

'Don't worry,' Spurlock said. 'There's no way they'll know who it is.' He paused, then added, 'There's a point to this. You'll see.' He began dialing, and after another second's hesitation Peter did too – what the hell, how much worse could things be?

Spurlock's call went through first. 'Mike Ovitz calling for Mr Geffen,' he said.

Peter's phone rang twice and a receptionist answered in a business-like voice: 'Walt Disney Studios.'

'David Geffen for Mr Ovitz,' Peter said.

The receptionist put him through to Ovitz's secretary. Again he said Geffen was calling, and Ovitz's secretary said she would see if he was available. A moment later she said Ovitz would take the call and Peter said he'd connect Geffen.

But Spurlock was shaking his head – his call hadn't gone through! And now Peter heard a voice in his ear – the calm, tight voice of Mike Ovitz himself. 'Hello? David?'

Peter hesitated. Spurlock raised his finger: Coming, coming.

'Connecting you, sir. I'm experiencing a . . . technical difficulty.'

'Who is this?' Ovitz said.

Spurlock brought his hand down like the starting flag at a race, punching two buttons simultaneously. Both of them held the phones, listening.

'Mike?'

'David?'

79

'How are you?' Geffen asked.

'Fine. And you?'

'Doing great.'

There was a pause.

'Well, what can I do for you?' Ovitz finally said.

'Didn't you call me?' Geffen said.

'I thought you called me.'

Another pause.

'Listen, David, I know you have nothing to do but count your money, but I've got a business to run.'

Geffen chuckled. Ovitz knew perfectly well that Geffen had a business to run, too – hell, the whole world knew about Dreamworks. But it amused him to imply that Geffen was really nothing but a rich dilettante. 'I thought that was Eisner's job,' he said.

Touché: You may be chairman of a huge company, sucker, but to a guy with my money you're still just punching a clock. You work for Michael Eisner.

'I try to help where I can,' Ovitz said, keeping his voice perfectly calm. 'But seriously, I do have another call coming in.'

'You better take it, then,' Geffen said, amused: *He* didn't have to take calls.

'Nice talking to you,' Ovitz said. 'Keep in touch.'

Which was a reminder that they had business pending, and would always have business pending. Then Peter heard a click, and Spurlock started putting his phone down. But Peter thought he heard the soft hiss of an open line, and hesitated. He was about to hang up when he heard the voice in his ear, as intimate as a tongue. 'Who is this?' Geffen asked.

Peter held his breath.

'I hope you had fun,' Geffen said, gently but with enough of an edge to make it a warning.

The line went dead.

'Didn't you love the way Ovitz didn't react?' Spurlock crowed. ' "*Keep in touch*." Mikey's a *machine*.'

'Jesus,' Peter said.

'Do you understand?' Spurlock asked, hopping off the table as Peter sat there recovering. 'I'm not taking Barry's side – he's just as crazy as Max. They're *all* crazy. It's just a strategic move. You got to fight in one army or another until you can start your own.'

He gave Peter the satisfied grin of a man who has figured out all the angles. 'We all gotta spend the requisite period eating shit.'

'How long is that?' Peter said.

'As long as it takes, boyo,' Spurlock said, grinning. Peter found himself remembering again how warm everyone had been when he first came to town . . . such a long time ago. Even Ovitz had been nice – 'Call me anytime,' he'd said. And now what had he gone and done? 'I'm experiencing . . . a technical difficulty.' What a moron he was. What a *jerk*!

When Peter got back to the office, Max was on the phone. 'What the hell is he doing up in Montana, anyway?' he shouted. 'If one more actor buys a ranch up there, they'll have to rename the fucking place Malibu *North*.' He looked up at Peter. 'Where have you been?'

Peter handed over the Olympus, hoping it would be enough. All he wanted was to get through the rest of this day and lie down.

'Listen to this,' Max said, half to Peter and half into the phone. 'The second biggest box-office star in the world, and his own agent, my friend, can't give me a fucking phone number. All right, Jay, call me back.'

Max slammed down the phone and shouted through the doorway. 'Sarah, is Mosely still there?'

Peter looked at his watch. It was three-thirty. By now Mosely had been waiting almost three hours. 'I sent him to lunch,' Sarah said, raising her voice to cut through the distance. 'Felt sorry for him.'

'Get him. Send a runner.'

Max looked at Peter and sighed, shaking his head: What a day we're having. He let the Hanks problem go unmentioned.

'Did you eat?' Peter asked.

'Pasta.'

This was the moment. In this pause, he could blurt it out: Max, I have to tell you something. Last night, I didn't go home. That was a lie. The truth is, I went to Tracy's. She was wasted, I was horny, and the fact is I was pissed off from being with you, from being kept prisoner, from being ranted at and ordered around, from being weak and powerless and miserable all those years you were

81

making those movies in your own veiny, throbbing, purple-headed self-image . . .

But he couldn't. It was too complicated. He needed more time to think it through. He picked up a stack of pencil sketches from the coffee table. 'How'd it go with the lawyer?' he asked.

Max nodded at the sketches. 'What do you think?' he asked.

Then Peter realized what he was holding – sketches for the Fischer Pictures, softball uniforms, drawn by Max's favorite costume designer. One uniform was traditional, with stripes and those high white baseball socks that looked like the hocks of racehorses. The other was very Japanese, all flared hips and carefully modulated shades of charcoal. Peter didn't hesitate; it was good to appear decisive, especially when the stakes were low. 'The traditional.'

'Ordered them last week,' Max said.

'I thought you would go for the Japanese thing,' Peter said.

'Are you kidding – this is *baseball*. The fucking media would get ahold of it and make us sound like a bunch of Hollywood fags – "And at the climax of the game, Max Fischer slid into home in a design reminiscent of Issey Miyake" . . . *please*.'

'I didn't know you were going to play,' Peter said, numbly carrying on the conversation.

'I'm not going to *play*,' Max snapped. 'It's just an example.' He looked at Peter and frowned. 'The first game's this Saturday,' he said. 'I hope you've been working out.' Then he jumped back to Peter's first question. 'He fucking *deposed* me.'

Ah – finally. They were talking about it. 'Did you reach the Ripper?' Peter asked.

'He said not to worry. Routine.'

'Some routine.'

'Stop pouting, will you?'

Peter felt a stab of hatred – here Max was all recovered, his obnoxious old self again. He was much nicer nervous. 'So who were you with last night?' Peter asked.

Max tilted his head, as if considering the possibility that Peter was smarter than he thought. Or more dangerous.

After the tiniest of pauses, Peter added: 'I'm assuming it *wasn't* Tracy.'

Max's face went sour. 'If it becomes necessary, you'll know.' Then he softened. 'Anyway, Tracy'll snap out of it. It's only been, what . . .'

He looked at the clock on his desk. 'Seven hours? Right now she's still pissed off, probably still high.'

Still high? How do you know she was high, Max? And still pissed off? Pissed off about what, Max?

Before Peter could think of what to say next, Mosely poked his wheelchair through the office door. 'Hey,' Max said, waving him in. As the ritual small talk restarted, Peter could see Max's anxiety evaporate – he was working again, and nothing else existed.

They were just getting warmed up when Sarah buzzed again. 'The Ripper on line one.'

Max smiled apologetically, holding up a finger: just a sec. 'I gotta take this,' he said.

Mosely shrugged. By that time Max already had the phone to his ear. 'Hey,' he said.

Then he listened, intently. 'Who said that?' he demanded. He listened some more. '*Shit*! Goddamnit.' He held the phone away from his ear for a moment, contemplating the world's infinite injustice. 'Of course it's *important*. What else did he say? What else have you heard? What is everyone saying?'

Evidently the news got no better. '*Shit*! *Fuck*! *God damn*!' Finally he slammed down the phone. 'Word's out,' he told Peter, in a voice that sounded shocked and numb. 'Everybody in town knows.'

For a moment Max looked so hurt and worried, Peter felt sorry for him. It was amazing he could still feel that way, he thought, but no matter what Max did there was still an eager little kid inside him, and that part was hard to hate. Besides, it was downright comical – Max was more upset about the town finding out than he was about the rape charge itself.

But Max recovered quickly, turning to Mosely with a professionally apologetic smile. 'Sorry, Flip. It gets crazy around here,' he said. 'So let's talk. You want a soda, something to drink?'

Jerked out of his sympathy before he got a chance to enjoy it, Peter felt a little miffed.

Without waiting for an answer, Max yelled: 'Sarah, get a . . . what do you want? Evian? You like the bubbles? How about the stuff in the blue bottle. Sarah – get that stuff in the blue bottle!'

Sarah punched a button on her phone. 'Lovett on six,' she said.

'Shit,' Max said. He hesitated, gave Mosely a long-suffering look, then yelled: 'Tell him I'll call back.'

Mosely looked stricken. 'No, no – take it.'

Max waved a hand. 'We've been interrupted enough.'

'No, please,' Mosely said.

Max shrugged. 'You're sure?'

'I'm begging.'

Max shrugged and grabbed the phone, swiveling his chair around without waiting to see Mosely wheel himself back out. 'Hey,' he said, then waited while he was patched through. 'Hey,' he said again, as if he were sipping a Mai Tai on a sunny day. 'How you doing? Still playing with Java?'

He listened for a bit, verbally nodding now and again: 'Hmmm . . . Yeah . . . It's amazing . . . Sure, everything's going digital. Someday we'll be able to have digital *sex*.'

Then Lovett asked a question. 'Yeah . . . forty,' Max said. 'Thanks. Yeah, the big four-oh. But I'm still a child at heart.'

When enough time had passed – Max didn't rush it, because each wasted second was a calibration of his power – Max swiveled back around and got to business, leaning forward with one elbow on the desk and one hand waving in the air. 'I mean, what the fuck, Mike? He disappears up some river *fishing* and then I hear he's reading a Barry Rose script?'

It wasn't what Peter expected. But it made perfect sense. Max would act as if all he cared about was business, and the rest was just a minor irritant.

Lovett must have tried to interrupt, but Max just powered over: 'I heard it. I got sources. I mean, come on, we're in the middle of a *deal* here.'

He listened for a moment, then used his stunned-and-hurt voice: 'What does he want to think about?'

Another pause.

'I'm telling you, it's not true. It's not true. It's not even semitrue. You tell Tom – there's another side to this. I'm being *fucked* – *that's* the other side.'

For a minute or two Max listened, nodding his head every so often and saying, 'Yeah, okay.'

Then he changed his tone, and Peter noted the careful modulation of yield to push, calibrated to fit the pressure on the other end of the line. 'Richard, this is *bullshit*. Listen listen listen – I ask *one* thing. Before you make any decisions – let me *talk* to him . . . I'll *fly to fucking Montana*! Come on! I'm a salesman, I'm a closer – that's what I do! I'll buy a rod and – what-do-you-call-it, one of those wicker baskets – a *creel*. I'll probably be the first Jew in the state! I'll be the amazing fishing Jew! I'll throw out my line and reel in *Nova*!'

He was laughing as he hung up, but the second the phone clicked down he jumped to his feet. 'Goddamn it! My fucking life is falling apart.' He tore open the door. 'Sarah, get me the Ripper. Peter, get me Jay Maloney. Get me Dick Donner. Come on, come on, come on! Let's run the calls!'

Two hours later, they were still working the phones and telling everyone they could how silly and vicious the rumors were, it was insane to think Max would do such a thing, just a pathetic revenge attempt by the rapidly dwindling Barry Rose – and still trying to get a number for Hanks in Montana, without success – when Sarah poked her head in. 'You're going to be late for your birthday party,' she said. 'And Flip Mosely is still here.'

'Shit!' Max said. 'I forgot. Send him in.'

He sounded almost happy. Surprised, Peter checked his own emotional temperature and realized he felt better too, energized by the work and a sense of real progress. Everyone was so supportive – *I'm with you, Max. I believe in you, Max. Fuck Barry Rose anyway, Max.*

'What about the party?'

'Ten minutes,' he said. 'We'll just be ten minutes.'

Sarah looked at Peter: We've heard that before. Half of Hollywood would be at Max's party – the top half – and it wouldn't be smart to be too late. Especially today.

'Come on, come on, what's the matter with you?' Max said. 'It's *my* party! And I'll be late if I want to.'

Sarah left, her expression skeptical, and a moment later Mosely wheeled himself in again. He was getting that dazed expression people sometimes got when they'd been around Max too long, like shell-shocked soldiers staggering around a misty battlefield.

'Can I get you something?' Max said.

Mosely looked pained and shook his head, and Max wasted no more time. 'I loved your student film,' he said. 'What was it called, *Ozzie and . . . ?*'

'*Ozzie and Harriet Must Die.*'

'Right. Great title. My favorite shot – toward the end, where you have the Steadicam going around and around and then slowly tilt up, just like the last shot in *Nashville*.'

Mosely gave a cautious smile, surprised. 'Thanks. You were supposed to think of *Nashville*.'

'What am I, a shmuck?' Max said. 'We're a very intellectual outfit. I even have an on-staff semiotician here. Peter used to give *lectures* – "Intertextuality in Altman: The Early Oeuvre." '

'It was the late oeuvre, actually,' Peter said, deadpan. This was fun. They were a team, working for a living.

'I know you don't usually do this kind of picture,' Mosely said, shifting nervously in his chair.

'How about never,' Max said.

Mosely looked embarrassed. He'd been trying to get a new picture started for months, almost since the day he got out of the hospital, but his moment of heat had passed and his wheelchair seemed to make people nervous. Could he get around a set? Did he have the stamina? Max was not his first stop.

'Relax,' Max said. Then he stepped back, surveying his room. The Ruscha was an ocean horizon in black and white, the word BEAUTIFUL floating above the water like a wisp of sunset. Max concentrated on it for a moment, then snapped his eyes away and went behind his desk. 'A tortured-soul movie,' he said, musing. 'It's definitely not . . .'

For once he seemed at a loss for words.

Mosely's movie was about a shy blind man who wanders into a strip joint. He becomes a regular, and one day a stripper asks him why he comes since he can't see anything, and he says he listens to the music and uses his imagination, and it helps to know that there really is a naked girl . . . sometimes he can even hear the lingerie rustle. Soon all the girls love him because they know that in his mind's eager eye they are beautiful. But then the strippers start getting murdered. Will the blind man solve the crime . . . or is he the killer? The working title was *The Blind Voyeur*. It would have to go, of course.

Max pursed his lips, then shot Mosely a matter-of-fact look. 'What I like about it,' he said, 'is that it's one big whipped-cream bikini.'

Mosely looked puzzled, raising his eyes.

'It's a phrase we use,' Peter explained. 'One of Max's Maxims. We call—'

Max cut him off. 'What it means is something very suggestive but totally G-rated. There's no difference between a whipped-cream bikini and a regular bikini in terms of what you see – but in terms of what you *think* . . .'

'Uh huh,' Mosely said. He didn't seem too happy.

'So if we can get inside that blind guy's head – if we can see what he doesn't see. See the stripper world the way he thinks it is, the way he *dreams* it is . . .'

Peter jumped in: 'All soft focus, sometimes just a blur . . .'

'A *flesh*-colored blur . . .'

'But sometimes cutting to the audience POV,' Peter said.

Mosely was weakening. 'She could tell him what she was doing, and he could . . .'

'Picture it,' Max said.

Mosely nodded. 'A whipped-cream bikini.'

'So who do you see as the guy?' Max said.

Mosely didn't hesitate, fitting himself to Max's abrupt rhythms. 'For the man, I want someone who is actually blind.'

Max tossed a beseeching glance to the ceiling. 'Why me, Lord?' he said.

'But that's the whole point,' Mosely said, 'the gulf between the pretty surface and the inner truth. If he's not blind, we lose a whole level of meaning.'

'*Fuck* a whole level of meaning!' Max shouted. 'The point is to *make the fucking movie!*'

Mosely shrugged, giving in.

But Max still wasn't happy. 'The real problem is, I don't like the guy.'

Now Mosely was offended. 'What do you mean?' he asked.

'He's lonely. He's sad.'

'But he's blind.'

'I know he's blind! It doesn't mean he has to be a *loser*!'

'He's not a loser. He's going through—'

Max chopped the air with a hand, cutting Mosely off. 'Listen to me, Flip,' he said, a sudden anger in his voice. 'I am telling you, this man is a loser! He doesn't know who he is. He doesn't know what he wants. And women can smell that. Therefore he is alone. And now you have to listen to me very carefully. Alone is good. Lonely is bad. Do you understand me? Alone – *good*! Lonely – *bad*!'

'Yes, I *understand*,' Mosely said, his voice precise in anger.

'I know what you think. You think lonely is touching. That's why you sat around all day like a fucking loser. You should have told me to fuck off!'

Mosely gripped the arms of his wheelchair. 'Okay,' he said. 'Fuck off.'

'Say it again!'

'Fuck off!'

'Say it like you mean it!'

'*Fuck off*, Max Fischer, you big puckered asshole.'

Max patted his belly happily. 'Maybe there's some hope for you yet.' Then he smiled, raising his eyebrows, cocking his head to one side and shooting out the last question, the question that bonded them in their travail, that always kissed the whole wispy dream with such sweet promise: 'And who,' he asked, 'do you see as the girl?'

The whiplash mood change left Mosely momentarily silent, but he quickly caught on, tossed out some names, and they spoke for another half hour, increasingly enthusiastic. Finally Sarah came in again. 'I'm sorry, Max, but—'

'I'm in a *meeting* here, for chrissake,' Max said.

'Alan Kramer called. He's at your party, wondering where the hell you are.'

Max looked at Mosely, shaking his head. 'See the way they talk to me.' But he was happy, visibly pleased with his own grand gesture – he'd kept the head of a studio waiting while he talked to a nobody. Because he was a producer, and that's what producers did. They talked to dreamers about their dreams. What a great business we're in, his smile said. Then he got up and stretched. 'Better get going,' he said to Peter, as if he were somehow to blame. He shook Mosely's hand again. 'Nice to see you. Let's talk again.'

Mosely started to wheel himself toward the door, but then he stopped, puzzled. 'I don't understand,' he said. 'Are we making the movie?'

Max looked at his Ruscha. BEAUTIFUL hovered on the wall, rippling like a mirage. 'Not without a rewrite,' he answered, his mind on to the next thing.

'What are you saying? A development deal?'

Max's head came around. He focused on Mosely, as if surprised that he was still there. 'No deal,' he said. 'Rewrite it, make him less of a shmuck, work on the whipped-cream bikinis. *Then* we have a deal.'

'What if I decide to sell it to someone else?'

Max shrugged. 'I'll take my chances.'

Mosely gripped the arms of his chair and shook his head, as if seeing the ugly truth for the first time. 'You want a free rewrite,' he said. 'You're worse than Disney.'

Max smiled. 'Stop trying to get on my good side,' he said. Then he snapped his fingers at Peter. 'Let's move! Sarah, *go home!*'

'Let's go!' Peter shouted. 'We're outa here!' Then he realized he was pumping himself up by acting like Max, and blushed.

'Move move move!' Max shouted.

Mosely and Sarah watched them go. Mosely shook his head, exhausted by it all. Sarah raised her eyebrows and shrugged. 'Elvis has left the building,' she said.

Max was silent in the car, brooding again, which made Peter so nervous he cut around traffic like a madman, using both the turning and the parking lanes. He gunned through the fading seconds of a half-dozen orange lights. Max didn't say a word.

When they got to the house, Max threw open the door and started walking toward the stairs . . . then came to a dead stop in front of the fireplace. It was one of those free-standing California-modern fireplaces, with a brick base and a funnel-shaped copper flue coming down from the ceiling. 'I hate this fucking thing,' Max said. 'Call Yoji.'

'Now?'

'Yeah, *now*. It's fucking *tacky*. I can't stand it in this house *one more minute.*'

'But we're already so la—'

'*Call the fucker!*'

Peter went to the kitchen and called. There was no answer. When he came back Max was still standing there.

'I want glass,' he said, caught by a vision. 'That way you can *see* the flames.'

'I've never heard of a glass fireplace.'

'So what? Where is he?'

'Out of the office.'

'Call him again! Try him at home!'

'I think if it was possible to have a glass fireplace, somebody would have done it already,' Peter ventured.

That did it. '*Anything* is possible,' Max shouted. 'Call fucking NASA – what do they use on the *shuttle*?' He glared at Peter as if astonished that he was still standing there. 'Jesus fucking Christ, I'll do it myself.' He marched to the kitchen, then whirled around. 'Look, go home. Take a shower or something. Change. I'll meet you there.'

'I've got my party clothes in the trunk,' he protested. Part of him was desperate to leave, hoping Max was serious and trying not to show joy, but the stronger part was terrified: Why was Max trying to get rid of him?

But Max just waved him away. '*Go*, I said.'

'Max, I—'

'Save it,' Max said, heading for the stairs.

Peter followed, determined. 'I wanted to talk to you about something.'

'*Later*.'

'But—'

'What do I have to *do*?' Max exploded. 'Send up *smoke signals*? Should I try *semaphore*?' He waved his hands in big circles in air, like a lost hiker trying to catch the attention of a passing pilot. 'GET THE FUCK OUT OF HERE! Yes, you, the one with the stupid-ass dumbfuck look on your face. *Go beat off or something*!'

Okay, Peter thought. Have it your way. But he still didn't want to let Max go. 'How are you going to get to the party?' he asked.

Max spun around, actual hate in his eyes. 'I *can* drive, you know.'

The orange sky turned violet as night fell. Peter drove down from the hills into the stucco wasteland that fringed the San Diego freeway, left his car under his apartment (which hung over its parking space like some huge air-conditioner), and charged up the stairs to his door. *Move move move!*

Then he saw a familiar body at his neighbor's door. He heard a rumble of thanks, saw the door close, and then the man turned and saw him . . . and smiled.

'Dog,' Peter said, not even trying to conceal his surprise. 'What are you doing here?'

'Just checking,' Dogosta said.

'Checking what?'

'Checking your story, Peter.'

'But what if the cops find out?' Peter said, keeping his voice low. 'I mean, Max said I was with him. You work for Max. It's going to look . . .'

Dogosta didn't say anything, just kept watching him.

'. . . It'll look weird,' Peter finished. 'Like Max was lying.'

Max. Not him. Get the point?

'See, Peter, I was worried. In this business you always get fucked by details, and I started thinking – what if one of the tenants remembers your car?'

Jesus – his car. Peter's heart started pounding so hard he could feel it in his throat.

'I mean if you parked in the same place all the time, and you came home last night like you said, and your neighbors saw your car . . . well, what would Spinks make of that?'

Dogosta put a little spin on 'like you said', just enough.

'But guess what?' he continued. 'Martin' – he pointed at a door as they passed it – 'just told me he was sure your car wasn't parked there when he got home, one hundred percent sure, and he just told Spinks the same thing. Stroke of luck, eh?'

'Spinks was here?'

'Just left.'

Peter paused to absorb the news. It had been just ten hours since she left Max's house, and already Spinks had *interviewed* his *neighbors*.

Dogosta nodded at another door. 'Susanna in Two C even told Spinks she was positive you didn't come home last night.'

Peter tried to keep his face impassive. He took his keys out and started walking toward his door.

91

'She's a restless sleeper,' Dogosta continued, following him. 'Says she always knows when you come home 'cause you stomp up the stairs. You really shouldn't do that, you know. It's inconsiderate.'

'I gotta get to the party,' Peter said, putting the key in the lock.

Dogosta smiled, leaning in. 'Guess she wasn't restless last night. Maybe somebody relaxed her, eh? That's a girl whose rent is paid, if you know what I mean.'

'Yeah,' Peter said, putting his key in his door. He hesitated, not wanting to invite the Dog inside.

'So what about the car, Peter?' Dogosta was right behind him, surprisingly close, almost whispering in his ear.

'Like I said, I was here.'

He half turned, the key still in the lock, and Dogosta suddenly jammed his face just inches in front of Peter's nose. He hissed in a low voice. 'Don't fuck with me, you punk. I catch you in a lie, I'll come after you.'

Peter's throat went completely dry. The doorknob jabbed him in the back. There was salami on Dogosta's breath, and he could see the pores in his shiny nose. 'I'm not lying,' he croaked.

Dogosta grabbed him by the arm. 'If I find out you're playing some kind of fucking game here, it'll be between you and me,' the Dog hissed again, shaking his arm. 'I won't even tell Max. I'll just handle it. I'll handle it my way. I'll make you *afraid of the dark*. You hear me? *Afraid of the dark*.'

He was squeezing hard enough to leave bruises. Peter fought the urge to shake his arm free. 'Are you finished?' he said.

Dogosta let go and stepped back. He looked Peter up and down and up again, holding his eyes for a moment. Then he smiled and walked away without another word.

Inside at last, Peter closed the door behind him. His eyes went to the stack of empty suitcases against the wall, then drifted across the still-unpacked boxes filled with old class notebooks and papers, the wooden thrift shop desk stacked high with new hardback books, his new Powerbook computer half hidden in the mess. There was a letter on it to his parents that he'd started and never finished.

You know what's the matter with you?

He stripped, throwing his clothes on the bed and heading for the shower, twisting it to hot, and leaned in, letting the needles drill against his skull and trying not to think. But memories came at him, like a sewer backing up: looking out the window back in high school, surrounded by sports fans and Bruce Springsteen wanna-bes, wanting to be anywhere but in that seat; the feeling that there wasn't enough air in the world, of being bored out of his mind (another weekend, another golden opportunity to cruise the supermarket parking lot and drink till you puke); the sight of his father at the dinner table, his sharp nose and dull hair, always putting the flatware at right angles (he was an engineer, obsessed with order, so Peter put a Disaster Area sticker on his bedroom door and tried to live up to it); his mother flipping through the *Ladies Home Journal* . . .

You don't know what you think . . .

His mother: beauty-shop hair accessorized by a phony smile. She's one of those vague Harriet Nelson housewives who seem to be repressing something but really aren't, he used to say, getting laughs he regretted. The truth was that she had been unhappy all her life, and learned to live with it much too well – which scared the hell out of him.

You're changing fast . . .

'Ah, fuck it,' Peter said aloud. He turned off the water and dried off, then picked up the stupid blow-dryer and began giving himself that smooth studio-lizard look, occasionally stopping to sneer at the face in the mirror. The soft brown eyes, furtive and unformed. The lips that were too big, too sensual: sign of weakness. People said he was good-looking, but he couldn't see it. And wasn't that the start of a double chin?

He sighed and went to his closet, and sighed again. On the plane out from New York he'd studied a satirical article about power dressing in *Hollywood, Inc.*, marking it up like a class assignment, then went out his first weekend and loaded up his credit card: four new suits (Mani's and Hugo Boss – he couldn't afford Le Collezioni, even on sale), ten pairs of Boss trousers, a couple of sports jackets, eight Armani shirts, eight ties by various designers, four pairs of thin-soled Italian shoes, and a dozen pairs of discreetly patterned socks. He planned to wear them only to work, like pieces of armor. The new Peter James was going to be cold and practical about the project of life. He wasn't going to sabotage himself with romantic notions about modesty or idealism. He was going to *win*.

You don't know what you think . . .

But now he leaned against the closet door and stared into the closet. All this stupid, overpriced crap. He learned his first week that any assistant who wore Armani during the day risked getting laughed all the way to Iowa. What if he lost his job? He'd be out at Venice Beach panhandling in an Armani suit . . .

If you lie to the grand jury . . .

And look at the way they hung there, all the shirts turned in the same direction and all the pants dangling from squeeze hangers. In college, he'd left his jeans crumpled on the floor, the way Nature intended . . .

I'll make you afraid of the dark . . .

What a nightmare! He was totally dependent on the whims of a teeming hive of sociopaths! And what made it worse was this feeling that he deserved it, that *this* was the doom that had always been lurking just around the corner, his punishment for wanting too much and being too little . . .

I'll make you afraid . . .

Knotting his tie, Peter wandered over to his desk and stared down at the Powerbook, thinking what he would say if he ever did finish that letter. Most of it was bragging about all the famous people he had met. He'd have to cut that, because it would just annoy them. And he couldn't talk about his fears, or they'd throw themselves into a fit of worrying.

I'll make you . . .

Ah, to hell with it. Do like Max, get dressed, go to the party, don't give a shit, be a man of action . . . a man of action movies.

Chapter Five

It started before Peter even got to the door: '*There* you are. Where have you been? Where's Max?' That was Mark Hill, Columbia's boyish head of publicity, a cheerfully cynical thirty-year-old whose office was decorated with cartoons from *The New Yorker* making fun of publicists (a self-deprecating touch that fooled only the more credulous reporters). Peter was stunned. 'You mean he's not here already?'

'Don't torture me,' Hill said. 'A hundred of his closest friends are in there trashing him.'

They were standing in the parking lot of Morton's, the moguls' cafeteria, where the food wasn't particularly good because it didn't have to be: The patrons came only for each other. What's on the menu? The special this evening is broiled Geffen in a light béarnaise sauce, garnished with his usual T-shirt, jeans, and jacket – and the unmistakable silky sheen of that billion dollars in his wallet. And for dessert, perhaps a Schwarzenegger blintz, stuffed with the richest cheese.

As Peter began to cut through the restaurant, he saw Alan Kramer coming his way. Damn, he thought, controlling a flinch. Just his luck – no Max in sight, almost two hours late, and here comes the chairman of the studio. Kramer's eyes drooped to half mast, as if he were on some kind of anti-psychotic drug, but at the same time he was wired, almost jumpy. Kramer was always like that, like a five-year-old overdosing on sugar, so you never knew whether he was about to fall asleep or pounce on you and wrap himself around your leg.

Tonight he was in pouncing mode. 'Where *is* he? He's two and a half fucking hours fucking late. I've never *known* anyone so dilatant.'

He probably meant dilatory, Peter guessed. Kramer was always mangling the English language – said penultimate when he meant ultimate, exorbitant when he meant luxurious. 'You know Max,' Peter said.

'I thought he was with *you*.' Kramer examined him quickly for signs of Max's presence.

Peter answered with a shrug, telling himself to stay cool. 'He said he wanted to make an entrance.'

'Entrance, schmentrance,' Kramer said. 'You tell him – this kind of behavior is indefeasible.' Then he spotted Michael Douglas coming out of the bathroom, and shot towards him so fast he practically left behind a puff of smoke.

Peter stood by the door and watched Kramer shake the famous hand. Sleepy and goofy as he seemed, Kramer couldn't hide his boundless ambition. He didn't even bother to try. As Peter watched him, he realized that the sleepiness and the ambition were joined, like a body to its shadow. In fact, he could say the same thing of almost everyone he'd met in Hollywood – at least the successful ones. Mike Ovitz came off restrained, Jeff Berg (head of the ICM agency) came off abstracted, and Brian Grazer (the producer of *Splash* and *Parenthood*) seemed downright goofy – and they were, but the opposites were also true. Ovitz could be as temperamental as an actor, Berg as rapacious as one of the larger Mongol hordes, and Grazer as calculating as the most ambitious banker. The mistake was thinking they were one or the other, of putting their contradictions down to hypocrisy or mere protective coloration. You could even make a rule out of it – pick an actor who seems to be a saint, say Jerry Lewis with his crippled-kid telethon, and you can assume a mean streak a mile wide. Pick one who's known as a sinner, and assume unknown acts of kindness. It was the secret of Hollywood, the reason its movies and TV shows were so popular throughout the world – the people who survived its battles were all built like the old carbon-arc bulbs in projectors, with positive and negative poles – and a hot spark jumping between them.

Or so Peter thought, watching the guests work the room. They were all there, Hollywood from Arnold to Zemeckis. They all looked healthy, they all were thin, all the men wore Armani and all the women Alaïa. There was a Rolex on every wrist. Peter heard the occasional break over the surf of conversation, like froth on a wave: *. . . lawyer who handled . . . heard the police . . . date rape . . .* It seemed like they were whispering. Every now and then they stopped whispering and looked up at him. He saw Kramer go up to groups of people, and suddenly they raised their voices to normal, giving him hearty hellos. Here and there around the room, people glanced at their watches and then at the door.

Twice Peter walked past the maître d' and called Max from the pay phones. Both times it kicked over to the guesthouse and the housekeeper picked up. 'He's still gone,' she said. She was an old woman, and she always treated Peter and Max as if they were just boys playing games.

And there was the Ripper, wearing a sweater made out of some kind of thick natural fiber, probably from an endangered species. A mat of silky black hair climbed out of his shirt right up to his throat, like moss around a tree. 'Haay, kid,' he said.

'Geez,' Peter said.

Rippert squeezed his shoulder. 'Dawn't wooory, kid. A little excitement, good for the circulaaytion. Getting any?'

'Here and there,' Peter said.

'It's a fucking great business, ain't it?'

With another squeeze, Rippert was gone. Peter could hear him as he cut through the crowd, saying, 'Sawwry, that's privileged,' and laughing.

Then a voice murmured in Peter's ear. 'You're going to take the fall, boyo.'

An insect ran up Peter's spine, an electric centipede with a hundred hot little feet. It wasn't just the words in his ear, but something about the voice, its tone of warm, tropical corruption. Peter turned slowly, preparing just the right smile, polite but impersonal, and found himself facing one of the oddest characters in modern Hollywood. Fifteen years ago Jennings West had been one of the most promising directors in Hollywood, but drugs and a long string of flops had left him dusted with failure, like an expensive piece of furniture forgotten in the window of a bankrupt store. He still dressed completely in white, with white Pat Boone shoes and a white tuxedo jacket and white Sansabelt pants *and* a white silk scarf coiled around his neck. 'You failed to produce your boss,' West continued. 'That's your job, to keep him on track, to deliver him. Make sure he's dressed right' – he wagged a finger – 'with no stains on his pants.'

There was something wrong about West. After a minute Peter realized that his face looked slightly malformed, as if it had been squeezed in a vise. His eyes were full of needling intensity, like someone with fantasies of being a master hypnotist, and he grinned at Peter as if they were complicit in some amusing crime.

Peter kept his face wooden. 'So that's my reason for being,' he said. 'I'm a pants inspector.'

West nodded. 'You got it, boyo – and your boss has dirty pants.'

Peter couldn't help glancing down at West's pants. They were immaculate. He didn't know what to say, so he said what came to mind: 'I loved *Running on Fumes*. What a great movie.'

Almost imperceptibly, West winced, and Peter remembered the rest: *Fumes* was West's first directing job, a dark road story about an escaped con who gets a ride from a nun. The nun is all forgiveness, which softens the con's bitterness, and they fall in love and even have sex – it was the seventies – but in the end the nun turns him in anyway, because she must. At the time there were huge arguments about whether the movie was old-fashioned or modern, on the nun's side or against her, and the Vatican even issued a statement condemning it. *Fumes* made West's name. After that he flopped with a couple of middle-brow 'issue' movies before giving up Meaning altogether and making a fortune off a string of sex comedies.

'Thanks,' West said, graciously. 'But I always hated the ending of that movie.' He winked. 'They should have kept running.'

Then he nudged Peter, leaning in with a confidential whisper. 'I have one tip for you – don't call your first movie *Running on Fumes*. Makes the sequel a bitch.'

As West grinned, Marlon Spurlock came up and slipped an arm around his shoulders. West's grin went even wider. 'Homeboy!' he cried, as the two fell into a mock tussle. Peter kept his face solemn, thinking: how ludicrous, this Sansabelt-clad sonofabitch calling Spurlock *homeboy*. A real pair of hardened ghetto dwellers, all right.

And Spurlock didn't look very good. He was so pale and pockmarked and furtive, like the villain in a German expressionist movie. Sweat kept beading his forehead.

'You're getting here late,' West said. 'And all sweaty too. *What* have you been doing?'

Spurlock didn't answer. After giving him another lurid smile, West turned to Peter. 'Do you know Marlon?'

'We've met,' Peter said, sticking out his hand.

West squeezed Spurlock's shoulder. 'Marlon is writing a very
funny script.'

'What's it about?'

Spurlock frowned, then sighed. 'Hollywood,' he finally said, throwing the word away, as if to make it clear that he knew the conventional
wisdom, which was that Hollywood stories didn't work. This was a
deeply held conviction on all levels of the town, which was puzzling
since it not only ignored hits like *A Star Is Born*, *Sunset Boulevard*,
and *Whatever Happened to Baby Jane?*, but also the rabid fasci-
nation of tabloid readers everywhere with Hollywood gossip of
any kind. It was almost as if Hollywood insiders, out of some
instinctual wisdom, had to believe that Hollywood movies didn't
work in order to keep their own limitless self-enchantment in
check – or else all movies would become Hollywood movies.

Peter tried to think of something to say, but West broke in, nodding
toward the two far ends of the tent. 'Geffen in one corner, Ovitz
in the other,' he said. 'Both of them getting pissed off, but neither
wants to be the first to leave.'

With that he patted Spurlock on the back and plunged back into
the crowd, aimed like a heat-seeking missile at a Lycra-clad starlet.
Peter watched him go, remembering the day he saw *Running on
Fumes*. It was at the Thalia in New York City, in a double feature
with *The Last Picture Show*. He was about sixteen, had ridden in on
the bus from Jersey, telling his parents he was going to a friend's
house for the day, and he was sure there was nothing so fine and
magical in all the world as the bleak black-and-white landscapes
on the screen. Odd that such depressing movies would give him so
much of a lift. Just as the squalid tumult of Manhattan made him
so much happier than the green lawns of suburbia. But that was all
he liked then, the more depressing the better: depressing was *truth*.

And there was the man who produced the movie, hunched over
some bimbo and wearing a *cravat*, for chrissake.

'So where is Max, anyway?' Spurlock said. 'I didn't think he'd
miss this.'

'I better go call,' Peter said.

Spurlock put his hand on Peter's arm, and leaned in. 'I just
can't see Max hurting Tracy,' he said, as if he really meant it,
as if he was deeply concerned. 'Definitely not raping her. Can
you?' Without waiting for an answer, Spurlock went on: 'I can

see why the *cops* would believe it. Throw a rock in this town and you'll hit someone with a Max-and-Barry story.' He pointed to himself, the perfect illustration.

'So why'd you stay with him so long?' Peter asked.

'He begged me,' Spurlock answered. 'I was always good with story – I'd give him script notes and then he'd go into a meeting and just repeat them word for word. That's why he wouldn't let me go.'

Peter wondered if it was true, or if it was something Spurlock needed to believe. Certainly, in his experience, Max had no lack of story ideas. And if you believed what people said about themselves, every creative exec, agent, scriptreader, secretary, waiter, valet, and busboy south of Sacramento was *good with story* – Peter had heard people say it so often in the last three months he couldn't remember if the phrase was peculiar naturally or by repetition.

'So what's your script about, really?' Peter asked, curious now.

Spurlock looked right into him. 'It's about an assistant who gets driven crazy by his boss,' he said.

'Very funny,' Peter said.

'No, really. That's what it's about.'

'What's it called?'

'*The Buddy System.*'

'And Max is paying for this?'

'He doesn't care,' Spurlock said. 'He'll never even read it. He'll make *you* read it.'

Spurlock was so bitter. Peter saw Mark Hill come scowling across the room, and felt a surge of relief. 'Listen, I really have to work now,' he said. 'Let's talk later, okay?'

Spurlock nodded, and Peter hurried to meet Hill halfway. Hill was shaking his head: more trouble. 'Just checked my answering machine,' he said. 'Message from Kit Bradley at *Hollywood, Inc.* "Where's Max?" she says. Then she cackles and hangs up.'

'How could she *know* that?'

Hill shrugged. 'Somebody must have called her from the bathroom. Lot of media junkies in this place.'

Peter shifted nervously. 'He should *be* here,' he said.

'Ovitz will last fifteen more minutes, tops.'

At that moment the door opened . . . and a king appeared. A red velvet cape hung from his shoulders to the floor, the collar trimmed in ermine, and in his hand he held a glittering golden scepter. On his head perched a crown that glinted and flashed in the light. The band caught on and stumbled into a jazzy version of 'God Save the King'. The crowd quieted for a stunned moment, then broke into scattered applause. Peter heard the buzz go through the crowd: walla *rape* walla walla **rape**.

It was Max, of course. He raised his scepter for quiet. As he began speaking, his voice cracked. 'Someone told me this was a come-as-you-are party,' he said.

Laughter.

'So I just wore what I usually wear around the house.'

More laughter. People were nervous, so they were happy to laugh.

'Yes, this is my secret self-image,' Max continued. 'Now you know the truth – I don't want to be just a producer. That's not enough for me. I wanna be a *potentate*. An *emperor*. I think I'm going to shave my head and wear those shoes that turn up at the toes.'

More laughter, less nervous now. Max was winning them over.

'No, but seriously. What this really is, I decided to come as all of you *think* of me – as a *royal asshole*.'

Now the laugh was big, and there was more applause, and Max threw up his hands to receive it, wading into the crowd to accept hugs and handshakes. He was like a prizefighter after a fight, or a star after a hot premiere. Peter watched from the sidelines with a half-smile. Even under this dark cloud, Max was still at the center of his world, this tight little clique, as if they had all gone to the same school together for twenty years and Max was their perennial all-star.

And Peter, meanwhile, remained on the sidelines. He'd been feeling very sympathetic up to the moment Max made his big entrance and charmed the rabid crowd. Now he sighed and tried to forgive. After all, it *was* his birthday . . .

Then a waiter went by with a tray, and Peter grabbed a glass of Pellegrino. He carried it to Max. 'Water?'

'Thanks,' Max said.

Kramer joined the group, giving Max's hand a two-fisted shake. 'Some of us didn't think you'd make it,' he said. 'To forty, I mean.'

'Yeah,' West said, smiling his friendliest smile. 'We thought somebody would have killed you by now. A studio production executive, an agent . . . an assistant.' He winked at Peter, then turned back to Max, smiling brazenly and saying what no one else would say. 'So tell us, Max, what everybody wants to know. No beating around the bush – *have you been beating around the bush*?'

Laughing at his own joke, he put his arm around Max and squeezed. 'Sorry, I just couldn't resist that. But you know I love you.'

Kramer shook his head, like a weary schoolteacher. His droopy eyelids slid up a millimeter, and he raised his voice above the crowd noise: '*And now, let's go to the videotape*,' he said, waving his hand. After a slight delay, the band quit playing, then the lights came down and a projector shot a beam toward a screen at the back of the room. The Columbia lady appeared, holding her torch against the heavens, and the scroll began: *Columbia Pictures Presents: The Max Fischer 40th Birthday Video. Starring Max Fischer and a cast of dozens*.

The crowd laughed. They were used to this – in recent years the birthday video had become virtually a Hollywood requisite. They leaned toward the roast, and always came chockful of cameos by every actor and big shot ever to cross the path of the birthday boy. This one began in black and white, with a slanting shaft of light cutting through a dusty soundstage. Sitting in the light was a man in a fedora, his voice a *noir*-ish gravel. 'Who's a busy man? Me? I'm chairman of the board. I got nothing but time.'

It was a parody of *Citizen Kane*.

Cut to the reporter – played by Kit Bradley. 'We thought maybe, if we can find out what he meant by those last words . . . as he was dying . . . ?' she asked.

Cut to a shot of a kid's sled. Instead of ROSEBUD it read BACK END.

Then another shot of the man in the fedora. 'I never knew what it meant,' he said. He tilted his face so you could see him, and it turned out to be Kramer. 'At least,' he grinned, 'that's what I always told Business Affairs.'

Cut to Arnold Schwarzenegger smoking a cigar. 'Max,' he said, stabbing at the camera with the cigar, 'you *fucked* me. You said if I did your movie I vould get a plane.' Arnold reached down and picked up a carpenter's plane. He looked back at the camera, grinning. 'So now for your birthday, Max, I have a good present – I'm giving you a pretty little bird.'

He gave the camera the finger.

And so it went, with just enough edge on the gags to keep people a little uncomfortable, especially when several female stars appeared with big bellies and teased Max about 'that night'. One asked if she was going to end up like Sigourney Weaver in *Alien 3*. And then Michael Douglas went on and on about what a great guy Max was, until someone off camera handed him a note. Douglas read it and looked enormously relieved. 'Not only is Max Fischer a truly wonderful human being,' he concluded, with a perfect comic pause, 'but I've just received word that my wife and child have been released unharmed.'

The video was just ending when the guests heard someone roaring out in front, something about being a regular goddamn patron of this fucking pretentious-ass restaurant. Another voice overlapped it, obviously the maître d' in maximum soothing mode: 'I am very sorry, Mr Rose, it is a private party . . . But sir, you can't—'

Then something crashed, and the loud voice picked up again. 'Goddamnit . . .'

The door opened, and Barry Rose lurched into the room. Peter had never seen him in the flesh before, only in pictures. He was very tall, at least six four, and at least a decade older than Max, in his early or mid-fifties. But he was still lean and athletic, with a weathered face that puckered around hard black eyes, and he looked dangerous, like someone untouched by ordinary human scruples. He glowered at the crowd. 'Look at this,' he said. 'Max and all his pals, all *my* pals. Hi, Alan. Hi, Michael. Hi, David. Dan, nice to see you. This is great – this fuck *rapes* my daughter, and the same night everyone wishes him *happy fucking birthday*. At Morton's! I love this town.'

Max stood up, fixing a cold eye on his former mentor. '*Barry*,' he sneered, pausing long enough for the voices to die down again. Then he hissed into the silence: 'I wouldn't put it past you to rape her yourself just so you could blame me.'

For a moment Rose looked stunned. Then he exploded in a roar and charged at Max, scattering chairs and moguls as he crossed the room. With both hands he seized Max's throat. For a long moment not one person breathed. Then Max's crown fell to the floor and the plastic jewels scattered, and everyone started to move at once – backing away, stepping forward, edging to the side. Only Peter stood frozen to the floor, watching Max flap his hands against Rose's head. He looked up at the crowd – there was West, moving close and grinning – Hill, watching with horror as he shifted side to side – Spurlock, his eyes narrowed and his lips compressed in a thin smile – Ovitz, retreating toward the kitchen door. Rose's hands were still on Max's throat, and Max was turning red, slapping at Rose's shoulders. He brought a knee up and Rose gasped and kept choking.

Finally Peter jumped forward. From the corner of his eye he saw the doorman coming, followed by two or three white-coated valets. But when he reached Max and Rose, the doorman and the valets were still behind him and he didn't know what to do. He touched Rose's shoulder, started to say something – 'Uh, Mr, uh' – when Rose ducked his head and butted Peter on the chin. A red explosion stung his eyes, and he tasted blood. He had to do something – Max's knees were going soft. Dimly he was aware of the bouncer reaching Rose and tearing at his hands.

Then they were pulling Rose back, and Max stood bent over, rubbing his throat. He straightened up, coughing, glared once at Peter and then saw the bouncer and the valets holding Rose – and leaped! He landed on Rose, his fingers clawing for his eyes.

'You *fuck*,' Max shouted. 'I'll *kill* you.'

Rose lifted his feet and kicked Max in the chest, and Max staggered backward and fell down, flat on his ass.

The bouncer and valets kept dragging Rose back toward the door. He didn't fight them – he had a big smile on his face. 'You'd have to *hire* somebody to do it, fat boy,' he shouted. 'You don't have the *cojones*.'

Max got up, but he didn't charge again. He watched them drag Rose out of the restaurant. 'Get the old drunk out of here,' he said, dismissing Rose with a wave of his hand and turning back to his guests. 'Sorry for the interruption, folks. Drinks are on me.'

Rubbing his throat, Max met Peter's eyes. Then West came up to him, patting him on the back, and others joined them. Peter heard laughter and then Max started laughing too – telling the story of his shock and amazement, exactly how Rose grabbed him. Peter watched, almost numb, hoping that the laughter really meant that everything was all right. But he knew it wasn't. Until Rose came into the restaurant, he almost didn't believe the whole thing was real. Or that Rose was just the old has-been Max always said he was, nothing to really worry about. He just hadn't thought about Rose. But now he knew that Barry Rose was tough, and vital, and full of the most violent rage. He probably had private detectives of his own, working the case right now. He'd been the head of a studio, for God's sake – he'd lunched with the governor, dined with the president, negotiated with Teamsters. They were in trouble – deep trouble. Peter leaned against a pillar and loosened his tie.

Then Max slipped away from the crowd and came up to him.

'You all right?'

'What about you?'

'Been better,' he said, stroking his neck. 'I want you to call the cops. Call that bitch Spinks. I want that sonofabitch arrested for assault.'

Before Peter could say a word, Max turned and approached another guest. '*David*,' Peter heard him say. 'How'd you like the fight? Stick around, later tonight I'm going to take on Mike Tyson – I need a new challenge.'

Chapter Six

Sharp on the dot of nine, as if it were any other day, Peter opened Max's kitchen door and found old Mrs Berger making the morning fruit salad. 'On the patio,' she said without looking up, and Peter continued through the living room. The fireplace was gone, pulled like a giant tooth, and Yoji the architect was studying the red brick wound. '*Ohayo gozaimasu*,' Peter said, passing. Yoji nodded but remained fixed on the absent hearth. And there was Max, still wearing his bathrobe, his feet wrapped in white tissue, ripping his way through the *Daily Variety*. A pile of shredded newspapers and magazines rose a foot off the ground beside him. A middle-aged woman knelt before him, finishing up Max's regular Friday morning pedicure.

'Next week?' the woman said, putting her tools away in a tackle box.

Max nodded, barely flicking his eyes in her direction. 'You'll bill the office?' he said.

He looked tired, Peter thought. 'How're you doing?' Peter asked.

Max pointed to his neck. 'I have *bruises*,' he said.

Mrs Berger brought Max's fruit salad on a tray.

'I couldn't believe it when he came in like that,' Peter said. 'Like he was out of his fucking mind . . .'

Peter expected Max to take up the theme, but he just picked up the spoon and dug in without a word.

'. . . or drunk or something . . .'

Without looking up, Max snapped: 'Just give me your report. Have you talked to anybody?'

Peter took a deep breath and obeyed: Yes, dammit, he'd been on the phone since he got up that morning, and everybody was talking about the fight, which meant they were also talking about the rape, and the consensus was: Max Fischer was capable of anything.

Max blanched, then shoveled in another spoonful of fruit, hunching over his bowl like a dog. If I tried to touch it, Peter thought, he'd growl and bite my hand.

One good bit of news: Nothing had hit the press so far. Peter made a 6:00 A.M. run to Robertson's newsstand, first checking the trades and Page Six of the *New York Post*, the most likely overnight possibilities, then the *Daily News* and *USA Today* and the *L.A. Times*, which generally treated Hollywood with the deference of an in-house newsletter and made no exception to that rule today. The only media pest actually present during the events was George Christy of *The Hollywood Reporter*, and he had promised Peter in the parking lot that he wouldn't write anything too specific – just that you could always count on Max Fischer to deliver sparks, 'on the screen and even at a party'.

Peter waited for a compliment but Max was too preoccupied, so he started his rundown of the call list, taking a certain pleasure in the litany of bad news: 'As of 9:24 this morning we have calls from *Variety*, *The Hollywood Reporter*, *Entertainment Tonight*, *The Post*, George Rush at the *Daily News*, *Fox News*, *Hard Copy*, Marilyn Beck, Liz Smith, Mitchell Fink at *People*, *Inside Edition*, *The Star*, the *Enquirer*, *The New Yorker*, and *The Washington Post*. And your friend Kit Bradley has called three times.'

Max looked down at the flagstones. Peter watched his bent head and felt a twinge of pity . . . and guilt. *Tell the truth.*

Just then, Max looked up, a puzzled expression on his face. '*The New York Times* didn't call?'

Peter shook his head. 'Nope.'

'What the fuck is the matter with them? Aren't I *important* enough?'

Caught off guard, Peter laughed.

'I mean, Jesus Christ, *The New York Times* – they're probably writing about the Middle East or some dumbfuck thing like that. The *deficit*. Why don't they *get on the ball*?'

'Clearly they have no news sense whatsoever,' Peter said.

Max put his spoon down and got up, kicking the white tissues off his feet. He slipped his clean pink tootsies into a pair of Moroccan slippers and headed toward the stairs. 'I guess I should have just let the bastard choke me to death – then, *no story*. An obit in the back of the D section.'

Peter bit back the I told you so. They all had told him. When he found out Max had sent for the cops without checking with him first, the Ripper just about burst a vein: We have enough trouble as it is, gaaawdaaaamnit. But Max was unstoppable. *I want the sonofabitch charged with assault!* And then he'd spent another forty-five minutes arguing with the detectives, who didn't seem to appreciate the effort he was putting into producing their investigation – *You don't want a statement from him, he's a fucking waiter.* And when he found out it was up to the cops to press charges, which they would only do if they thought there was a case . . . well, he was damn lucky he didn't get arrested himself, if only for exceeding the permissible decibel level.

'Also talked to the Ripper's office,' Peter said. 'They said—'

'What about *Hanks*?' Max barked. 'Have you gotten anywhere with that?'

Peter considered: He could strike him with a blunt object. With all the construction, there were plenty lying around. He pictured Barry Rose with his fingers on Max's throat and felt a pang of envy. But instead he followed Max up the stairs like a good little doggie. In the bedroom Max ripped off his bathrobe and tossed it on a chair, then crossed to the closet in his boxer shorts.

'Talk to the Ripper yet?' Max asked.

Peter glanced at his clipboard, a vaguely military-looking thing shaped out of brushed stainless steel. It held the call sheet, the master list of studio executives, the auto-dial codes. 'You have a three o'clock – on the phone, but he's teleconferencing in the criminal attorney.'

'I hope it's Roy Cohn. Tell him I want Roy Cohn.'

'I think he's dead,' Peter said.

Max didn't miss a beat. 'Then let's get that guy from *Reversal of Fortune*, what's his name – Dershowitz.'

'The Ripper got someone already,' Peter said. 'I don't think it's Dershowitz.'

'Who is it?'

'Hey, what about an attorney for me?' Peter asked. He'd been waiting for a chance to slip that particular question. But Max just scowled.

'Who *is* it?'

'Some big guy,' Peter said.

'*Some big guy?*'

Peter shrugged. He was tired too, not that anyone cared. He didn't get home till two in the morning, and even then he couldn't sleep. 'I don't know,' he said. 'I just talked to his secretary. I didn't think it was my place to question Mr Rippert's decisions.'

'But I want *Roy Cohn*,' Max shouted. 'Who gave him permission to die? For the kind of money I'm paying any self-respecting attorney would *rise from the dead*.'

So it was a joke. Which made Peter's snittiness seem churlish. But Max didn't give him enough time to de-snit. 'We should think about getting some kind of media consultant too,' he continued. 'Who was the guy who handled Oliver Stone on *JFK*, the Kennedy guy?'

Peter searched his mind but came up blank.

Max snapped his fingers. '*Frank Mankiewicz*,' he said. 'Works for some firm in Washington. Find him. Next.'

'That's it,' Peter said, blinking his eyes and dreaming about coffee.

'That's it? I thought I was having dinner with what's-his-name.'

'He cancelled.'

Max tucked in his shirt – a relatively modest Missoni Uomo, at $250 one of his cheapest items of clothing – and cinched his belt. 'He cancelled? What's-his-name cancelled? I can't even remember his name, how could he fucking cancel on me?'

Peter checked the clipboard. 'Said his mom was sick.'

'His *mom*?' Calmly, Max sat down on the ottoman and pulled on a shoe. When he was finished he looked up and stabbed a finger at Peter. His voice was very quiet. 'I want you to call every fucking hospital in town,' he said. 'Every fucking one! Call every room if you have to. If his fucking mother isn't *terminal* I'll . . . I'll kill her!' He jerked the lace tight on his other shoe and stood up and headed for the door, muttering in disgust. 'His *mom* . . .'

Max shot down the stairs at a dangerous forward angle, Peter jumping two steps at a time to keep up with him. As they crossed the living room, Yoji turned to Max and held two beseeching arms out toward the raw brick hole where the fireplace used to be. 'Max,' he said mournfully, 'why you didn't call me?'

Max looked at Peter, who raised his clipboard and flipped back the call sheet. 'We called twice,' Peter said. 'Eight thirty-two P.M. and eight thirty-seven P.M. Office and home.'

'Why you in such hurry?' Yoji asked. 'All the time go fast.'

Max stopped, looking pained, almost embarrassed. Although Yoji was only about twenty-eight – a *genius* Max had discovered on a recent trip to Tokyo – he was massively serious, as serious as a stone, so controlled in every movement he was almost ceremonial, and Max treated him with the wary deference the frenetic accord the calm. Now, caught by Yoji's grave face, Max searched for a good answer, then gave up and threw his hands up in the air, shaking them as if they were dripping hot oil. 'Because I *hated* it,' he said. Yoji continued to study him, the disappointed schoolteacher, until Max made a fist and shook it and spoke in a violent whisper. 'It became *ugly* to me,' he said.

Yoji and Max locked eyes. For a moment neither of them looked away. Then Yoji nodded once and turned back to the fireplace. Max watched him for a second or two, then marched for Peter's Fiat. 'Get the Ripper,' he ordered, slipping into his seat and slamming the door. After fifteen or twenty seconds, without even looking to see if Peter had made the connection, he held out his left hand for the phone; when it was not immediately placed in his palm, he shook his hand impatiently.

'I'm on hold,' Peter said.

Max shook his hand again.

Finally Rippert's voice came on and Peter handed Max the phone.

'How bad is it?' Max demanded, his tone of voice a mixture of anger, worry, urgency, irritation and professional detachment, an almost military attention to strategic detail. 'What did David say?' he asked. 'What about Jeffrey? . . . I should call him. Should I call him? . . . What about Kramer?'

Whatever Rippert said on the other end of the line set him off. 'You're goddamn right I want charges pressed – *you* saw what he did. In front of everybody I know, in front of the whole fucking town, the scrawny old pathetic low life *loser—*'

Max stopped, yielding for a moment. But only a moment. 'If I hadn't tried to press charges,' he shouted, 'everybody would have said, *he's guilty, he got what he deserved . . .*'

He listened again, and his expression changed to white-lipped anger. 'Then why didn't you *stop* me? Of course you could have stopped me! *You're my lawyer.* You *chose* not to stop me!'

Max pushed the hang-up button and handed the phone to Peter. 'Get Kramer,' he snapped.

Peter dialed, then listened to Kramer's secretary make excuses. She sounded nervous.

'In a meeting,' he said.

Max slapped his open palm on the side of the car door, and Peter snuck a glance at him. He looked worried.

'What's up?'

'You know what he told the cops? My pal, Alan Kramer? He didn't see a fucking thing.'

'You're kidding.'

'Happened to be looking the other way. Missed the whole fight.'

The rest of the way to the studio, Max kept slapping the side of the car, sometimes hard enough to make a metallic whoomp that sounded like a distant pile driver. Peter offered to make more calls, but Max just shook his head.

At the lot, as they threaded the alleys to the office, people called out hesitant or overly cheerful hellos. Max just nodded and kept moving. When they got to the bungalow, everyone looked up at once. 'Bradley on line three,' Sarah said. 'And you've got—'

'Put her through!'

Max was already behind his desk with the phone to his ear by the time Peter slid to the end of the sofa, picking up the phone and punching line three all in one motion. 'So let me get this straight,' Bradley was saying. 'First you force your attentions on demure and innocent Tracy Rose, who looks so much better since she got out of rehab, and then you viciously attack her sainted father – the man who gave you your start in the business – at your own birthday party. While all of Hollywood watches. And then *you* charge *him* with assault. Is that about it, or is there more?'

By this time Max had picked up his letter-opener and was stabbing at the desk pad with it – only to get a little too enthusiastic and stab right through the pad, deep into the three-hundred-year-old wood. 'Shit,' he said.

'Can I quote that?' Bradley said.

'I slipped and stabbed my desk,' Max said.

'So you *do* have a violent streak,' Bradley said, teasingly. One of her peculiar charms was the undisguised pleasure she took in human suffering.

'It's nuts, Kit,' Max said. 'I'm telling you. It's *insane*. None of it *happened*.'

'I heard Alan Kramer personally pulled you away from the cops and tried to get you to chill the assault charge, and you told him to fuck off.'

'It's *insane*, Kit,' Max said. 'Does that even sound like me?'

'So tell me the real story.'

Grimacing, Max flipped through the pile of magazines on his desk – *People*, *US*, *Artnews*. The Los Angeles County Museum was giving a show called 'Kitsch and Kulture'.

'*Some* of it has to be true, Max,' Bradley prodded. 'I'm hearing it from too many people.'

'Kit, you *know* me. Would I lie to you?'

Bradley hesitated only for a second. 'Of course you would.'

Max murdered the desk a little more. 'You're so *mean* to me,' he said. Then he launched into his version of last night's events, and ten minutes later he was just winding down. 'Me they take down to a shitty police station for questioning, but to him they're polite – "Excuse me, Mr Rose did you *strain your fingers on his neck?*" '

Bradley saw her opening and pounced. 'So they did question you about this Tracy thing?'

Max jabbed through the desk pad again, chipping out a chunk of wood, angry with himself for giving her the opening. 'I haven't been *arrested*. I haven't been *charged*. There's no truth to it at all.'

Peter watched him. The great Max Fischer was starting to sweat. If he wasn't so worried himself, it would have been great fun to watch.

'But they did question you?'

'I'm telling you it's not true! And the Ripper will sue the crap out of anyone who says it is!'

'But they did question you?'

'They questioned me, and they *let me go*.'

Score one for Bradley, Peter thought.

'Don't bullshit me, Max.'

'*Check it out!*' Max shouted. '*Call the fucking cops!*'

Bradley's voice stiffened, just enough to let Max know she didn't like being yelled at. 'I'll do that,' she said.

*   *   *

After Bradley, Max worked the rest of the press, telling them all the same thing – no charge, no arrest, the Ripper poised to tear out their throats at the hint of libel. After listening to a few of the calls, Peter clicked on to another line to check his messages. 'Hi, Peter, everyone's talking about you. Call me.' That was Marcie, a luscious young actress he met his first week in town, the kind of woman he would have been much too shy to talk to before. There was another message from a friend in New York, who heard about the fight from someone who worked at the *Post* and wanted all the details. Ten were from other assistants, all begging for quick returns about you-know-what. And there was another call from John Sayles, returning Peter's return call. He probably just wanted Max anyway.

The last message was from Detective Spinks. 'I have a few more questions I'd like to go over.' The voice was matter-of-fact, almost curt. 'Are you free at lunchtime? Today?'

It wasn't a question. Peter wrote down the number and looked up at Max, who was just wrapping a call with yet another reporter, wielding the paper-opener like an ice-pick. The desk pad was completely shredded now, and there was a series of deep gouges in the desk. 'You *do* have a choice, Rod,' he shouted. '*I* don't have a choice. *You're* the reporter! *I'm* the target! But I'm not a little duckie at the state fair! I shoot back, Rod! I don't just fall over! *I shoot back*!' He slammed the phone down. '*Shit*,' he said. 'That was bad. That was bad. *Never* lose your temper with a reporter.' Then he noticed the expression on Peter's face. 'What?' he demanded.

Peter hesitated. What a time to tell him about Spinks. Then the Amtel toned and Sarah called out: 'Jennings West on five.'

Saved by the tone. But Max was hesitating. In the last three months, he'd spoken to West maybe five times, strictly courtesy calls, although he had a copy of *Running on Fumes* in his private video library and had once said that West would have been a great director – if he'd been born without a dick or a nose. Then he shrugged. 'Okay, put it through,' he said.

Relieved, Peter picked up the line and listened in.

'Maaax,' West said, 'my favorite prizefighter. Has Don King called yet?'

'You're a piece of shit,' Max said. 'Here my life is falling apart and you're . . .'

'That's when the fun begins,' West said.

'Is that what this is? Fun? That must be my problem – I can never tell the difference between fun and *wishing I was dead*.' Max didn't sound upset though; in fact, he sounded the calmest he had all morning, almost soothed by West's lilting voice. 'So this is a nice thing, you calling me in my travail. I'll have to revise my negative opinion of you.'

West chuckled. 'I just hate to see you and Barry fighting,' he said. 'I mean, he has no talent and no taste, but he's a friend of mine.'

Max sat up straight. 'Did he ask you to call?'

'Max, that hurts my feelings,' West said. 'I'm calling to invite you to a little party. A screening up at my house. A little *divertissement*.' He chuckled lewdly.

'I'll try to make it,' Max said, sounding grateful. 'Have your girl call Peter, give him the details.'

Hanging up the phone, he gave Peter a weary smile. 'Can you believe this town?' he said. 'I'm accused of raping a young girl who was practically my sister, and he wants to invite me to a party. Now he *likes* me.'

Joe Dogosta strolled into the office like he owned it, nodding to Max and giving Peter a sarcastic smile. He slid into the armchair next to Max's desk. 'We gotta talk,' he said.

Max hit the button under his desk, releasing the door. They all watched while it swung shut.

'Bottom line, the cops don't believe you,' Dogosta said. 'They're all over this thing, and they ain't gonna let go, either. Looks like Detective Spinks has a real hard-on for you, Max.'

'What do you know about her?'

'Started out in homicide. Worked the Hillside Strangler case, the Billionaire Boys' Club. Switched to sex crimes on her own request after her six-year-old niece was raped. Takes this shit real serious. They call her the Terminator.' Turning to Peter, he added: 'She's asking a lot of questions about you too.'

'Like what?' Peter asked, trying to be casual.

Dogosta looked at him through narrow, unfriendly eyes. 'Where you came from, who your friends are. If anybody saw you two nights ago when you said you were with Max.'

'Max said it, I didn't.'

Peter just blurted the words out, annoyed that Dogosta was giving him such a hard time. But they caused an ominous silence.

'She just called me,' Peter said.

Max bugged his eyes out. 'What? Why didn't you *tell me*?'

'You were on the phone. Then he came in.'

'What does she want?'

'Lunch.'

'*Lunch*?'

Peter nodded. 'Look, I didn't call her,' he said. He could tell that Max was starting to wonder about him, as if he was picking up the Dog's suspicion by osmosis, and for the first time he wondered what his parents would say if the scandal reached southern Jersey. 'So what do I do?' he asked, humbly. 'Do I go?'

Max looked at Dogosta, then back at Peter. 'Let's call the Ripper, get him in on this.'

While Peter put the call through, Max shook his head at Dogosta. 'Do you *believe* this fucking cop?' he said. 'Lunch *today*? In half an hour? What does she think – the studio's *lunch bell* goes off at twelve-oh-five?'

Peter forced out a laugh.

'Put it on speaker,' Max said.

Rippert's considered legal opinion took less than ten seconds: 'Fuuuuck her,' he said. 'She got her freebie Thursday morning. She wants more, let her get a fuuggin' subpeeena.'

Peter left a message at Spinks's number saying he couldn't get away on such short notice, and tried not to worry about whether she'd hold it against him.

Then Dogosta went back to work and Max turned to other problems, first among them the potential perfidy of Tom Hanks. He kept Peter dialing the phone until they found one of Hanks's pals, then tenderized him like Japanese beef. 'Is he worried about the script? The director? Is it me? Come on, dammit, help me, please, I'm *suffering* here.' By 5:30 Max had talked five times to Jay Maloney, three times to Ronnie Meyer, three times each to Jon Dolgen and David Geffen and Jeffrey Katzenberg. He called Rippert twice before and three times after the three P.M. meeting, just to mull over what the criminal attorney had said. In between he worked on other Hollywood powers like attorney Jake Bloom and producer Ray Stark, even dipping down into the lower ranks with calls to production executives and the lesser agents. And none of it was wasted effort – as the day passed, Peter could feel the town weakening. This was what Max was best at, drawing people in, firing them up, making them part of his army. By the third call, Maloney was practically weeping: Yes, keeping the Fischer account was important to CAA. It was vitally important, crucially important, *critically* important! By the fifth call he sounded like he was ready to burn incense in front of Max's photograph.

As the day passed, Peter felt his worries fall away. Max was right. Max was wise. Work would save them. That was the great thing about the movie business – it was so complicated and urgent that it could expand to fill any vacuum. And there were so many vacuums to fill . . .

And when Max hit a wall, he just smashed through it, scorching the skeptics with bursts of anger as unyielding and fierce as the California noon. Nothing they could say would make any difference. Nothing could change his mind. Nothing could slow him down. There was something inhuman about that, Peter thought, but also something powerful. Normal people huddle together for warmth and learn to ignore each other's bad smells; men like Max rise above the smells, or think they have, and lose all human patience. But the joke was, even that worked for them, just strengthening their will to conquer. And therein lay the mystery: Was Max so unyielding because he was powerful or so powerful because he was unyielding? Had Hollywood changed him, or did he succeed in Hollywood because he came that way?

Finally it was time for the six o'clock news, the first local broadcast of the day. 'Let's see what they've got,' Max said, with a grim sigh.

Peter crossed to the corner of the room and opened an antique mahogany cabinet. Inside stood a 26-inch Mitsubishi, black and sleek. Under it were three VCRs – (VHS, Beta, and three-quarter-inch) and a laserdisc player, along with an impressive array of remote devices. He picked up a remote and clicked on the TV. Channel 9 crackled on, and L.A. institution Jerry Dunphy – craggy and white-haired, the poor man's Walter Cronkite – zipped off the day's summary: fire in the hills, a mudslide in Malibu, trouble in the EEC . . . 'and in Hollywood, a fracas at the world-famous Morton's restaurant shows that the beautiful people . . .' – Dunphy paused, ducking in his chin for somber emphasis – 'are not *always* so beautiful.'

Max tilted forward in the chair, slamming his hand down on the desk. 'Listen to that shit,' he said, waving his hand at Peter. '*Switch*!' he said.

On Channel 7, a frosted blonde in an authoritative blue suit somehow mixed professional detachment with concern. 'Top story this evening,' she said, 'Fire Rages in the Hills. Reporter Tim Milligan helicopters through the flames to bring you the story . . . and in local news, the body of a nude woman washes up on a Malibu Beach . . .'

'*Switch*,' Max said.

Click.

'Thank you, Donna,' another hairspray victim said. 'The first story tonight – a brawl broke out among the beautiful people at the elegant Morton's restaurant last night, as *Blood Hunt* producer Max Fischer took a swing at his old friend and partner Barry Rose, a former chairman of Columbia Pictures. When we come back—'

Peter switched channels fast. Commercial. Commercial. Commercial.

'Why do they *do* this?' Max asked. ' "The beautiful people are not always so beautiful" – they *love* saying that. They *hate* us. They're media versions of those psychos who stalk celebrities. Did you see them smirking? Every fucking one of them smirked. They *smirked*!'

Three months ago Peter would have smirked too, laughing at the rich Hollywood assholes. But after seeing Max wince every time he came across a snide reference to his movies, or heard one of those wretched puns the media liked so much – 'Bottom Fischer' was a perennial favorite – it wasn't so easy.

'It's never going to stop!' Max yelled. 'George Bush deserved what he got, the gutless lying bastard, but the smartest thing he ever did was that bumper sticker that said ANNOY THE MEDIA, VOTE GEORGE BUSH. Everyone loved it – even the *media* loved it. It almost won the election! *Annoy the media, win the election*! Because we have the money and the cars and the women, and they'll never forgive us for it – I'm telling you, the only way to get these fuckers off our backs is to give them each *ten million dollars*.'

Finally, the commercial ended.

'. . . and police sources report that the dead woman was a prostitute who may have had ties to Japan's Yakuza crime syndicate . . .'

'*Switch it*,' Max snapped.

'. . . Japan. Police say they have no motive for the crime, but sources within the police department say the investigation is centering on . . .'

Anticipating, Peter started to switch back to Fox. But just as his thumb pressed the button, a photograph of the dead girl flashed on the screen. She was turning away from the camera, black hair hung over one eye. The newsreader was giving out the number of the homicide police and asking for help identifying the victim.

'Wait,' Max said, frowning. 'Go back to that.'

Peter switched back just as the picture flashed off. They caught a glimpse of a high, almost Indian cheekbone . . .

'. . . and now in sports . . .'

'*Switch*,' Max said. 'Find that murder story.'

Peter clicked fast, and there was the picture again. The camera zoomed in, turning the cheekbone into a white smear, abstracting the visible eye into a half-dozen Lichtenstein dots.

'Jesus Christ,' Max said.

It was her. Marina Lake. Max sat with his mouth open.

'. . . have no leads. The body was found near the *Splash* nightclub, which police have linked in the past to organized crime . . .'

Keeping his voice neutral, concentrating as hard as he could – *how could this have happened? She was alive **yesterday*** – Peter asked if Max wanted him to switch channels again. After a slight hesitation, Max nodded, then cleared his throat. 'Yeah,' he said, sounding a little faint.

Jerry Dunphy was back, grinning at Pat Harvey. Behind them, in an inset box, a limo pulled up to Morton's and a valet parker rushed forward to open the door. 'I don't know, Pat,' Dunphy said. 'Too much money on their hands, I guess.'

Pat grinned back. 'Maybe they should reduce the ticket prices.'

Dunphy grinned and turned back to the camera. 'And now, a look at tomorrow's weath—'

'*Switch*!'

But it was too late – they'd finished reading the headlines and were settling in for the usual lengthy report on the fire. Max got up from the desk and grabbed the clicker from Peter, turning off the TV himself. 'Sarah, get me copies of all tonight's news shows,' he shouted.

Sarah yelled back. 'L.A.?'

'Yeah. Get New York too.'

For a moment he stood there, frowning, with the clicker forgotten in his hand. Then he started pacing – and continued to pace in silence for a good two minutes. When he finally looked up he seemed surprised to see Peter there. 'Try Kramer again,' he said, almost automatically. But before Peter could get to the phone he changed his mind. 'No, call the Ripper.' Then he changed his mind again. 'No, don't call anyone.' Instead he clicked a few keys on his keyboard and called up the computerized call sheet's pink and blue bars. He frowned.

'Fuck it,' he said. 'Take me home.'

And he just walked out, before Peter could even get up off the sofa. The whole way home, he didn't say a word. When they pulled into the driveway, he put one leg out and remembered Peter. 'Why don't you take the night off,' he said.

'You okay?'

'We're both tapped out,' he said, his voice distant. 'Get some rest. Got a baseball game tomorrow.'

Peter had completely forgotten. The Producers' League was starting its spring baseball season. He watched Max walk up the steps to his house, taking each one in slow motion, like he'd just come back from a funeral.

For the next twenty minutes Peter drove on autopilot, barely aware of where he was, thinking of Marina and Tracy and Marlon Spurlock and Barry Rose and Max and Jennings West . . . were they all connected in some way? Was Marina really a prostitute? And what was she doing at Tracy's, anyway? Not exactly providing sympathy, from what he could see. And what was all that about Japan and the Yakuza?

Then the first hunger pang hit him – God, it was past eight, and he hadn't eaten since breakfast. He was so hungry he was shaking, on the verge of nausea. He registered the street he was driving down – Motor Avenue – and laughed. He'd driven around in circles and, like a homing pigeon, come right back to the studio. Which meant he was right near Ships, his favorite cheesy coffee shop, so ordinary and dull it was comforting, like eating macaroni and cheese with a glass of chocolate milk. In fact, he just might order macaroni and cheese and chocolate milk. They probably had it on the menu.

He parked the car, found a booth and smiled at the toaster as he sat down. That was Ships' trademark, a toaster at every table, so the fierce individualists of Los Angeles could customize their bread. The first time he saw the toasters he thought they were goofy, tacky, pathetic, but tonight he loved them. How dumb! How precious! By God, he was going to toast up some bread tonight! He looked up to signal the waitress . . .

. . . and found himself looking right into the square face of Detective Spinks. 'Mind if I sit down?' she said.

'What – what are you doing here?'

'Just lucky, I guess.'

She was already sliding into the seat across from him.

'I'm . . . I was . . .'

'Alone for dinner,' she said. 'But now you're not.'

Peter stared at her nose, a real Karl Malden special. What an icebreaker it was, pure Americana, like something out of *Let Us Now Praise Famous Men*.

'I'm not supposed to talk to you.'

Spinks shrugged. 'You always do as you're told?'

The waitress arrived with menus and a plate of white bread. Peter popped two slices into the toaster – he *had* to eat, no matter what else happened – and waited for Spinks to say something. But she didn't. She snatched up a piece of bread, slabbed butter on it and chomped it down. Then she hooked a finger at the waitress, a doughy knish of a woman who looked as if she might be a relative, and begged her for a cup of coffee.

'So . . . Detective Spinks,' Peter finally said, just to break the silence. 'What's your first name?'

'Patty,' Spinks answered, tearing off another chunk of bread. Then she raised her chin and swallowed, and the wad of bread bulged down her throat like a rat in a snake.

'I'm starving,' she said. 'Tossed my cookies at a murder scene this morning, nothing in my belly but acid.'

'Excuse me?' Peter said.

'Threw up,' Spinks said. The knishy waitress came back with coffee, pulled out her pad and pen. Spinks continued: 'Caucasian female, throat crushed, naked and bashed up pretty bad on the rocks,' she said. 'Not a pretty sight.' She looked up at the waitress. 'I'll have the spaghetti meat sauce, garlic bread, another coffee.'

Was it Marina? It had to be.

Peter saw macaroni and cheese on the menu and ordered it. But he skipped the chocolate milk – on the verge of ordering it, he had the ridiculous idea that it would be suspicious.

'I thought you were on sex crimes,' he said, when the waitress left.

'Related case,' Spinks said. She lifted her eyes.

She put the paper napkin in her lap and arranged her silverware so the knife and fork were exactly straight, just the way Peter's father always did. Then she looked back across the table, studying him as if he were something quite unusual. She did not smile, which would have clashed with her disconcerting habit of making matter-of-fact statements. This was a woman who flattened the drama in her life, Peter thought . . . which was probably a useful trait in her line of work. The exact opposite of Max, who heightened the drama and even the tedium, no doubt some weird occupational disease: Producer's Syndrome.

'What are you thinking about?' Spinks said.

'Me?' Peter repeated, automatically. Spinks didn't answer, just kept boring in with those unsettlingly cold eyes. 'I guess, that you and my boss are opposites,' he stumbled. 'You're very restrained, and he's . . . unrestrained.'

Spinks nodded, swabbed down another chunk of bread. 'Like at his birthday party,' she said.

Peter flushed, and started fooling with the silverware, pivoting his knife on the slick Formica. He had to be more careful what he said. Spinks seemed to read his mind, tipping a hand and shrugging like it was no big revelation. 'He made a lot of noise about pressing charges.'

Peter nodded. 'I told him not to do that.'

'Why's that?'

'The press will just . . .'

'Make your boss more famous,' Spinks said, chewing away on a fresh wad of bread.

'Nobody wants to get famous that way,' Peter said.

Spinks didn't look convinced, but the waitress was there with the plates. When she left, Spinks got to the point. 'I need your help,' she said.

That was a surprise. 'Yeah?'

'It's all up to you, you know,' she said.

Peter tried not to react. What did she mean by that? Had Tracy told her?

'What do you mean?' he said. 'How can it be up to me?'

'Let me be straight with you, Peter. Can I call you Peter?'

Peter shrugged. There was the macaroni and cheese, and suddenly he couldn't eat. So he stared at it.

'Fact is we're in a bind. We have no physical evidence. Zero. Tracy took a shower before going to the hospital. Put on makeup. Douched too.'

Peter nodded his head, tried to look grave and serious.

'Almost like she was deliberately covering up evidence,' Spinks said, still studying him. 'And she hasn't been very cooperative. Wants to drop the charges, doesn't want to drop the charges. Won't answer certain questions.' Then she shrugged, adding casually: 'Of course, the investigation continues. Something might still turn up.'

Peter nodded. It was like a scene in a movie, just another game of cat and mouse in another greasy spoon, life imitating pulp. That was all. Nothing to worry about.

'But right now . . . we could really use your help.'

As Spinks waited, Peter nodded again. What should I say, he thought? I could just tell the truth and beg for mercy, try to make her see it how it really was, but if I did that Max would find out sooner or later – the Dog would dig it out of his police sources – and then Max would fire me and that would be it, it would—

It would be over.

Peter took a deep breath. 'Look,' he began. 'I—'

'Don't say anything yet,' Spinks said, raising a pale slab of a hand to stop him. 'Don't do anything right now. Just listen. This dead female I was telling you about, out in Malibu. She was a friend of Tracy's. Grew up a few houses away. What if she's connected to this?'

Peter took another breath and started to speak . . . but then Spinks held up that slab of suet again. 'This might turn out to be more than rape, is what I'm saying.'

Spinks was watching him, as if she'd like to slice him right open with those sharp little eyes. Peter shook his head, still feeling like he was acting even though this time he was genuinely innocent: He definitely hadn't killed anybody.

'At the hospital Tracy got into a fight with her father,' Spinks continued. 'He left a car for her, but she wouldn't take the car. An hour later an unidentified woman picked her up. She won't tell us who.' Spinks frowned. 'My guess is she spilled her guts to that woman. I would. Friendly face, traumatic moment.'

'Didn't the nurses or doctors or anyone see—'

'Yeah, we got a description. Beautiful young woman. Chinese eyes.' She watched him while she said the words.

'You think that was this girl – woman – out in Malibu?'

Spinks kept watching him. When she spoke, she seemed disappointed, almost sad. 'Peter, listen. I can tell when a man is lying to me. If you don't drop this bullshit story of yours' – she rolled the *story* around in her mouth like a bad anchovy – 'I promise to chase you down just like you raped and killed her yourself.' She wiped her plate with a piece of bread, staining it red and folding it into her mouth. Peter watched, resentful of the theatrics. He didn't kill Marina Lake.

Spinks started talking again with a full mouth. 'Mmramgdtmmammathb.'

'Excuse me?'

'I said, I'm good at my job. I may not look like Columbo to you, but I will catch your boss just the same. And then you will wish you stayed at Columbia University In The City of New York.'

Jesus Christ, the fucking cop even knew where he'd taught, to the point of knowing the school's unusual full name. They were working hard on this. If it wasn't the murder, if that was just a ruse to make him nervous, then Rose must be calling in a lot of markers.

Then Spinks looked up from her plate again, and the room seemed to go quiet. Peter had seen enough movies to know what was coming next: the big question.

'Where did you go, Peter?'

'When?'

'After you left Fischer's house.'

'I told you, I was there the whole night.'

She just stared at him.

'I didn't leave,' Peter said. He tried to look as innocent as he could, but in his mind he was panting down an alley, looking over his shoulder: Did Tracy pay for the hotel with a credit card? Could anyone at the hotel identify him? Where did she say she was raped, anyway?

Spinks nodded, and signaled for the check. 'Things are moving fast, aren't they?' she said. She seemed sympathetic. 'I know what you're thinking – I didn't do anything. I'm just the assistant. Why me?'

Peter laughed, and Spinks continued: 'Maybe I can worm my way out of this. Deny deny deny.'

Sounded plausible to him. Or at least delay delay delay. Until the Dog came up with something, or Tracy came to her senses.

'But you did do something, Peter,' Spinks said, her voice almost kind. 'You did.' Her eyes glinted. Tiny as they were, they held secrets. 'You're *in* this,' she said.

She's just guessing, Peter thought. But Spinks held the look, as if she wanted to plant something in his brain. 'How much do you trust your boss? He's got a hell of a temper, doesn't he?'

It was insane. Max would never . . .

'And he's got the Dog too. You know why he left the force? Got too physical too many times. They let him take early retirement.'

Was Spinks on to something? Did the Dog find out about Tracy and Marina? That Marina had been at Tracy's house that morning? She must have picked her up, that explained what she was doing there.

Spinks just kept staring at him, her eyes boring in. 'Think about it,' she said.

The waitress put the check down and Spinks picked it up and pulled her billfold out of her purse. Peter watched her leaf slowly through the bills. She was as methodical as an old man. They walked to the door. As Peter opened it, Spinks put her hand on his shoulder and gave him a look that was almost kind: her attempt at maternal. In the light from the door, Peter noticed two long hairs on the side of Spinks's chin. Why didn't she pluck them?

Then Peter found himself walking. He left his car at the restaurant and cut across the street into the residential neighborhood south of Washington Boulevard – shoebox houses slathered with brown stucco, peaked windows stuck on like afterthoughts, halfhearted homages to homes left behind. Mean little brown lawns and faded Japanese cars in every driveway. And palm trees, regular as lampposts, dead fronds hanging down scrawny chicken necks. They were full of rats, people said, and Peter pictured baby rats sitting in nests like birds. Rats were everywhere here. At night the ivy rustled with them, and in the morning the rich people woke up to find them floating in their pools.

Think about it.

Everything was so dry. All day long the sun bore down, forcing that white Los Angeles light through everything. It really was a desert, and all the greenery the Mexican gardeners coaxed out of the dirt couldn't dress up the stony truth.

Think about it.

When you thought about it, the light really was hateful. He had read about how its pure glare had influenced the West Coast school of painters and given birth to the movie industry, and so he had tried to like it, but it really wasn't human light. Back east the sunlight was yellow, nicely filtered through humidity and plant spores. The light of Los Angeles was white and cruel.

Think about it.

Guy watering his lawn. Old guy standing there with his hose, eighty years old and still can't accept the fact that he's living in a fucking desert. Stupid hose, stupid lawn, stupid guy. Peter clenched his fists, suppressing a sudden urge to jump the old bastard and pummel him to the ground.

Think about it.

Obstruction of justice. Making a false report. Bogus wanky charges. Why not go all the way and make a *really* false report. *Yes, your lordship, the foul beast pushed the lassie to the ground and forced himself upon her, I saw it with me own eyes . . .* And then he'd take over Fischer Pictures and become the star of his own personal film fantasy, *Max Fischer 2: The Sequel.* With a female cast of thousands.

Stupid. Spinks was right, he had to *think.* First off, hard as it was to remember sometimes, he owed Max. Max believed in him. Max opened the door for him. The idea that he could rape or . . . *kill* someone . . .

Think about it.

Damn Tracy to hell, anyway. Really, when you thought about it, it was all her fault. She was psychotic and careless and self-pitying. It's tough all over, babe. Think you had it rough? – get in line! And you knew she was loving every minute of it. She got to punish all of them at once. Max became a gossip target, maybe lost Hanks, got arrested or worse. And her father got a real kick in the ass – guess what your worst enemy did, Daddy? Climbed aboard your innocent little daughter, aimed his slimy pistol between her thighs, and *shot* . . . Nice girl, Tracy. Hell, maybe *she* killed Marina Lake . . .

Think about it.

But did Spinks really mean it, that Marina's murder might be a related case? Or was she just trying to rattle him? Because really it was just a coincidence, right? It *had* to be a coincidence. The definition of bad luck. The Yakuza or something was behind it. Not the Dog. And anyway Max didn't react watching the TV, not until he saw Marina's face, so he wasn't expecting anything, he *couldn't* have . . .

Think about it.

So, to review. His options were:

1. Betray Max again.
2. Tell the truth and lose everything.
3. Wait passively while events swept along.
4. ————————————————————————

One thing was sure – the first three options sucked. But how to fill in the blank?

Chapter Seven

Eleven P.M. on Sunset Boulevard, Friday night, the festivities just beginning: Peter walked past a pair of headbangers with hair like helmets of black straw, stopped at a doorway where a boy in a dark suit and thin tie checked his name off a clipboard and waved him up a narrow and drab flight of stairs. On the second floor a private little bar hung like a shelf above the Strip. It had been there forever, through a dozen different owners, but it was always just a dark box with a bar on one side and sectional sofas against the other wall, and it always operated by guest list only, and you had to know somebody to get your name on the list. It was Tracy's hangout, the place they'd met, and since she didn't seem to be answering her phone he had come here hoping to find her. Get some answers. Failing that, he could at least get drunk.

Inside, everybody seemed to be from the same college class, each one dean's list in aerobicizing – all twenty, all beautiful, all slim, all blow-dried to perfection. They wore hand-tooled cowboy boots heavy with silver and Gap T-shirts under Matsuda jackets. There was Charlie Sheen, drinking a bottle of Tŷ Nant in the corner with a lovely *model, actress, whatever* at each elbow. And there was Kiefer Sutherland, waving to someone in the doorway with such an easy grin.

'It's Peter James,' a lilting voice called.

Peter turned his head: the dread Marlon Spurlock. 'How's it going?' Peter said, pretending indifference. He didn't want Spurlock to think he was worried about anything.

'What are you doing here?' Spurlock asked, his voice unnaturally jovial. Peter noticed that he looked especially pasty, his grey face damp and his hair askew, as if he'd just dug up a fresh corpse and dropped it off at the lab.

'I'm looking for a blonde,' Peter said. It was the truth.

Spurlock watched him, eyes intent. 'I would have thought you'd be working tonight.'

Peter shrugged and took a sip of his drink, giving the room more careful study, as if he really came there to pick up girls. It was certainly a good place for it – most of the women seemed to be alone or in pairs, not with other men. Over in the corner six or seven real beauties sat around an anorexic-looking brunette with carved cheekbones and full lips. She was older than the rest and seemed to be in charge, a queen bee surrounded by her drones. Probably a casting agent, Peter thought.

'So what, did Max fire you already?'

Peter pursed his lips, considering how to react. Spurlock was such an asshole. Why wouldn't he take a hint and drop it? Any minute now he'd be gassing on about how he was *good with story*.

Spurlock tried again. 'Or did he go on the lam?'

Peter let out one flat laugh, thinking how pathetic it was, Spurlock resorting to bad movie dialogue – go on the lam, indeed. I guess he isn't *good with dialogue*.

'He went to the *Edward Ford* screening and then to the party at Cicada,' Peter said. 'With about ten close friends.'

'And he gave you the night off out of deep human feeling,' Spurlock said.

Peter kept watching the queen bee. A muscular little redhead left a guy at the bar and crossed over to her, bent down to say something, then headed for the door. The guy met her on the way out.

'I don't know . . . maybe he thought I needed some time to myself. Maybe he was just being a nice guy.'

'*Not*,' Spurlock said.

Terrific, Peter thought, sucking down the rest of his drink – the Great American Medium is in the hands of guys who quote *Wayne's World*. Read André Bazin – *not*. Study Eisenstein – *not*. Kurosawa was the guy who made the Japanese version of the *The Magnificent Seven*, and Fassbinder didn't even exist, because his films didn't make money, they were strictly art house, not exploitable, remake possibilities nil. At least Max cared about the tradition, studied it, loved it, and even if his movies were closer to *Captain Blood* than *Citizen Kane*, he made them with real love and a passion for excellence. It was downright weird how people despised him for serving up corn – the Irwin Allen of the '90s, they sneered. But who were they kidding? They were all making corn. They weren't Kuro*fucking*sawa, they weren't John Ford or Hitchcock or even William *fucking* Wyler, and there was something so touching about the passion Max poured into his Karo syrup, so touching and sad – that this volcanic desire would burn to make such fluff. Why couldn't they see it?

But why was he getting so upset?

'So what kind of blonde are you looking for?' Spurlock said.

'Moist,' Peter said, turning to signal the bartender.

Spurlock turned with him, his mad-scientist's bouffant bouncing as he nodded toward the corner. 'So,' he said. 'Have you learned the *critical* importance of pink and blue markers?'

Now he was trying to bond. One of Max's many obsessions was the proper use of markers on the call sheet – since blue came out black on a fax, you used blue if you wanted to cover something up, like a call that had already been returned. But if it was a new name or number you didn't want to lose, you marked returned calls with pink marker, which didn't show up on faxes at all. And if you failed to have both pink and blue markers in your possession at all times – well, that was no minor error. It was evidence of a deep flaw in your nature, absence of spirit, failure to anticipate. 'Repeat after me,' Spurlock said, ' "Yes, obi wan Max, I will use the mystic pink and blue markers." '

Peter rewarded him with a weak grin. 'I guess you know Max better than anyone,' he said. Maybe he could draw him into a conversation that would lead unobtrusively to Marina Lake. But just then Spurlock came alert, and Peter followed his eyes back toward the woman in the corner. A girl with short black hair bent over her now. Peter couldn't see her face, but she seemed familiar, and sexy too, with black tights running up long legs into a pair of coal-colored bicycle shorts, a black leather jacket hanging open over a beaded red bra . . . *The Wild Ones* meets *The Lost Boys*.

'I want you to meet someone,' Spurlock said, grabbing his elbow and pulling him toward the corner. Then the girl shifted position and Peter saw her face, the dark eyes looking for trouble, the newborn, milky kind of skin that bruised easily – the small bandage above her left eyebrow: Tracy. With her hair dyed. He felt the familiar twinge in his belly, fear mixed with desire, and his throat went dry.

Somebody cranked the music up as they were crossing the room, and then somebody else turned it down again almost immediately, which was why Peter caught the last few shouted words: '. . . *fucking* cops,' the Queen Bee was saying. 'Like I had anything to do with it. I *loved* Marina.' She lowered her voice. 'At least when she wasn't being a total cunt.'

Then Tracy saw them and straightened up. She nodded at Spurlock without smiling, then shifted her eyes to Peter. She waited. There was a question in her eyes, and Spurlock thought he knew the answer. 'Guess who this is,' he said. '*Peter James.*' Then he stepped back, clearly thrilled at the chance to observe – and later report to all his cronies, no doubt – the reaction he'd set in motion. An explosion? A meltdown?

Peter held his breath. With a word, Tracy could destroy him. She gave him a long, cool look, Barbara Stanwyck circa *Double Indemnity*, taking her time before speaking, the importance of dramatic timing bred in her bones.

'So,' she finally said, even more blasé than usual, 'you're the assistant.'

Her voice was a little too steady. She was stoned.

'I am,' Peter said.

Tracy looked him over. 'I heard you were gay,' she said.

Peter laughed, actually more of a blast of exhaled tension. 'I don't think so,' he said.

'Really?' Tracy said. 'Because I heard you were. I heard you liked young boys.' She slurred a little on the last three words, but it was hardly noticeable.

'Nope,' Peter said. 'I could get you references.'

Spurlock was still watching, now with a grin on his face. He wouldn't dream of interrupting the conversation, or even joining. He was *consuming* their performances, like watching a video, and the Queen Bee was watching, and so were all the people sitting with her, and suddenly Peter and Tracy were putting on a show. They couldn't help it. The audience made them into actors. People from the bar were looking over too, and Peter could hear the murmurs: 'Look, it's Tracy Rose, talking to Peter James.' . . . 'He's Max Fischer's new assistant, stupid.' . . . 'Now that's what I call a perfect couple . . .'

Tracy gave Peter a half smile and pulled out a cigarette, milking the moment. Peter quickly fumbled for a match.

'So show me how you pucker,' Tracy said.

Peter looked confused.

'When you kiss his ass.'

Peter heard a few chuckles around him, then felt the wave of heat that meant he was blushing. Tracy kept teasing him with that half smile, Mona Lisa with a mean streak, until Peter shrugged and did an abashed little shuffle on the floor.

But then neither one of them could go on with it. The pause went on too long, and Peter looked back into Tracy's eyes and saw something worried – whether it was fear or sorrow, he couldn't tell, and Tracy probably couldn't either, with her emotions so muffled by whatever drugs she'd taken. People looked away, returning to their conversations, or at least pretending to. Tracy let the fake smile fade and blew smoke across the room. 'This place is so *boring*,' she said, to no one in particular, and walked to the bar.

Spurlock took Peter's arm and pulled him along after her, picador at the bullfight. 'Peter was just telling me that he thinks Max is – "basically a nice guy", I believe your words were?' He put on an expression of abstract scientific inquiry. 'Would that be your assessment as well?'

The half smile came back. She let her eyes drift to Peter's throat, then blatantly slid them down his body to his crotch. 'Well I'm not sure I'd go quite that far – basically a *guy*, maybe.'

Peter felt the urge to give Spurlock a good shove. The bastard was standing there smirking over every word, gloating over Peter's dilemma. He didn't even try to hide it.

'Joking aside,' Peter said to Tracy, shifting just enough to block Spurlock's view, 'I'd really love to get your point of view. I mean, I just got off the bus from New York three months ago. I don't know *what's* going on.' He tilted his head forward, just a hair, and narrowed his eyes, trying to get her to understand his meaning without it being obvious to everyone in the bar. 'I'm an innocent, a suckling child, a babe in arms. A *virgin*.'

Tracy licked her lips, doing a vamp number. 'Mmmm,' she said. 'I like virgins.'

She turned her smile to Spurlock, who had edged his way back in, checking to see if he appreciated the line. This would all be retold and retold, and she wanted to be sure none of her effects were missed.

Peter edged another half-step in front of Spurlock, who once again quickly shifted to compensate, the tenacious bastard. 'I'd be so grateful,' Peter said, tucking in his chin and giving her his boyish under-the-eyebrow look, with just a touch of sexual smoke. 'If you're gentle.'

Tracy laughed for the first time, throwing her head back and displaying her long marble neck, her clipped black hair made witchy by the gesture: They shaved it, revealed my skull, and even now the tar heats in a bucket . . . Then she stopped, and with a glance at Spurlock to confirm the moment, she looked back at Peter with the same practiced half smile.

'But it wouldn't work,' she said, pretending to be sad about it.

'Why's that?'

'Because I'm *never* gentle,' she said, sneering and her voice was suddenly so bitter that Peter was startled. 'You better watch out for me,' she added. 'I'm dangerous.'

'She is,' Spurlock agreed.

'You might get hurt,' Tracy continued.

'I can take care of myself,' Peter said.

Tracy laughed, then gave a sideways suck on her cigarette.

Then she stopped laughing. Peter followed her eyes. She was looking at a man who was standing in the doorway. He was so tall the arch over the door threw a shadow on his face, but Tracy seemed to recognize him anyway. There was surprise in her eyes, even a bit of sudden furtive guilt. She stared at the man, and so did Peter, and so did Spurlock, all of them frozen in place like looters paralyzed by a sudden flash bulb. Peter noticed the clock above the kitchen door: The hand clicked from 11:59 to midnight, and the man stepped forward into the light.

It was Barry Rose. He looked determined and unstoppable, his eyes scanning the room with fierce purpose. They stopped at his daughter. Then he headed straight for them, pushing through the crowd like a surly bouncer bearing down on a drunk.

As Rose marched across the crowded room, a boy with slicked-back hair murmured his name reverentially – it's *Barry Rose*. 'Who's he?' his girl asked, and contempt crossed the boy's face. 'He used to run Columbia,' he said. 'It's a studio.'

Rose heard the murmurs and ignored them, heading straight for Tracy. His eyes skated over Peter and Spurlock before focusing hard on her, silently demanding an answer to the obvious question: Why in God's name are you wearing black leather in a dubious nightclub two days after getting raped? The voiced question came as mere emphasis: 'What the *hell* are you doing in this dump?'

'Tripping the dump fantastic,' Tracy said, her tone infinitely bored, her eyes flicking over to Peter and Spurlock to make sure they were taking it all in. When her father said nothing, she added: 'Trying to drown my many sorrows.'

Rose studied her for a moment. And Peter, astonished to be so suddenly face to face with Max's nemesis, studied Rose. Although he must have been almost sixty he didn't seem old, just weathered, with grey cowboy bristle on his cheeks and those black, timeless eyes. A hard guy to have for a father. Which gave him new respect for Tracy, who was returning his look with her head cocked back in full adolescent defiance: Give me all you got, Pops.

'What'd you do to your hair?' Rose said, his voice casual.

Tracy displayed both profiles. The black dye job had a purplish tinge. 'Do you like it?'

'No.'

Then, slowly, he turned to Peter, raised his eyebrows, and waited. Peter cleared his throat and held out his hand. 'Mr Rose, I, uh, I'm happy to . . . I didn't . . .'

Rose ignored the hand. 'Do I know you?'

Yeah, he thought, I'm the guy who was trying to break your grip on Max's throat last night. But then his brain stalled and he let his hand fall back down.

'Peter works for *Merwin*,' Tracy said. Rose ignored her, looking down at Peter (he had six inches on him) as if he were studying something on the bottom of his shoe.

'What are you trying to do?' he said.

'Do?' Peter said.

'Did Fischer send you here?'

'Max?' Peter said, his voice sounding stupid in his own ears. But even under the best circumstances, meeting Barry Rose for the first time would have been unnerving – his legend was potent, one of the classic Hollywood stories: how, at sixteen, he kissed his grandmother good-bye at the bus station in Corpus Christi (she worked at Sears, behind the counter) and came to L.A., working construction for three years until he landed that first job with Roger Corman, making giant houseflies out of spit and fiberglass. Then came the move to Columbia and the fateful meeting with producer-intriguer

Ray Stark – *A crew jacket, Ray? It'll be on your desk before lunch* – and a few years later the critical moment when Stark introduced him to Herbie Allen, the investment banker who had bought and sold Columbia a half-dozen times, pulling strings most people in Hollywood didn't even know existed. That was when Rose started to *get it*, as they like to say in Hollywood, to distinguish themselves from the vast herd of losers who don't. At some point during that time he started becoming difficult, developing a sour and testy air, making it immediately clear to everyone who met him that he was almost always disappointed and had no intention of taking it well. He undercut the sourness with a wry tone, playing the curmudgeon, which gave it a certain charm and made him into a character. It also made him formidable. He made president of production before he reached thirty. By thirty-three he was chairman.

Rose looked at his daughter. 'Is there something *wrong* with this boy? Is he *stupid?*'

So that was where Max got his habit of talking in italics.

'Don't ask me,' Tracy said.

Now they were all examining Peter. Spurlock was so alert he seemed almost sexually excited.

Finally Peter snapped into gear. 'I just happened to . . . Marlon just introduced us.' From the corner of his eye, he saw Tracy smirk.

Without warning Rose jabbed out an arm, and out of reflex Peter jerked backward, bumping into the boy behind him and spilling his drink. '*Hey,*' the boy said. Peter tried to mumble an apology but found himself staring at the hanging silver tongue on the boy's belt. It swung, catching the light. Before he could snap out of it he heard the boy talking. 'Mr Rose,' he was saying. 'Nice to see you again. Steve Sterling? I work for Art Linson?'

Rose gave the boy an absent nod and reached out again, slowly this time, taking hold of Peter's shoulder with strong fingers, smiling as if he were just giving him a friendly squeeze.

'So you work for Max Fischer,' he said.

'Three months now,' Peter nodded.

'Three months,' Rose repeated, staring into Peter's eyes.

Staring back, almost hypnotized, Peter found himself thinking about Rose's deep tan. He didn't seem the type to lie in the sun to make himself more attractive. No, Peter decided, Rose's tan was aggressive, a suit of armor – almost a form of hostility.

'Your boss had a busy week,' Rose said.

Peter shrugged and tried to come up with a response, but before he could think of what to say Rose loosened his grip and patted him on the shoulder. He flashed Peter a complicated grin, at once wry, suggestive, accusatory, pitying and infinitely unsurprised. He turned to Spurlock. 'He hasn't got a clue, does he?'

Visibly happy to be consulted, Spurlock immediately shook his head: nope.

Then Rose gave Peter's shoulder one more hard squeeze and turned his face to his daughter. 'Go home,' he said. His hand stayed on Peter's shoulder.

Tracy looked right in her father's eyes. 'No,' she said.

'Tracy . . .'

Rose's voice had a warning tone, but Tracy shook her head. '*No*,' she repeated.

'Marlon,' Rose said, 'take her home.'

And damn if Spurlock didn't hop right to it, dragging Tracy toward the door. But she shook loose and crossed her arms, thrusting her chin forward and glaring at her father.

Rose spoke slowly, emphasizing each word. 'I want you to go home,' he said.

'Aren't you a little out of place here, Daddy?' Tracy sneered. 'Shouldn't you be at Chasen's?'

Thirty years ago Chasen's was Hollywood's hot spot, renowned for the chili that Liz Taylor had flown to her on location. But those stars had fallen, gone to Palm Springs every one, and Tracy knew perfectly well that it had finally closed down for good. Rose's eyes narrowed.

'Why are you following me, anyway?'

Everyone in the club was watching. Rose glared at them, and they shifted away, small talk rising obediently.

'I'm not following you,' Rose said, his voice so controlled it was menacing. 'I have an appointment here.'

'I have an appointment too,' Tracy said.

Rose studied his daughter, then scanned the room, as if to see just what business she might have. His eyes came to rest on the gathering in the corner. The Queen Bee was laughing at something, her head tilted back in theatrical delight.

'Do you know Angie?' Tracy said, disdain in her voice.

'Do *you* know her?' her father barked.

For a second, Tracy looked hurt. Peter glanced back at Angie and caught her watching them. The hair on his neck tickled. There was something feral about her, as if she had night vision or could smell blood at long distances.

'I asked first.'

Peter saw the fingers curl up again. There was a long pause. 'I know people,' Rose said. 'It's my job.'

'I know people too,' Tracy said.

For a moment neither one of them spoke. Embarrassed at watching, Peter let his eyes drift to the bar. A pudgy blonde in her thirties sat on a stool, alone and out of place. Obviously she didn't get it. Peter felt tenderness and contempt, in equal doses.

When he looked back, Peter saw that Rose's lips had gone white. He seemed on the verge of exploding. Instead he hesitated, and Peter was touched by the momentary doubt he saw in the old man's eyes. Barry Rose, in doubt. Barry Rose, who was famous for storming out of business negotiations – he would stand up and shout, either give me what I want or this conversation is over. *Over*. I'm outta here. Max told Peter about it, laughing, the closest he ever got to affectionate on the subject of his ex-boss. And nine times out of ten, Max said, Rose's simple willingness to walk inspired such panic – *What? You don't need us?* – that he got exactly what he wanted. The one thing he learned from Barry Rose, Max always said, was *hondeling* – Yiddish for being a giant pain in the ass until you get your way.

But Rose couldn't *hondel* Tracy. She knew all his tricks.

'Let's *both* go,' he said, his voice suddenly gentle. 'We'll go together. How's that?'

Tracy looked suspicious.

'We need to talk. We can talk in the big house, in the TV room. Like the old da—'

Tracy cut him off. 'Is *she* there?'

Instantly, Rose snapped back: 'She *lives* there.'

They were talking about the new wife, Peter guessed. The wedding had been in George Christy's column a few months ago. She was a production assistant in her early thirties, determined-looking, with big hair.

'Just please come along,' her father said, sounding weary and reaching for her again. But Tracy stepped back quickly, a bullfighter dodging horns.

'This is so boring,' Tracy said, clutching her elbows so there would be nothing to grab.

'Tracy . . .'

'Why don't you just criticize me here, and we can skip the trip home,' Tracy said. She imitated her father's gruff voice: '"You know, Tracy, I'm very concerned about your erratic behavior. Drinking in bars, associating with bottom feeders, especially at a time like this. You've got to understand, I'm a public figure. And that's spelled m-e-d-i-a t-a-r-g-e-t."'

Rose nodded his head slowly, tallying the digs. 'I guess I'm very boring and predictable,' he said.

Tracy returned to her own voice. 'Let's not get all sentimental,' she said.

Rose turned back to Peter, shaking his head sadly. 'When she was two years old, she slammed the door in my face,' he said, glancing back at Tracy. 'Remember that story?'

Tracy rolled her eyes, but she didn't try to stop him. 'She hated going to sleep,' Rose continued. 'I learned I could shut her up by saying *One more word out of you and I close the door*, which worked for maybe six months. Then one night I said *One more word and I'll close the door*, and damn if she doesn't get up out of her bed – we'd just moved her from the crib, and a chunky little thing she was too, a little milk-fed sumo wrestler—'

He let his voice get sentimental for a second.

'—and she waddled right up to the door and looked me right in the eye – *and slammed the fucking door right in my face.*'

Rose looked back at his daughter. She had been listening closely, almost with hunger, but now she put back on her exquisitely bored look. Rose's face went somber. 'You were good at slamming that door,' he said.

'Thank you,' she said.

'You're still good at it.'

'Stop, I'll blush,' Tracy said.

Rose turned to Peter again, very intent this time. Peter could feel his force. 'Two nights ago she comes home, she's a mess,' he said. 'Clothes torn, face all bloody. She had bruises on her *wrists*.'

Tracy laughed, tossing her head back and blowing out a column of blue smoke. 'Stop, Dad, you'll get him all excited.' But she sounded nervous.

Her father didn't even turn his head, kept bearing down on Peter. 'That's what Max Fischer did. Your *boss*.'

Peter shifted. 'I, uh . . .'

'The man you work for.'

'This is so stupid,' Tracy said.

'Now there's another little girl who's *dead*,' Rose said. 'I guess my daughter got off easy. And that's the man you work for.'

Tracy's eyes widened. '*Da'ad*,' she said, with that double-syllable dip teenage girls use when their fathers are being ridiculous. 'You don't really think Max had anything to do with Marina.'

'I'd say he's capable of anything.'

Tracy studied him for a moment, then turned to Peter. 'My father is obsessed with Merwin Fischer,' she said. 'It's kind of pathetic, actually. All because once upon a time, after my sainted brother ascended, Daddy became a dead man. He got up in the morning dead, he went to work dead, he shuffled around the house dead. I hear he even fucked the occasional starlet dead, which must have been a lot of fun for her.'

Rose bristled and reached for her wrist, but Tracy dodged away. 'And then Max Fischer came along and brought him back to life. And Daddy will never forgive him for it.'

Peter had heard the story before, from Max. The short, unhappy life of Barry Rose, Jr, the perfect Bel Air boychik until he was found up in Will Rogers Park one morning, translucent junkie skin rubbed thin by the embrace of angels, and after the funeral Rose stepped down from chairman to a production deal on the lot, his fire to succeed as dead as his son . . . until the day Max walked into the office and grabbed his hand, literally going down on his knees, saying, 'I love your movies, I will do *anything* for you,' and Rose said, 'Well, you're in the right position' and started unzipping his pants, and without a beat Max said, 'Well, *almost* anything – but I know a hairdresser you might like.' They spent the next two hours talking about *The Searchers* and *Sullivan's Travels* and *All About Eve*. But what clinched it was when Max said his real favorite film of all time was *The Great Escape*. 'I mean, Dustin Hoffman is a genius, but the real question isn't who do I wanna *see* but who do I wanna *be* – and the answer's Steve McQueen, no question.' Rose gave him a job on the spot, and six months later they were in production.

'He didn't give me life,' Rose growled. He *used* me and then he *fucked* me, just like—'

'*Max Max Max Max Max Max Max Max Max Max*,' Tracy teased, eyes blinking madly. When she stopped, father and daughter glared at each other again, and Tracy's defiance was so total it seemed almost murderous, as if she were seconds from pulling a knife. Slowly, a look of amazement spread over her father's face.

'Incredible,' he said. 'Max Fischer rapes you, and *I'm* the bad guy.'

Tracy made her voice world-weary. 'If it weren't Max, would you care? It would just be some minor property damage.'

Her father shook his head, looking down at the floor. 'I'd say that property was already pretty well damaged.'

Tracy gave him a tight, twisted smile. 'Condemned, practically,' she said.

Rose's face sagged. For the first time, he looked his age, with a hangover. 'I wish you would come home,' he said.

'I know.'

Her tone was almost forgiving: What can we do, a pair like us?

Spurlock put his arm around Tracy. 'I'll keep an eye on her,' he said. There was a tenderness in his voice Peter had never heard before.

Tracy smirked. 'Yeah. Marlon will keep an eye on me.'

Rose looked at Peter, as if wondering what to do about him.

'Don't worry about the assistant,' Tracy said. 'He's harmless.'

Peter felt relieved . . . but insulted.

Then Rose looked down, concentrating so hard that he actually seemed to expand. There was still a frightening amount of power left in him, when he cared to focus it. 'I can't change the past,' he said, his eyes still down, 'but I promise you one thing' – and now he raised them, and they *burned* – 'I will *destroy* Max Fischer.' He paused, and a smile teased his lips. 'I can, you know.'

Tracy locked eyes with her father, and for a moment no one spoke. Even the ambient nightclub hum seemed to dim a little. 'When I'm done with him,' Rose finished, 'he'll be living out of his *car*.'

He pointed a finger at Peter, cocked it and fired. Then he blew on it, smiling at Peter through the imaginary gunsmoke.

'You better learn to duck,' he said. 'I might hit you by accident.'

Rose turned away. He walked over to Angie, bent down and whispered quickly into her ear. She looked at her wristwatch and nodded. Then he straightened up and marched for the door, ignoring the young people who shifted out of his way.

The minute he was out of sight, the air seemed to go out of Tracy. 'Let's get out of here,' she said. She sucked up the last of her drink and put out her cigarette on the floor. Then Spurlock took her arm, and they left Peter standing there without even a good-bye.

At the doorway, Tracy gave Angie a quick wave.

Chapter Eight

The next morning Peter woke up with a scorched-earth hangover: black skeletons of burned trees, scattered wisps rising from hidden beds of coals. Snapping off the alarm with a groan, he remembered making a fool of himself the night before, the specifics returning in wet, vomitous chunks: sitting on a bar stool, slugging double gin-and-tonics . . . first just chatting with . . . then trying to impress . . . a blonde – no, not the – God, it was the pudgy blonde, the one who looked so out of place, the one he'd *pitied* . . . he remembered her eyes, looking at him with absolute blank indifference, like he was a television tuned to a game show. God, she shot him down – the pudgy blonde shot him down! Shot down by the pudgy blonde!

He sat on the edge of the bed and stared at his bare feet. It was stupid, but nothing that had happened to him in the last few days made him feel quite as bad as this – getting rejected by someone he didn't even want, and getting so drunk . . . What a loser. He rubbed his face with both hands, trying to knead away the nausea. When he realized it wasn't going to do any good, he took a shower and went out to get some coffee and a newspaper.

On page two of the metro section there was a picture of Marina, an 8 x 10 actress headshot, and a brief story: Beverly Hills woman found dead in Malibu, foul play suspected. Age nineteen, daughter of a noted Beverly Hills plastic surgeon, parents could not be reached for comment but had been notified by police. Attended but did not graduate Beverly Hills High. No suspects, police investigation continues . . .

That was it. No mention of prostitution or the Yakuza. Probably that was the invention of some overheated television reporter.

Peter looked closely at the picture. She really had been an extraordinary beauty. He wondered if her father helped any, then felt instantly ashamed of himself: She's *dead*, you jerk.

When he got to the house, Max came out the minute Peter's wheels touched the driveway. 'About fucking time,' he said, plopping into the passenger seat. 'Let's go.' He had black circles under his eyes, and looked thinner. He hadn't shaved. Peter guessed he hadn't slept at all. He didn't try to make conversation, and neither did Max. About halfway to the studio Peter couldn't stand the silence any longer. 'Did you ever reach Kramer?' he asked.

'No.'

'How about Hanks?'

Max just gave him a sour look. They drove the rest of the way in silence.

Through the gate they went, down one alley and up another, past the buildings that mutated daily, sprouting a new facade or sign, a sudden lamppost in a period style . . . until they reached a long, low building punctuated by a series of doors like changing rooms at an old-fashioned beach club. These were the cutting rooms, as the sign still said, decades after cutters started calling themselves editors. Max banged on one of the doors. '*Billy!*' he called. He waited and banged again, and again. '*Billy! Open the fucking door!*'

A face appeared in the glass, pale and startled, the face of Billy 'Buck' Fargo. When Max hired him to direct *Romulux*, he had fifteen three-minute MTV epics on his résumé, and rumor had it he'd actually slept with Madonna. Now he was mouthing the word *no*.

'Let me *in*,' Max yelled.

Fargo slowly shook his head, flipping his little ponytail side to side.

'You've had your ten weeks, asshole,' Max said.

Fargo shook his head faster, holding up a finger – one more day; he was pleading. In fact he did have the rest of the day in the ten-week producer-free editing schedule mandated by the Directors Guild. Most directors let their producers in the editing room all through postproduction, but Fargo had sat on his rights, as they say, barring Max for the entire ten weeks. In the past few days he'd even started begging for a little more time – the opticals hadn't come, the temp dub wasn't finished . . .

Now Max was drawing his finger across his throat, and finally Fargo opened the door. 'I have till *midnight*,' he whined.

'I'm the *producer*!' Max shouted.

Fargo tried to look pitiful, which at that point wasn't too much of a stretch. Even his ponytail drooped. 'I'm afraid of you,' he whined. 'You're too strong. I need the time. I need to nurture my little bird.'

Max's eyes widened and he started breathing heavily. In a second he would start snorting like a bull. Fargo had picked up this phrase from some actor, and he'd been using it all through the shoot – Max, I have to nurture my little bird. Max, my little bird needs air. It was the one thing he could have said that was guaranteed to make Max more insane.

Max shook a finger in Fargo's face. 'I'm going to *kill* your little bird,' he hissed. 'I'll snap its neck and twist its *fucking* head off.'

Fargo's eyes pinched tight. 'Talk to my agent,' he said, slamming the door.

Max beat on the door with his fist. 'I'll eat it for *dinner*! Do you hear me? I'm going to eat your fucking bird for *dinner*!'

Fargo studied Max for a last moment through the glass and then his face disappeared.

'He's a dead man,' Max said.

Up the alley! Past the lingering Teamsters, the smoking grips, and face-stuffing gaffers! Into the office! Call Ronnie, call Alan, call Donner and Blitzen! *What have you heard*? *What are people saying*? And between calls, tend to all the other details that need tending, never mind the crisis du jour: Any new word from Hanks? How is the *Romulux* ad campaign coming? Party tonight at West's? Tell him maybe, but no promises. And get the Ripper on the phone, goddamnit, I want to talk to him *now* . . . and then the mail, with Max wincing as he always did when he got to the hate letters – your movies are sexist, racist, show too many people hurting animals/smoking cigarettes/promoting evolution . . . they're so violent they make me want to *kill*, to kill *you*, you fucking *Jew* . . .

'Jesus Christ,' he said, dropping the last one.

Sarah came to the door. 'It's Joe Dogosta,' she said. She kept standing there, worried about her boss.

Max didn't notice. He glanced at the last few letters, then got up to grip the private detective's hand. 'Hey, Dog,' he said. 'What's shaking?'

'My tail,' Dogosta said, with a grudging smile. 'Cops don't have shit. Pretty soon they'll be canvassing the homeless community.'

He sat down and only then did he bother to look Peter's way. He didn't say hello.

'That's *good*,' Max said, half asking.

'Someone's putting a lot of pressure on them, a shitty case like this.'

'Someone?' Max spat.

'Let's just say your former employer is having a lot of meetings.'

Max frowned. 'With who?'

'Played golf with the chief of police. Had a drink at *On the Rox* with that piece-of-shit madam, Angie. Even hanging with your buddy Alan Kramer, from what I hear.'

'My buddy Alan Kramer,' Max repeated.

'He's getting a lot of mileage off this new thing, this dead girl,' Dogosta said, casual as could be, as if they'd all talked about it for hours and hours and were bored with the subject already. But he was watching Max carefully when he said her name: 'Marina Lake.'

Max didn't answer, but it was obvious from his expression that the name troubled him.

'You know about it?' Dogosta said.

'Saw it on the news last night.'

'It's got the cops all excited,' Dogosta said.

'They think there's a connection?'

'They hope. Otherwise, like I say, there's no case.'

Max gave a nervous chuckle. 'So what, they think *I* did it?'

Dogosta nodded.

'That's insane.'

Dogosta shrugged. 'And it looks like Barry's doing everything he can to prove it. Apparently Lake worked for Miss Angie, and Barry's been working on her to—'

Max shot out of his chair. 'It's fucking *ridiculous*. This is *insane*. You gotta *stop* this.'

'The cops are gonna do what they're gonna do, Max.'

'What about Barry? Can't you stop him?'

'What do you want me to do?'

'I want you to—' Max was on the verge of a tantrum, Peter could see the urge welling up in him. But he stopped himself, evidently deciding it was strategically incorrect; Dogosta wasn't the type of person you could abuse. 'What about the DA?' he said, back to practical mode. 'Any luck there?'

Dogosta shook his head: more bad news. 'They've got some chick assistant DA on it, sex-crime specialist, Katie something. Member of the National Organization for Women, on the board of the Rape Crisis Center. I think she's hoping you'll be her O.J.'

'Great,' Max said.

Dogosta looked at Peter, sitting at his traditional perch on the TV end of the sofa. 'Well, I gotta get back to it,' he said, standing up. 'Checking out a lead that Tracy and the Lake girl used to hang out at this S&M club, Sin-a-Matic. Maybe the killer's some whips-and-chains fan. Maybe the rapist too – that would make life *real* simple.'

'Jennings West,' Max croaked.

The Dog cocked his head, waiting for more.

'Marina was friends with him too. Worked for him or something.'

As Peter tried to process this – Was that why West invited them to the party? But he'd invited them that morning, way before the news hit – the Dog just nodded, unsurprised. 'I'll do that,' he said. At the door he turned for a last comment. 'By the way, you ought to have a conversation with your little assistant.'

Max looked at Peter, then back at Dogosta, furrowing his forehead. 'What?'

'Let's just say that Mr Barry Rose has been talking to a lot of people, not just Kramer and the cops.'

Max turned on Peter, slowly. 'What's this?'

Peter hesitated. How much did the Dog know?

'He's a regular night crawler, this kid,' Dogosta said.

Peter exhaled, carefully paying out the held breath. This was a chance to tell the truth, to get it over with once and for all. 'I talked to him for, like, two minutes last night. I was at *On the Rox*, Marlon Spurlock introduced us.'

Max looked stunned. 'Why didn't you *tell* me?'

'I was going to,' Peter said.

'But you *didn't*,' Max said.

'You were in such a shitty mood. I didn't want to make you any more upset.'

Max stared at him, trying to decide whether to believe him.

'Its not like we were making friends. He threatened me.'

Max mollified. 'He did? What did he say?'

'Said I better learn to duck. He was going to get you and I better learn to duck.'

'What else?' Max said.

'That was pretty much it.' Peter snuck a look at the Dog, who was still watching him. There was something unnerving about the way he breathed – the steady rise and fall of his chest beneath his stare. 'I was talking to his daughter when he came in,' Peter added.

'*What*? Now you're talking to her too?'

'It was Spurlock,' Peter said. 'His idea of a joke, to introduce me.'

'What did you *say* to her?' Max demanded.

'*Nothing*. She called me a fag. Said the club was boring.'

Max nodded, with bitter satisfaction. 'That's Tracy.'

Evidently deciding he'd seen enough, Dogosta waved a good-bye, giving Peter one last smirk as he left. But Max kept staring at him. A long miserable moment passed before he spoke. 'So what'd you think of her?' he said.

It was the one question Peter hadn't expected. 'She was . . . interesting,' he said. 'Smart. Fucked up. Kind of sexy.'

Max pursed his lips and nodded, processing the information. Then he sighed. 'It's her father's fault. I blame him. He treated her like shit, just like he treated me.' Then he sighed again and got up. 'Come on,' he said, 'fuck all this, it's Saturday. Let's go to the ball game.'

If only Max had yelled. Forgiving him was the cruelest thing he could have done. How could he ever tell the truth now?

That year, the producers' softball league used a field at the University High School, a hop and a skip northwest of the Columbia lot. When Peter and Max arrived, the game had already started. Max immediately stalked out to the diamond, his chest puffed out, chomping on an imaginary cigar, transforming himself into the image of the big-league baseball team owner, while Peter went off to the bathrooms to change into costume – or rather, uniform. When he came out, Max was pacing around behind the backstop, talking on his cellular phone. 'You're kidding,' he said. 'Goddamnit. Shit.'

Peter assumed he was talking about the case, so he tried to change the subject to the game. 'How we doing?'

'Down four runs,' Max said, shaking his phone at Peter. 'And the Thorns are three fucking runs ahead.'

That was Rose's team, of course: another hour, another crisis.

'Who are they playing?' Peter asked.

'*Castle Rock*,' Max spat, as if those were the two most disgusting words in the language.

Peter stepped into the dugout and sat down with his teammates, who were crew members and actors from Max's movies. The rule in the Producers' League was that anybody who ever worked on any movie made by a given producer could play on his team. Peter was considered something of a ringer, since he'd played ball in college – there were even some jokes that this was the real reason he got his job. So the ribbing went when they saw him: 'Hey, the game's going to turn around now,' one said. 'Yeah,' answered another, 'if Peter doesn't get a home run every time up, Max is going to have him *stuffed*.' There were some nervous chuckles, and after that everyone was very careful to avoid any sensitive topics – like sex, women, violence, Barry Rose, and the Los Angeles Police Department.

The game did pick up. The competing team was a gang of aggress-ive young technoids from Lightstorm Entertainment, the company headed by director Jim Cameron, who made *The Terminator*, *T2* and *Aliens*. Each of them had a combustive gleam in his eye: half laid-back, blue-jean normalcy, half dangerous, cyber-preppy fanaticism. The team uniform was jeans and a T-shirt with a pair of burning eyes staring out of it, with the logo YOU CAN´T SCARE ME – I WORK WITH JIM CAMERON. Peter caught a snatch of an argument out near third base. 'I'm telling you, the Baby Bells are going to get creamed on this. Remember two words: *dark fiber*.'

The third baseman spat. 'Wrong, dude – it's gonna be cellular.'

By the bottom of the seventh inning they were almost tied, though. Max's presence alone seemed to fire up his team, not to speak of his frequent pep talks, threats, and bribes. At least one lucky hitter got a battlefield promotion, from runner to creative executive – or would if Max chose to honor it the next day.

Then it was Peter's turn up at bat. He'd been hitting fairly well every time, plus once he got a double and once a triple. 'Come on,' Max said. 'Get a homer, and I'll give you tomorrow off.'

'Tomorrow's Sunday,' Peter said.

'So – wouldn't you like it off?'

Peter tested his bat, giving a significant look to the Fischer King player standing on third, a comely young D-girl named Anne. Before

Tracy, Peter had thought about asking her out – she had an intriguing way of breaking out in gusts of embarrassed laughter, hinting of innocence and unexpressed passions. Not to speak of natural blond hair and a spectacular pair of breasts. But that was then. Peter squinted against the sun and waited for the pitch . . .

Then it came, and Anne started running, and he popped it up, right along the first baseline. He ran under the ball, stumbling against the first baseman . . . 'That's batter's interference, you son of a bitch!' shouted the Lightstorm team captain, a steamy little fireplug named Connie, kicking up the dirt next to the baseline. But the first baseman recovered . . . and *caught* it, sprawling to the ground behind first base. And Anne reached home, blonde pigtails flying. The first baseman stood and whipped the ball to third. The third baseman stomped on the base.

'Double play!' Connie shouted. 'Our game!'

'What the fuck are you talking about?' Max, screaming, marching up to Connie with hands waving. 'She tagged up! Score's even!'

'She left the base early!'

'The hell she did.'

'She did too!' Connie screamed, as far gone as Max. 'You cheating bastard.'

Max let a stunned, hurt expression come over his face. 'Jesus H. Christ, Connie – it's *softball*. It's a *game*. We're having *fun* here. Besides, I'm telling you, she *tagged up*! Every softball game I ever played, you could tag up on a foul pop.'

Caught off guard, Connie hesitated.

Then Peter acted – on impulse, not so much making a decision as just launching himself forward into motion, off the base and toward the argument. 'Max,' he said.

'Not now!'

'But Max, she's right. Anne left the base early.'

Both Max and Connie looked at Peter, amazed. Then Connie turned back to Max. 'Oh,' he said, as if he just hadn't realized the facts. Pleasantly, he said, 'Well, I have to apologize. It's your game.' He shook her hand and walked off the field.

Peter followed, feeling nervous. Max nice was always Max dangerous. 'Sorry, Max,' he said.

'Why are you sorry?'

'Muffed the hit,' he said. 'Lost the game.'

'And that's all?'

'She left the base early, Max.'

'So? What's your *point*?'

'Point of ethics, I guess,' he said, with a sad smile: there were ironies here Max would never understand . . . not if he could help it.

Max cocked his head back, disgusted. 'Ethics? You're not *successful* enough to have ethics.'

On the drive home, Max kept up a generalized fuming: losing to those obnoxious *Lightstormtroopers*, what a pain, and how did you like that dyke manager they had, and thank God at least Barry's team lost too, a minor consolation, only better check the chart, I think that means we'll actually have to *play* that sonofabitch next Saturday. He was talking to keep from thinking, that much was obvious, and Peter found that he was glad to listen for much the same reason. After a while, Max turned to trashing various people they both knew, starting with Kramer – fucking *moron*, only thing he knows how to do is attach his lips to celebrity butt. Then Peter told him the Kramer joke that was raging through town. Man jumps out of window in Century City, falls fifty stories, lands in a mattress truck. As he gets up somebody says, man, you must be the luckiest guy in the world. No, the guy says, brushing himself off – that's Alan Kramer. The gag being that Kramer didn't deserve his obscenely high salary. Max chuckled, and by the time they got to the house they were a team again.

After showers and an hour or so on the phone, the usual evening routine, they got in the car again and drove to the crest of Mulholland Drive, heading to Chez West. Max said it was to get intelligence, the sense of the town, to show their faces, to see what West's motive was in inviting them, but Peter thought there must be more to it, especially if West had some connection to the Marina business. Anyway, it was a lift to drive along Mulholland, high up on the crest of the Santa Monica mountains. From there the city below was a lake of buildings, the Valley on one side and Los Angeles on the other, two huge basins brimming with rooftops and windows that lapped against the spring-green hillsides. After a short drive they pulled off Mulholland and down a winding driveway, passing through a large wrought-iron gate onto a cobblestone courtyard. They came to a stop in front of West's Italianate villa, a sumptuous palace swept by a giant weeping willow. Professional set painters had artificially aged it, giving it that dried-in-the-golden-sun look beloved of interior decorators, and it was capped by a red-tiled roof that may or may not have been spotted by actual moss. The usual white-jacketed valets waited to whisk away the car, then West's assistant – a fiesty young NYU graduate named Rachel Levy, who always wore a black leather jacket and at least six earrings – led them out to the pool, which hung so far out on the hillside it seemed to float in the sky.

'Max! Amigo mio!'

It was West, waving from the opposite side of the pool, flanked by a matched set of women (one blonde, the other brunette) as a Roman emperor by lions. He was wearing the same white buck shoes and white Sansabelt pants, only tonight accessorized with a black scarf. Sitting across from him was none other than Marlon Spurlock, who was getting to be as ubiquitous as God. He also waved, flashing them a hearty grin. Rolling her eyes at the spectacle, Levy left Peter and Max and headed back to cover the door. She treated it all as theater, but word around town was that (despite her nearly doctrinaire feminism) she would lead West's hookers right to his bedroom door, and wait nearby until he was finished. Apparently he liked it that way.

As Max greeted a few of the guests, Peter quickly scanned the party: There was Jack Nicholson, standing at poolside with a drink in his hand, a pleasantly dazed expression on his face. There was Helmut Newton, talking to an Amazon in a thong bikini. Max whispered in Peter's ear: 'In the seventies, she would have been topless.'

'So much for the notion of progress,' Peter said, trying to do Noel Coward.

Most of the men were in their forties and fifties, gold watches glittering on their wrists, shirts open to tanned throats. Peter recognized a few producers, directors, executives of West's generation, most of them either sidelined or eking out a project here and there. A few were still major players – a director of production, a business affairs chief, a fast-rising executive in his thirties who had a reputation for cheating on his Playmate wife. They all had one thing in common, which brought them to this particular party in this particular house: They liked women. And West always had plenty of women around, all of them so very congenial. Some were upscale hookers, some genuine party girls attracted to the money and glamour, and some were young actresses taking charge of their careers. They were all in their twenties, all 'model quality'. Although West still directed a film every few years, this was the thing he was known for now. 'He has five or six who live here all the time,' Max said. 'Pays their expenses, buys them clothes. All they have to do is swim naked in his pool.'

As Peter looked them over, trying to distinguish the professionals from the, um, amateurs, a limp and friendly hand clapped down on his shoulder. 'It's Pants Inspector. Hello, Max. Welcome to Sangria-la. What can I get you?'

'Diet Coke,' Max said.

West mugged disappointment.

'I'll try the sangria,' Peter said.

Now West really looked disappointed. 'Sangria is a *whore's* drink. Have some Glenlivet and soda. Or an Absolut martini.' He winked. 'Or some iced vaginal secretions, perhaps?'

'Sounds great,' Peter said. 'With an olive and a splash of gin.'

West stopped at the various tables to introduce them. Finally he got to where he was sitting when they came in. 'Alexandra, Leela,' he said. 'Meet Max Fischer and Peter James, as fine a pair of troublemakers as ever you've seen.'

Peter nodded and smiled at the two women, or at least at their eyebrows. Beauty still made him very uncomfortable, though he was getting more used to it every day. Max, on the other hand, examined them casually and thoroughly. Then he turned to Spurlock. 'Hello, Marlon,' he said. 'You're looking healthy.'

He was being facetious. If anything, Spurlock looked more damp and pasty than usual, as if he'd spent the last few nights dreaming about children in sordid postures.

Spurlock waved a hand without getting up, which struck Peter as a bit impertinent. Even deliberately so. 'Wheat germ has been veddy, veddy good to me,' he joked, in an Indian accent.

A geisha appeared with drinks, and Peter accepted his gratefully, sucking half of it down before stopping to notice that it was vodka. As he took another long pull, saying good-bye to the lingering malaise left by his hangover, he watched West sit down at the end of Alexandra's chaise longue and bend over to kiss her toffee feet – he sat, he saw, he kissed, Peter thought, sucking down the last of his drink. 'God, I was thirsty,' he apologized. 'Just played seven innings of baseball.'

With a flip of his hand, West ordered Peter a replacement, then turned his soft gray eyes on Max – eyes from an opium den, languorous and amused, as if he were studying him through a veil of smoke. 'So I hear you're a murderer now,' he said, with an amused smile.

Max did a take, pulling his head back and holding a beat. 'A murderer?'

'That's what they say.'

'Gee,' said Max, the soul of innocent confusion. 'I don't remember killing anyone.'

Spurlock pretended to frown. 'Maybe it was one of those *Morning After*, *Tough Guys Don't Dance* kind of things,' he said. 'You did it in a blackout.'

Peter consulted his hand, pretending it was his clipboard. 'He's right, Max. Here it is – Friday, twelve forty-five, murder enemy number four two one. You must have just forgotten.'

West and Spurlock chuckled, and Max gave a tiny nod to acknowledge the joke, but now he was finished displaying his lack of concern. 'So what have you heard?' he asked, in a matter-of-fact tone that carried the message: For business reasons, I have to be concerned with this nonsense.

West shrugged. 'It's going around – this girl they fished out of the water off Malibu. Marina Lake. You did her.'

'I *did* her?'

'The night of your party,' West said. He didn't seem so amused any more.

Max frowned, and darkness settled on his features.

'You did know her, Max,' Spurlock prodded. 'You're not going to deny that?'

Max stared at him, and Peter felt tension shoot between them. He also noticed that West was watching the exchange very carefully. Then, slowly, Max nodded. 'Yeah,' he said. 'I knew her.'

'Really?' West said.

'I met her when she was about fifteen,' Max said. 'I think you were there, Marlon. She and Tracy had just come back from the beach, still wearing their bikinis. Even then, she was . . .'

'A piece of ass,' Spurlock said.

'A beautiful young woman,' Max finished. He turned to West. 'Didn't you know her too? Wasn't she one of your . . .' He passed a hand over the scene.

West shrugged. 'She might have come by once or twice,' he said. Then he pushed a leather-bound photo album across the table. 'Hey, Peter, take a look at these,' he said. 'Helmut took 'em.' He was changing the subject, or at least taking some of the pressure off it – we're all friends here, jes' havin' a few drinks . . .

Taking a sip of his fresh drink, Peter flipped open the front cover. The first picture, glued to black paper, under a plastic sleeve, was a shot of two stunning Amazons lying naked beside a swimming pool. One was lowering her head between the other's legs, her tongue arched out to a point and a look of intent concentration in her black eyes, her wet blonde hair plastered like rubber against her skull. The other woman had her head thrown back and mouth open. Her hair was black and wet, hanging in thick clumps like the hair of a statue. You could see every goosebump on their bodies, and the pointed tongue was as textured as a ripe strawberry.

'Look familiar?'

Peter blinked and realized that the pool in the picture was the pool at his feet. And the women . . .

Leela turned back and grinned. She was truly lovely, with a long Modigliani face and green eyes flashing, hair the color of midnight. 'Like it?'

Peter looked back down at the picture. The eyes were the same. 'You look different with a mustache,' he said.

Leela threw back her head and laughed. Her muscular little belly shook. And Peter, feeling light for the first time in ages, knocked back another slug of vodka. God knows he deserved it – *Popeye* couldn't have tied the knots in his shoulders.

Spurlock turned back to Max. 'I always wondered – did you ever fuck her?' He hesitated just a second, then added: 'Marina, I mean.'

Max pulled back, offended. 'The girl is *dead*,' he said.

Spurlock shrugged, giving him that much. Peter flipped through the rest of the album: Leela and Alexandra, Alexandra and Leela, hills and hollows in high relief, as alabaster as the Parthenon by moonlight, yet braced by the alienating grit of porn. Then he handed it to Max, who glanced at the first few pictures and pushed it back to West.

'So where did you hear this rumor?'

West smiled, answering airily: 'I never reveal a source.'

'Sounds like Barry.'

West shook his head, smiling a froggy smile: mmmm, *juicy* fly.

'Was it Barry?'

West waved across the pool at another arrival, a young executive from TriStar. 'Of course, Barry's very upset about all this,' he allowed.

'Have you talked to him?'

West shrugged.

'He knows it's not true, doesn't he? I mean, bottom line, no matter what fights we've had, I can't believe he would really think that of me.'

Max was sending his messages, using Hollywood's version of semaphore or smoke. Maybe he was more worried than he seemed.

'You did accuse him of forcing himself on his own daughter, as I recall,' West said.

Max scowled. 'But I didn't *mean* it.'

Half an hour later, Max had gone to the bathroom and Peter was slumped into a deck chair, trying to think and not to think. How did Max react when he saw the murder news on the TV? Switch it. But then he ordered copies of all the shows. For the party news? But why was he so late to the party? Could he have gone to Malibu? If Marina tried to blackmail him or something? Or maybe the Dog did it. Maybe he was just trying to make her afraid of the dark.

Behind him, he overheard West talking to someone. 'He's an invert,' West was saying. 'Don't you love that word? Invert. A pity it's fallen out of use – it's so much more evocative than *per*vert.' Then West called out his name, and Peter turned to see him patting the chair next to him. 'Come sit with me and Leela and . . . what's your name again?'

'Alexandra,' the girl said. She was so blond her eyebrows were practically white – an Icelandic blonde.

'*Alexandra*,' West repeated. He smiled his lizard smile. Then he smiled up at Peter. 'Another drink?'

'Sure, thanks.'

They made small talk until the drink appeared, then West clinked glasses with him. 'So, what's your next move, boyo?'

'Excuse me?'

'You must be planning something. Max is about to do a Fatty Arbuckle, poor man, and I hear he's broke too.'

Peter answered automatically: 'Are you kidding? He must be spending five hundred grand just on renovations on his house.'

'Of course he's broke,' West said, rolling his eyes. 'He's always broke. Why do you think he makes so many pictures – he calls it slicing salami.' He imitated Max's voice perfectly – ' "I gotta *slice* me some more *salami*" ' – and smiled, running his hand up Alexandra's endless leg. Alexandra kept chatting to Leela, paying no attention, as if her leg was something she had donated to charity.

For some reason the news that Max was broke – he was immediately sure West was right – disturbed Peter almost as much as anything else that had happened. If Max was broke, then nothing was as it seemed. 'I'm honestly not planning a move,' Peter said. 'I don't think he did anything, you know, wrong . . .'

West watched him carefully, looking for something.

'He brought me in.'

West nodded, evidently giving him a passing grade, then made a steeple with his fingers. 'I wonder if Max knows what Barry is really up to?' he said.

'You mean beyond trying to put his ass in jail.'

But West shook his head, with a patronizing smile. 'That would be the fringe benefit.'

'Steal Hanks.'

'Getting warm.'

Peter tried to think, but he couldn't figure it out.

Finally West helped: 'Did you know his contract at Fox is up soon?'

'Barry's?'

West nodded.

And of course, so was Max's. Peter put the rest together: 'Barry wants to move back to Columbia?'

'And with *Romulux* in the toilet and the Hanks picture evaporating as we speak, that's a hell of a lot of overhead Kramer doesn't need.'

'Especially if Barry can deliver Hanks.'

West nodded.

Peter waited. Wondered what West's motives were – if West had been friends with Marina Lake, if he had invited Max up to get information? 'So why are you telling me all this?'

West smiled again, and stroked Alexandra's thigh. 'I like to help young people,' he said.

Sick of cat and mouse, Peter allowed himself to be brusque. 'Then tell me about Marina Lake,' he said.

The smile left West's face. He sighed and looked across the pool, his eyes settling on each of his beauties in turn, as if he were drawing sustenance from the sight of them. But before he could answer, another blindingly perfect young woman emerged from the house, and in one smooth motion she opened her robe and let it fall. She stood there for a moment, bare breasts thrust forward, her naked body honeyed by the fading sunlight, then dove into the pool and swam underwater, straight for Peter and West, kicking the water into a mosaic of blue and tan . . .

West smiled, happy again. 'I think of myself as one of God's gardeners,' he said. 'I tend his precious blooms.'

Then the swimmer broke out of the water, holding up her hands like a presenter on a game show. 'The screening begins,' she said, perky to the point of parody. The moment had obviously been choreographed.

In the screening room Peter grabbed a chair and found himself sitting next to Jack Nicholson. They made some amiable small talk about the weather and New York, and Nicholson couldn't have been nicer. For a moment Peter forgot everything else. He was talking to Jake Gittes! He pictured Nicholson younger, thinner, with a white bandage on his nose, and the mental picture made him feel disassociated from the man sitting beside him, almost as if he were seeing double. He had to force himself to concentrate on the conversation.

Then the lights came down and the movie began: *The Godfather, Part 2*. It was a particular favorite in Hollywood, where people liked to think it was really about them. In the last three months Peter must have heard at least two dozen people quote from it, always the same line, and always with great satisfaction: *This is the business that we chose.*

After five minutes, Rachel Levy came down the aisle and crouched down next to Peter. 'Jennings thought you'd enjoy the picture more from the Playroom,' she said. Her voice was neutral, all business.

Peter didn't know quite what to say. The Playroom? Was West gay? What would Max think if he walked out? What would Rachel think? Besides, he was sitting next to *Jack Nicholson*.

'I'm fine here,' he said.

'Suit yourself.'

Two minutes later she was back. 'Jennings *really* thinks you'll enjoy the movie better from the Playroom,' she said. So he got up and followed her, past the pool, down a little path, past a pair of orange trees to a little bungalow hidden in foliage. 'Jennings likes to watch from here,' she explained, leading him down a small hall. 'The movie comes in on closed circuit.' Her face was a mask.

She knocked once and opened the door for him. Inside, he found a large room with a sunken floor and one of the most elaborate home entertainment units he had ever seen built into one wall. A wraparound bedlike sofa spanned two more walls, every inch of it covered with mink. The fourth wall was all mirror. Jennings was splayed out on the sofa in a red silk bathrobe, the woman who had dived into the pool to announce the movie draped beside him. Her hair was still a little damp and her robe (white silk) lay loose, exposing a long line of flesh from neck to belly.

'Come in, me boyo,' West said. 'Join the party.'

He patted the sofa, and Peter sat down on the edge, hooking his foot under his knee so he was more or less on the bed without actually putting his shoes on the fur. Levy waited by the door.

'Kick off your shoes,' West said. 'Get comfy. Make him a drink, sweetie.'

Levy went to the mirrored wall, waved her hand in front of one panel, and a small but very well stocked bar came hovering out. While she mixed, West produced a small mirror with six fat lines of cocaine laid out on it.

'Haven't seen that for a while,' Peter said.

'Some of us keep up the traditions,' West answered. He passed Peter the mirror, and Peter gingerly sucked half a line into each nostril. He hadn't done this since his junior year of college. He'd been surprised, actually, to find so few drugs in Hollywood. Max didn't even drink – it got in the way of work.

After everyone (except Levy) had a turn at the mirror, they turned their eyes to the movie for a few minutes, making comments and cracks like any other tribe gathered around the electronic fire. Levy stood to the side, waiting to be dismissed. Then West turned his amiable grin on Peter. 'So tell me, boyo, did you like any of those girls?'

Peter hesitated, looked at Rachel.

'You liked Leela, didn't you?'

'Well, uh, yeah,' Peter said, trying not to look at Rachel. His lungs ached. His head was a cold buzzing elbow, that had just been jabbed in the funny bone.

West was delighted. 'Isn't she lovely? Mmmm. And so lively too.' He gave Peter a coquettish pucker. 'She could help you with all your terrible problems.'

While Peter wondered exactly what that meant, West turned to Levy. 'Sweetie, why don't you go get Leela. And send Kate and Marie along too. We'll have a little *costume* party.'

As Levy left, West grinned and punched Peter in the arm, locker-room style. The gesture seemed out of place, too hearty and all-American. Peter tried to smile and then fell back against a pillow. For a few moments they watched the movie. Peter didn't remember it being so slow . . .

Peter gave his head a little shake. Snap out of it, *boyo*, he told himself. Best to put this time to use. Sensing that a question about Marina would be wrong, he asked if Max was really broke.

West didn't take his eyes off the screen. 'Hasn't got a dime.'

'What about all his hits?'

'Max Fischer never had a hit.' He teased open the swimmer's robe with a finger, peeking inside, then let it fall back. She kept watching the movie. There was a little white crust around her adorable nostril.

'What about *Blood Hunt*? It made a hundred and fifty million domestic.'

'But Max didn't see a penny.'

'That's impossible.'

'You really don't understand the business yet, do you?' West said, with the *faux* exhaustion of someone forced to explain the glaringly obvious.

'I guess not.'

'Max Fischer is not a gross player. He gets a fee.'

'But his fee's a million five,' Peter said.

West shook his head, draping his disappointment with a delicate glace of contempt. 'I'm telling you, boyo, he's never had a payday.'

The door opened and the three women came in. Leela had changed into a short black dress. She posed against the door, giving Peter another wink.

'They're twins, you see,' West was saying, indicating the other two, a pair of perky California girls with curly Orphan Annie hair. 'But not exact twins. Show him, girls.'

Without hesitation, the two redheads pulled up their shirts . . . and it was true, they were not identical. Peter blushed, but then the grins on their faces comforted him – amused grins saying *go ahead and look, you know you want to, it's only human – and anyway, we get a kick out of them too . . .*

Rachel Levy was still standing in the hall, watching him. 'I'll be in the office,' she said.

Without taking his eyes from the twins, West waved her off. 'Put on something pretty,' he told the twins, beckoning Leela to the sofa with his other hand. She sat down next to Peter, smiling at him and then resting her head on his shoulder. Meanwhile Marie passed her hand over another part of the mirrored wall and a row of previously invisible doors popped open, exposing an array of girl clothes that ran almost the full length of the wall – girl clothes in silk and satin and Lycra and leather, dress girl clothes and sports girl clothes and slinky little nightclub girl dresses. And a hundred shades and types of lingerie. Quickly and without shame the two girls stripped to panties and started rifling through the outfits. West watched, flicking his eyes between Pacino and the twins.

Peter cleared his dry throat, but tried not to move. He let his eyes fall to Leela's long brown legs. She cuddled against him and let out a little sigh, as if she were relaxing at last, all because of him. With his other hand, Peter rubbed his nose and snuffled, tasting bitter coke in the back of his throat. Leela shifted again, this time flattening her breast against his arm, and Kate was stepping into a little pink skirt, her knee raised, the little puckered hammock at the crotch of her panties pulling tight. Then a cool hand took his chin and pulled his face to the side and he felt wet lips, warm lips . . .

'Look at that, boyo!' West punched him in the arm, and Peter looked back to see the twins dressed in matching cheerleader outfits. 'Get out the pom-poms, girls!' West shouted. The twins giggled and then, to Peter's amazement, actually pulled pom-poms out of the closet and started a cheer: 'Two, four, six, eight, hurry up and copulate!'

Peter laughed, tension leaking out of him.

'Three, five, seven, nine, give it to her one more time!'

'I taught them that,' West said, proudly.

The twins began to pose, turning various angles and lifting their little pink skirts. But by then Peter was concentrating on the tongue in his mouth. 'Let's go somewhere,' he said.

Leela shook her head. 'He doesn't want me to leave?' she whispered, phrasing it like a question, as if she were worried about offending him. Then she took his hand and put it on her breast.

Peter left his hand there, with an almost intravenous awareness of the softness in his hand. The nipple against his palm. But the smell of perfume was suddenly much too strong, and the top of his head was set to launch: ten, nine, eight, seven, six, five, four . . . 'I need some air,' he said, taking his hand back. He got up, not without difficulty, and headed to the door.

'Where you going, kid?' West called from the bed. Peter looked back and noticed for the first time that the girl who dove into the pool was now naked, her white robe in folds beside her, like she was sitting in melting snow.

'I need some air,' Peter said, as graciously as he could. But he was angry now – at West for pulling him into his harem fantasy and at himself for falling into it. How could he be so stupid, with all that was going on? He remembered an article he read about a certain species of fish that only had one male per school. All the others were either female or neuter. But when the dominant male died all the neuters grew sex organs and fought it out. The new winner got all the women, and the losers got to watch their little fish dicks atrophy and fall off. He had a creepy feeling West was making him neuter.

But nothing was falling off him. Quite the contrary: There was a pit bull in his pants, straining at the leash. Dizzy from drugs and lust, he lurched past the antiques, past the collections of jade and ivory, past the cabinets filled with ornate silver plates, over Persian carpets, until when the cool air hit he felt the blood humming in his veins, and he wanted to jump a fence, or butt his head against a tree. He turned and turned again and imagined himself a dervish, reeling his head back with eyes half closed, and as he made the dramatic gesture he observed himself, thinking how he must look, which only made him feel more dramatic and passionate: I am in torment! I am a man in torment! The sweet flowered air sweeping up the hills added poignancy. *Ah life, at once so hungry and so full. . .*

He made a quick mental calculation: The movie had been playing just half an hour. It was nearly three hours long. So on the safe side he had maybe two hours left. If he could be back by midnight . . .

Without another thought he ran to the valet stand, took down the box and searched for his keys. 'Can I help you, sir?' a valet asked. But there they were, and he was running for the car. He had just enough presence of mind not to gun the engine as he slipped past the rolling electric gate.

Chapter Nine

The little red Fiat hugged the curves of Mulholland all the way to Beverly Glen, and then Peter pulled a hard left and plunged down toward the city lights, wheels screeching as the car fishtailed – down, down through the hills, toward the ocean. 'Come on, be nice,' he said, into the car phone. 'I need to see you.'

Tracy laughed. 'What's the matter, horny?'

'As a matter of fact . . .'

'At least you're honest.'

There was give in her voice – she wanted to see him, she just didn't want to admit it.

'Sometimes,' he said.

She gave a short, surprised laugh. He was winning her over.

'I need practice,' he said.

'I don't know,' she said.

'I'm on my way. Hear those tires squeal? I'm risking my *life*.'

'Where's Max?'

'Fuck Max.'

'Now that's a thought.'

She said it teasingly, putting him down again: Max might be worthy of me, but you're just an assistant.

'Tracy, please,' he said. No games now, just honest pleading.

She hesitated for a second, then made up her mind. 'Come on over,' she said, and hung up the phone.

Left on Sunset and left again, and back up the winding hills past the walls and hedges and once again into the upper lot of the Bel-Air Hotel. And again through the bushes and trees, ignoring the branches that slapped him, pulling cobwebs off his face and moving on. There was the tree. Up! Up and over!

He dashed behind the tennis court and up to the guest house door. The second he got there, it opened.

'You're sweating,' Tracy said.

'I wanted to see you.'

He walked through the door and she closed it after him. 'I almost didn't answer the phone,' she said. After a slight hesitation, she confessed: 'I'm a little fucked up.'

But she didn't seem ashamed of it. Her eyes were blurry, distant.

'I don't mind.'

He put lechery into his voice, hoping for comic relief. There were so many . . . *issues* between them. He knew that he should ask about Marina, ask about Max, get intelligence, but that shit would drag them down, and that's not what he wanted now. No, no. She was wearing the same blue robe she wore the last time, only this time he caught a glimpse of something black underneath. Forget Marina. Forget Max. *La vida es sueño*, and hope springs nocturnal . . .

'You actually left Max in the screening room?'

'Yeah.'

'What are they watching?'

Peter told her.

' "This is the business that we chose",' she quoted.

'They love that line, don't they?'

'They wish they were outlaws, instead of a bunch of butt-licking ass-kissers. Gin and tonic, right?'

He nodded. She was dropping ice cubes into glasses, acting so removed. 'Wanna smoke some pot?'

Peter shook his head. He was wasted enough already, and paranoid enough for a Thorazine transfusion.

Tracy brought his drink and leaned in close. She swayed there, grinning vaguely, smelling of gin and perfume.

'Do you want to play, Peter? Do you want to play with me?'

The question threw Peter off balance – and so did the distant way she asked it. It sounded too much like 'toy with me'. Was she going to go off on him again?

Tracy shrugged out of the robe, stood there waiting in bra and panties. 'Come play,' she said.

Peter was beginning to suspect she didn't really like sex. That's why she needed all these theatrics, to distract herself from what she wasn't feeling. But there she was, standing before him in lingerie, so close he could smell her perfume. He leaned in and kissed her neck, inhaling deeply, trying to lose himself in her smell, thinking maybe just maybe he could fuck his way through her defenses. Before she had never let him do anything for her, not even with fingers, but this time he would make her come and maybe then she'd just be normal. Drop all this rape bullshit and crazy anger and just be . . .

Her hands went to his shoulders. Pulling him closer.

Then away. She watched him, a mischievous smile on her lips. He was about to say, Okay, I'll go, this wasn't a good idea, when she put a finger on his lips.

'Wanna see something?' she asked.

He gave her a humble little nod: anything, just have mercy . . .

She hunched her shoulders to unclasp her bra, which joined in the front. Then she held it open like a curtain, taking a deep breath to make her breasts rise. The theatrical gesture thrilled Peter so much that it was a second before he noticed the small white bandage next to one nipple. Tracy peeled it down. Underneath was a tattoo, a tiny bumblebee nuzzling the edge of her aureole.

'Like it?' she said.

He nodded, licking his dry lips.

'Kiss it.'

He leaned forward. But she pulled back.

'It might sting,' she warned.

He looked in her eyes, meaningfully: I don't *care* if it stings. Then he kissed the bumblebee. When he was finished he grazed upward and let his lips close over her nipple. He felt it harden in his mouth, but then she giggled and pulled away. Patting the bandage back in place – 'You got it all wet,' she said – she started up the stairs. Peter watched her naked back, the stunted wings of her shoulder blades shifting under the skin. She disappeared into the upstairs living room. When Peter got to the top of the stairs she was bending over by the coffee table – probably snorting a line, he thought – but she quickly turned and walked up to him and kept walking, circling him and then pushing him back onto the sofa and yanking down his zipper all in one smooth motion, like a dance in some Janet Jackson video. Then she had his erection out and with one practiced hand guided it between her thighs, pulled her panties aside with the other, then gave a little shivering wiggle of her hips to ease him inside. She was like a guy about it, rough and ready, no foreplay, no tenderness. His clothes were still on, even his belt was buckled. She started moving above him, her eyes closed. But maybe he was wrong – she seemed, if anything, *transported* . . .

Then he felt her hand move over the arm of the sofa, heard a fingernail click against plastic, then the electronic death rattle of a telephone autodialing. 'Don't move,' she ordered.

On the speaker, a distant phone rang. A girl picked up.

'West residence.'

Peter sucked in his breath.

'Max Fischer, please.'

'He's—'

'In the screening room, I know,' Tracy said. 'Transfer me there.'

She kept moving. She put her hands on Peter's wrists and pinned them to the sofa. After a minute, eighty seconds at the most, a harsh voice rasped onto the speaker.

'*Yes?*'

'Hello, Max,' Tracy said, breathing heavily and rolling her hips.

'Tracy?' He hissed it, keeping his voice low.

She breathed some more. 'Enjoying the movie?'

'I've seen it before.'

'You should be doing what I'm doing.'

'What are you doing?'

She gave a little moan. 'Can't you guess?'

Max didn't answer. Peter felt a sudden surge of excitement, and pushed hard into her. Tracy responded with another moan. Their bodies slapped together.

'What are you doing, Tracy?'

'Don't you hear?'

She let out a little grunt. Max didn't answer. But he didn't put the phone down either.

'What's the matter, Max?'

Again there was no answer, and Tracy laughed. Peter felt the laugh from the inside, shuddering like an orgasm.

The speaker rasped: 'You're crazy,' Max said, his voice hissing like a kung fu villain.

'Yesss,' she said.

She was grinding her hips harder now, and Peter was squeezing, biting . . .

'You're a psychotic *bitch*.'

'Max. I – *oh* – didn't know you cared.'

Max didn't answer. Peter could picture him, biting his lips. Clenching his teeth. Maybe the vein at his temple would throb.

Tracy moaned again. 'That's gooood, baby,' she said. 'Do it *harder*.'

And he did. Their bodies slapped together. Peter lunged and lunged again. He was close.

'He's young, Max. And hard. Hard all over.'

She moaned again. Their bellies slapped. Both were wet with sweat. Thighs sliding against thighs.

'He's in me so deep.'

'God*dammit*,' Max exploded.

But he didn't hang up. They could hear the movie in the back-ground, the sound of glasses clinking and men grunting in low mournful tones. Now the sound of Max's breathing was starting to come through the phone, rasping like Velcro. Tracy smiled, leaning across Peter to whisper at the phone in a voice that trembled with deep feeling – arousal mixed with anguish. 'Come on, Max,' she groaned. 'Talk to me.'

'You're crazy,' Max hissed.

'Help me.'

'A crazy bitch.'

'Yes.'

'A fucking crazy bitch.'

'Yes, that's—'

Max slammed down the phone, and Tracy collapsed in a series of shudders that started in her neck and echoed right down through her thighs. When it was over she patted Peter on the neck.

'. . . perfect,' she finished.

Peter let himself out and padded to the wall. After the sex, he had tried to talk to her. *Why did you do that? What's going on between you and Max? Who was Marina, and is all this just a big coincidence or what?* But she just shook her head and looked away. Maybe she was about to cry. It was hard to tell. Instead she pulled out a joint and lit it, but he'd had enough – too much – and said it was time to go. He was cold about it. Maybe she *was* the most fucked-up and unhappy female in the entire Western world, but look what she was doing to him! He was just a big human dildo

in her weird Maxodrama. She walked him to the door and gave
him a kiss on the cheek, but by that time he couldn't tell if it was
a peace offering or just another black joke.

He jumped at the wall and caught the top, then hung there for a
second, gathering strength. He felt so dazed. As he started scrambling
up, he heard a rustle and a cough. 'Well, well, well. Look at this.'

It was Barry Rose, in a burgundy smoking jacket with his hands
in the pockets as if he were merely taking a casual stroll around his
grounds. He squinted at Peter, a cowboy deciding whether to waste
a bullet.

Peter let go of the wall and dropped back to the ground.

'It looks like a young man sneaking from my daughter's door,'
Rose said. 'Pretty damn suspicious, if you ask me.'

'I was, uh . . .'

Rose held up a hand – don't even bother. He became very quiet.
'Not so many years ago,' he said. 'I could have *shot* you for this.'

He pulled his hand out of his pocket, and with the hand came
a cute little nickel-plated gun.

'In fact,' Rose said, smiling at a happy new thought, 'I probably
still can.'

'But sir, I didn't mean . . .'

'What's the matter, is Max afraid to come himself?'

'No, I—'

Rose cut in again, the snarl in his voice thick with cigars past. 'He
should be. Because I *would* shoot him. I had the chance once and I
still can't believe I wasted it.'

'It was my idea,' Peter said.

'Let me guess – you were *worried* about her. After meeting her for
the very first time just last night, tender human feelings overcame
you.'

'Maybe,' Peter said, coldly, mustering dignity.

Rose didn't let the sarcasm linger – his style was quick slashes
followed by abrupt subject changes, keeping his quarry off balance.
'So,' he asked, with a smile, 'are you happy in your work?'

Peter shrugged.

'Didn't expect all this, did you? Rape – now murder.'

Peter shook his head.

'I almost feel sorry for you.'

Peter sighed.

'What's the matter, you nervous?' Rose said. He looked at his gun, dangling on one finger, as if he were a little surprised to see it there.

Peter cleared his throat. 'It's just that, well, I've heard so much about you . . .'

Rose smiled knowingly, as if he saw through Peter's feeble attempt at diversionary flattery. 'Has Merwin been talking about me?'

'A little.'

'I'm sure it's all been good.'

'*Warm*, I'd say. It's amazing how much he admires you.'

Rose laughed and slipped the gun back into his pocket. 'Now tell me about that swamp land in Florida,' he said.

Peter didn't hesitate. 'Make a damn nice retirement home,' he answered. Then he realized one possible implication of his joke and quickly tried to cover: 'I mean, if someone were thinking of retiring.' And he blushed, angry with himself for blowing his one smooth moment.

But Rose smiled again, and this time it was genuine. 'You're okay, kid.' He reached out a hand and grasped Peter's shoulder. His fingers felt dry and hard, and Peter imagined being grabbed by one of those enchanted trees in *The Wizard of Oz.* 'Maybe you ought to come work for me.'

Peter gave a shy little smile and ducked his head, trying to hide the surge of hope that ran through him: Maybe it will all work out after all, maybe I am the hero of my story, maybe I don't have to sacrifice years of my life to Max's baroque version of a Zen enlightenment ordeal. Maybe I will win the prize and the glory . . . and the girl.

'Well,' he began.

Rose interrupted him with a scowl, another whiplash mood change. 'Or maybe you still need to get to know Merwin a little better.'

Peter took in a breath and held it while trying to think of a response.

'God knows, it took me long enough,' Rose continued, his scowl deepening into darkness.

'I'm *getting* to know him,' Peter said, with a nervous chuckle. 'And believe me, it's an experience – like working for *Torquemada.*'

Rose smiled, and again his face changed completely. Now he seemed friendly, understanding, wise, with a survivor's scrappy dignity. He cocked his head and turned his smile down to low wattage.

'Well, you can stick with him and learn to make movies the wrong way, or come work for me and learn to make them the right way.'

Yup, that sounded like a job offer all right. But something was wrong . . . Peter glanced quickly in the direction of the guest house, not even sure why he was doing it, but the involuntarily furtive gesture reminded him of the real situation: Barry Rose had just caught him sneaking out of his daughter's house in the middle of the night, just a few days after her alleged rape, which meant that he probably knew by now that they were just pretending before to be strangers in the nightclub. Or worse, he thought they were strangers that night, and he didn't care. Not very fatherly behavior, was it?

Unless Tracy told him everything. It was hard to tell how much of their relationship was real warfare and how much theatrics. Weren't they on the same side, against Max?

Peter pretended to be deeply concerned about something. 'Well, first I'd have to know something. How do you feel about the correct use of pink and blue markers?'

Rose grinned and slapped him on the shoulder. 'Don't fuck up the markers, kid, or you're history.' He slid his arm around Peter's shoulders and gently pulled him toward the big house. 'That's *my* gag. I taught Max about the markers ten *years* ago, at the dawn of the Age of Fax. He had no *concept*. The guy is a fucking slob, that's one of the things I always hated about him.'

Peter felt himself dragged along, and hated himself for it. Rose's power left him feeling clumsy, almost helpless. He knew it was getting dangerously late, but how could he get out of this? Rose led him like a child through the door, past a huge kitchen (Peter caught a glimpse of an industrial-size refrigerator, stainless steel with a glass door, the same fucking Subzero everyone in Hollywood had) and down an aisle (was that a real Rothko?) into an old-fashioned study, with red leather chairs and hardback books lining the walls. There was a piranha on the desk, dried and mounted – a popular ornament in Hollywood offices – and a miniature guillotine.

There was also a picture of a boy. He was painfully thin and angelic, with long Jesus hair and the wounded, wondering eyes to go with it.

'Your son?'

Rose nodded, and pointed at a chair next to the desk. Suddenly he was all business. 'First thing you have to do is tell me your marching orders,' he said.

'Excuse me?'

'You work for Max Fischer. Max Fischer raped my daughter. What exactly are you doing climbing over my fucking wall? Did he send you to make some kind of deal – because I'm telling you, I'm not making any deal. I'm going to see his fat ass in jail. You understand me?'

'I'm telling you the truth,' Peter said. 'Max didn't send me. He doesn't know where I am.'

'So what are you doing here? And *don't lie.*'

He didn't say it, but Peter could hear the implication in his voice: You've lied to me enough already. He took a breath and exhaled slowly. 'I've known your daughter for a few weeks,' he said, and it felt good – confession, balm for the soul. 'Last night we pretended to be strangers because we didn't want Marlon to know we . . . knew each other. It's not clear whose side he's on.'

He waited, hoping Rose would clear up that little mystery. But Rose didn't say anything, or even change expression. So Peter continued.

'I *care* for Tracy,' he said. 'I also care for Max . . . sometimes. He gave me a chance. He believed in me.'

He'd been saying that a lot lately. This time he felt as if he were throwing arguments into a void, trying a little too hard. Was he trying to convince himself? And yet he felt the truth in what he was saying, and the truth felt good. It was something you could hold on to, even just a little piece. He found himself thinking of Jennings West, how he flaunted his women and joked with such casual contempt about pants-inspecting – wasn't he, in his way, throwing off the burden of lies, the hypocrisy that life, and especially The Business, demanded? Only by airing your dirty laundry can you clean it of those telltale spots. He felt a flash of guilt for his revulsion, back at the party, when Leela said West wanted her to stay in the Playroom. Maybe what had revolted him was his own desire. 'I guess I just wanted to know what was really going on,' he finished.

And it was sort of true, or at least it was true the last time he came here. But tonight he came for something else.

He felt something drifting inside, just above his stomach, guilt falling like a black snowflake.

'You know him,' Rose said. 'What do you think?'

Peter hesitated. 'I just find it hard to believe.'

'I don't,' Rose said. He looked off, into the books. Peter followed his gaze, then turned his eyes to the desk. The only modern thing in the room was the phone, a gunmetal grey saucer with four concave buttons for different lines and a digital strip across the top. Peter found himself admiring Rose's ability to leave silence alone. He was the opposite of Max – Max threw off sparks, but Rose held them in, radiating so much restrained tension that he almost generated heat.

'He's never done anything – not that I've seen – anything,' Peter stumbled, 'like this.'

Rose pointed to the floor. 'There's a rattlesnake,' he said. He waited.

'Yes?'

'You've never seen a rattlesnake before, so you've never seen a rattlesnake *hurt* anyone before,' he continued. 'Do you pick up that rattlesnake?'

'Well . . .'

'*Do you pick up the rattlesnake?*'

Peter felt ridiculous, a schoolboy forced into an idiot catechism.

'*Do you pick up the rattlesnake?*'

'No, I do not pick up the rattlesnake.'

Rose hooked a thumb toward his own chest. 'I know Max Fischer better than anyone in this town, and even when he was eating dinner every night at my house, I *knew* what was wrong with him – the son of a bitch has no ethics. He'll do anything, *anything* to fill that hole inside.'

Rose glared at Peter, and the intensity of his eyes and the way he underlined the word *anything* seemed full of the darkest implication. 'And it's a black fucking hole, believe me,' he finished. 'Everything gets *sucked into Max.*'

He kept on glaring and Peter stared back, nodding like a good student. But the truth was he didn't understand – why was Rose so obsessed with Max? What had really happened between them?

The phone rang and Rose snatched it up. 'Yeah, he's here,' he said, without even waiting for the other person to speak. Peter frowned, puzzled – how did he know who was calling?

'Nah, I'm being friendly,' Rose said. 'I just wanted to talk to him.'

Then he figured it out: Caller ID. In fact, from where he was sitting he could even read the last three numbers displayed on the digital strip at the top of the phone.

Rose cupped the phone. 'Tracy. She's worried about you.'

When he hung up Peter said it was time for him to get going. Max was waiting.

Rose stood up. 'I'll walk you out,' he said. 'Front or back?'

Peter blushed. 'My car's parked down by the hotel.'

They walked toward the back door. 'I'll let you in on a secret, kid,' Rose said, casually. 'For the last few years I've been running a fairly lean operation, a small office with five or six people. But I'm about to sign a new deal. If everything goes through, I'm going to need a director of development, maybe someone in production. Can't pay too much – a hundred, maybe a hundred and fifty to the right person . . .'

He meant thousand. A hundred and fifty *thousand*. More than twice what he was making with Max.

They reached the door, and Rose held it while Peter walked through, out into the soft perfumed air.

'Of course, we shouldn't even be talking,' Rose said, smiling. 'Detective Spinks tells me you're Max's principal witness. If it wasn't for your alibi they might have arrested him already.' Without losing his smile, Rose patted him on the shoulder. 'But you're loyal. That's a good thing.' He smiled.

At that moment a maid came out of the big house holding a black portable phone up in one hand. 'Señor Rose,' she shouted. 'Is Señor Hanks! Calling from pay phone, collect!'

Rose patted Peter's shoulder again, giving it one last friendly squeeze. 'I gotta take this one, kid.' He grabbed the phone and bent his head down, as if for privacy. 'You cheap son of a bitch! I can't believe this! I got *Apollo Three Hundred Million* calling me collect!'

Peter pointed toward the house and mouthed a silent question: Can I use your bathroom? Rose waved a hand impatiently – do whatever you want – then turned away, smiling into the phone. 'What are you fishing for up there, anyway? Trout? Hell, you oughta try Madison – I got a *cabin* up there.'

Peter hurried back into the house.

*   *   *

Back at West's compound, Peter waited for a car to come out of the driveway. The gate was just closing. Luckily, he managed to veer around it. He hadn't even thought about how he was going to get back in, but it looked like this was going to be his lucky night. Aside from a little of that sucking-at-your-lungs after-coke emptiness, he felt great . . .

There were still a half dozen cars in the driveway, but now the house was quiet and ominously dark. The valets were all gone. Something was wrong.

As Peter hopped out, West's front door flew open, swinging 180 degrees and hitting the stuccoed wall. Out came a skinny woman who looked just like . . . Angie, the woman from the nightclub! The Queen Bee. Yes, it was her, with the same feral look, like a prison guard gone sadistic, thinking of private pleasures. And she was dragging someone along behind her . . .

Leela! Stumbling in a pair of high heels, still in that crotch-high black dress, letting Angie drag her by the elbow, her arm hanging limp beneath it as if she were a kid hoping that Mom would just take the damn elbow and leave the rest of her behind . . .

West fluttered around them. 'You better not do this, Angie,' West said. His eyes looked like they were propped open by invisible toothpicks.

Angie shook her head and held up a hand: Stop! 'Look, Jennings, I like you, but business is business.'

'She's a *guest*,' West said.

Angie wheeled around, suddenly angry. 'As long as she owes me money, she's *nobody's* guest,' Angie said. She pushed Leela toward the Mercedes and finished her thought, muttering to herself, confirming her good judgement: 'You pay or she don't play, simple as that. Those are the rules.'

She was wired on something. Twice she jerked her head, as if she'd just heard her name called by a distant, mysterious voice.

'How much does she owe you?' Jennings asked.

Angie didn't seem to have heard. 'If you have trouble filling the room, Jennings, why don't you call me? I got my shit *computerized*. That scaggy old whore you do business with is *over*.'

She was almost whining now, eager to please despite the situation, treating West with respect. But then she wheeled on Leela, who was

standing by the open door of the Mercedes looking like she wanted
to apologize to everyone. 'I told you, get in the fucking car!'

Leela ducked her head instantly, obeying.

'Wait!' West ordered, flinging out a hand.

Again, Leela obeyed, freezing in mid-crouch. Peter smiled at her,
and she rolled her eyes at him, grateful for the smile and embarrassed
to be alive.

'I said, how much does she owe you?'

'Total?'

West nodded.

'Forty grand. And change, but for you I'll forget the change.'
Angie smiled, as if that was funny.

'All right,' West said.

Her face tightened. 'You're going to pay her debt?'

'Yes.'

'Why?'

'I like her.'

Angie gave him a knowing smile. 'I know what you like. You like
watching her do your friends.'

West was not amused. 'I'll messenger a check over in the morning.
Just let her go.'

Angie moved her head side to side very slowly, tempted and
sorry but simply not programmed to accept this concept. 'Can't,'
she said. 'Already promised her to someone else.' She shot a nasty
look at Leela. 'If she'd been where she was supposed to be, or
answered her *fucking beeper*. . .'

'Who?' West asked.

'That's my business.' She looked at her watch. 'And it's getting
pretty late.'

'Listen – I'll pay you *fifty*. Leave her with me.'

Startled, Angie tried to focus. But she shook her head again in the
same slow, pained way. 'Can't.' Then she smiled. 'You don't care
about her. This is about Marina.'

Peter's skin prickled. *Marina again*. What did she have to do with
Leela? He sidled up to the car, where Leela was still standing by the
open door, waiting for her fate to be disposed.

'You okay?'

'*God*,' she said.

'What's going on?'

'I don't know how she found out I was here.'

But now West was giving in. 'All right, go ahead,' he said. 'You don't want to make a deal, you don't want to make a deal. This is why we can't do business . . .'

'I want to make a deal,' Angie said. 'But I already have a commitment. What can I do?'

They could have been talking about a screenplay.

'It's up to you.'

'I'll bring her over tomorrow.'

West shook his head. 'Too late.'

Angie shot a look toward the Mercedes. Leela was still talking to Peter. 'Get in the fucking car, I said.'

Leela gave West one last look – it's okay, I understand – and then offered Peter a weak, apologetic smile before getting in the car. As the Mercedes pulled out, West stood in his place, watching it go. Peter did the same. Not until it disappeared onto Mulholland did West break the silence. 'Well, let's go have a drink, shall we?'

Questions sizzled through Peter's brain. If Marina was a prostitute, she may very well have known Leela from that world. What did West say? *She can help you with all your terrible problems.* And why had West tried to hook them up, anyway? What did he want? And why did Angie come in the middle of the night to drag Leela away? And who was the customer who wanted her so badly? And why was West willing to pay fifty thousand dollars to keep her – fifty thousand dollars!

'What was all that about?' Peter asked.

'The Whore Wars,' West said. He seemed drained.

'What?'

'Never mind.'

'What's it got to do with Marina Lake?'

West patted his shoulder, absently. 'You should talk to Madame Meursault,' he said. 'Meursault knows all.' To Peter's questioning look, he returned a sly smile. 'Call me tomorrow, I'll give you her number.'

Through West's French doors, they saw Max sitting in a deck chair by the pool, staring into the water. 'I'll join you in a minute,' West said. 'Help yourself to anything.' He went off toward his bedroom.

Peter went out to join Max, who looked up at him without moving or saying hello.

'Where the fuck have you been?'

Peter tried to put everything else out of his mind and concentrate on the job in hand, which was making his voice blasé. 'Doctor's appointment,' he said.

Max looked up at Peter and frowned. 'Doctor's appointment?'

'Yup,' he said. 'Had to have an operation.'

'Oh, really?'

Peter waited just another second, then launched the gag he'd been preparing ever since he left Rose: 'To get my thumb taken out of my ass.'

Max didn't blink an eye, just kept looking at him. His eyebrows went up thoughtfully. 'There's a medical procedure for that now?'

Peter nodded.

'And was it successful?'

Peter leaned over with a very self-satisfied smile – still acting, trying to show he had nothing to hide – and handed Max a piece of paper. He knew he was taking a risk, a huge risk, but how could he resist?

Max studied the paper and then looked up. Later Max would even chuckle about Peter's joke, repeat it to others, though never without observing that the operation was *clearly not a complete success*. But now he was still incredulous.

'Is this what I think it is?' he said.

'Indeed it is,' Peter said.

'How'd you get it?'

'Don't ask. He's at a pay phone – better hurry.'

'At one in the morning?'

Peter nodded. 'In some bar. He goes there at night, has a few beers, makes a few calls, goes back to nature.'

Peter had his lie prepared – restless and upset by something that happened in West's bedroom (I'll explain that later, he'd say, rolling his eyes significantly), he went for a drive, and while he was cruising he'd turned on the scanner and damn if he hadn't heard some woman talking to Hanks on her car phone. She was losing him in the hills and he gave her the number to call back. You could hear the country music and clinking bottles in the background.

But Max didn't ask. Without another word, he got up and walked straight for the house. Peter followed, waiting for Max to ask the obvious question. He found the telephone and dialed. There was some kind of problem with the line, so it took about a half a minute to get through – a half minute that Peter would brood over later: *That* was my mistake. I should have *volunteered* the scanner story. But I got too fucking *cute* . . .

'I'm looking for Tom Hanks,' Max said.

Someone must have asked him to wait a sec, because he gave Peter the happiest, most amazed, and most approving grin: This is great, I can't believe it.

Then all his attention got sucked into the phone. 'Hey,' he said. 'Whaddaya doing in a fucking bar? I thought you were getting away from it all. We got bars down here.'

He listened for a moment, then laughed. 'It was easy, I got sources you wouldn't believe. I'm plugged in, I tell ya.'

He covered the phone with his hand. 'He says nobody has this number.'

Peter smiled modestly.

'So what's this thing you Gentiles have with fishing, anyway?' Max said. 'You want fish, buy it in a store.' Max listened and laughed. 'Yeah, thanks,' he said. 'Forty. You missed my party, you son of a bitch . . . But listen, I gotta tell you, I'm calling because I heard Barry Rose gave you a script. What happened to ours?'

He listened for a moment, then allowed just a touch of anger in his voice. 'You know I'm working like a motherfucker trying to put this thing together – I got Alan *this close* to signing off on your new deal.'

He listened.

'But ours is still your first choice, right? . . . That's good. *Then what are you reading Rose's script for?*'

Peter heard the mournful howl of Hank Williams, Jr, singing 'All My Friends Are Going to Be Strangers'.

'No, I'm just kidding – go ahead, read the script. Maybe it's a good script. Maybe it's a better choice for you . . . You gotta do what's best for you . . . All right, all right. Have a beer on me. Catch some fish.'

He clicked off the phone. '*Son of a bitch*!' he shouted.

West appeared in the doorway, as if conjured by the scent of drama. He had his terribly amused smile back on, and some more white crust around his nose. 'Bad news?'

Max shook his head, confirming it by denial. 'We gotta go,' he said.

The twins appeared behind West, now wearing plaid Catholic schoolgirl dresses, complete with white socks and saddle shoes. 'Come on, have a drink, relax,' West cajoled.

Max shook his head, making for the door. 'I got to think,' he said.

'At one in the morning? Who thinks at one in the morning?'

Max kept cutting through the house, trailing Peter and West and the schoolgirls behind him.

Then West dashed in front of them and held both hands out like the one smart camper in a horror movie. 'Ingrid Bergman!' he shouted.

'What the fuck are you talking about?'

'Ingrid Bergman leaves her husband for Roberto Rossellini – end of career! Exile! Disgrace! That's what happened to me – I was *crucified for love*. And that's what's happening to you too – crucifixion! Disgrace!'

Max stopped at the front door, shaking his head with mock dismay. 'This is what happens to people here,' he began.

'You're Ingrid Bergman! I'm Ingrid Bergman! America wants us to die!'

'They make too much money,' Max continued. 'Sit on their butts all day, start to rot from the head.'

West stood behind one of the twins, took her white dress shirt in both hands and ripped it open. Breasts spilled out, jiggling.

'Look at those boobs!' West said. 'Isn't that the most beautiful sight in the world?' He lifted her skirt, exposing white panties. 'And this cunt – it's *life*, goddamnit! It's *life*! That's why it smells the way it does, humid and mulchy like you turned up a spadeful of dirt deep in some dark cave where secret mushrooms grow – potent fucking, hallucinogenic mushrooms strong enough to give you visions of fucking *eternity*. Guys'll die for that, get fat and old overnight when they lose hope of getting it, sit in front of the TV and drink beer until they choke on it. Maybe for ten minutes when they're in high school they get a chance, and they're too damn scared and confused to enjoy it, and society has fucked them up with a lot of bullshit about how you're not supposed to enjoy it because that wouldn't be *nice*, and then they get shitty jobs and they know they're never going to have another chance so they drink and they get bitter and little by little they die and then they get up in some pulpit and tell me I can't have it either. *Because they can't*! Fuck that, I say. I'm going to take all I want and I ain't gonna apologize for it neither. I got *nothing to apologize for*.'

Max sighed and headed across the driveway for the car, still trailing his peculiar brood. He opened the car door and then stopped, speaking across the car. 'Jennings, I appreciate the invite. You're probably not a bad guy. But you're making it all way too fucking complicated. I don't know if it's the drugs or just because you're nuts.' He said this without anger, as a statement of fact. 'Yes, people hate us. But they don't care who we fuck, not that much anyway. They hate us for one simple reason – because *we have the stuff*. Like Barry hates me because I'm making movies and he isn't. I've got the stuff, he doesn't. Simple as that. Human fucking nature.'

West nodded energetically, so happy he couldn't speak. Never mind the details – Max understood. Max was a brother! Peter took his place in the driver's seat, and by that time West was able to get a few words out, spacing each of them ritualistically, like some crackpot liturgy: 'We spew – our spunk – on Ingrid – Bergman,' he said.

Max waved. ''Bye, Jennings,' he said.

Only when they were safely on Mulholland and halfway to Laurel Canyon did Max finally sigh and shake his head. 'What a fucking lunatic,' he said.

Peter didn't say anything, not wanting to disturb the peace.

Later Max sighed again. 'What I don't understand is why these sleazy bastards like whores so much,' he said. 'I mean, why pay for it? All the women in Hollywood are whores already.'

Chapter Ten

Usually Peter got Sunday off, but today there was work to do – specifically and most important, the long-delayed rough-cut screening of *Romulux*. By now an awful lot was riding on Max's little *Romeo and Juliet* knock-off – if it flopped, Barry Rose's end run to a Columbia contract was practically a done deal. Max was pumping away on his StairMaster when Peter got there, and kept on pumping without a word for another fifteen minutes. Afterward he didn't make any calls at all, just read the papers – there was a longer article about Marina Lake, with quotes from some of her high school friends (ranging from 'such a nice girl' to 'trouble at home') and also from her father's customers, some of whom were suing him over problems with their silicone implants. Max read without saying a word, gruff and preoccupied. But just before they got in the car, Max put his hand on Peter's shoulder and squeezed. 'You came through for me last night,' he said. 'I'm pleased. You're really working out.'

Peter smiled, feeling a warm gush of pride and gratitude. From Max, a little kindness went a long way.

'I got lucky,' he said.

'You *anticipated*.'

On the drive to the studio, Peter felt growing hope. Max had been right all along. Anticipation was the key. He had to talk to this Madame Meursault, find Leela, and have a *real* conversation with Ms Tracy Rose. If he could fix all this, he was made. If not . . .

They got to the studio five minutes before ten, plenty of time to make the screening, except there were TV camera crews at the parking lot entrance. Only a few, but it was still alarming the way they jolted to life at the sight of Max: 'Mr Fischer, have you been charged with rape?' and 'Max – did you do it?' The questions got more blunt and more hungry the closer he came. Max stared straight ahead, ignoring the cameras, giving them as dull a shot as possible, but Peter couldn't help skulking a little. As the guard waved them through, one reporter called out: 'Max – did you do it to get back at Barry Rose?'

Max flinched and kept staring.

When they got to the screening room, Buck Fargo was already down in the second row. He turned around and said hello, but Max ignored him and went straight to the control console, picked up the intercom phone, and gave the projectionist the order to begin. The lights dimmed and the curtains parted.

It was the first time Peter had been in a theater in a week, but it felt like a month. He felt immediate, almost narcotic, pleasure. It's almost a religious thing, he thought, when the lights go down. I feel like I should get down on my knees.

There were no credits, no title. The movie just started, with a surprisingly small spaceship crashing in L.A., right near the Griffith Observatory. A handsome young alien got out of it, looking perfectly human in every respect, aside from his clothes and his green-tinged skin. He took a look around, breathed deeply, and smiled. Then another alien got out after him, and together they went to explore this new world.

They had just run into their first earthlings, a gang of local toughs – and the fight that would kill the alien Mercutio was just beginning – when a red light on the phone console pulsed. Peter picked up, cupping his hand around the receiver. Max hated calls during screenings. Which was quite a tribute to his love of movies, since Peter figured he'd even take a phone call during sex.

'We're just watching it now,' Peter said. 'The opticals didn't come in.'

'Who is it?' Max hissed.

'Kramer.'

Max frowned. *Now* he calls him.

'Tell him I'll call him back when it's over.'

Peter cupped his hand over the phone and relayed the message. When he hung up the phone, he told Max: 'He wants to see it tonight, at seven. He says don't be difficult – it's time for you to be paradigmatic.'

Max let out a black chuckle.

The opening sequence was almost over. Now the handsome young alien was staring in a mirror, looking lonely and determined, using a flesh-colored latex flap to try to cover his gills. But the flap wouldn't stick, and finally he got frustrated and threw it down.

Peter looked down four rows at Fargo, the director, cowering down there with his editors, his ratty dork-knob ponytail quivering like the tail of a terrified dog. No doubt he was hoping he could get through the screening without a Mad Max Moment. Peter hadn't been here to see it, but he'd heard that Max started hating Fargo on the second week of shooting, when he yelled at Fargo for going too slow and Fargo yelled back loud enough for everyone on the set to hear: '*Too bad.*' The next day Fargo's girlfriend got fired from her job making rock videos. Nobody ever proved a connection, but everyone knew Max did a lot of soundtrack business. Kit Bradley even wrote it up in her *Hollywood, Inc.* column under the headline *Born 2 B Bad.* On screen, another group of aliens approached Earth in a larger spaceship, coming to get poor Romulux. Only the optical house was still working on the backgrounds, so 'space' was still just bluescreen. Max leaned over and whispered: 'We gotta cut two minutes out of the first reel – it should be *bang! bang! bang!*'

Peter made a note on his pad: cut 1st rl 2 min. He always carried a pen with a tiny flashlight built in just for these occasions.

The red light pulsed again, and Max let out a blast of air: 'What, are they giving the fucking number out on *QVC*?'

Peter shrugged. 'Screening Room B,' he said.

'Is that my favorite pants inspector?'

'That's me,' said Peter.

'So how are the pants in question? Staying clean?'

Onscreen, the aliens were hustling across a broad bluescreen. It was disorienting to watch: an alienation effect.

'We're in a screening,' Peter whispered. 'Can we call you back?'

'I've got that number for you, boyo.'

He hesitated. He was beginning to feel like a rowboat drifting among three supertankers – one good wave and he'd be ground to pulp. 'Okay,' he said. He wrote the number down.

'Say thank you,' West said.

'Thank you.'

The phone went dead. Peter looked up at Max, who was completely absorbed in the movie, smiles of delight alternating with undiluted loathing – the masks of comedy and drama come to life. Now the alien was lost in suburbia and happened to glance in a window as a beautiful teenage girl was getting ready for bed. Caught by a backlight, her nightie turned transparent. The alien stopped in his tracks. His gills opened and shut, opened and shut.

Fargo looked around nervously. 'Don't even listen to the temp dub,' he said. 'I hear something more John Williamsy. Da dum dum!'

Max gave Fargo a cold look and leaned toward Peter. 'Thinks he's making *The Last Temptation of Christ.*'

They watched the rest of the movie in almost complete silence, interrupted occasionally by a note from Max or an explanation from Fargo of the missing bluescreen scenes. It looked beautiful – gorgeously shot, with an aquamarine color scheme that gave it an otherworldly, underwater quality. But it was long and illogical and the action scenes didn't work at all.

Then it was over – the last two minutes all blank screen, scene missing, scene missing, scene missing. The lights went up, and everyone looked at Max.

Max made a steeple of his fingers, holding them under his chin. He let the moment lengthen just long enough, then lowered his eyes to Fargo.

Fargo couldn't stay quiet any longer. 'When the opticals come in, it's gonna be . . .' His voice trailed off.

Max allowed the moment to lengthen again. Timing is all. Finally he spoke: 'You're *fired.*'

Fargo looked stunned. 'Max . . .'

Max turned to Peter. 'Call a guard,' he said, loud enough so everyone could hear. 'Walk the fucker off the lot, pack up his office, send it UP fucking S. Before lunch is over I want his name *off his parking space.*'

Fargo was about to cry. He couldn't believe it. 'But Max . . .'

Max ignored him, speaking to Peter. 'Do you have any brothers or sisters?'

'No,' Peter said.

'Grandparents?'

'Just a mom and dad,' Peter said.

'How old is your father?'

'Sixty-two,' Peter said, knowing exactly where Max was going. 'Engineer. Lives in Jersey.'

Max nodded his head in satisfaction. 'Your *sixty-two-year-old father* could have edited a better picture. At least he's alive!' He turned to the others. 'This picture was edited by a *dead* person. What happened to chop chop chop music video? I thought the one thing *Buck* here could do was *cut fast!*'

Fargo stood up now, hesitating. 'But Max, listen, please, if you don't like it, I'll work with you. That's how the system works, right? I get my chance, you get your chance . . . like lawyers. Right?'

Max stood up too, facing him with Olympian coldness. It was a side of Max people rarely saw, and Peter felt a chill: *This is the real Max*, he thought, much more so than Mad Max or even Max Morose. You got a hint of it in his total indifference to former friends and ex-girlfriends – once they were out of his life, they were *dead*. He barely even recognized them in the street. Which is not as easy as it sounds. It takes a special talent, an almost imperial self-absorption. After this Max would never think about Fargo again. Now Max looked down at him and uttered the words he'd been saving for just this moment. *'Too bad,'* he said and turned his back.

Peter followed Max out the screening room and up the alley, past two huge soundstages big as airplane hangars. 'Do you believe that fucking guy?' Max ranted. 'Little prick locks me out of my own fucking editing room and then wants to work with me. I could kill him.'

'We should return Kramer's call,' Peter said. Why was Max blowing off the chairman of the studio? Was this the start of some self-destructive rampage?

As Max barreled on, crew members waved to him, smiled, called out his name – *it's Max* – *it's Max Fischer*, they said, men who scorned actors and patronized directors. *Max Fischer, the producer*. Max nodded and half smiled back, clearly not paying attention, but that was okay with the guys. He was busy and important. They didn't expect much.

When they reached the bungalow, Max swept into his office. Sarah was there, working on a Sunday, knowing Max was in crisis mode and wanting to be there for him. Nobody had to call her either; she just knew. 'Get me Richard Edlund,' Max snapped. He jumped on his StairMaster and started furiously pumping away. He kept at it on the phone. 'Richard,' he panted. *'You gotta help me . . .* Kramer wants to see the picture *tonight*. We gotta get these fucking opticals or I'm a *dead* man. You might as well just start saying *Kaddish* . . .' Sarah brought him a Diet Coke, anticipating nicely. 'I don't care if they're not perfect – I need some kinda fucking effects slapped into that print *tonight* . . .'

With that Max jumped off the StairMaster, knocking the Diet Coke all over Peter's pants. He didn't seem to notice. 'Do the ones you *can*, that's all I'm asking, and we'll put the rest in later. You and me, Dick – we'll turn chicken shit into chicken salad.' (This was one of the two most common Hollywood phrases. The other was: don't try to make me put twelve pounds of shit into a ten-pound bag. That the two most common Hollywood phrases turned on excrement was purely a coincidence, of course.) But when Max hung up he called out to Sarah: 'Get Peter some new pants. Send out, go to *Fred Segal's*.'

Only then did Max sit back down. Putting both hands flat on his desk, he gave Peter a grim nod. 'Okay, get me Kramer,' he said.

This would be their first phone call since the rape investigation began three days ago, an unprecedented delay – usually they talked three or four times a day. And Max was in such a mood . . . Peter took a deep breath and dialed Malibu.

A moment later he nodded, waving a finger like a flagman at a racetrack, and Max punched the button on his line. '*Alan*,' Max said. 'How're ya doing? . . . With Stallone? . . . Tell him I say hi, tell him thanks for the tip on the milkshake diet . . . Yeah, he gave us a whole fucking *infomercial* on it at Planet Hollywood . . .'

While Kramer passed the message, Max covered the mouthpiece and whispered: 'Stallone on his couch – he'll probably have the thing *bronzed*.' Then he went back to the conversation: 'Sly, how ya doin'? . . . Yeah, about five pounds . . . That's very nice of you, but I still have this fucking gut . . . Yeah, that's why I'm *punishing* my inner child . . .'

Then Kramer came back on. 'Listen, this is the situation,' Max said. 'I ain't gonna lie to you, the opticals are late, and the temp dub sounds like, like, like – I dunno, *John Cage* or something . . . but the film is *great*, it looks *awesome*, it's gonna be *Star Wars* . . . I just want you to get a good first impression . . . Of *course* you know how to watch a rough cut, I trust you . . . three days, can you just give me three days? I mean, we've been through a lot together, Alan . . .'

Kramer must have given in, because Max said thanks. Then he nodded his head three times, each more impatiently, like a boy getting a lecture. 'You know Tracy, she's a teenage psycho,' he said. 'This is all just Barry Rose making a Hail Mary, trying to get back to where he left his career . . . It's one for the record books – makes the Zanucks look like a happy family . . .'

Max's face went sour again. But this time he was really mad. 'He *won't* be working with a rapist,' he snapped. 'There *is* no rapist . . . I honestly think Tom is smarter than that. He won't fall for this McCarthyite bullshit. Unlike some people I know.'

Again, Kramer must have backed down. The conversation drifted off to technical issues, winding down instead of cutting off, Kramer evidently hedging his bets with a little no-cost schmoozing. 'Yeah, I got a good cutter,' Max said. 'Stuart Baird gave me his right-hand guy, a kid named Andy Potter, promised to step in if he fucks up. So worst-case scenario, I get Baird to cut my movie for free.'

That bit of deviousness must have pleased Kramer, because Max chuckled with him before ending the conversation with a few verbal backslaps.

Late that afternoon Peter dropped Max off to get ready for a dinner, a typical Fischer affair for twelve. Peter usually went along but tonight he begged off, and twenty minutes later he found himself picking up a blue teacup in Madame Meursault's bedroom. His new pants – three hundred dollars' worth of linen from a designer with the unlikely name of Paul Smith – felt scratchy on his legs. Thank God Sarah had thrown in a pair of silk boxer shorts.

'Try some of the cookies,' Meursault said, giving him a grandmotherly smile.

Peter chose a white powdery thing and smiled back. He had been sitting with Meursault for ten minutes, making small talk, and she made him very nervous. To begin with, she was half naked, sitting cross-legged on her bed wearing nothing but the nylon shift a particularly sodden hausfrau might wear, and it was virtually see-through, with no underwear beneath. He kept having to look away when she shifted. And she was practically a dwarf, with arms like swollen sausages and alarmingly large breasts, and these bruises and *scabs* all over her. The overall effect was lumpish and pale, like something plucked out of a seashell. 'Don't you love them? I get them at an Arab bakery around the corner. They make the loveliest pastries, don't you think?'

Peter agreed that they were lovely pastries. Then Madame Meursault barked in laughter – literally barked, like a seal. *Orrr orrr orrr . . .*

'But not as lovely as *my* pastries. *Orrr orrr orrr . . .*'

Peter smiled again. The bedroom was overheated, each surface covered with knickknacks – china figurines of poodles, girls in full skirts, a man holding a monocle to his eye, a full bowl of candy on each table. It was a room decorated for a maiden aunt, some lace-doily Englishwoman trying to keep things up in the tropics. Meursault sat on the bed in the middle of it all as if she were riding on a palanquin, surrounded by magazines and newspapers, a box of candies, a tray to hold her teacup and saucer, an ivory telephone. Peter unwrapped a Hershey's Kiss as Meursault launched into a joke about a bull who saw a cow across a barbed-wire fence and tried to jump over the fence only to catch his balls on the barbed wire. The point seemed to be that bulls without balls didn't jump fences, but it was hard to follow because Meursault took an impressionistic approach to the English language, sketching in pieces of sentences and then letting her listener's imagination do the rest. And she seemed to love irrelevance, perhaps as a kind of kin to immorality. So Peter didn't pick things up as much as he acquired them by osmosis – after she talked for a while, for example, he realized he'd learned that she was born in Marseilles and raised by a strict mother in South Africa, even went to Catholic schools. The nuns were compassionate about her affliction, so naturally she hated them. *Orrr orrr orrr.*

He wanted to ask a question, get her on the subject of Marina Lake, but he was finding it very hard to break into her monologue. What was the strongest thing in the world? she asked, and leaned forward to answer her own question: 'The strongest thing in the world is a pussy hair – it can tow an ocean liner. *Orrr orrr orrr.*' Then she looked down at her phone and frowned again. 'These damn *phones*,' she whined. 'I've been calling the company all day – they say there's nothing wrong. So why aren't they ringing?'

She'd been complaining about the phone lines since he got there. She was convinced someone had stolen them, which seemed a bit crazy. Could phone lines be stolen? And besides, *he* had gotten through – could they be stolen for an hour or two, then switched back?

'I was hoping we could talk about – I mean Jennings said you knew about—'

'Yes yes yes,' Meursault said. 'Little Marina. So sad.'

'So you knew her?'

'I can tell you all about that one,' she said. She started laughing. 'The prince had such a thing for her – he was one of my Arabs. He said, "Merry . . ."' Then she stopped in mid-anecdote and launched into a long story about how the Arabs checked into hospitals and then snuck out after visiting hours to go debauch California girls, so that when their wives called, the nurses said they were safe in their beds and couldn't be disturbed. When she finished, Meursault gave him a smile, and winked a froggy eye. 'Wouldn't you like to try one of my creatures? I can give you the house discount.'

There was just a touch of flirtatiousness in her voice, sexual not in content but in form, the better to establish their kinship. It reminded Peter of his first week in Los Angeles, when he visited the American Film Market. Max laughed at him for going, since it was the kind of thing starving independents went to – 'a trade fair,' Max said, 'a bunch of two-bit merchants making deals.' But that was what Peter liked about it. It was the perfect good-bye kiss to his academic notions of movies as art – all the posters and flyers and photo displays in every suite showed half-naked young women, Nurses and Cheerleaders and Co-eds and Schoolgirls and Schoolteachers and Prostitutes and Career Women and Actresses and Dancers. It was so crass! He felt like sticking a big cigar in his mouth and finding a starlet to dandle on his knee. Why not? When you thought about it, the movies just got in the way, just packaged desire so it could be sold. So why not just toss out the celluloid and seize the thing itself – grab the Cheerleaders and Nurses and Teachers and Co-eds and *have at them*!

'Soon,' Peter said, deflecting the offer with a smile. 'When I start making a little more money.' He winked back, then tried steering the conversation back to what he wanted. 'So, how long have you known Marina?'

But Meursault went off again, this time gassing on about Hollywood men and how so few of them actually liked normal sex. The most popular kink was watching two girls together – 'One time I kidded Jennings about it, I said, "You old pervert, you love girls so much you always want two of them." And he said, "I don't consider it a perversion, I consider it an interest." *Orrr orrr orrr.*'

A fat gray cat jumped on the bed, and Meursault cooed, 'Come to Mommy.'

Then Peter heard a knock at the front door, followed by the noises of the maid opening it, and after a moment footsteps padded down the carpeted hall. Peter looked up into a familiar face, although he wasn't sure for a second if he recognized it from life or from some fashion layout in a magazine. Leela gave him an enthusiastic hug, happily surprised, crushing her breasts against his chest.

'You know each other?' Meursault said.

Peter couldn't help feeling a bit more manly, a welcome change. 'We met at a party last night.'

She shook a finger at him. 'You snuck off somewhere,' she said teasingly, like a teenage girl at the mall. 'Just when things were getting fun.'

'You left pretty suddenly yourself.'

She pretended she hadn't heard.

Picking a grain of tobacco from her tongue, Meursault raised a palm along Leela's long body, a gesture halfway between appraisal and display: breasts jellied into a skin-tight white leotard, hips set off by puffy peach shorts made out of some scalloped fabric. 'She's not one of mine,' Meursault said, regretfully. 'I sold her to Angie. But she still comes to me for advice – *orrr orrr orrr*. I moonlight as a career counselor.'

Leela bent down, and the two women touched cheeks. Then Meursault sat forward and fluffed her pillows, putting one in her lap and resting her breasts on it like two sleeping cats. Pretending impatience, she demanded: 'Come on and tell me, what's the problem now?'

Sitting down, Leela shot a dubious look at Peter.

'He's all right,' Meursault said.

'But I can't,' Leela pleaded.

'Go on, go on,' she said. 'Don't waste my time, girl.'

Head down like a scolded child, Leela chirped: 'She's making me do things? Things I don't want to do?'

Meursault patted her hand. 'Honey, just close your eyes and think of money,' she said.

Leela squirmed in her seat, then leaned forward to grab a Hershey's Kiss. Before eating it she sat up straight and touched her belly, checking to see if it was flat enough. Satisfied, she started peeling away the tinfoil with a long red nail. 'It's not that,' she said.

'Come on, girl, out with it,' Meursault ordered. 'Time is money – *orrr orrr orrr*.' Then she frowned, picked up her phone, listened, and frowned again. She reminded Peter of a poisonous fish in a rich man's aquarium, one of those rocky things with spines. 'These *phones*,' she whined.

'It's not a sex thing?' Leela said. 'It's something else?'

She was so tentative, with that schoolgirl habit of ending every other sentence with a question mark. How could a woman so beautiful be so insecure, Peter wondered. With her cap of black hair, she looked like one of those twenties flappers, like a sunlit nymph from an old Maxfield Parrish painting. What had happened to her? Even Meursualt looked a little closer. 'You want a drink, honey? Something to smoke?' She lifted up a box from her bedside table, giving it a little shake.

Leela shook her head. 'Angie said I might end up like Marina? It was the smartest thing to do?'

Peter sat at attention.

'That Angie,' Meursault said. 'Just when I think I like her again, she acts like such a *cunt*. When she came to me she was a dirty little thing in torn blue jeans – I had to give her a shower! And she was such a lousy whore – she wanted *them* to do *her*. *Orrr orrr orrr*. That's why I had to make her my assistant.' A whining tone came into her voice. 'Then I let her go into business for herself, just to get rid of her, and now she tells everybody she's bigger than I am. Can you believe that? She's such a braggart.' Finally she worked her way back around to asking Leela what it was that Angie was having her do, exactly.

'Talk?' Leela said.

Meursault nodded. She seemed to understand exactly what Leela meant. But Peter didn't have a clue, and he couldn't hold back any longer. 'Talk to who?' he asked.

Leela turned pleading, worried eyes at Meursault, who nodded reassuringly.

'To Barry Rose,' Meursault said. 'To the cops.'

'What about?'

This time Leela answered. 'My roommate.'

'Who's that?' Peter asked, now thoroughly mystified.

Meursault answered again, as if it were so boringly obvious. 'Marina,' she said.

'Marina Lake?'

Meursault nodded.

'Angie introduced us?' Leela continued, more willing now. At least *she* hadn't told the secret. 'The cops still don't know? But now Angie wants me to talk to them? She and . . .'

She stopped, and began wringing her hands, working the fingers hard. 'Can't I just come back to you?' she asked Meursault. 'Can't you talk to Angie? Please?'

'Why don't you get *Jennings* to buy you,' Meursault asked, purring the question like a jungle cat enjoying a late-night snack, some peasant child who wandered too far from the hut – *delicious* – if you don't mind picking a few bones out of your teeth. She turned to Peter. 'He's such a sweetheart, Jennings. The girls all love him – he can't get it up much anymore, so he pays them to screw their boyfriends. It's every who-aah's dream. All he wants to do is watch.' She went off into her barking laugh again, so hard this time she rocked the bed.

'Why does anybody have to buy her?' Peter demanded. 'Why can't she just quit?'

'I sent her to Gambler's Anonymous and what does she do?' Meursault asked, shaking a schoolmarm's finger at Leela. 'She meets five new bookies. *Orrr orrr orrr.*'

Leela hung her silken head. Under the cover of the moment, as if examining the evidence at hand, Peter looked her up and down. She was so . . . so crystalline. The green eyes, the carved face, the endless cartoon legs. It was incredible to think that she could be bought – *bought* – for forty thousand dollars. But then he pulled his eyes away. He had to figure out a way to get the conversation back to Marina.

'So what does she want you to tell them, the cops?'

Leela looked to Meursault for help, and Meursault picked up her silent phone again. 'I have a *dial* tone,' she whined. 'Why isn't anyone *calling?*' She shook her head, going from exasperation to worry, looking much older. 'I'm going to have to go down there, to the phone company.' The thought seemed to upset her terribly. She started to get up, then fell back down, as if exhausted by the effort. 'You two better go now,' she said, waving them away and cradling the phone in her lap like a sick baby.

Perfect! Now he could talk to Leela alone. Peter wondered if Meursault was just acting, and had planned it this way. Leela had seemed surprised to see him, but she gave in on the public confession awfully quickly. What deal had Jennings West made with Meursault? What did this have to do with Meursault's apparent war against Angie?

At that moment, as if reading his mind, Meursault looked up and winked. 'Why don't *you* buy poor Leela? *Orrr orrr orrr orrr orrr.*'

The laugh shredded into a hacking cough.

Outside Meursault's house, Leela gave Peter a shy smile and said, almost wistfully, that it was nice to see him again. It was dark already, the time families sat down to the dinner table. Heck of a sermon today, eh, Marge? Sure was, honey. Pass the peas.

'You okay?' Peter asked.

'I'll be fine. I'll just get a cab.'

'You don't have a car?'

Leela shook her head, smiling again as if to say: Can you believe it? Silly me.

Peter stared at her, more to fix her face in his mind than anything else. Her lips were full and defined by a pronounced outlining ridge – a ridge that set them off and made them into an object, like a tribal fetish she carried around on her face. Her green eyes gleamed with a hint of mischief. And if that was not enough, there was the ripe swell filling out her white leotard: blinding.

'I'll give you a lift,' Peter said.

In his car, he asked her where she wanted to go. He felt awkward, remembering that just a few hours ago he had kissed her on Jennings West's mink sofa.

'I don't know?' she said.

And she had kissed back.

'Home?'

'I don't want to go there,' she said.

Peter put the car in gear and started driving. Men stared at Leela from passing cars, craning around to keep her in their sight. They also checked him out, to see what kind of a guy he was. She didn't even seem to notice. At Santa Monica Boulevard, he aimed the car toward the beach.

'Do you have some friend's house or something?'

'Can we just drive for a while?'

Leela didn't talk much, leaving long spaces between sentences, and by the time Peter had gotten her to say that she was from Albuquerque and her father was in jail on a drug charge, they had gone all the way to the 405 freeway. Which was okay: It gave him time to get used to her. They passed Patrick's Roadhouse before she volunteered anything. 'I'm sorry about the other night?' she said. 'I do wish you hadn't left.'

'I wish *you* hadn't left,' Peter said.

She laughed, not happily, and Peter felt like a schmuck for trying to flirt. They lapsed back into silence. A few minutes more and they passed Topanga Canyon, and then they couldn't see the ocean anymore, except in the gaps between the rich people's houses lining the shore. When they passed the Malibu sign Peter thought he noticed Leela flinch.

'Want me to turn back?'

She thought for a moment, then shrugged.

'So you knew her pretty well? Marina?'

Slowly, Leela nodded her head.

'Close friend?'

'Not really.'

'What was she like?'

'Most people thought she was a bitch.'

'And you?'

Leela looked away, up into the brown hills. 'She had tattoos? She had a tiger on her back, got it in Japan.'

'What was she doing in Japan, anyway?'

'Hostess,' Leela said.

'Why'd she go there?'

Leela shrugged. 'Something about some guy. The usual thing. Some older guy.'

'Was his name Max? The older guy?'

Leela shrugged.

'Was it Barry?'

She looked away, up into the hills. Then they came to a gap in the row of houses along the shoreline and for a moment there was a space where they could see the ocean. The moon shone on the water, casting down a silver path.

'Maybe we should go back,' Peter said.

'Let's park for a little while,' she said. Peter slowed down and pulled into the center lane, then made a U turn and pulled onto the shoulder. For a moment they just sat there, watching the moonlight glitter in the waves.

'Can you turn on the radio?' Leela asked.

Peter cranked the knob. The radio was tuned to an oldies station, and Chrissie Hynde came on singing: *I went back to Ohio, but my city was gone* . . . After a while, Leela began talking about how she got started in 'this', a confused story that involved Satanists, a body shop, and big car-repair bills. Then she switched subjects without being asked. 'She liked to party. You wouldn't think it, 'cause she was so tight-assed and pissed off all the time, but she could party.'

'Marina?'

'And she was smart too? She liked to read books.'

'Really?' Peter pictured Marina curled up in bed with a book, the tattooed tiger reading over her shoulder. 'What books?'

'I don't know. Books.'

Then the song finished, and Springsteen started singing about the boardwalk. Leela sighed.

'Are you okay?' Peter asked.

She didn't answer, but she shifted the seat and laid her head down on Peter's chest. They sat there like that for the rest of the Springsteen, and then there was a commercial. Leela reached over and turned down the volume. 'I'd like to tell you,' she said.

'Tell me what?'

'What you want to know.'

'What do I want to know?'

'You know.'

'So tell me.'

She moved back, her face pleading. 'I can't.'

'Why not, Leela? You can talk to me. I'd never do anything to hurt you.'

'It's not that,' she said, as if that was a given. 'I'm so broke.'

He didn't understand at first. Then he stammered, 'You mean you, uh, you need . . .'

'Fifty thousand dollars,' she said. 'I need it really bad. Angie said she'd give me ten to talk to Rose, but . . .'

'What?'

197

She squirmed, looked away. 'He wants me to talk to the cops. Then I get fifteen. *If* I say the right thing. And I can't say what Angie wants me to say.'

'Why not?'

'I just can't.' Then her eyes became completely focused. 'Can't you help me?'

So that's what it was all about. Why she was at Meursault's, why she accepted the ride. To let him bid. 'I don't have that kind of money,' he said.

'What about Max?'

'I, I don't know. I'll see.'

'I really need the money, Peter,' she said, putting her hand on his leg. 'I don't know what they'll make me do for it. I don't want to know. Please, Peter. I need a friend bad.'

All I have to do is push, Peter thought. Not even hard. Just a little push and she'll tell me everything. All I have to do is maybe squeeze her wrist a little, make a promise nobody has to believe. She wants to please so badly. It's there in the hesitant angle of her shoulders, her body calling out: Take command, please, relieve me of this burden. So he reached out, taking her wrist in his hand, and she looked up at him, eyes shining into his, vulnerable and expectant as a child waiting to hear the last line of a story, but he felt ashamed and dropped his eyes. The wrist in his hand was so narrow, fine black hairs feathering off the bone. Acting on instinct, he lifted it up and kissed it, softly. And put it back down. 'I'll see what I can do,' he said.

Leela started to shiver and rub her arms. Night fell cold in California, always a surprise. 'Will you take me home now?' she asked. 'I'm so tired.'

Peter started the car, waiting for a gap in the stream of cars behind him. 'What about Jennings,' he said, over his shoulder. 'How does he fit into all this?'

'He's just a friend.' She was unconcerned, so he knew it was true.

'He wanted to watch us, didn't he?'

'That's what he's into,' she said, giggling.

'What a sick fuck.'

'That's nothing,' Leela said. 'There's this one guy in Hollywood, real famous, he likes you to . . .' She whispered it in his ear.

'*Gross.*'

She laughed, the first truly light laugh he'd heard out of her. Was it the comfort of being on home ground again?

'So Jennings is just a friend?'

She nodded. 'He's . . . on my side,' she explained.

Peter felt a little sting of jealousy, and turned back to the traffic. *On my side*. Jennings West, of all people. And why did she say it that way, as if the concept were hard to grasp? He craned his head, looking for his opening, but the traffic just wouldn't stop. Red taillights strobed down the highway. In his rearview mirror he saw the ocean, ragged black rocks, black waves sagging with kelp, and the cold moon shining on the water. Suddenly he felt like crying. He didn't know why exactly – for Leela, for Tracy, for himself. But he'd never been able to cry, except at the movies, and always at the same scenes, when parents and children overcame their bitterness and embraced each other. *On my side*. That was what was making him want to cry. It was so hard to find, so fragile when you found it. Even for Max. *You came through for me last night*, he had said. *You're working out*.

He reached out a hand to stroke Leela's hair, but just before his hand made contact he stopped. He didn't want her to misunderstand. He wanted her to know he was on her side too. And then there was an opening in the stream of traffic and he jumped into it, gunning the car for Santa Monica. The wind off the ocean was icy now, and Leela huddled against him, hugging his arm.

'You can stay with me if you want,' Peter said. 'I won't touch you.'

He had meant to say 'I won't *hurt* you'. But maybe it amounted to the same thing.

Part Two:

The Bluescreen

Chapter Eleven

Max was talking to his lawyer, holding a cellular phone to his ear. 'I don't want to sue them, Jack,' he was saying, his tone all sweet reason. 'I want to *destroy* them. I want them *erased*. All I want left is a *wet stain on the pavement.*'

As he spoke, Max shook his fist in the converted school-bus window, glaring through heavy wire mesh down at the black Mercedes cruising alongside. His lawyer was just visible in the back window, a cellular phone at his ear.

Next to Max sat a guy whose footsteps probably registered on the seismographs at Cal Tech, a guy with tectonic arms and a back the approximate size and texture of Arizona. He was wearing handcuffs, and he was listening to Max and smiling.

'I want them reduced to *gristle*,' Max said. 'Gristle and little pieces of bone.'

Arizona nodded: *Tell* it, brother. Hallelujah.

But Max, still glaring down at the black Mercedes, didn't notice him. He was listening now, shifting the cellular phone from one ear to the other, clicking his handcuffs as the unused hand dangled uselessly by his collarbone. They were rattling through the dead zone of Sunset, below Silver Lake, heading downtown to the Criminal Courts building. The cops told him that the bus left the Hollywood substation only once a day, so he was lucky they arrested him before dawn. 'Yeah, real lucky,' said Max, putting his keys and money clip onto the stainless steel counter. When the cop who'd frisked him looked away, Max palmed his cellular phone, certain he'd lose it when they searched him. But the guard turned out to have worked a couple of Max's movies – and Max *always* took care of the cops who worked his movies. Right now the guy was sitting in the front seat, shotgun standing on the seat beside him, looking fixedly through the windshield.

'Of *course* they're being pressured,' Max hissed. 'But they're cops. They gotta have *evidence*. Don't they?'

Now the giant black man shook his head, as if saddened. Max looked up to see him pointing at the phone. 'Yo, can I use that?'

Max studied him for an instant. 'When I'm through,' he said, lowering his head again and listening intently.

Peter watched the exchange from the seat behind, thinking, Max, Max, *pay attention*. Look at the size of this guy. We're on a prison bus. A bus to *hell*. This isn't Hollywood. We've been *arrested*. These are *criminals*. Peter looked around the bus, counting the broken teeth, bloodshot eyes, and teardrop tattoos. If Mad Max manifested himself today, they were both dead.

He couldn't believe they'd arrested him too. Until that moment he'd still thought Spinks was bluffing.

'Meanwhile, I want you working on the assault charges,' Max said. 'Don't drop that – I want Barry Rose's ass on this bus, too.'

He listened a moment, then literally dropped his jaw. 'What are you talking about?' he said. 'He attacked me in front of three hundred people. You're telling me none of them were looking?'

Max covered the phone and half turned his head, speaking to Peter. 'Every single son of a bitch at my party says they weren't looking when Barry attacked me.'

He talked back into the phone. 'What about Geffen? What about Ovitz? . . . Well, Jesus – if they haven't talked to Ovitz or Geffen, what the fuck kind of investigation are they running?'

'Yo,' the black guy said.

'I'm *not* yelling at you,' Max yelled. 'I'm *telling* you! I want Barry Rose on this bus! I want his ass in this seat! Get on the goddamn phone, get Ovitz, get Geffen, get Kramer, and tell them to be stand-up guys. Why are they scared of a loser like Barry Rose? He's over! He's history!'

'Yo,' the black guy said again, tapping Max on the shoulder. 'My turn.'

Max glared at him. 'Do you mind? I'm fighting for my life here.' Without waiting for a response, he turned back toward the window. 'Just get it done, Jack,' he said. 'You're supposed to be the hot-shit attorney. *Get it done*.'

He listened for a second, then exploded. '*Fuck* you, Jack! You're supposed to be my *spear*! When I throw you, you *kill*!'

Then Max sat up straight. '*What*?' he said. 'What did you say?'

Like someone who has heard of a death in the family, Max slowly repeated what he'd heard, trying out its taste in his mouth: '*Where do I want you to send the files*?' He held the phone away from his ear, turned back, and looked at Peter – and for the first time since Peter had known him, Max looked genuinely thrown. Without saying anything, he turned back. 'Are you *dumping* me, Jack?' he said.

He listened. When he spoke he was very calm, with a tone of almost rabbinical resignation, awe before the mystery.

'I'm facing criminal charges, and I'm on the bus, and you're firing me?'

But now Max was almost playful, and Peter could tell that Rippert was protesting, saying he wasn't dumping him, never meant to imply anything like that . . .

'You asked me where I want you to send the files. Here I am surrounded by the cast of a Walter Hill movie, the worst moment of my life to date, and you ask me where do I want you to send the files?'

Peter saw the black guy's eyes narrow, heard a few criminals shifting. I'm going to die, Peter thought. They know who Walter Hill is, and I'm going to die. I'm going to die because of the auteur theory. If I get through this, I swear I'll never read *Cahiers du Cinema* again. I'll *kill* Andrew Sarris.

'Okay, then,' Max said. 'Get *Rose* arrested. Get his ass on this bus. Then I'll be happy.'

Max flipped up the mouthpiece, and the Mercedes pulled forward. From behind, Peter could see his jaw clench and unclench.

'Yo – it's *my* turn, motherfucker.'

'When I'm *finished*,' Max said. But he continued staring ahead, clutching the phone, his jaw working. After a minute, the bodybuilder swiveled his huge shiny face around toward Peter, fixing him with two immense white eyes, a pair of hard-boiled eggs in a puddle of oil. 'Who *is* this dude?' he asked.

Peter considered for a moment. 'Elvis,' he said.

As if he hadn't heard, Max snapped open his phone again and stabbed out a number. As the circuits mated, he turned to Peter and spoke in a tone as grim and definite as Peter had ever heard. 'Someday I'm going to call up that son of a bitch and say, "*This* is where I want my files sent, asshole." '

Then he put the phone back to his ear. 'Andy Potter,' he said. 'He should be in Editing Room B.'

At that moment, the bus tilted down into the garage of the Criminal Courts, an anonymous gray box until you got close enough to see the shadow of grime left behind by the millions of criminals come before. 'Andy, Andy, are you getting that piece of shit to make any sense?'

Then Max's face went *noir*. 'Reshoot *what*, Andy? Reshoot what? Andy, I'm going to lose you, I'm going into a tunnel . . .'

They actually did look like characters in a Walter Hill movie, Peter thought, glancing over his new cellmates, most of whom had come off the bus with them. In fact, *all* the Walter Hill movies – the porcine white guy in the Jack Daniel's T-shirt was right out of *Another 48 Hrs.*, the Mexican with cheekbones that jabbed out like elbows was from *Extreme Prejudice*, and the feral white kid with skinny red sideburns was a Warrior all the way. They surrounded Max. '*Hey*,' the giant from the bus said, pointing at Max's pants pocket, where he'd hidden the phone. '*The phone*.'

'Sure,' Max said, casually pulling it free. 'But make it quick. I'm expecting some calls.'

The man took the phone but kept staring at Max, not at all sure what to make of him.

'I'm *working*,' Max said. 'Use the fucking thing and give it back to me.'

Peter flinched, and Arizona straightened up, glaring at Max and crossing his arms, tensing the muscles until they gleamed and rippled like loaves of challah bread. Max glared back at him, a small grin playing across his lips. 'Try one-eight hundred-Jacoby & Meyers,' he said.

The pecs twitched. Seismographs at Cal Tech trembled.

Just then the guard called Peter, and he found himself winding down a maze of grimy halls and up dank staircases crowded with prisoners handcuffed to the railings. After another forty minutes in a holding cell, he was finally led into a courtroom and told the charge against him: obstruction of justice. Rippert was there, pleading him not guilty and telling him not to worry, and Peter thought: Why don't they plead innocent? Why is it always not guilty? He'd seen this scene in a thousand movies and never thought of that . . . funny how personal experience focuses your imagination. As Kit Bradley and a half-dozen other reporters scribbled away, the judge set bail at two thousand dollars and listlessly dropped the gavel. A few flashbulbs went off. It all happened so quickly.

The guard was leading him back down the hall when Detective Spinks appeared out of nowhere. She made a gesture to the guard, and he stepped aside a few feet to let them talk in privacy.

'How do you like it so far?'

'It sucks.'

'Wait'll you do some real time,' she said. She didn't smile, but there was pleasure in her voice. Again, Peter noticed the two long hairs on her chin. He understood now: She didn't pluck them because she didn't want to be nice, because she was beyond playing the please-like-me game. She was an avenging angel. 'I've never had a case like this before,' she said. 'Never had so much interference. Private detectives messing up the trail. Colleagues taking me aside to give me friendly advice. I don't like it.' She looked Peter over, then came abruptly to the point: 'This is officially a joint investigation now,' she said. 'I'm working with the homicide division.'

She waited for him to respond. When he didn't, she continued. 'Marina Lake was a hooker, working for a madam named Meursault. She was also involved either professionally or otherwise with a man named Jennings West.' She waited for a second, watching his reaction, then added: 'You remember him, don't you? From the party the other night?'

Peter didn't answer, trying to think. Spinks knew about that night? Who had told her? And how much? 'Marina who?' he said.

'I think you know who I'm talking about,' Spinks said. She glanced once up the hall, at the prisoners chained to the railings. Then back at him.

Angie, it must have been Angie. Or Leela. Or Leela who talked to Barry who talked to the cops.

'It looks like Marina Lake was the woman who picked Tracy up at the hospital,' Spinks continued. Then she waited, as if to let the implications sink in.

'I think I better talk to my lawyer,' Peter said.

She was disappointed, but not surprised: another bad feeling about mankind confirmed. She nodded to the guard. 'We'll talk again,' she said.

Walking away, Peter found his heart thumping away like a trapped miner trying to signal for help. *I'm sure you remember him, don't you Peter*? *From the party the other night*? The contempt in her voice sent such a clear message – she knew just what kind of party it was, and she despised him for it. She was going to make nailing him a personal project.

Back at the basement cell, Peter found Max in the center of a group of prisoners. 'You made *Cyberkill* too?' Arizona was asking. 'Man, that was ug-leee. That movie *flared*.'

Jack Daniel's nodded his head, solemn as a drunk. 'That cat got shredded to the *bone*, man,' he said. 'I mean, you could see the bone, the white goddamn bone. That was some sick shit.'

All the prisoners exhaled in appreciation.

'Well,' Max said, slowly nodding, almost taking a bow. 'If it grossed *you* guys out, I guess I can feel a real sense of accomplishment.'

Peter laughed. 'Max, you've found your audience.'

The Walter Hill guys gave Peter a battery of suspicious looks. Who the fuck was he?

'*Really*,' Peter continued, feeling a little giddy. 'This is it – this is your public.'

Max looked over at him as if noticing him for the first time. 'So what'd *you* get charged with?' he said without a smile. 'Suspicion of being a fuck-up?'

After a theatrical beat, Max grinned at the Walter Hill brigade. 'My assistant,' he said. 'Used to be a college professor.'

Everyone laughed.

Hours later, they were in yet another holding cell, in yet another building, when a guard came with a clipboard and called Peter's name.

'What about me?' Max asked. The guard ignored him. 'What the hell is the Ripper doing?' Max said.

Peter hesitated just a moment before following the guard, and after one more round of moving and waiting they gave him back his wallet and his belt.

Tracy was waiting outside the door, smiling just for him. 'Poor Peter,' she said, linking her arm in his.

'What are you doing here?' Peter said.

Was she worried about him? Did she rush down when she heard they'd arrested him too?

Tracy's face twisted in a bitter smile. 'I wanted him to be *alone*,' she said. 'Not with an assistant. Alone in jail is a bad feeling.'

Again Peter felt that swirling dizziness, as if the rules of life were melting around him. You're damn right the rich are different from you and me – they're fucking *psychotic*. He watched Tracy's taunting lips and found himself remembering the title of a book he'd read in college: *The Imperial Self*. The idea was that every American is the absolute ruler of a crazed and lonely kingdom of one, perpetually setting off in his or her personal covered wagon, escaping it all with a dash for the Great Frontier. And here at the end of the frontier the smartest ones figured out how to throw the covered wagons *up*, onto movie screens. They took America to its logical conclusion and became monsters of self – the Marlboro Man stared into the mirror, saw that he was beautiful, and pulled out his gun . . .

'Are you mad at me?' Tracy asked, tugging on his arm.

'What do you think?'

'Come on. I'm parked illegally.'

Of course you are, Peter thought. 'I better wait for Max,' he said.

'Fuck Max.'

'Easy for you to say.'

'Come on, Peter. Pretty please?'

Peter shook his head. Tracy pouted, a scolded child. 'Okay,' she said.

'Okay what?'

'Okay I didn't want you to rot in jail.' She waited a beat, then added: 'At least not for the whole day.'

It may have been the nicest thing she'd ever said to him. 'Just half a day?'

'Maybe three-quarters.'

He let out a mock sigh, but really he was glad to see her. It would be good to talk to her. Smart too. 'Where are you parked?'

Tracy took his elbow and led him to her car, one of those red Saab convertibles that look like particularly well made children's toys, a caboose for the Super Chunky Railroad. She even opened the door for him, a parody of male gallantry. 'How was jail?'

'Broadened my horizons.'

They got on Sunset, driving toward Hollywood, away from the surprisingly urban downtown. And good riddance. It was the first time Peter had been down there, and it seemed even grittier than New York.

'And how's Max taking it?'

'Just fine,' Peter said. 'Has his phone and the cast of his next picture.'

She laughed. Then she did a double take. 'He has a phone? Are you serious?'

Peter nodded.

'What's the number?'

'Tracy, you're not going to—'

'What's the *number*?' she said, grabbing her car phone.

'Tracy, please . . .'

'Oh, come on,' she said. She waited, but when he didn't give it her she opened her bag and pulled out a little red phone book. 'Never mind, I've got it.'

Tracy found the number and dialed it, holding the phone to her ear and driving with one hand. 'Hello,' she said, then frowned. Peter could hear the voice barking – 'Miss? *Yo*, miss?' – and then Tracy snapped, 'Can I talk to Max, please,' her tone stuck between annoyed and respectful, carrying traces of each.

She held the phone away from her ear and smiled at Peter, returning his weary look with a flourish of eyelashes. 'Some criminal talking to his lawyer. Says can I hold?'

Red light. Tracy kept the phone to her ear, braking to a stop and turning her rearview mirror so she could check herself out. She rubbed a sliver of lipstick off a white tooth, preparing her face for the phone call. Peter turned his eyes away from her the way you look away from a traffic accident, ashamed at how much you really want to watch.

Then Tracy smiled (checking it in the mirror as she did). 'Merwin,' she said. 'It's so nice to hear your voice.'

Peter heard, even from three feet away, a snarl like a chain saw cutting into wet teak. But Tracy jumped right in, her voice as cool as second-act Doris Day. 'And it was so nice of your *lover* to let you use the phone.'

Peter heard Max laugh. Tracy kept the *Pillow Talk* bit going, her false laugh tinkling. 'I have him right here,' she said. 'Sitting right beside me.'

Now a touch of Katharine Hepburn, New England backbone . . . and then her tone degenerated into early Bette Davis, with that hint of ominous sexuality. 'I think I'm going to take him home,' she said. 'Teach him about the picture business. Just like you taught me.'

Peter felt that he could evaporate from the seat at that moment and Tracy wouldn't notice. She would look at the lingering smoky mist and give it no thought. They were bumping down the hill, about to pass the very transgressive Amok bookstore, L.A.'s headquarters for the literature of recreational body mutilation, which Peter had visited on the advice that it would remind him of New York.

'Maybe I'll introduce him to Daddy,' Tracy said.

The chain saw exploded with a rip and a roar, and Tracy laughed. 'Max, I can't hear you. I'm going behind a hill. I'm losing you.'

She clicked off the phone with an evil chortle and stared out the windshield.

'Why do you *do* that?' Peter asked.

'It's fun,' she said.

'Seriously – why, Tracy? What's it all about? Just explain it to me so I understand.'

There was hurt in his voice, and real pleading. She gave it some thought, as if trying to decide whether he deserved an answer, then spoke in a definitive, almost lecturing way: 'The only way to get Max's *attention* is to torture him a little,' she said. 'If you're loyal, if you act like a loyal little dog, Max just takes you for granted. But if you betray him or hurt him, he'll get obsessed with you – he'll probably think about you more in the next half hour than he has since the day he hired you.'

Clearly, she had given this a lot of thought. And she was right, of course.

'But why do you care? What is it between you two, anyway?'

Again she gave it some thought, then gave him the definitive answer. 'We're in hate,' she said. This time her voice was kind, as if she really was sorry about all this – but there was also a certain amount of grim satisfaction.

Ah, hell, Peter sighed. They were all sociopaths. He spoke without thinking, saying the first thing that came to mind: 'Pull over,' he said.

'What?'

'Just pull over.'

Tracy looked surprised, and for that matter so was Peter. He knew he needed to talk to her some more, that this was as good a time as any to ask about Marina and Max and all the other things he'd been thinking about. And they were still miles from his car, in a crappy part of Sunset near Western Avenue. But he was tired and sick of it all.

'What's the matter?'

'Just let me out,' Peter said.

'Peter . . .'

'*Pull over.*'

She did, then turned in her seat to study him. Peter noticed that she looked interested, more than she had since the fateful night. Evidently Max wasn't the only one who took loyalty for granted.

'What are you, jealous?'

'I can't be jealous. I don't exist.'

Tracy grimaced. They both knew who he was quoting.

'I need some air,' he said, pouting.

'It's a *convertible.*'

Peter got out, slamming the door behind him. 'Don't blame me if you get mugged,' Tracy said. But she sounded a little apologetic.

'Next time, leave me in jail, okay? I feel *safer* there.'

He turned away, thinking: good exit line. He knew Tracy was trying to come up with a better one. Then he heard the tires of the convertible squeal, and he smiled and stepped up onto the sidewalk and started heading west.

Peter walked all the way to the police station, where he'd left his car, stopping to eat from a fast chicken place along the way. Altogether it took him almost two hours. He passed old men shuffling along, women carrying laundry, bikers parked by the curb, rockers carrying guitars, Latin American kids chatting in groups, and not one of them cared a damn what anyone in Hollywood was doing. By the time he turned the Fiat up Max's driveway – no media pests, thank God – he felt almost relaxed. By then he had finally figured out what Tracy had done. Why hadn't he appreciated the gesture for what it was? Why had he stormed out of the car?

Love's a bitch.

He parked next to Jack Rippert's black Mercedes. Night was moving in – the sky dark blue above, but still dirty orange around the horizon. The transition gave him a sense of calm, as if the troubled day was passing and now he was entering a time of contemplation. The cool air coming up the canyon helped. Now he was able to face certain facts – that he was jealous, for example. It was true, no getting around it – clearly Tracy was still . . . working out a few unresolved feelings for Max, as they said here in Therapy Nation. But she was also reaching out to Peter, and that was the important thing . . .

Come to think of it, why hadn't he just told Max he had a date that night, and walked out of the house? *Here's your fucking sandwich, I'm out of here, fire me if you don't like it.* No wonder she was mad at him.

Then he heard a strangled scream – the sound of someone being attacked! The sound of *Max* being attacked! And the door was hanging open! Peter glanced around the car for some kind of weapon, saw nothing but his aluminum clipboard, grabbed it and raced for the house, hit the door with the heel of his hand and ran inside . . . and there, in the living room, stood Max, his chest plumped out like an emperor, stalking around a chest-high pile of boxes in the middle of the living room floor. 'I'm not going to keep them! I'm just going to sort *through* them. And what the fuck difference does it make what I do with them! They're mine! It's all mine! *Mine!*'

Yoji the architect was staring at the boxes, disapproval etched into every line of his face. He pointed to an arcade-style pinball machine featuring the characters from *Blood Hunt*. 'You tell me you want simple,' he said. 'This not simple.'

'I'm not keeping it!' Max half yelled. 'The girl sent it over! Jesus Christ!'

Yoji looked over at Peter, allowing himself the subtlest possible version of a skeptical eyebrow-lift.

'Listen to me,' Max continued, ignoring him. 'I'm *not keeping it*. I'll send some to the office, some to Palm Springs. This is just *temporary*.'

Jack Rippert stood watching the scene, his arms crossed over his trademark T-shirt (with blue jeans – the top Hollywood lawyers always dressed casually to emphasize that they too were stars). Max looked at Rippert as if to say: You're my lawyer, back me up.

'Are you finished yet?' the Ripper asked, contempt in his voice.

But Max didn't notice. He kept trying to stare down Yoji, who crossed his arms just like Rippert, clearly not buying it. And Yoji's instincts were solid – the birthday gifts had been coming into the office for the last two weeks, and this pile represented the culled favorites. Max had even said something about working some into the design, which maybe didn't have to be so Zen after all. Max's voice went to pleading. 'Come on, Yoji – they're my *birthday* presents.'

The young architect looked away, gazing through the patio doors at the garden. The beginnings of a glass fireplace – glass bricks – stood near the red socket left by Max's last interior-design tantrum.

'Max,' Peter said, trying to get his attention. This was starting to piss him off. There were more serious things to do than fight with his architect.

Max just glared at him and turned back to Yoji. 'I mean, there are a *few* pieces I'll want to keep,' he said.

Yoji unfolded his arms and wiped his hands once, a definitive gesture. 'You come to Yoji, say, "I want house simple, my life too much clazy." Then you smash fireplace, now all pile up toys' – he waved a hand in frustration, the beginning of his own Maxamania. 'Now design no good. Design *long*.'

Peter had never heard four consecutive words from the architect before – in fact, he half suspected Yoji was just a hustler using inscrutability to cover for having nothing to say. But he was clearly passionate at this moment, his black eyes boring into Max as if he were trying to reprogram him telepathically.

And it seemed to work. 'The design's good – it's great,' Max said. 'I *love* the design.'

'Design *long*,' Yoji said. 'Better you hire Gary Panter!' Panter was the 'downtown' New York artist who designed *Pee Wee's Playhouse*, a surprisingly hip reference. Max seemed thrown for a second.

'I just brought home some goddamn birthday presents!' he yelled.

Yoji crossed his arms again. Max hesitated.

'*Max*,' Peter said again. 'We really have to—'

Then Max saw a two-by-four from the carpenter's sawhorse table and snatched it up, swinging it over his head. Peter and Yoji both stepped backward. 'I got some *gifts* from a bunch of my *friends*,' Max said, swinging the two-by-four down on a box – *crrraaaakkk!!* 'A buncha *suck-up bastards* who only return my calls *as long as I make hits* decided to give me some *presents*!' The two-by-four came down again and again, denting the boxes and breaking the gifts inside. 'And I *brought them home! So shoot me! I brought them home!*'

The boxes were all destroyed now, and a few of them had tipped over, spilling chips of Styrofoam and pottery. Yoji uncrossed his arms and took a dignified breath, then gave Max a little half bow. Panting, Max returned the bow.

Rippert pulled his car keys out of his pocket and headed for the front door. 'Well, it's been fun,' he said. 'We'll talk later.' He was visibly angry, doubtless thinking this little performance was for his benefit, to keep him waiting like any other servant. And maybe it was.

'Make some coffee,' Max said. 'I'm taking a shower.'

But Peter just stood there, watching him climb the stairs. It would be very easy to get in the car and go back to his little hovel. The sheets on his bed would be cool, and the room would be dark. Instead he tossed his clipboard on the marble countertop and went to the refrigerator, staring at the glass door. There were bottles of Pellegrino and Tŷ Nant, various cheeses, a roast chicken, leftover fruit salad. He tore off a wing of chicken and stood there chewing it. Then he remembered that he'd completely forgotten to check his machine. He dialed home, and found that he had thirty-three messages, right to the end of the tape – eighteen from reporters, ten from other assistants, two from Marlon Spurlock, saying he had information that Peter would find interesting, one from Flip Mosely, a return from John Sayles . . . and one from Tracy: 'Hi, this is me, call me.' He wasn't sure when she left it. But Peter was far too tired to talk to any of them. What he wanted was a cup of coffee. And a lawyer.

So he made the coffee, because he wanted it. While it brewed he considered the problem of the lawyer. He needed a criminal lawyer, not some dealmaker in tasseled loafers. A litigator. Tomorrow he'd call around, ask for recommendations, first thing.

But what about money? His entire bank account would buy about a half hour of mediocre legal time.

He was pouring his first when Max came in, toweling wet hair. 'This place is a disaster,' Max said, taking the mug. 'The glass fireplace idea – I must have been on *drugs*. It's like something some *actress* would do. I ought to just tear the whole thing out. Cream?'

He seemed tired, maybe even contrite. Something was eating at him.

'Not tonight, I hope,' Peter said, handing over the cream. Then he took down another mug.

'I want *space*. Just four white walls and nothing inside. Emptiness. Purity.'

For a moment he contemplated emptiness – a brief moment. Then he looked at Peter. 'So you walked all the way from Western, huh?' Max said. 'Why didn't you get a fucking cab? You abandoned me for *hours*. I got *finger bruises* from dialing the phone.'

Peter realized that Max, in his own way, was patting him on the back, even apologizing, the finger-bruise line a gift of self-ridicule: In penance, I abase myself for you. But it was only a matter of time, Peter knew, before Max would begin to resent the apology and begin to make him pay for it.

'Did you bring the project list?' Max asked.

Automatically, Peter flicked his head toward the counter, where he'd put down the clipboard. As always, the project list was there, in the back behind the latest call sheets, all one hundred and twelve projects. 'Let's sit down with it,' Max said. 'I want to think things through.'

'It's been a *long* day, Max.'

'We live and die by that list.'

'I know Max, but—'

'Why keep your heartbeat going, after such a long day?' Max said, starting to build a fresh temper. 'Why bother *breathing*?'

'We shou—'

'We gotta find what's been out to rewrite the longest and *jam* these guys. Fucking writers, neurotic bastards, they're hanging me up. I want to get stuff out to other studios. I need to set up some *deals*.'

Peter drank his coffee, staring out the kitchen window into the driveway. He was so tired. It was like he'd been on a forced march, like he'd gone numb but just kept moving.

'What's the matter with you?' Max said.

'"Come to Hollywood", he says. Three months later I'm a *convict*.'

Max snorted. '*Stop*,' he said.

'I guess I'm just tired.'

'Tired? You're a *farm animal*. Let's get to work.'

Suddenly Peter found he wasn't in the mood for Maxisms. 'Do you mind talking about the actual situation before us?' he snapped. 'What the Ripper said, before you chased him out with your latest infantile tantrum? Are we going to jail? Are you a murderer?'

Max scowled, but instead of going on the attack, he let the words slip by. He glanced around the room for something else to worry about and stopped when he saw a yellow booklet on the dining table. 'Did you see this?' he demanded, snatching it up. 'The Kagen Report, came this morning. Do you know what that is – you, who don't know the difference between Greenblatt's and Canter's?'

The Kagen company did financial analysis of Hollywood for stock investors, putting out a weekly sheet of number-crunching and predictions. Peter had been studying their reports since the day he got off the plane, as Max well knew. But he ignored the question.

'This is the *actual situation before us*,' Max said, turning to a dog-eared page. 'Grosses for the years nineteen eighty to nineteen ninety – for the whole decade, I'm *number one*. As a pure producer, I mean, not counting director-producers like Spielberg. *That's* what's real – as a pure producer I'm the top grosser for the *whole fucking decade*.' Then he frowned. 'Unless you count Kathy Kennedy.'

Max glanced up to make sure Peter was not counting Kathy Kennedy. He didn't have to say that in the 1980s she only existed at the whim of Steven Spielberg, the difference between pure producers and relationship-producers having been discussed at length already, many times. A relationship-producer was really just an extremely lucky flunky, someone whose power was bestowed on him by an 800-pound star. A pure producer made shit happen. He found the property, roped in the talent, made the deal. Maybe Kathy was doing that now, but she *wasn't* during the eighties. She was just an assistant with a fancy title. Max held the chart sideways so Peter could see it. 'See? My grosses are the highest.'

'You're huge,' Peter said.

'I'm higher in *rentals* too,' Max cried, flipping another page. 'Here's the chart for that.'

'You're a god,' Peter said.

Max didn't even seem to notice the sarcasm. 'And look at profitability,' he said. 'When you count gross participations and overhead against the negative and everything else, my pictures are the *most profitable of all*! Nobody can touch me except Spielberg, and Spielberg is Spielberg!'

He was insatiable, Peter thought. It was truly an illness.

'But didn't you share credit on a few of your movies?' Peter said. 'Wasn't there some guy named . . .'

Max stared at him, open-mouthed.

'. . . uh, what was it? Barry something?'

Peter knew he was asking for it, but he couldn't stop himself. Darn that testosterone. Why couldn't he just accept life as Max's personal castrato?

To his surprise, though, Max just put down his coffee cup and walked past him into the living room. After a minute Peter heard a thud and the tinkle of broken glass. Max was poking through his broken presents. Peter finished his coffee, then wandered out. Max was holding something that looked like a high-tech radio.

'Mini-disc,' Max said.

'Insured.'

'How would I claim it? Earthquake damage?'

'Act of God.'

Max tore at another crumpled box. He pulled out a tin man, slightly crunched. It was a fifties' advertisement icon for some long-forgotten product. He held it in his hand, then turned it around looking for a logo.

'So what did you do to her, anyway?'

'Who?'

'Back when she was sweet sixteen.'

Max put the tin man down and grabbed another box. 'Tracy was never sweet sixteen,' he said.

'Sweet fourteen then.'

'How could she be, growing up with *that*?'

'Come on, Max,' Peter said. 'You did something. One night you got pissed off at her old man and . . .'

'What? What is it you think I did?'

Peter didn't move his eyes or change expression. The look turned into a stare. 'Fucked her.'

Max pushed away the half-open box and stood up. 'Let's go outside,' he said.

There was no moon out, but the lights glittering far below gave the patio a candlelit glow. It was another balmy, perfumed evening – a night that should have found them stretched out on silk pillows, smoking hookahs and watching dancing girls clink finger cymbals. Instead Max settled into one of the outdoor chaises, trouble in his face, and Peter turned one of the wrought-iron chairs backward and sat down, crossing his arms over the back. He waited while Max looked off over his city.

'Look, I always liked Tracy,' Max said. 'She was a good kid. Like you said: smart, fucked-up, sexy. That was well put. I felt sorry for her. Hell, I was practically her *babysitter*. I can't tell you how many nights I took care of her while her father was out trying to get actresses to fuck him. And not having much fucking luck at it either.'

'So you were like, Mary Poppins?' Peter said. 'Did you float down on a little umbrella?'

Max's lips went white, crimping into welts. 'She was throwing herself at me for years,' he hissed. 'When she was sweet fourteen she was playing *footsie* with me under the table.'

'And you never footsied her back?'

'You want to take a deposition?' Max snarled. '*Get in line.*'

Peter changed the subject, not without a certain relief. 'What about the Ripper,' he said. 'What's he doing?'

'You know as much as I do,' Max said. 'Spinks says she's got some kind of witness or source or some damn thing. The Ripper says she's got some piece of evidence, something circumstantial. But it *has* to be bullshit. There *is* no evidence. There *is* no witness. *Nothing happened.*'

'Something happened,' Peter pointed out. 'Marina Lake is dead.'

Using her name like that, complete and out loud, made it official. They both paused to take note of the change. Then Max waved a hand, as if batting away flies: Don't want to think about that. 'Anyway,' he said, 'we got months before anything happens now. The worst is over.'

He didn't sound too sure of it, though. Peter was sure he was keeping something to himself, some detail that was bothering him and he didn't want anyone to know. Peter pictured him with the two-by-four again, smashing all those presents. What if Marina had gone to Max after picking up Tracy, needled him in some way . . . taunted him . . .

'So what do you say? Have I answered enough questions? Can we do the project list now?'

Peter reached for the clipboard, giving in.

'And check the calls,' Max said.

Peter got as far as the dining room before he stopped. He turned around and went back as far as the patio door. 'I can't do it, Max. I'm beat.'

Max looked up at him without expression, waiting to hear more.

'I'll see you in the morning, okay?'

Max waited.

'You want me to leave it?' he asked, holding up his clipboard. 'You can—'

'Yes,' Max said, coldly interrupting. 'Leave it.'

Peter shrugged. He put the clipboard down on the patio table. 'See you in the morning,' he said. The second he stepped out of the kitchen door and felt the cool air, he was just like a teenager again, escaping the house on a Friday night. Anything could happen. For a few hours the world would be his.

Chapter Twelve

Dawn blushed over Los Angeles, and already gleeful voices were flying invisibly over buildings and through trees, into kitchens and bathrooms and cars all over the southland. *Did you see today's paper?* . . . I can't believe Max Fischer, he thinks he can get away with anything . . . *Got what he deserved, the little weenie* . . . Nothing Max Fischer does surprises me . . . *He probably just did it for the publicity* . . . I'm confused – did he kill her or rape her? . . . *I heard he was fucking both of them* . . . They went to high school together, then started turning tricks for whatshername, that madam . . . *On the news they said it was a peeping Tom thing. Isn't he one of those guys who likes to watch?* . . . I told you so, didn't I tell you – when I took that pitch meeting, I thought, this guy is a classic Hollywood sociopath . . . *Killed one, raped another – what's he gonna do for a third act?* . . .

Peter slept blissfully unaware. Until: *rrrrrnnnngg . . . rrrrrrnnnng . . . rrrrrrrnng . . . rrrrrrnnnng.*

He rolled over, grabbing the phone just before the answering machine kicked in and casting a bleary eye at the digital clock: 7:03 A.M. *Shit!* He could have slept another hour. This was beginning to feel like sleep-deprivation torture, and it was only Tuesday.

'The press is going bananas. Max is going to have to talk *today.*'

It was Mark Hill, the Columbia publicity chief. The previous afternoon, when Max refused to cooperate in any way whatsoever, Hill had released a bland denial about Columbia standing by its man and innocent until proven guilty, a one-day placebo to keep the media beast at bay.

'Ugh,' Peter said.

'How bad is he?'

'Same as ever.'

'I'm going up now,' Hill said. 'Meet me there.'

'What's going on at the studio? What does Kramer say?'

Hill gave a dry chuckle. 'He supports Max Fischer one hundred percent. As he does everyone in the Columbia family.'

'On my way,' Peter said.

Rrrrrrnng. Rrrrnnng. 'Hello.'

'Good morning Peter,' said a cooing voice.

It was Kit Bradley. 'Can't talk, gotta go,' Peter said.

'Of course you do. But if you'd ju—'

'This is off the record,' Peter said. 'I'm *innocent*. I know *nothing*. Please be kind.'

Bradley changed her tone to solemn, rushing her words out to get them all in: 'This is serious, Peter, it's in the courts now, it's not going away, people are going to write about it, and you're better off if you talk to me. I'll be fair, I'll tell the whole story, I swear to God on a stack of Bibles.'

Peter took a deep breath and looked out the window: palm trees in a pewter sky, the morning haze spinning its dull cocoon. 'Let me think about it, Kit,' he said. The call waiting tone sounded. 'I got another call. I'll get back to you.'

'Thi—'

He tapped the switch-hook to change lines. 'Yeah, I'm coming,' he said, expecting Max this time. Not that many people had his home number, and it was still awful damn early.

'I haven't even asked you yet.'

It was Spinks, trying to soften her voice so she sounded human.

'I can't talk,' Peter said.

'There are some new developments,' Spinks said. 'Last night we interviewed one of Marina Lake's boyfriends. He says that your boss—'

'I don't *care* what he says. Why do you keep telling me all this! Leave me *alone!*'

He slammed down the phone and walked directly into the shower stall, bending his head like a supplicant and twisting the cold knob all the way. Ahhh. Brrrr. Shouting at Spinks like that was childish and stupid, and he already wished he'd let her finish her sentence, but it felt good. Really good. Maybe he would shout some more later. The phone rang again and he ignored it. When he left the apartment seven minutes later, hair still wet, there were five messages on the machine and the phone was still ringing.

*   *   *

Max was about to be the lead story on the *Today* show. While
Peter dragged the TV out from under a pile of boxes and plugged
it in, Max stomped from the patio to the kitchen and back again,
barreling past startled construction workers and absolutely refusing
to talk to the press at all – ever – about anything. His bathrobe
flapped around his legs like a cape. 'Fuck 'em, they just want to
burn me *at the stake*. Fuck 'em all!'

Hill was following him, furrowing his forehead to show how very
concerned he was. 'They'll just think you're guilty,' he said, over and
over. Occasionally he alternated with part two of his message: Smile
for the reporters, act like it's no big deal, plant the seed of doubt.
In a situation like this, Hill programmed himself just as he would
program a client: Stick to two or three messages, repeat them over
and over until the morons get it.

But every time Hill spoke it just set Max off. 'They're having *fun!*'
he shouted. 'I'm not going to play! It's not a game! *It's my life!*'

Dogosta watched them argue. He leaned against a wall, sipping
from a mug of coffee, with the spare and unhurried gestures of a
man who knows how to wait.

Then *Today* came on, Bryant Gumbel giving the camera a particularly somber look: '. . . And our lead story this morning:
megaproducer Max Fischer is the chief suspect in an explosive
case of alleged rape – and possibly murder – that has mesmerized
Hollywood. Here with the story is NBC's Martin Masters.'

Max stalked to the TV, followed by Hill and Dogosta. Masters
appeared, a middle-aged reporter wearing a polyester tie. 'Hollywood
Boulevard,' he began, as the camera panned down the legendary
street. 'The Chamber of Commerce calls this stretch of pavement
the Walk of Fame, but poets call it the Boulevard of Broken
Dreams.' The unseen editors cut to an 8 x 10 shot of Marina,
with long black hair and tragic knowledge in her eyes. 'For this
young woman, an aspiring actress named Marina Lake, the poets
got it right. Her dreams stopped short Thursday night – and the
prime suspect in her death is a man whose dreams all came true.
A man who knew her from the time she was a child. A man with
his own star in the Walk of Fame.'

Insert: a head shot of Max, looking pampered and arrogant.
'Max Fischer,' Masters intoned. 'The quintessential modern

Hollywood producer, whose wealth and power grew out of cinema
sex and celluloid violence, whose movies are all about men jolted
out of sleepwalking lives by acts of horrible brutality. Was he acting
out one of his own plots – or were his movies a way of enjoying
murderous fantasies without getting caught . . . until now?'

Max threw his coffee cup against a wall, the sudden *crack* startling
everyone in the room. 'What sappy bullshit,' he shouted. 'Walk of
Fame, Broken Dreams – get those jerks on the phone.'

'It's taped,' Hill said, with the soothing voice of a police hostage
negotiator.

'I *know* it's taped,' Max blasted. 'Call the studio. Get the
kid producer, what's his name, Zucker. I want to go on the
air!'

'Zucker's gone,' said Hill. 'It's Friedman again. Besides, I don't
think—' But Peter was already dialing the office. Sarah was
there early, wisely anticipating a troubled day. 'Get Friedman
at Thirty Rock,' Peter whispered, 'patch him through to the
house.'

'There's reporters outside the studio gates,' Sarah said.

'How many?'

'Twenty. Maybe thirty. With camera crews.'

On the TV, Masters was talking over a shot of the Sony sign.
'Several sources within the studio said the growing scandal is causing
concern among the studio's Japanese owners.'

Peter hung up, turning his attention back to the TV. Max,
Hill, and Dogosta were still standing in front of the screen,
surrounded by white drop cloths that gave everything a vaguely
medical look, as if they were scientists watching something emerge
from an alien pod. Masters had moved on to specifics about
the crime and was now discussing 'the Peeping Tom theory' –
evidently the new rumor was that Marina had been killed by
someone who liked to watch.

Max bit his lip. He leaned toward Dogosta. 'What'd you get on
this?'

Before Dogosta could answer, Gumbel got off one last line:
'Curiously, insiders say that Fischer's latest picture, *Romulux
147*, contains a Peeping Tom scene. According to one source,
Fischer insisted on keeping the scene even after studio chairman Alan Kramer objected to it.'

That turned Max's flame up to broil: *One source*? Could his name be *Alan Kramer*?

Max was still howling when the phone rang – Sarah, patching through Friedman. Max grabbed the phone. 'I want to respond,' he said. 'No, no, no, no, you're *playing* it that way, you *want* it to look that way . . . We're not talking a flop at the box office here, we're talking about my *life* – how are you going to feel when you find out you're *wrong*? . . . I *know* it's eleven fifteen in New York. Haven't you ever heard of a *news bulletin*? I don't want to go tomorrow, I want to go *today*. It's the *Today* show, right? It's not the *Tomorrow* show!'

As soon as he hung up, Max nodded to Dogosta. 'Tell me,' he said.

'The cops are asking questions about guys who like to watch. Apparently Lake reported some guy looking in her window a few days before she got whacked.'

'And they think that's *me*?' Max said, almost laughing, looking at Peter and Hill. 'Some geek who lurks around in *alleys* looking in *windows*?'

They all shook their heads at the insanity of it.

'And just because of this scene in my movie? It's the *balcony* scene, goddamnit. *Shakespeare* wrote it.' Max sighed once, then headed for the door. 'Enough of this,' he said. 'Let's get to *work*.'

Hill actually blocked his way. 'I need a statement,' he said.

'This is the statement,' Max said, leaning in and blaring it right in Hill's teeth. 'I'm innocent. It's an outrage, a miscarriage of justice, and we will sue for false arrest. I have the greatest admiration for Barry Rose, a producer who did great work in his time, and I profoundly regret what happened to his lovely and troubled daughter and her friend. *But I didn't do it.*'

'You need to hold a press conference,' Hill said, inching back just a step. 'You have to let them see you.'

'I've got *work* to do,' Max snapped.

Hill backed off. 'In that case, ignore me completely,' he said.

Which advice Max took, starting up the stairs and barking out a list of people he had to speak to *immediately*, without even looking to see if Peter was following. But Hill managed to stop him with one last question. 'About this murder, Max. You knew her, right? That's a fact? We don't want to deny things that—'

Max stopped halfway up the stairs, and for a moment he looked almost sad. 'I knew her,' he said. 'But I didn't *kill* her. I know a lot of people, and I kill very few of them.' Then he turned and took two more steps before turning again and stabbing a finger at Hill. 'And don't soften the Barry Rose line – I want it to say 'a producer *who did great work in his time* . . .'

The next three hours were pure *Key Largo*, palm fronds flying through the air and windows breaking, wind blowing in a ceaseless howl, with Max playing both Edward G. Robinson and the hurricane. When he got out of the shower, he told Peter to run the calls, which he took while riding the exercise bike – not too fast, wouldn't want to pant. Geffen had called first, ever the early bird, and from there the call sheet spanned Hollywood – Steven and Jeffrey and Joel and Jon and Peter, Jerry, Terry, Andy, Dawn, Mario, Arnon, Jake, Bert, and all the others, the West Coast and the East Coast and, touchingly, several major cities in the Far East (the Asians were still passionate about their cinema, God bless them). Everyone was concerned, everyone said how much they were *there for him*. To hell with Barry Rose, they all said, he was over, stick a fork in him. Sure they'd talk to the cops about the party assault, no problem, except they didn't see that much, really. They were looking away, in the bathroom, at the bar. Only Alan Kramer continued to be unavailable. Max chuckled along as casual as could be, it'll all work out, the new picture looks great. He moved from the bike to the StairMaster, then to sit-ups and crouches. A crew from the *Today* show came and went, shooting ambient footage of the house for the next day's interview. And Alan Kramer continued to be unavailable.

At 10:30 Max jumped up. 'Let's go,' he said. They drove down the hill to the studio, past the reporters at the main gate, slipping into the Thalberg lot. They rode up to the third floor in the Thalberg's tiny Deco elevators. Kramer's senior secretary (he had two, each with a desk flanking the door) told Max that the chairman was still unavailable.

'I'll wait,' Max said.

Peter followed him into the waiting room, which was like a little living room, with two armchairs and a sofa. The sofa pillow was embroidered with the word *Chairman*, the walls were covered with one-sheets of Kramer's hits, and the counters were covered with

Kramer's memorabilia: framed shots of him with Barbra, Arnold, and President Bill. Max sat and fumed, kicking his foot.

Ten minutes later – ten minutes of absolute silence – Max got up and walked firmly out the door, without a word to either of the secretaries.

Behind him, Peter paused. 'Please, Sam, have him call,' he said, with a family-size smile.

Max was silent as they rode down in the little silver elevator. Peter studied the Art Deco engravings: That was one of the things he loved about the studio, all the Deco lines and figures built into the massive soundstages and offices, as if the studio itself were just one big set for a musical comedy about The Business – *Singing in the Rain 2: The Deluge.*

The second they got out of the Thalberg Building, Max exploded. 'What the *fuck* do you think you're doing? How could you say that? *Please, Samantha, pretty please.* Don't you *ever* do that! Don't ever beg! Don't ever *apologize* for me!'

'But . . . I . . .'

Max shot down the alley, and Peter broke into a trot to keep up, skittering sideways next to him. 'Max, I didn't mean . . .'

Max ignored him. 'Look at this, I'm *sweating.*'

'What are we going to do now?' Peter said.

'I'm a blimp.'

Running backward now, Peter almost bumped into Chevy Chase, who looked surly enough already. 'Sorry,' he mumbled.

'Kiss my ass,' Chase said.

Max scowled at the actor. '*I* was going to say that,' he said.

Chase registered Max and crackled to life; in an instant, his expression went from surly to his trademark smirk. 'I was just saying it *for* you,' he said. 'A man in your position shouldn't have to say "Kiss my ass" himself.' Chase shook a finger at a gaffer walking by with big rolls of colored tape hanging off his belt. 'You – kiss his ass!' Chase ordered. A guard looked over, wondering what was up. 'Guard,' Chase said officiously, '*Kiss Mr Fischer's ass.*'

Everyone laughed, recognizing Chase and figuring whatever it was, it must be funny. And Max smiled a big fake smile. It was another of the Maxisms: Always smile at actors – they need it.

Then the moment was over and Max was starting the charge again, faster this time, until Peter scuffed his shoes keeping up.

He followed Max right through the gate, into the parking lot and up to his little Fiat. If he had known he was going to use it so much, he would have bought a hard-top, with air-conditioning. Hell, he would have bought a Mercedes.

'Let's get out of here,' Max said.

Peter kept his mouth shut until they passed through the gate. 'Where to?'

'Just *go*. Take a left here.'

They were heading toward the beach, where Max never went, citing some ancient aversion of Jews to water. Max was silent, no doubt thinking over the Kramer situation, so Peter called the office for messages. Sarah answered. 'The lawyer's here,' she said.

'Who, Rippert?'

'No, the studio guy. Asking everybody about this murdered girl. Wants to talk to Max.'

Great, Peter thought. 'Give me the calls.'

'Jennings West, said it was urgent. Also Ronnie Meyer and Jeff Berg and—'

'What about Kramer?'

'No.'

'Get Meyer then,' Peter said, clicking off the phone and cradling it in his lap.

Max stared out the window. They were passing a long series of postwar apartment buildings, every one a basic stucco box with some kind of filigree trim, from Googie to Tiki. Peter told him about the studio lawyer and Max just nodded, as if he'd expected it.

Then the phone buzzed. 'Patching you through,' Sarah said, and Peter waited until Meyer's secretary made the transfer, then handed the phone to Max. He took it listlessly.

'Hmmm . . . Really?' Max said. 'So when is he going to call me? . . . Okay, Ronnie, thanks, I know that's not your job anymore . . . Yeah, you're a fucking Olympian . . . How's Kelly? . . . Yeah, no, I'm fine . . . going for a drive . . . I'm fine, really.'

Clearly, the news was not good.

Max handed over the phone. 'Says Hanks is shaky. Lovett's going to call me later and explain. Translation: It's over.'

Max was so grim, Peter searched his brain for something encouraging to say. 'Flip Mosely says his script is coming along great.'

Max frowned. 'You talked to him?'

'He called me.'

'He called *you*?'

'He didn't want to bother you.'

'So what did he want to ask?'

'Just, you know, story stuff.'

'Story *stuff*?'

The phone rang. Saved by the proverbial bell. Sarah sounded breathless. 'It's Kramer,' she said.

'Patch it through.'

It was only ten minutes after they left his office.

'Hello, Alan,' Max said, his voice cool. It was the first time Peter had ever heard him say hello on the phone. 'Yes,' he said. 'Well, that's nice to hear.' He covered the phone. 'The studio is behind me a hundred percent,' he told Peter. 'I'm sorry to hear that. The flu? . . . Oh . . .'

He covered the phone again. 'His kid has an ear infection and Bruce Willis is driving him nuts.'

Then Max's face clenched like a fist. 'Alan, it's not *ready*,' he said. 'You've got to give me a couple of days, I mean the kid didn't know what he was doing in the cutting room, he was a disaster, I want to get a good temp dub together . . .'

Peter couldn't believe it. So that was it, the extent of Max's long-delayed meaningful conversation with Kramer about their legal situation. They were already off on the stupid movie, and Max was as upset as he'd been in days, as upset as he was on the bus to jail, maybe even more upset – he stared out the window, tension turning his lips into two pale scars. 'I *know* the ten weeks are up,' he said sharply.

He listened for one more moment and took a deep breath. 'Eight P.M. it is,' he said, and hung up.

Peter was driving past the pier, uncurling down the ramp onto the Pacific Coast Highway. Max gave Peter a critical, suspicious look, and for a moment Peter thought the Mosely issue was about to resurface. Or worse.

Then, gazing over the Santa Monica pier, Max broke into a smile. 'Didja ever see that movie, *Crime and Punishment U.S.A.*? Terrible thing, real piece of shit, George Hamilton as Raskolnikov – Raskolnikov in *Santa Monica*.'

He laughed, all clouds momentarily banished, and for a moment Peter felt the same lift: nothing like a bad movie to cheer you up.

'That's what'll happen to us,' Max said. 'We'll find God on the way to prison.'

Peter grinned. 'What you mean *we*, white man?'

In the editing room they scrambled like assembly-line laborers in a comedy sketch, ignoring hunger and thirst and even phone calls, including three from Jennings West with the message *incredibly urgent, call back*. Max didn't even take the call from Lovett when it came in just after five. There were seven people working, all sitting around the flatbed like lost explorers studying the map home – the screenwriter, Max, Peter, Potter, and his two assistants. 'We may want to loop that whole thing,' Max said as the film ran through the flatbed, lighting up a small screen. 'It's not the same track. You guys figure it out – either you want to loop it or you use the same track.'

'You wanna cut this line at "donuts"?' asked Potter.

'No, I like it,' Max said. 'But there is something slow. Should she come . . .?'

'Later?' suggested the screenwriter, a preppy-looking guy in jeans and a Gap T-shirt.

'Sooner,' Max said. 'And the guy, he has look, look, look. I don't think he needs all those looks.'

They were trying to fix the ending, which still didn't work. Max adjusted the flatbed knobs himself, rewinding the scene and playing it over and over. At one point he tried to clean some lint out of the reel and nicked himself, but he kept working, dabbing at his wound with a paper towel. 'If you cut him off,' said Potter, 'it looks like he's killing the girl himself. We tried that.'

'Let's just trim the tail a bit,' Max said.

The film end ran off the reel with a flash of white light, and Max switched to the other bay, where one of the assistants had set up the next reel. 'I don't like it when he holds on the razor, it's so *TV* . . . and trim this a few seconds – it takes so long for him to get the line out, it's such a stage wait.'

When that reel was finished they had to wait for the cutter, so they turned on the lights for a second. The paper towel in Max's hand was soaked with blood. 'It's a film cut,' joked the screenwriter. 'Much worse than a paper cut. That's why I stick to writing – less bloodshed.'

Max shrugged it off and went back to work.

During the next break Max returned the call from Lovett, nodded his head, said 'Yes, uh-huh, thanks for doing what you could.' When he put down the phone he stared at the reels of film on the rack and no one said anything to him, just kept up the business-as-usual chatter. If people came with warning labels, Peter thought, Max's would read CONTENTS UNDER PRESSURE. Then Max snatched up the phone himself, punching in a number so fast Peter couldn't even read it. 'Get me Yoji,' he barked.

'That wall, the one between the library and the living room? Take it down . . . No, I *want* it open! . . . It was *your* idea, I'm just saying I want it done . . . When you have time, I don't care, no rush . . . and probably we'll do what you said on the patio wall too, half-shojis, to open it up in good weather. I love that idea.'

He hung up and turned back to work.

When he got a minute, Peter called Jennings West. 'He's work-ing,' he said. 'Can't come to the phone. But he wanted to connect. When's a good time to call?'

This was a standard blow-off; the call to set up a future call. Depending on how much Max cared, there would be one or two more before the effort was abandoned.

'I'm beginning to lose faith in you,' West said.

'I'm sorry,' Peter said.

'I keep trying to help you. I fixed you up with Leela, then Meursault. What more do I have to do?'

'I'm only trying—'

'Just bring Max up here tonight. I've got a little show-and-tell demonstration he's going to *love*.'

'But—'

'We'll clean those pants, boyo. You and me. Dry cleaners of the gods.'

They screened the movie at 8:05 P.M., exactly one minute after Alan Kramer arrived. Max took a deep breath as the lights went down, and nobody heard him exhale.

When the lights came up, Kramer sighed. His face looked slack and empty, but there was nothing unusual about that; he always looked as if he'd stayed up till dawn rereading his press clips. 'We'll put a new editor on it,' he said, speaking casually, as if power bored him.

'Andy's doing a great job,' Max said.

'Maaaax,' Kramer said, calling for sanity.

An expression of mild, almost abstract curiosity came into Max's face. 'Are you taking over the picture, Alan?' he said.

Kramer looked pained. 'Max, I wouldn't say—'

'*Are you taking over the picture*?'

Kramer shrugged: He had tried to be kind, hadn't he? 'Let's face it, Max,' he said. 'The studio has to protect its investment.' Then he turned to the studio's head of postproduction, who sat next to Kramer with a clipboard that held the list of studio-recommended cuts. At this point in the filmmaking process, the head of postproduction became a very powerful man. 'Let's get together first thing in the morning,' Kramer said.

'Eight-thirty in your office?'

Kramer nodded, then turned back to Max. 'You'll be there?' he said. It wasn't a question. Then Kramer got up. 'Don't worry, Max. When we take thirty, forty minutes out of it, it'll—'

Max stopped. '*Forty minutes*?'

'We lose the subplot, bring it down to ninety minutes.'

'That'll kill it,' Max said. 'It'll fucking kill it. Nothing will make sense.'

'This is not the best time for you to be difficult, Max,' Kramer said, an edge coming into his voice. 'Did you see the news this morning? Do you know how many calls I've gotten? And this thing's going international now. I'm getting clips from Paris, London, Japan. Even *Moscow*.'

'Is that what this is about? A little bad publicity?'

'I'm just trying to make the picture better, Max.'

'You wouldn't know *how* to make it better.'

'Max,' Kramer said, with an alligator smile, 'even if I hated you more than life itself, I still couldn't embrocate my responsibilities as studio chief.'

'*Abdicate*,' Max hissed. 'It's *abdicate*, not *embrocate*.'

Kramer shrugged. 'Whatever.' He gave Max a fatuous grin deliberately calculated to infuriate him: Maybe I am an idiot, but I'm still the idiot who decides your fate, suckah.

Max took a deep breath, drawing himself up to full striking height. They all watched him, waiting for the pounce. Instead Max spoke with rigid control. 'I want to sneak it,' he said.

Kramer's mouth opened. Technically, if a producer didn't like the notes the studio gave him, he could demand to sneak his picture and let the audience decide. This had evolved over the years as a way of settling arguments with a minimum of screaming, and was now a matter of standard contract. But it was risky. There were always so many hard feelings, and preview audiences could be quirky.

'You sure that's—' Kramer began.

'*I want to sneak it*,' Max said, emphasizing each word.

For a long moment, Kramer and Max stared each other down. Then Kramer nodded and let his face go slack again. 'Okay, Max, have it your way. We'll screen it on Friday.'

'Sunday,' Max said.

Kramer hesitated, looking at his colleagues: After all, his expression said, I do want to be fair . . .

'I need the time,' Max said.

Kramer waited.

'Please.'

Kramer smiled, happy now. Max Fischer had pleaded. 'Saturday,' he said, pushing through the door without another word.

Max moved through the alley, first slowly, then picking up speed. And there was the bungalow, Max's beloved bungalow, flanked by mutant Quonset huts built for an army of giants. '*Sarah*!' Max barked, banging through the door. 'Call Barry Rose! I want that bastard on the phone!'

Then he stopped midstride and whipped back around, so that Peter almost bumped into him. 'No – no, wait. Cancel that. *Don't* call.' He stepped around Peter and headed for the door. 'Come on, come on, come on.'

'Where are we going?' Peter asked.

'Hurry!'

'Where to?'

'Barry's house.'

The drive took less than twenty minutes. All the way through the flatlands, Max picked at his scabs. Why was Kramer turning against him? Just the rape? Or was he negotiating with Barry? Was it the Hanks picture? Was that why CAA couldn't seem to get him on the goddamn phone? Because Max's own studio chairman was against him! Conspiring with Barry fucking Rose!

'I heard his contract at Fox was coming up,' Peter said.

Max nodded, unsurprised. Yes, it made sense. And Max's contract was coming up too! So Kramer could get rid of a public relations problem and still keep Hanks! It was perfect! It was evil! He was being framed! He'd get them all! He'd have their jobs! Their houses! Their cars! He would *kill and eat their children*!

By the time they got to Bel Air it was almost eleven. The streets were quiet and empty. 'Maybe we should try this in the morning,' Peter said, afraid of what Max might do. How would this look in tomorrow's paper? But Max just lowered his head like he was planning on battering down Rose's gate with it.

As it turned out, the gate was open. 'Go on, go ahead,' Max said, and Peter obeyed, driving past the big brick house to the garage. He pulled to a stop behind Barry Rose's old Rolls-Royce, a car so fat and shiny it looked like a ceremonial barge for a Chinese emperor.

'Look at that fucking thing,' Max said. 'It's like something Zsa Zsa Gabor would drive. It's *pathetic*.'

But Rose's Mercedes was gone, and so was the Mercedes coupe his wife drove. They were probably out having separate dinners together, enjoying the life of a two-career couple. Peter exhaled pure tension. 'Let's come back in the morning,' he said.

Max ignored him. He went to the back door and banged on it until the maid came.

'Mr Rose no here,' she said.

'I know that! Where is he!'

'He no here.'

'Tell me where he is!'

Max seemed ready to storm the house, his own one-man invasion party . . . until the creak of another door pulled his head around. Tracy stood on the guest house steps, her black hair gleaming under the doorlight.

Max peered at her.

'He's not home,' she called.

Max hesitated, then started across the lawn. This time Peter was right behind him.

'Where is he?'

'You got me,' Tracy said.

They stared at each other. Tracy had a faint smile on her face, Max just a cold burn.

'I'm sure he'll be sorry he missed you,' Tracy said.

Peter looked closer at her, saw that her eyes were red. Her nose was too. It looked like tears, but with Tracy you never knew.

Max didn't notice. 'Are you happy?' he asked. 'I've been to jail, the studio's trying to take my picture away from me, your father is busily *fucking* me in various orifi . . .'

Then he stopped himself and looked a little closer. 'Are you okay?'

Tracy laughed: Don't get sentimental on me now. 'Hello, Peter,' she said.

'Nice to see you again.'

'It's been so long.'

Max broke in, impatient. 'I got a theory, Tracy,' he said.

She cocked her head: how original.

'It wasn't your idea at all. One of your little boyfriends got rough with you or something, and Barry decided it was me.'

Tracy gave a reluctant shrug: not bad.

'You just went along with it,' Max added, not very nicely. 'Is that right? So Daddy would love you?'

Tracy met Max's eyes, reflecting his anger right back. 'I got a theory too,' she said. 'Marina went over to your house, maybe she asked you for a favor, maybe just a ride somewhere, but you were too busy adding up your total lifetime grosses in Czechoslovakia. So you killed her. Or you had your little flunky kill her.'

'That's a *shitty* theory,' Max said.

'I like it.'

'It's *mean*.'

'Now I like it better.'

'Why don't you grow up already? Be a little *tougher*.'

Tracy looked up at the sky and started singing, in a high-pitched off-key voice: '*La la la la, la la la la, la la la la* . . .'

Max listened, smiling bitterly: Go ahead, be that way. So Tracy stopped and gave him the same smile back, with a twist. At that moment Peter saw a moving silver gleam in the corner of his eye, something coming down the driveway.

'Guys,' he said.

The oh-shit sound in his voice turned both their heads. Together they watched the gleam turn into the bumper of Rose's Mercedes, inching past the corner of the house. He was staring at them from behind the wheel, in disbelief, and they all straightened up a little, like schoolkids caught misbehaving. Rose parked his car and got out, standing for a moment to consider again the improbable sight. Then he shook his head and started moving toward them, clenching his fists.

Peter stepped toward Rose, thinking maybe he could slow him down, give them all a minute to think, but he felt frozen, underwater, as if he were moving in such extreme slow motion that it would take whole minutes for his lips to form words. In his belly he felt that sudden yaw, the greasy tug of fear.

'Mr Rose,' Peter said. 'Uh, we . . . uh . . .'

Rose reached out, catching Peter in the collarbone with the heel of his hand. It wasn't particularly aggressive, just a casual stiff-arm, as if Peter were not important enough for any more than that. But it caught Peter off guard, knocking him back. He stumbled and fell against a bush, which had recently been pruned, and tore a deep scratch above his left eye. From his knees, feeling the wet blood trickling down his face, he saw Max straightening his hair. It was funny, straightening his hair for a fight – did he think he was on camera? Or was he worried about leaving a handsome corpse? After all, Max might be fifteen years younger, and he might have the edge in bulk, but Rose had that leathery desert-rat strength, like he'd been dried and cured and could last forever. Peter's bet was on him.

Then Rose stopped, three paces away. The two men studied each other silently. Finally Rose asked, in a tone that was oddly polite, 'What the fuck are you doing here?'

Max didn't answer, just stared back with an emotionless chill, as if the situation were so revolting to him that he had chosen to let his brain operate his body from a distance, by remote control. Attack, his face said, and I'll be forced to instruct my body to retaliate.

Tracy watched the confrontation with fascinated disgust. 'I think he missed you,' she said.

236

Rose flicked his eyes at her – I'll deal with you later, girl – then back at Max. 'I'm gonna ask you again – what the *fuck* are you doing here?'

'I heard you were in negotiations with Alan Kramer,' Max said. Like a lion tamer, he kept his eyes on Rose's face, letting peripheral vision monitor the rest. 'Is that true?'

'Don't you have more important things to worry about?'

'Is it true?'

'That's my private business,' Rose said.

Max shook his head. 'I can't believe it,' he said. He wasn't angry, or blustering, or bitter – he seemed genuinely thrown. 'I can't believe that even *you* would take advantage of this ugly situation' – he indicated Tracy – 'for a lousy production deal.'

Dabbing at his cut with the palm of his hand, Peter watched Max. He had never heard him like this before – Max was always full of theatrical moans and self-mocking anguish, but it never seemed quite real. Now he heard honest pain in his voice, even anguish. Was this the fuse that lit the Fischer fireworks? 'As much as we've hated each other, I just can't believe it,' Max finished.

Rose's expression didn't change, but Peter thought he could see a little doubt there. Had he gone too far?

Then Max continued, and the grieving tone in his voice took on a slight theatrical twist. 'I didn't know things were so desperate,' he said. 'To frame someone for a lousy production deal, you must be really – I mean, is it the mortgage? Is it that bad? You gonna have to give back the Mercedes, drive around in that goofy old Rolls?'

By the time Max got to the word *mortgage*, Rose started to smile. When Max was finished he let himself look puzzled. 'Max, tell me something,' he said. 'Didn't I once tell you to get your ass out of my house and don't ever come back? Didn't I say that to you once?'

To Peter's astonishment, Max actually smiled a little. 'Actually, I remember it a little differently,' he said.

'Oh, really?'

'You said, "Get your *fat* ass out of my house."'

Rose almost laughed, but that made him angry, so he moved forward. Max moved forward too, matching him step for step, so that suddenly the two men were nose to nose.

Peter moved between them, one hand held to his bleeding cut. 'Come on, Max,' he pleaded, 'we just got *out* of jail. Let's not go right back.'

Rose snorted, and Max let himself be pulled sideways. The sight of Peter's blood seemed to impress them somehow, giving him more authority. Or maybe they were just glad some blood had been spilled.

'At least not until we pass go and collect two hundred dollars,' Peter babbled, pulling Max toward the car. 'We were just leaving, anyway. Right? Good-bye, Tracy. Nice seeing you again. We'll have to do this again sometime.'

Then Max shook his arm loose. 'Tell him the truth, Tracy,' he said. 'End this.'

Tracy hesitated. She looked at Peter. They had twin cuts now, each over the same eye.

Rose took her arm, turning her to face him, and not gently either. What he saw in her face surprised him. 'What the hell . . .?'

His voice went low and quiet: the power voice, compelling obedience. 'What is this?' he said.

'It's between me and Max,' Tracy said.

'And the state of California,' her father snapped.

Max took a step forward. 'Tell him, Tracy,' he said.

Rose glared at his daughter. 'It's gonna be pretty damn embarrassing if you keep changing your story. People are going to think—'

'*She made it all up*,' Max shouted, finishing the sentence. 'And you cheered her on, Barry, you cheered her on. So you could *hurt* me. So you could *steal Hanks*.'

Now Rose turned his glare on Max. 'She was *bleeding*,' he shouted. 'I *saw* her. She was *brutalized*.'

'Maybe she just had a rough night at Sin-a-Matic,' Max sneered.

'She was *bleeding*,' Rose repeated, almost quivering with anger. The two men glared at each other until Peter felt that he and Tracy might as well have disappeared, that time was frozen and no one existed anymore but these two mythic warriors locked in their unending death grip. A word popped out of Peter's past: *diachronic*. It meant across time. It was a big word when he was a graduate student, along with *valorize*, *reify*, and *proleptic*.

'I don't need to *frame* you to make a deal with Tom Hanks,' Rose was shouting, jabbing the finger again. 'All I had to do was *fire* you. Then everybody in town wanted to work with me.'

'Sure, *I* was holding you back,' Max shouted. 'It was my *unpleasant personality* making you such an ancient failure.'

Tracy stepped back, looking from one to the other like victim number five in a horror movie, face to face with Freddy at last.

'Your unpleasant personality didn't hurt me,' Rose shouted. 'It just made me sick to my stomach on a daily basis. What hurt me was your vicious and treacherous nature.'

'*Treacherous*?' Max said, as if that was the deepest blow of all.

'Nobody wanted to work with you. Nobody wanted to be near you. I *carried* you.'

'*I* carried *you*,' Max said.

'Sure. And you produced *Cyberkill*. You produced *Blood Hunt*. I know that's what you tell your cronies.'

'I always acknowledged your contribution.'

'The fuck you did. The day you started working for me, you started producing the pictures. I was just the guy opening the doors for you. The old fart getting in your way.'

Peter stepped forward and took Tracy's elbow, since she suddenly seemed nauseated, on the verge of vomiting. Her face went pale and damp.

Abruptly Rose turned to Peter. '*You're* the one I feel sorry for now,' he said. 'For putting up with this' – he pointed at Max – 'you should at least get a step into the business. That's the trade-off. But he's going down, and you're going down with him.'

Max waved a dismissive hand. 'You should put that line in one of your movies. It's crappy enough.'

'We'll just be going now,' Tracy said, linking her arm with Peter's. 'You lovebirds have so much to talk about.' She turned him and started steering him toward his car. Peter looked back at Max, but Max didn't say anything, just watched Tracy lead him away. Peter fantasized about going off with her for good – why not just leave the two bitter, obsessed, scheming bastards behind and go off *with the girl*? Tracy might not be the girl of the movies, all promise, but she was so fiery and sad, and maybe he could heal her, heal them both. Let the bastards stay and lock their jaws on each other and shift in the dirt like bulldogs probing for veins. And Tracy felt the same way, he could feel it. She'd seen through them at last and wanted to leave it all behind. 'I got a good idea,' she said, cheerful and excited as a girl about to ride her first pony. 'Let's go to Sin-a-Matic,' she said, eyes wide. 'After all, I'm on the list.'

But she was acting again, doing middle-period Goldie Hawn. Max turned in disgust, off to the car without waiting to see if Peter would follow him, and Tracy held on to Peter's arm one second longer than the joke required. Then she let go.

Chapter Thirteen

'Back to the house,' Max said, after they left Casa Rose.

'No,' said Peter. He still felt Tracy's hand tugging on his arm, and hated himself for leaving her.

'No?'

'Jennings wants us to come over.'

'That pervert.'

'He's got something,' Peter said. 'He knows that world.'

'Let the Dog handle it,' Max said. 'Don't start playing junior detective, like some crappy movie.'

'Excuse me, but it's my ass too.'

The next intersection was Beverly Glen. Peter turned the wheel left, cutting up toward Mulholland and West's house. Max stared at him, but didn't object, and Peter felt a little thrill: I am the captain of my Fiat. It wasn't far, ten minutes up the canyon and another five to West's palazzo. The front door opened one second before Max stepped onto the stoop, Rachel the assistant standing there in her black leather jacket and torn jeans. She led them into the living room.

'What happened to your eye?' she asked Peter.

'Ran into a door.'

'That's original.'

'You're so mean to me,' Peter said.

'Poor Peter,' Rachel said, smiling at Max. 'In town three months, with an actual working penis, and still not a studio chief.'

'How do you know it's working?' Peter asked.

Rachel looked him over, not pleasantly. 'I hear it's working overtime.'

Max glanced from Peter to Rachel, and back again. This little repartee bothered him, but he didn't seem to know quite why it bothered him . . . yet. He was working on it when West came out, rubbing his nose. 'Let's go out back, shall we?'

'Peter said you had something for us,' Max said.

But West pretended not to hear. 'Hey, did you ever tell the kid that story about working with Fred Astaire? I love that story.'

West knew the way to Max's heart. Working with Astaire, even though it was just on a television tribute to old Hollywood (Astaire narrated the dance section), was one of Max's favorite memories. He started out grudgingly, but quickly warmed up as West tossed in his own details and followed up with an anecdote of his own, and before long they were off, topping each other with tales of the living legends they had met back when. Hearing the love and nostalgia in their voices, Peter felt a stab of envy – would he ever love anything the way they loved Hollywood?

They kept talking as they got settled in the Playroom on the mink sofas, as Rachel brought a tray with bottles and ice and glasses. For the first time in days, Max seemed to relax. Prompted by West's first name, he launched into an involved tale about the legendary Jennings Lang, and West jumped in with encouraging flourishes. They were directing it all at Peter, and he understood that this was as it must be, because new blood kept Hollywood alive, fed its fading hopes, affirmed through fresh desire the choices they had made. In the same way, the photos-with on the walls of every Hollywood office helped validate the life they documented. But it all left a vampiric aftertaste. Why such a need for fresh blood? Why such a big hole to fill?

'So anyway, Lang is fucking Joan Bennett,' Max was saying, 'who's married to Walter Wanger.' He looked at Peter. 'Wanger used to *rule* Warner Brothers, the hottest producer on the lot.'

'I know who Walter Wanger is,' Peter said. '*Invasion of the Body Snatchers.*'

Max gave a tiny nod, not very impressed. 'He produced *The Cocoanuts* too, didya know that? So Wanger tells Lang, who is an agent then, stop fucking my wife or I'll kill you. Bennett is Lang's client. And Lang doesn't stop. One day Wanger is walking on the Warner Brothers lot and he sees Lang and what does he do? Whatever the fuck he *wants* to do – he's the *king of the lot*. So he pulls out a gun and *shoots him in the balls*.'

'You're kidding,' Peter says.

'*Shoots him in the balls*,' Max said. 'And do you know who the surgeon was? Tom Pollock's father.'

'You're kidding,' Peter said again. 'Tom Pollock's father?'

Pollock was a lawyer who became head of Universal Studios. It was amazing, and somehow reassuring, that his father popped up in this old story; it was truly a small town.

'And Pollock's father ends up cutting off one of Jennings Lang's balls,' West said, taking over. 'So after that everybody called him—'

Max joined in, finishing it in stereo: '*Jennings* Lang.'

Max and West broke into laughter, and Peter felt a flush of privilege, caught up in a sense of legend, prompting him to cast himself in a future anecdote: and then Max and Jennings West and I walked down to that old bungalow he had below the pool – oh yeah, West didn't spend much time in the big house, that was for his ego. His *id* lived out back . . .

Peter made a mental note to think about this later, how the story itself conferred importance. Maybe that had something to do with the power of movies, that the mere organization of material into a tale is some kind of compliment to reality. Another essay, for another life.

'And the capper is, then *Wanger remarries Joan Bennett*,' West said, choking the words out through his laughter. 'It's a . . . *Hollywood . . . love . . . story*.'

'I thought you said they were married,' Peter said.

Max snapped out the answer: 'They were, but they got divorced.'

Peter decided to take charge again. 'Maybe we should get to it?' he suggested.

West leaned over and pushed the button on his phone. 'Send her in, doll.'

Peter saw Max raise his eyebrows: Now what? West grinned again. 'Max, you're going to be thanking me for this for years. So give me a break, okay? Let me do it my way.'

Max let out an aggravated sigh.

'Just wait,' West said.

They heard clicking on the flagstones outside, then the door opened and they heard the rustle of clothes in the hall. A woman appeared, striking a pose in the doorway. Her face was turned away, hidden in the shadows, as if better to display the body in the black cat suit. Then she rolled her head and her black hair gleamed in the light.

It was Leela. She giggled and crossed over to the sofa, sitting down on the end, at West's feet.

'Hi, Peter?' she said, ending the greeting with her usual question mark.

Max let his eyes bug out. 'He knows *everybody*!'

'We met here, at the party.'

'I was trying to help you out, boyo,' West said. 'Twice.' Finally Peter understood: that West had set up his meeting with Leela at Meursault's, the one he thought was a wonderful coincidence. But he had blown it, and now it was time for the big boys to take over. West asked Leela what she wanted to drink, and she arched her eyebrows in an imitation of sophistication. 'Crystal,' she said, accent on the -*al*. No question mark this time.

West picked up the phone and pushed the intercom button, gave orders to Rachel. They made small talk until Rachel brought in a bottle of champagne in a silver bucket. West opened the champagne first and poured some for Leela, then started pouring Max a glass of whiskey. Laphroaig, the label said.

'Not for me,' Max said.

'Fischer, you're wrapped so tight it's amazing you don't just explode and flutter down in little pieces,' West said. 'Now, I am about to save your life, and in exchange you *must* take some kind of intoxicating substance and *try to have a good time*.'

Max's face actually puckered, as if he had drunk lemon juice. 'I feel like I need my wits about me,' he said.

'That's exactly what you don't need. You're a producer, you need to go by instinct – guys like you and me, boyo, we gotta be out front where the new ideas are. We can't follow the rules. We're *outlaws*!'

Finishing his speech with a flourish, West splashed some Laphroaig into Peter's glass. 'Sorry I don't have any heroin,' he said.

'I know that's the fashionable drug these days, but call me old-fashioned.'

Max looked weary, as if he didn't see why he had to go through this.

'Okay,' West said, nodding to Leela: Let the games begin.

Leela shifted, the catsuit stretched. She sipped her champagne, then laughed and covered her mouth with a hand, palm out. 'I'm so nervous,' she said.

'You can trust them,' West cooed, giving her his two best producer's tricks: the snake charmer's soothing voice and the hypnotist's burning eyes. Leela took a deep breath, and another sip of her Crystal.

Then she started in. It was the same story she had told Peter in Malibu, about the Satanists and the car shop. But West, unlike Peter, didn't let her get very far with it. 'C'mon, Leela,' he interrupted. 'Cut to the chase.'

Leela brushed strands of her thin black hair away from her eyes and went through a small adjustment. Realizing that this was not her moment, not her story, she ducked her head as if putting her self away one more time. When she looked back at them she was transformed: Her eyes shone with service. 'Well, you know how Meursault and Angie are kinda not friends?' She stopped, looking doubtfully at Max.

Impatient, West supplied the backstory: 'Angie used to work for Madame Meursault, then she went into business for herself. Now they hate each other – just like you and Barry, Max.'

'Nice comparison,' Max said.

West cued Leela with a nod.

'So anyway, about six months ago, this individual came to work for Angie, and since she needed a place to stay—'

West held up a finger, looking like the Shao Lin master of decadence. 'Marina Lake,' he explained. 'Tell the boys about what happened Thursday morning, Leela honey.' He took a big sip of his drink.

Leela ducked her head. When she looked up, Peter saw that her lip was trembling and her eyes were scared.

'I could get killed,' she said.

'Nobody's going to kill you,' West said, in his soothing voice.

'But Angie . . .'

245

'Don't worry about it.'

Leela swallowed, then took a deep breath and continued. But she was clearly terrified. 'I was there, in the apartment.'

'Go ahead,' West ordered.

Leela gave another small nod, a prim little gesture that didn't quite go with the black cat suit. 'Then we get a phone call? It's this girl, and the answering machine picks up, and she's asking for Marina, real upset, crying and stuff? Talking about men in Hollywood, what assholes they are.'

'Then what happened?' West prompted, drinking some more and nodding his head happily.

'So finally I pick up the phone, 'cause she seems so upset. And she asks for Marina and since Marina's not there, she asks me to come pick her up at the hospital.'

Another mystery solved.

'Then what?' Max asked.

Leela gave a sensual little stretch, lifting one shoulder, then the other, and rolling her head. She had their attention now, which seemed to relax her. 'Well, she didn't want to go home. So I took her back to my place. And then Marina came back and we all sat around for a while. Then she and Marina started arguing, I don't really remember what about, just little digs about who was the biggest slut. After a while I just went into my bedroom.' She stopped for a second, but a look from West prodded her. 'I did hear one name – she was shouting it so loud you could hear it right through the wall.'

Peter waited, expecting the worst: that it would be his.

'Max,' Leela said, looking at the floor.

For a moment no one spoke, letting it all sink in.

'That's all?' Max said, disappointed.

West nodded, ready to sum it up now. 'And that's what she told the cops.'

Max did a double take. Leela ducked her head again, abashed.

'*That's* why they arrested you,' West crowed. 'She told them she heard Tracy shouting your name. Leela was the witness.'

Leela gave Peter an apologetic look: Sorry I couldn't tell you. You know how it is.

Max shook his head. He hated thinking about this stuff, wished with all his heart that it would just go away. West sighed in sympathy, then patted Max on the leg. 'You got caught in the whore wars, my friend.'

Max didn't seem to be listening anymore, so Peter supplied the obvious question. 'The whore wars?'

West couldn't help grinning – he enjoyed all this, the intrigue and sleaze and the glimpse of people's secret lives. 'The whorrre warrrs,' he repeated, stretching out the words like an old Shakespearean actor. 'Angie saw a chance to get close and personal with Tracy's dad, thus getting an edge on Meursault. All she had to do was trade information, which is half her business anyway. The information just happened to be about you.'

'She said she'd forgive some of my debt,' Leela said.

'That's all it was, Max,' West concluded. 'Just kids squabbling over toys.' His grin turned lecherous, and he turned it back toward Leela, reaching out a hand to pat her thigh. She dropped her eyes modestly. 'Just schoolgirls playing with their toys,' West repeated, still grinning, though his eyes had gone distant, off to the place where his fantasies were.

Max stood up: time to go.

'Wait a minute,' Peter said. 'Aren't we missing something here? Who's the killer?'

West shook his head sadly, disappointed by mankind once again. 'You still don't get it. This is big business, boyo. Angie's making a hundred thousand dollars a week, maybe more. And she's mobbed up, she's connected to the whole drug world. She's got to protect her investment and that means doing whatever she can to make friends and influence people. What I figure is, she ordered Marina to help Barry, say whatever he wanted to hear, no matter what really happened, and Marina told her to fuck off, so she sent one of her goons over to shake her up. Only the guy shook a little too hard.' He shrugged. 'The whore wars.'

Max poured himself another shot of Laphroaig, and downed it in one gulp. He was in some kind of shock. 'All I want to do is make my movies. Is that too much to ask?'

West chuckled, and sent his hand up Leela's thigh. She raised her knee to give him better access, and Peter understood: West had paid the debt. He owned her now.

Peter looked in her eyes, and she looked right back at him.

'I'll put the Dog on it,' Max said, in a tone of grudging gratitude. 'I just want to go back to work.'

Max got in the car without a word, and stayed silent halfway to Laurel Canyon. A drunk driver drifted in front of them, and Peter swerved around him, tires screeching. Max still didn't say a word. Peter figured he was still a little stunned by West's revelations. Or maybe it was just the whiskey. But as they cut down toward the flatlands Max turned to Peter, and spoke in a voice thick with anger. 'What the fuck was that about?'

'What do you mean? Jennings was—'

'I mean, what the fuck was that about? What did Rachel mean, your penis is working overtime? What was that thing between you and that sleazy hooker? Don't tell me you just met at the party, don't *tell* me that. And how did you and Jennings get to be such pals?'

Max was watching him, studying every twitch.

'Jesus Christ, Max. I was just trying to solve your murder for you. How about a little gratitude?'

'Bullshit. That's just some Jennings West coke dream. He *wants* that madam to be guilty. The only issue that matters is: What happened to Tracy? Everything starts with that. *Something* happened.'

Max was getting close. Peter could tell by the way he was watching him. The truth was teasing at him, trying to find an opening. He took a deep breath through his half-open mouth, trying not to move his chest.

'And that little scene back at Barry's – you trying to tell me you and Tracy just talked once in a nightclub for two minutes? She called you a fag?'

There was only one thing to do. He had studied with the master, and it was time to put his teachings into play. 'Fuck you, Max Fischer,' he said. 'I have been *so* loyal to you. I never get any sleep, I work twenty-four hours, I take shit from everybody, I go to fucking jail. I have other job offers, you know. I don't have to take this. You're just jealous because I've been figuring things out while you've been drifting around having *vapors* and throwing *tantrums*.'

For a moment Max didn't say anything, just kept up that X-ray stare. Peter waited, knowing this could be it, the end: *Finito Mussolini*.

'*What* job offers?'

Peter laughed, tension exploding. 'You're a psycho,' he said, hoping the moment was over.

'What job offers? Who would offer you a fucking job?'

'As a matter of fact' – he wouldn't mention Barry Rose, although it would give such pleasure – 'John Sayles.'

'John *Sayles*?' Max seemed even more furious now than before – this was a betrayal he could understand, one that went to the heart of what he was.

'I said no,' Peter added quickly, but Max's expression did not change. 'I mean I didn't even really think about it seriously.'

Finally Max pulled his eyes away, staring out the side window. They passed the house where Robert Mitchum got busted for pot-smoking, and Peter remembered Max pointing it out that first week. Everything was so exciting then. Into the silence, he started babbling: 'He read one of my old essays in *Film Comment*, called me up a couple of days ago, said that I seemed pretty smart so I should know that what the movie business was *really* about was, can you back up a 15-foot truck? And just for the hell of it I said I could, because I can, and he said, "Hell, I need an AD, come and work for me then." I thought it was pretty funny at the time, not that I considered it for a minute . . .'

He kept talking but lost contact with the part of his brain operating his voice. Instead he wondered what he would do if Max fired him. Where he would go? How would he explain it to his parents? Would Tracy still care about him? Finally he stopped talking and waited for the boom mike to fall.

'*John Sayles*? You're telling me you want to go work for *John Sayles*?'

'I turned him down. I was just mentioning it.'

'John Sayles doesn't even *exist*.'"

'I know, Max.' He used the placating voice, by now so well practiced.

'You're going to disappear, you'll go *extinct*, you'll *fall off the edge of the planet*! No one will ever hear of you again! They'll say, "Peter James? That *Gentile* with two first names? Who knows? Who cares? The guy *doesn't exist*."'

Again Peter opened his big mouth – the imp of the perverse was really working overtime tonight. 'You can't tell me you thought *Matewan* was a total piece of shit, Max,' Peter said.

'Obviously it's not a total piece of shit,' Max answered without hesitation. 'In fact, it's better than anything I've ever made. What I make is *really* shit. *Trivial* shit, as you once pointed out.'

'Max—'

'No wonder you want out,' he spat. 'No wonder you're going back to *New York City* to work for *John fucking Sayles.*'

'I'm not taking the job,' Peter said.

They reached the house, and Peter parked. Max kept badgering him up the driveway and into the living room.

'I mean, John *Sayles* – it's like telling me you've decided to go into *social work.* Why don't you just go to *India* and get a job washing the feet of *dead* people?'

'*I'm not going to take the job*!' Peter shouted, ready to burst with frustration. 'I'm too *afraid* of you to take the job.'

Inside, two construction workers were sweating away under Yoji's all-seeing eyes, hauling out debris with a wheelbarrow. Max nodded to Yoji and continued his tirade. 'You *have* to take it. You gotta do what's *best for you.*'

'What's going on?' Peter asked Yoji, like a soldier ducking enemy fire.

'Max say take down wall.' His voice aggressively serene, as if he'd accepted his fate and was determined to absorb each lesson this particular doom had to teach. He pointed at the wall between the living room and the patio, which had a line drawn waist-high across it. 'Tomorrow we chop outer wall to half. Soon have no walls at all.'

This was insane. Max Fischer was insane. Peter was trapped in a disappearing house with an insane man. He was so tired that his feet dragged on the heavy canvas drop cloth spread out over the living room floor, and the construction workers seemed to be figures from some surrealistic dream, carting off pieces of his crumbling brain. He took a deep breath and spoke calmly. 'I was *never going to take the job*. I don't want the job. I *hate* the job. If I ever see John Sayles, I may *kill* him just for *offering* me the job!'

Max ignored him. 'If you wanted to go work for a studio – at least that would make sense. At least I would feel like you *learned* something. A guy wants studio experience. But God, *John Sayles.*'

'Max . . .' Peter broke into mock sobs. 'Stop, please. Just stop. I'll do anything. What do you want me to do?'

'See, you still don't get it,' Max continued, still shouting. 'It's about *service*. You don't say to someone, "I've been working for you for three months, I got what I wanted, I'm going to go now." You haven't *delivered* yet. You have to *serve your boss*. You have to *pay the price of admission*.'

'Max—'

'But you don't want to pay! You want to get in free! You want to go to New York and work with *John fucking Sayles*!'

Then Max stopped. Suddenly. Something had just occurred to him, something horrifying. His face went slack, and for a flashing second Peter thought he'd never seen anyone so miserable. But an instant later Max's eyes tightened down so hard that Peter could almost feel them jabbing at him, like two angry little elbows. '*You*,' he said.

Max didn't have to finish the thought. Peter knew. He felt it in his belly, a sucker-punch.

'*It was you!*'

Peter started backing up over the construction rubble as Max advanced. 'Uh, I, I don't . . . Max . . .'

Max noticed the two-by-four he'd smashed the presents with, and picked it up. 'You *fucker*,' he said.

Yoji and the construction workers stopped what they were doing and watched.

'What did you do, suggest it? Did you say, "I know, let's get Max on the speaker phone! Let him share this beautiful moment!" '

Peter backed up, and Max swung the two-by-four, catching a lamp and knocking it to the floor with a crash.

'And then you bring me Hanks's number. How stupid do you think I am? You didn't get it off the police monitor. *She* gave it to you.'

This time he brought the two-by-four down on the dining table, knocking a chunk of wood off the side. Peter backed up into the middle of the room, picking up a sawhorse.

'You thought I wouldn't figure it out?' Max shouted, 'I mean, it's incredible. You treat me like an idiot, like a chump, like you want to rub it in my face. *Just like Tracy*. What is it with you two?'

'Max, I . . .'

Then another thought hit Max, and the two-by-four sagged. Sensing the worst, Peter backed up toward the patio.

'It was all you,' Max said.

'Max . . .'

'*You* were the rapist.'

'No Max, I . . . I was with her, but it wasn't, I didn't . . .'

Taking that as confirmation, Max charged forward, raising the two-by-four. 'You lied! You manipulated! You're a *sleazy little hustler*!'

Then Peter gave up. He stopped backing away and bowed his head, waiting for the blow. Yoji and the carpenters stood frozen, and Max froze too, the two-by-four suspended above his head. Peter had done the only thing that could have stopped him, and now Mad Max was stalled in full tantrum. What would he do? Where would all that energy go? The two-by-four quivered. Everyone waited.

And then Max brought the two-by-four straight down, not swinging it forward but straight down, as if he were doing a pull-up, so that it tapped his own head with a hollow *thunk*. He did it again: *thunk*. And again: *thunk*. And that charged him up enough that he pulled way back and went into his backswing, ready to hit Peter at last. The two-by-four came around . . . aiming for the bleachers . . . but at the last moment Max twisted it away from Peter's head and hit the curtains behind him. The two-by-four ripped into the fabric and got stuck, and Max tried to pull it loose, giving a hard tug, then another, and then with a crack and a rumble the entire curtain casement started to come down. Peter dodged it, but Max just stood there staring up at it, even tugging on the two-by-four to hurry it down until it fell right on top of him, swathing him in curtains. The casement landed on top of the whole pile with a muted thump. And then they heard a long inhuman howl – *Aaaaaaaaahhhhh*! – a sound like an opera singer with a razor stuck in his throat, and Yoji and the carpenters snapped out of their daze and rushed forward, lifting the casement off Max. The razor song continued as they tried to untangle the curtains, and when they finally got him uncovered they saw the problem: his ankle, twisted out at a distinctly Dutch angle. The razor song continued, an aria of pain . . . and then it suddenly stopped. With wide, disbelieving eyes, Max looked down at his leg. 'Goddamnit,' he shouted, glaring at Peter. 'Look what *you made me do*.' Then his eyes closed tight and sweat covered his face completely, as if someone had thrown a bucket of water over him, and his body began to quiver.

*   *   *

Peter followed the ambulance in his Fiat, signed the hospital forms, and made the pertinent phone calls. After Max came out of the operating room, he was asleep for a blissful four hours afterward. Peter slept in the chair next to the bed. He woke up and saw Max staring at him.

'I am *so* stupid,' he said.

'Max—'

Max held up a hand. 'Don't talk,' he said.

And then for a few minutes there was nothing but a long silence. Peter heard the nurses in the halls, making small talk.

'It must be me,' Max finally said. 'I must do something to people. Something that makes them want to hurt me.'

Peter felt deep shame. You betrayed him, he told himself. You told yourself you were just playing by Hollywood rules, but you acted just as bad as they do. Worse.

'Marlon did the same thing,' Max continued, in the same mildly stunned, wondering voice. 'He wanted to write, I let him write. And do you know what he says to me? He says, "Thanks, I couldn't take it anymore."'

'He didn't say that,' Peter said.

'Why, did you ask him? Is he another one of your pals?'

'He was probably just mad.'

'He said he *couldn't stand being with me*. He said he *never liked spending time with me*. And let me tell you, it's a black fucking lie – he *wanted* to spend time with me. He was always after me, wanting to go to clubs, wanting to go to Palm Springs. I don't need paid friends. I have *friends*. People like me. He could have gone home any time he wanted. But he *wanted* to be with me – he wanted to be at my side, learning the business. It was only when he realized that he was never going to make it that he began *resenting* me. Then he was thinking secretly, Why do I have to spend so much time with this loudmouth asshole? *I* could do what he does. But he *couldn't*. He *can't*. That's why he hates me. Like you. Like Barry. Like Tracy.'

'I don't hate you, Max.'

'Then *why*?'

Peter hesitated, wondering what to say. And wondering, why indeed? Why hadn't he just gone to Max right away, confessed, asked his help? Max continued watching him, with dead eyes.

'I'll have Sarah box up your stuff and send it to your house tomorrow,' he said, without emotion. 'Leave your key on the table.'

Peter nodded, accepting his fate.

'Hey, it's like working for Torquemada, right? Now you don't work for Torquemada anymore.'

Peter frowned. He said that to . . . Barry Rose. How the hell did Max find out? 'I was joking,' he said. 'I didn't mean it.'

'You blew it, babe,' Max said. His voice was relaxed and casual now. He could have been ordering dinner. 'You had a chance and you blew it. No harm done. Go back to writing essays.' He grinned. ' "Fingernails in the Work of Jonathan Demme." That could be a good one.'

'Max, if you'd just listen for a minute. I know I fucked up. But I didn't do it to hurt you. I, I, I thought we were—'

Friends, he was going to say, but he choked on the word. 'I thought we had a relationship,' he finished, using the Hollywood phrase. No wonder it was so popular; it was better to leave the relationship undefined.

Max snorted. 'You should have thought of that before you *fucked Tracy*.'

For a moment there, Max's anger peeked out, with yellow fangs and fire.

'Now go!'

Peter looked at Max, his eyes pleading.

'*Go!*'

Numbly, Peter obeyed. Without paying any attention to what he was doing, he made his way past the nurses, down the elevator to the basement, got in his car and drove to the hospital parking booth. But then he couldn't find his parking receipt. He dug out every pocket, leafed through every bill in his wallet. 'I lost it,' he said.

Without a word, the parking attendant – a solemn Hindu with a turban and a huge white beard – pointed at a sign on the wall: LOST TICKET PAYS MAX.

Chapter Fourteen

The first thing Peter was conscious of was the thorn, a huge mutant thorn off one of those alien Bel Air palms, jabbing him in the back . . . or was it a knife, slipping between the second and third ribs? He heard the sinister hiss of a *noir* villain, Peter Lorre meets Sidney Greenstreet: *Between the second and third ribs, then flick it twice to nick the heart.* And the most horrible thing was that he couldn't move. He was paralyzed. He had to just lie there while the blade slid slowly home.

You blew it, babe . . .

Then his eyes opened to slits, and he worked his jaw, cracking the dried drool in the corners of his mouth.

Leave your keys on the table . . .

God, it was true: He was fired, finished, fucked. With his luck he'd end up taking the murder rap too. Or the killer would be Max and he'd give Peter an associate murderer credit and they'd end up sharing a cell . . .

Propping himself up on an elbow, Peter reached behind his back and pulled out an ashtray. Hello, Mr Lorre. He rubbed his eyes and sat up, automatically raising his arm for a look at his watch: 11:02 A.M.

No sweat, no job to rush to. But that didn't stop the jab of guilt: Lazy boy, no-account, and just look at that bottle of Wild Turkey lying empty on the floor. He remembered picking up the whiskey at the liquor store last night instead of gin and tonic because this time he wanted to feel the burn going down. And it still burned. With a groan, he lay back on the sheets.

The worst had happened: *You blew it, babe . . .*

He didn't even have enough money to move back home. He pictured himself pushing a shopping cart, wearing two overcoats, his feet wrapped in old T-shirts, an image both frightening and seductive –

oh, to throw it all away, to stop this undignified struggling. It pulled at him like an undertow, had been there always, behind everything he did. Whenever he felt it sucking at him he jumped up and ran, usually into a movie theater, until the urge went away. That was why he took the job with Max, really, because the movie business was such a mixture of all the things that mattered – art, writing, music, acting, business, strategy, sex, love, hate, revenge, even simple hanging out . . . so it was big enough to be everything. And everything was what he wanted. Or nothing . . .

But all along the tickle of doubt had teased: You're not like him, you can't do it, you're destined to fail. Wasn't that why he'd courted disaster with Tracy? Who had been born to it, and threw it all away?

When the phone rang he stared at it, then decided to just let it ring. Whoever it was probably thought they were calling Max's assistant, and that person didn't live here anymore . . .

Finally the phone stopped ringing.

But then the damn thing started up again, and it became easier to pick it up than to go on not picking it up.

'James? That you?'

It was the gruff, unfriendly voice of Detective Spinks. And why not? Life is rich. Life is full.

'Yeah.'

'What's the matter? You don't sound so good.'

'I'm having a great time. Someday I'm going to look back on this as the best week of my life.'

'Anything you want to tell me?'

Peter tried to think of something witty to say, but he couldn't.

'You want to hear the latest?'

'Sure,' Peter said.

'On the night of the rape, Tracy stayed at the Château Marmont,' Spinks continued. 'At some point a young man came and joined her. Nobody got a good look at him, but around three-thirty or four in the morning other hotel guests heard a loud argument. She left about a half hour later.'

Peter gave a bored *mmm-hmmm*. How pleasantly numb he felt.

'At the corner of Sunset and La Cienega, she went to a pay phone and made a phone call. Want to know who she called?'

'More than life itself.'

'Max Fischer. Or at least his house.'

If he gave a shit, this might have been interesting information.

'This would have been when you were there, answering the phone. Supposedly.'

At this point Peter considered confessing. He really didn't care anymore. Even though he still didn't feel guilty of rape, a nice warm jail cell would solve a lot of problems. And maybe Tracy would even feel a little guilty about all the shit she'd put him through . . .

But then what Spinks said began to sink in: After she left the hotel, Tracy called *Max.*

'I didn't talk to her,' he blurted out.

'The records show she had a conversation that lasted seventeen seconds,' Spinks said.

'I swear to God, it wasn't with me.' It was important that she believe him. He was sick of being accused of things he hadn't done.

Spinks didn't say anything at first. When she did speak her voice was more human. 'Listen, Peter,' she said. 'Something happened in that hotel room, and Marina Lake found out about it, and now she's dead. For God's sake, she was just nineteen.'

'How do you know it happened in the hotel room?' Peter said. 'Maybe it happened afterward?'

There was silence on the other end of the line, but he knew he had made a mistake. Maybe it was the way he said it. Maybe the question came out too eager.

'Why do you say that?' Spinks asked.

'I don't know . . . I just . . . I mean, why would she call Max if Max had raped her in the hotel room?'

Good save.

'That's a very good question,' Spinks said. 'I've been asking that myself.'

Maybe not such a good save. Shit. Shit. 'Look, I gotta go,' Peter said.

'But it couldn't have happened afterwards,' Spinks continued. 'Because right after the first call, Tracy called a cab. It took her home, and from home she went straight to the hospital. So whatever happened to Tracy happened in the Château Marmont.'

Peter felt a distinct thump: falling hopes. Without being particularly aware of it, he'd been telling himself that something did happen, some kind of real rape, and someone else did it. But there was no arguing with it now. 'I gotta go,' he repeated.

'Why? Where are you going to go?'

'Work.'

'I heard you got fired.'

'I'll talk to you later,' Peter said, hanging up the phone. He sank down deep in the bed, curling up on his side and pulling the covers over his head. He switched on the answering machine. Maybe he could sleep . . .

Then the phone rang again, and the answering machine kicked in: 'Peter, are you there? This is Flip, Flip Mosely. I tried you at the office but nobody knew where you were. You won't believe it. I'm *finished*. I finished the script. I did a John Hughes, slept like ten hours all week. Max was right: I just had to make him less of a schmuck. Once I saw it, I was *smoking*! So call me, okay? I want you to read it first, make sure I'm not out of my mind. Your boss still scares me a little bit.'

As Mosely hung up, Peter felt a surge of regret. Max was right, Flip would have a career, and the movie would be made without him. He turned the volume all the way down on the answering machine, then crawled back down under the covers.

Somewhere far away, a . . . *banging*. Coming closer. Bang. Bang. Bang. '*Peter*.' He was dreaming about Max, a demon Max pursuing him beyond the grave . . . but he was in his cave, his warm cave, and it was dark, cold winter and all he wanted was to stay warm . . . 'Come on Peter, I know you're in there!'

Bang. Bang. Bang.

Peter rolled over and looked at the clock: 11:45 A.M., which meant that he had been asleep for twenty-four hours, the first real sleep he'd had in ages. It was Thursday morning, exactly seven days and seven hours after he fell asleep at the Château Marmont.

Bang. Bang.

'Come on, Peter, open the door,' a male voice was saying. 'I know you're in there. Your car's in the carport. Open up.'

Then he recognized the voice: Spurlock. What did he want? He dug down into the covers again, but Spurlock just kept knocking and braying in the hall, so finally he wrapped the sheet around him and opened the door. Then he backstepped to the bed and let himself fall back down.

'You look like shit,' Spurlock said.

'I am shit,' Peter said. 'I have a solemn duty to be shit.'

Spurlock looked around the room, taking in the squalor with a certain smug satisfaction. 'Well, at least you didn't unpack the boxes.'

Thank you for pointing out the bright side, Peter thought, but didn't say it. 'What do you want, Marlon?'

Spurlock chuckled. He looked better today, or at least less pasty, although his hair still floated up there like crusty foam, and nothing would make the pockmarks go away. '*Maax Fissscher*,' he said, savoring the name. 'Isn't he a piece of work? Just a ball of hate, rolling down the hill of life.'

Peter moaned.

'Oh, don't be so pathetic. He used to fire me all the time. It's the cost of doing business.'

'This isn't exactly business as usual,' Peter said. 'At least I hope not.'

Spurlock sat down at Peter's desk, began flipping through the books. He studied a copy of René Girard's *Violence and the Sacred*, a graduate-school leftover. It argued that we need crucifixions and sacrifices to lift us beyond ordinary life to the most intense religious feelings. Peter quoted it in several of his essays, including the one about Max, trying to explain why movie violence could be more than just pandering to the mob, how it could arouse the tragic feelings of pity and terror, which led to a classic bit of academic ju-jitsu criticizing Max Fischer for not being violent *enough*. Everything was so theoretical then. But now that he thought about it, that was probably why he got the job. Spurlock sniffed and threw the book back on the pile. 'All he wants to do is use you,' he said, in a voice sharp enough to cut through Peter's fog. 'If he has to, he'll get the Dog to plant some evidence and make it look like you did it.'

'Come on. That's nuts.'

'He's had the Dog out digging up stuff on you all along,' Spurlock said. 'He even interviewed me, asking about the night I introduced you to Tracy. Seemed to think you knew her already.'

Peter remembered the Dog's visit to his apartment, and how quickly he learned about Peter's meeting with Tracy at On the Rox.

'You know what I'm talking about,' Spurlock said. 'I can see it in your face. You don't want to believe Max would do that to you, but he would. Believe it. The Dog has a whole dossier on you. He thought you were working for Barry, trying to set Max up . . .'

'That's . . .'

'Bullshit, I know. Of *course* it's bullshit.' Spurlock sighed, then leaned forward in the chair and began speaking in an excessively patient voice, as if he were talking to a child. 'You have to understand the psychology of the town, Peter. Guys like Max, they come here from all over the country, all over the world. They're geeks in their home towns, their parents hate them, they couldn't get laid – and they come here and after ten or fifteen years of eating shit and taking the horrible abuse you and I know so well – bang! They become *gods*. Suddenly they're rich, they're powerful, women want to fuck them – and all because they're making movies, these *figments*. So naturally they can't believe it, and it eats at them. It's that am-I-a-fraud thing, the same thing that brought them here, still making them miserable, only now they're big successes so it's even worse. And now they see it in movie terms – the reason they're unhappy is because they're not *creative*. That must be it. The figment doesn't happen because of them. It happens by magic. And it starts to drive them *crazy*.'

Spurlock was up now, pacing the small room. Peter watched him with growing curiosity: Did he realize that he sounded exactly like Max? He was even throwing his arms around, mad-scientist style.

'See, in any other business a guy like Max would just be a happy predator, ripping the throats out of weaker animals and taking their women and their stuff,' Spurlock continued. 'He'd be the king, and he'd probably even be relatively happy. But in Hollywood Max is not the king – he's not the one who makes the magic happen. He's one step down from the artists, and he knows it, and it drives him fucking *crazy*. That's why all these guys hire writers in teams and tell them what to write, so they can con themselves into thinking they're the ones making the movies.'

Spurlock finished his sentence, staring at Peter with a wild and empty expression. Peter wasn't sure whether he'd forgotten where he was or if he was waiting for a prompt. Finally he asked, 'What does this have to do with Tracy and Marina?'

'*Everything*,' Spurlock cried. 'Because the real tragedy is they're not *stupid* – they can *see* it. They know what great movies are – that's why they got in the business. Some of them will tell you they got into it for the money, or the pussy, but they're lying. That might be their reason now, but I don't care if it's *Bambi*, at some point they saw a movie and they fell in love. And in their hearts they know they can't do that, they need the fucking artists to do it for them, and it's a canker in their souls – so they start to hate – *hate* the irresponsible, childish, fucking egomaniacal artists, *hate* spending day after day kissing artist butt because they *have* to, and because they *want* to because in the one uncorrupted part of their souls they *love* the artists, love what they *do* – and then they spend their nights twisting imaginary artist necks in their fat little hands, only they need actual flesh in there because as we have established they are not *creative* people so they twist the necks that are *available*, their rivals or their mentors or the women who only want to fuck them because they make movies – or *you*, the lowly assistant, because you're there and you want to *be* them, and that's the greatest insult of all!'

Spurlock shouted out the last of his soliloquy, spitting and flailing at the air, finishing with his hands raised up like some Shakespearean madman invoking dark and vengeful gods. René Girard would have approved. Then, wiping his mouth dry, he turned on Peter, his eyes coming into a distant focus. He seemed to have forgotten where he was. But then he snapped back, speaking with miserable and bitter precision. 'Women are just a way to keep score, understand?'

'All very interesting,' Peter said. 'But the fundamental mysteries remain. Like who killed Marina Lake.'

'*Max*! Haven't you been listening? *Max killed Marina.*'

'Why would he want to do that?'

'Because she knew the truth! She knew everything about him! Even when she and Tracy were teenagers, she would never buy his shit. She was sixteen and she had his number. And then she found out what he did to Tracy.' Spurlock sat down on the edge of the bed and lowered his voice to the muted drone of painful revelation: 'You know why I left Max? I made a choice. It cost me big, I took a huge pay cut, lost his support, made new enemies. But I knew what would happen if I didn't – I was going to turn *into* him.'

'He told me he fired you.'

'What else was he going to say?' Spurlock grabbed Peter's wrist, looking right into his eyes, a plea on his face: *Listen to me! Understand me!* 'Ask yourself – who could kill an innocent girl? A beautiful nineteen-year-old girl? Only someone who had no feelings, someone *blocked*, someone who fears that deep down inside there's nothing, someone who doesn't want to look inside, who will do anything not to look – he'll *conquer the world* so he doesn't risk the slightest glance into his *black, uncreative soul.*'

In the bitterness of Spurlock's voice, Peter heard truth. Whatever else might have happened, there was no doubt that Max had done something, humiliated and hurt him until he was beyond rage.

'But he didn't do it,' Peter said, very quietly.

'You have to think about yourself now,' Spurlock said. 'Barry can help you.'

So that was it, the reason for this little visit. 'I'll think about it,' Peter said.

'Good,' Spurlock said. He got up off the bed, took a few aimless steps around the apartment. Now that he'd done what he came to do, the energy had gone out of him. He moved toward the door, but when he touched the knob he stopped and turned. 'If you left . . .' he said, in a whisper.

'What?'

Spurlock swallowed. 'If you left, I wouldn't blame you.' He let out a twisted chuckle. 'Sometimes I wish I could . . . just go away. Somewhere. Home.'

He gave Peter a twisted smile, as it that was funny.

An hour later, Peter's head was throbbing, so tight at the back of his neck it felt like some vicious little troll was grabbing him with long, dirty claws. He cut the Fiat's wheel left, swinging around an old Mercedes and climbing up the flying ramp that hooked the Santa Monica Freeway with the San Diego Freeway, gunning the engine on the downslope to kick in a little adrenaline surge. He was Luke Skywalker skimming the surface of the Death Star, Superman threading his way between skyscrapers; in Los Angeles, he thought, gasoline should be tax-deductible as a mental health expense.

He had been so stupid. He hadn't really seen it until Spurlock started talking. It wasn't anything Spurlock said exactly, but the pain and anger in his voice. At last he understood: That was how Tracy felt. *You don't know what you think*, she had said, throwing it at him like a fist. She was saying he was capable of anything, even becoming Max. But she was wrong. Fuck the job, fuck Max, fuck the parents, fuck the shame of failure too. There was only one thing left, one clear desire.

That day Peter drove from one end of Los Angeles to the other. He visited all of Tracy's haunts and restaurants, barged in on all her friends. No one had seen her or heard from her. Finally he just said to hell with it and drove to her house. He parked on the street, and walked right up to the front door, and rang the bell. 'Mister on the patio,' the maid said, stepping aside to let him pass, as if he were expected.

Peter walked through the house and out the back door, where he found Barry Rose sitting at a patio table flanked by Alan Kramer and Jack Rippert. 'Peter James,' Rose said, amused. 'Marlon said you might be coming up. Boys, you know Peter James, don't you.'

Peter leaned forward and shook all the hands.

'Poor Peter,' Rose continued. 'Just look at him.'

'Actually, I was looking for Tracy,' Peter said.

The maid came out, and Rose leaned back in his rattan throne. He looked at Peter. 'Something for you?'

'No thanks.'

'Come on, have a drink. You look like you could use one.'

They were all drinking beer, which was so unusual in weight-conscious Hollywood that it had to be ceremonial, part of some celebration. Exactly what kind became clear when Spurlock came out of the house trailing a long uncut fax. 'Aha,' Rose said.

'Here it is,' said Spurlock. He laid the fax out on the table, and Rippert leaned over to study it.

'Sit down, sit down,' Rose said. 'Have a beer. Want to talk to you.'

The maid waited. A beer would be nice. 'Corona,' Peter said.

'Sit down,' Rose said again. This time Peter obeyed, and then the men ignored him, as if they took his presence for granted. Rippert ran his finger down the fax, Spurlock stood there waiting like a lackey, Kramer sat back with a smug expression and grinned at Peter when their eyes met. It was late afternoon and the sunlight had gone gold, but the air was still summer-warm. They could have been planning a picnic.

Then Rippert looked up. 'Looks all right. I'll go over it in the office later. Unless he asks for a trailer for his surfboard or something, we can close on this tomorrow.'

They all laughed, and Peter understood that they were talking about Tom Hanks, who loved surfing. Rose smiled and pushed his chair back, taking a tiny sip of beer. 'Did I ever tell you guys about the time I tried to kill Max Fischer?'

Spurlock pulled up a chair.

'We were on the set of *Too Tough to Quit*, up near Valencia, in this little canyon where they shot the opening of *M*A*S*H*. The firearms guy was a gun nut, had hundreds of weapons, all kinds of veiny-looking things – I mean you gotta wonder about these gun wranglers – and he got us started target shooting. So we were shooting every day at this range we'd set up. And one day we go up there and Max has set up a bunch of targets, dummies of all the people I hated at the time – very realistic, faces and everything. He had the prop guys do them. There was Kirk Kerkorian, who ripped the beating heart out of MGM, may he eat dirt in hell, and nightmare talent like Jimmy Caan and Streisand and Dreyfuss, asses I had to kiss and kiss and kiss. And Max handed me a machine gun, a huge fucking thing, looked like a chunk of an aircraft carrier.'

He laughed but turned instantly fierce. 'Then I said to him, "Very funny, but this is the stupidest fucking thing you ever did. Now get rid of them." Because I didn't want to *read about it in the paper*. It was childish. It was *immature*. So what do you think he did?'

Peter didn't have to think long. 'Shot them himself.'

Rose cocked a finger and mimed: bullseye. 'Cut Kerkorian in half, blew Streisand apart. So I said, "Fine. Now it's part of *your* legend. Let's get out of here." But he *kept shooting*. With a crazy, fuck-you look on his face. And for the first time I saw what he was capable of.'

Rose looked around the table, waiting for his meaning to sink in. Then he smiled. 'He just goes too far,' he said, almost sad about it, as if Max were a precious resource wasted.

Spurlock prompted him: 'So you grabbed the machine gun?'

Rose's eyebrows pinched: Don't rush me, kid. He took a breath, exhaled, and only then continued: 'The wrangler had this box of handguns, and I picked a revolver and pointed it at him. I told him to put down the machine gun. And he wouldn't do it. He blew Richard Dreyfuss into itty bits. So I aim at him and I say, "I am going to shoot you right now, in the leg. Hopefully I won't hit a vein."'

Now there was a glint in Rose's eye, and Peter had the idea the old lion was showing them what *he* was capable of.

'What did he do?' Peter asked.

'He just stood there like a jerk. So I *had* to shoot him. Missed. For a second he looked like he was about to shoot back, but he didn't have the balls. He started running, and I shot at him a couple more times while he ran down the hill. Then I drove away and made him walk back to the set.'

Peter nodded, as if he understood the point of the story, though he still wasn't sure he did – unless it was that Rose was even crazier than Max, and therefore more formidable.

'I can't tell you how many people said, "I won't work with Max, I won't do the picture if Max is on it," ' Rose continued. 'And I'd tell 'em, no matter who they were, that Max worked for *me*. I turned down pictures for him.'

'Really?' Peter said.

'I *turned 'em down*. Because *he worked for me*.'

'He's not lying,' the Ripper said.

'We've all had to make allowances for Max,' Kramer said.

Spurlock grinned at Peter, inviting him to share in the moment, and a phrase popped into Peter's head: the Vipers' Club. It was something Tracy had said. Unless he was completely deluded, he had just been asked to join. At the very least they assumed he was already a member.

'Ah, to hell with him,' Rose said, waving a hand. 'I'm too old and too rich to spend my time worrying about Max Fischer.' He finally took the sip of beer and looked off across his estate. The yard lights came on under their little green lampshades.

Peter put down his beer. 'Is Tracy home?' he asked.

Rose peered at him, a squinty glare that shut him right up. When he spoke again it was in a quiet, soft voice. 'Listen to me carefully,' he said. 'This is how you define character – by how a person treats the people he *doesn't* need. Do you understand that?'

Peter could see the muscle roll back and forth against Rose's jawbone. He caught a whiff of the sweet hillside jasmine, blooming for another night.

'Years ago, Max and Tracy were very close,' Rose continued. 'They saw each other every day. But the day I fired him, he stopped talking to her. He *never spoke to her again*. Until now. And do you know why? Because he didn't *need* her anymore.'

The bitterness made Peter uncomfortable. He wasn't sure why, but he didn't want things between the two men to be quite so cold and bitter. Wasn't that how all this got started? And he didn't want these men to think he was a complete turncoat either, like Spurlock. 'But you worked together for so many years, you and Max,' he said. 'There must have been some good things.'

'Let me explain something to you, kid,' Rose answered. 'I've been in this business for thirty years, and one thing I've learned is there's only two kinds of people in this town – humans and animals.'

'Humans and animals,' Peter repeated.

'Let me tell you one more thing. Of all the top people in this business, the twenty-five most successful? I know every one of them, and *not one of them is human*.'

Rose leaned back in his chair and watched Peter, waiting for his response. Peter realized then that he felt sorry for him. Rose had spent his life building up walls of judgment, and now he was stuck inside them, alone.

Peter got up. 'I just want to see Tracy,' he said.

Rose just sat there, looking up. 'She's out. She's always out.'

'Do you know where she is?'

Rose shook his head.

'I think I'll go look for her.'

Rose shrugged. 'Just consider your options,' he said. 'Human or animal? Which are you going to be?'

Chapter Fifteen

On the Rox was almost empty, just a handful of young executives at the bar and Angie in her usual corner booth, flanked by two of her girls. She looked up as Peter crossed over, breaking out in a smile as she recognized him. 'Peter James,' she said happily. 'I was wondering when you'd come to see me.'

'I'm looking for Tracy,' Peter said.

'It's been Grand Central Station around here lately,' Angie said, ignoring the question. 'Everybody coming to ask me what I know about Tracy and Marina. That pervert loser Jennings West, that fat pig detective, and that fat pig ex-detective, all of them. Even the great Barry Rose. Go on, sit down.'

Angie just kept on talking, pausing every so often to puff on one of those thin 'women's' cigarettes. 'They all wanted me to tell them what I know – and I know the whole fucking story, baby.' She leveled her eyes at him when she said it, a challenge and a threat. 'So I said to Barry, "Listen, I'm a businesswoman, make me a proposition." I'm sure it pissed him off, because these guys expect women to kiss their ass, but I get tired, you know? I'm not some cheap little whore, I got a *business* here. I've been doing this one year, and already I'm the biggest there ever was in this town.'

Finally Peter gave in and sat down. Angie was coked out of her mind, and if she did know where Tracy was, it would take a while to steer her around to telling him. She was like Meursault in that way – listening was the tribute she extracted before she would tell you what you wanted. A waitress came by with a tray, and Peter ordered a beer. He was starting to feel shaky; this was one of those hangovers that got worse as the day went on.

'What about Meursault?' Peter asked, because she irritated him.

'*Meursault*? That fat old skag? She's *over*. Put a tag on her toe and slide her in the fucking drawer, you know what I mean?'

She rolled her eyes at her girls, who both giggled agreement: Meursault was over, totally.

'Tracy too,' Angie continued. 'She came to me. Wanted me to tell her everything about Marina and Max because we're both women. *Excuse me*? *Hello*? Because we both have *vaginas*, I should be doing you favors? I'm a businesswoman, baby – *pay me*.' Angie put a simpering look on and changed her voice to mock-girlish: "Oh, but I don't have any money, I'm just a helpless little girl. Daddy won't let me *charge* it."' She reverted to her real voice. 'So fine, bitch. Turn a trick for me.'

'You didn't really say that,' Peter said.

'Fucking A I did. Turn a trick, like all the other Daddy's girls.'

The waitress brought over the beer. She studied his face while he paid, and he wanted to tell her he was just talking to Angie, not doing business. 'What did she say?'

'She said she'd think about it.'

'I can't believe it.'

But the fact was, he could believe it, all too vividly: Tracy, with her latest tattoo, ready for the rosy crucifixion.

'Am I lying? And you know what I'd do? I send her up to Max Fischer. I bet he'd pay a hundred fucking grand for one night with her. Get that pushy detective of his to take a few pictures, good-bye rape case. Shit, I bet he'd pay a million. *Two* million. He'd have ol' Barry in the bankruptcy court.'

'I thought you and Barry were pals,' Peter said, drawn in despite himself.

'Listen – I sell to the highest bidder, you know what I'm saying? Besides, Barry's pissed off because some little whore got a case of amnesia. I told him, it's just like Hollywood, baby – you got to *pay to play*. One thing I'll say for Jennings West, he's not afraid to write a check.'

She was talking about Leela.

'Or throw a party for me. What's the matter, you *ashamed*? You want my help, but you're *ashamed*?' Again she exchanged looks of understanding with her two girls, shaking her head in disgust. 'Well, fuck that.' She said it teasingly, stretching out her leg as she spoke. She was wearing open sandals, and Peter noticed she had unusually long toes.

Then he heard a muffled ringing. Angie reached into her handbag and took out a cellular phone. 'Hello? No, Meursault's not here. She went out – out of the business.' Angie cackled, then quickly switched to a soft and seductive voice. 'This is Angie, I'm taking over from her. Remember Lexie? Blonde, all-American type? Just like Cheryl Tiegs. She works for *me* now. I'm the best game in town, baby.' She waited for a second, then smiled. 'What's your room number? Good. She's on her way. Just remember my name – *Angie*.'

She tapped the phone dead, then nodded to one of her girls. 'It's Sheik Yerbootie time,' she said.

Bye bye, Lexie.

'She's a beautiful girl,' Peter said, watching her leave. Angie smiled, a mixture of pride and cynicism, accepting the compliment and correcting it: a beautiful whore.

'If I can ever help you, make a referral or anything, I'll do it.'

Angie looked at him, and waited.

'Can I buy you a drink?' he asked.

Angie waited another moment, meeting his eyes. Then she nodded her head: Good boy. Smart boy. I accept. 'Campari and soda,' she said. Then she turned to the girl sitting so quietly beside her, the one who did not look like Cheryl Tiegs. 'It's Friday, right? Isn't that the hot night at Sin-a-Matic?'

Just past midnight, Peter stood at the Sin-a-Matic bar, nervously rattling the ice cubes in his drink – not that he could hear the rattle in the industrial din. The music sounded like an earthquake in an echo chamber: Chlunk! Chlunk! Chlunk! Chlunk! Chlunk! He'd been there almost half an hour, with no sign of Tracy.

He'd never been in a place like this before. The dance floor was ringed by video monitors playing porno movies, and a row of leather boys danced on a narrow stage in the back. Everyone seemed to have at least one tattoo. It was so crowded Peter kept getting pushed down the bar, squeezed on both sides by sweaty, shouting people. It seemed scary at first . . . until he realized that the biggest chunk of the crowd was just the usual movie-yuppie gang wearing nose rings that looked suspiciously removable: deviance as fashion. 'No, you can't get it in Tibet anymore, you have to go to Nepal . . .' 'At Clothes Whore, five hundred bucks . . .'

Peter waved at the bartender, calling for a second drink. Or was it his third? A man in mascara jostled him, made eye contact and then curled his lip in a sneer. Why? Hostility as fashion? Did that explain the metal detector at the door?

But what was he going to say to Tracy, if and when he found her? Sorry for everything? You were right?

The music washed over him like waves, sucking his mind away.

'Thank you,' Peter said sarcastically, handing a twenty to the bartender . . . who didn't even hear him, just nodded. . . . Good God, why was that boy on the monitors greasing up that gigantic squash?

Where was she? What was she doing? No answer on her home phone all night.

A man in a Lone Ranger mask came up and peered right in Peter's face, eyes glinting from their sockets like a pair of wolves lurking in the mouths of matching caves. Peter put a hand on his chest and pushed him away. Hostility as fashion indeed. Whoops came from the dance floor, and Peter saw that one of the young women had taken off her top. People made room for her and she danced, tossing her hair in rhythm to the pounding noise, a smile of innocent bliss on her face. He tried to picture himself sweaty and free, shirt off, throwing a pair of fine breasts around. How great that would be . . . no thoughts, just feeling . . .

A man in black appeared at his elbow, mouthing a question: 'Want some X?'

Which would be Ecstasy. The Love Drug, they called it. Was that the route to topless bliss? Peter had never taken it. He'd spent the entire *Bright Lights, Big City* era back at Butler Library, feeling lonely and superior.

'How much?'

'Twenty-five.'

Without thinking, Peter dug out the money and handed it over. On the monitors, the boy slid to his knees, handing the squash to an older man dressed in a dark suit. And on the dance floor the topless girl tossed her head, her face bright with joy. Peter smiled in her direction. He was just about to pop the little white pill in his mouth when he got a brilliant idea – buy more! Get Tracy to take it with him! Make love all night and tell all their secrets! Break through all the walls . . .

He pushed away from the bar, looking for the man in black. There he was, rounding a corner, heading toward the back . . .

The back? Was there a room back there?

Without bothering to excuse himself, Peter shoved his way through the crowd, found the corner and the dark doorway previously invisible in the shadows. He found himself in a small room with a pool table. So this was where the authentic Sin-a-Maticians hid, the ones who put the sin into cinema. There were ten or fifteen of them, most dressed in leather, several wearing harnesslike outfits full of straps and studs. One bare-chested boy had big brass rings in both nipples. The walls were decorated with S&M murals, dominatrixes in their black leather uniforms, whips poised above the pale buttocks of Old White Males. Then Peter saw a narrow passageway at the back of the room, promising adventures still more extreme. He started for it, sure that was where he'd find Tracy . . .

Then he heard her call his name, and there she was, behind him, bent over the table, pumping a pool cue through her fingers. He'd missed her at first, since she'd dyed her hair again: red this time. She nodded at him and went right back to lining up the shot. There was something else new, glinting in her left nostril: a delicate thread of gold.

'I see you everywhere,' Tracy said.

She was at once sarcastic and almost friendly, like life was just one big Tracy–Hepburn movie combat just another form of affection.

'Thanks for not calling me "the assistant",' he said.

Tracy smiled sweetly. 'Well, you're not anymore, I hear.' She lowered her head and drove her cue: *Craaack*. She missed. A man in a leather vest took over, and Tracy came up to Peter. She didn't seem to be with anyone.

'What are you doing here, anyway?' she said.

'Came looking for you.'

'How romantic.'

'Can we go somewhere and talk?'

Tracy looked toward the passageway leading off into darkness. Then she looked back at him, lips pursed. 'Want to try the back room?'

Peter shrugged, and looked meaningfully into her eyes: anything you want.

Tracy looked back, hesitated, then just let her body go slack and leaned against him. It was such an odd gesture, between surrender and relief. He didn't care. He didn't move at all, except to press her shoulder with one hand. He could feel her breasts press against him, and one hipbone, and a thigh.

'I'm sorry,' he said.

'I know.'

For another moment she just leaned against him. Then she sighed. 'Let's get out of here,' she said.

In the parking lot, they looked at each other nervously, and it was clear that neither one of them knew what to do next. So Peter pulled out the tablet of Ecstasy. 'Wanna get high?' he said.

'What is it?'

'X,' Peter said, as if he did it all the time.

'Why?'

He shrugged, as if it didn't matter. He pictured the two of them on the road, in a big old American convertible, driving to Flagstaff, to Taos, to Lubbock, someplace where no one knew them.

'I don't know,' he croaked. 'It's probably a dumb idea. I guess I just wanted . . .'

He shrugged, embarrassed to say it.

But then he realized, this is it. The critical moment. Don't hide in your pose of confusion. Don't be inarticulate, like some damn teenager, hoping she'll take it for cool. You *know* what you want.

So he just said it:

'Everything. Love. Absolution. Understanding. Redemption.'

He looked at her, trying to read her reaction. But he couldn't. 'Pretty corny, huh?'

Tracy studied him intently. And Peter, realizing she was taking him seriously, instantly veered in the opposite direction: What the hell am I getting into? Tracy Rose is the textbook definition of a pain-in-the-ass, high-maintenance woman, the type who would cheat on you just because she was starting to like you too much. 'I only have one tab, though,' he said.

But as she kept staring at him, he saw that her eyes were quick and full of intelligent pain, and anger, and suspicion . . . and the distant possibility of kindness, if deserved. All the right emotions. Yes, he liked them. They went such a long way down. And finally Tracy stopped staring at him and started digging in her little black purse. 'I think I have some X in here someplace,' she said.

*   *   *

The minute they got in the door, Tracy stripped to her underwear. 'It's so *hot*,' she said, throwing herself across Peter's unmade bed.

Peter considered joining her, but he felt jumpy. The X was coming on.

'Sorry it's a mess,' he said.

'I don't care,' she said.

So he lay down next to her, and for a while all he could do was wait for the rush to pass. His chest was tight and the room was so full of heat – sun on ancient deserts, on lumbering dinosaurs and the leathery wings of giant lizardy birds. He reached out to Tracy, just to stroke her, but after a few limp pats on her thigh his hand fell to his side. After a long time he heard her voice coming from a distance.

'You went away,' she said.

An hour had passed. His lips were cracked, his throat parched. 'Had to . . .'

'Why?'

'Out of control,' he said. He pictured a glass of water, moisture beading and dripping, ice twisting light.

Tracy got up on one elbow and studied him.

'Gotta stay on top of things,' he said, forcing the words down his thick tongue. 'Especially now.'

She kept looking at him, displeased.

It suddenly seemed very important to explain. 'I can't be like you,' he said.

She waited. Time passed. Mountains crumbled.

'You had everything,' Peter said. As he spoke the words he felt sure they were true, the key to all their problems, and he lost himself in twists of the idea: To have nothing meant to want everything . . . like Max . . . to have everything meant to want nothing . . . like Tracy . . . and to have just a piece meant . . . you went in search of the lost pieces . . .

Tracy's voice brought him back.

'I had everything?' she asked.

Peter reached out and traced a line along her knee. He felt guilty for neglecting her body.

'Beautiful. Rich. Two up on me.'

She laughed. The glass of water was becoming a distinct possibility. He had visualized it, and soon it would become real. And there you go, pushing yourself up, padding to the bathroom, twisting the faucet. He drank two glasses before taking Tracy the third. 'Thanks,' she said, giving the word a little spin, keeping her ironic distance.

Peter stood looking down at her, poor thing, not nearly as tough as she acted, laugh lines around her eyes giving the lie to the teenage dose of mascara. He was wrong. She didn't have everything. She didn't want nothing. But she was going away from him now, just as he'd gone away from her on the X rush. 'You're not so tough,' he said.

'Yes I am,' she said.

'Still fighting their battles?'

'Still working?'

'Nah,' Peter said. Now that he had started talking, he was beginning to relax. Maybe things would still be okay. 'You were right the first time. I'm unemployed. You may now refer to me as the ex-assistant.' He giggled. 'The X-assistant.' When the giggle-fit passed he saw concern on Tracy's face, as if she was realizing for the first time how rough the last week had been on him. 'Did you know Detective Spinks's first name?' he asked.

She nodded.

'It's Patty,' he said anyway. As if it followed directly, he added: 'What I can't figure is who you really hate, me or Max. Or is it your Dad?'

Tracy kept looking right at him, dead-serious. 'Who do you want me to hate?'

Maybe it was the X but everything they said seemed so very important, and this the most important of all, because what she was really saying was – yes, the X made it all clear – who do you want me to love? In a way it was the same question.

'Me,' he said. 'Hate me.'

Somehow it had gotten to be dawn. The morning light was leaking in around the edges of the curtains, making the dark seem a little more decadent and private. It was time to kiss her. Tracy patted the bed next to her, and Peter rolled over against her. She helped him take off her panties and bra, but they just lay there, kissing vaguely, animals nuzzling on a hot day. He tasted her tongue, bitter with tobacco. He stroked her hair.

'What was he like, back at the beginning?' Peter asked. 'When you were a kid?'

Tracy hesitated. 'Back then?' she said. She paused so long Peter thought she'd drifted off to other thoughts. Then she started talking, in a detached storyteller voice: 'Well, at first it was always the three of us, Max, Marina, and me. We were like six or seven, and Max was twenty-six or twenty-seven, something like that. We called him The Fun Man because he made everything into an event. Did magic tricks. Filled entire rooms with balloons. Made chocolate soup. The old man was so out of it in those days, so Max drove us to the mall and helped with homework and even, a few years later, took me to the doctor to get a diaphragm – my idea, and he was so embarrassed it was cute. That was when Max was golden. Did he ever tell you about the time he spent in the hospital?' Tracy asked. 'When he was a kid?'

Peter shook his head. 'He never talks about his childhood. I didn't think he had one.'

Six months, Tracy said. Six months he was in the hospital with rheumatic fever. And all that time he watched the kids play in the park outside the hospital window. That was when he discovered movies. And before long he asked for a box of toy soldiers, though he was almost twelve and too old for them, because he had an idea – he wanted to arrange them, pose them for the 'camera', his eye. And the funny thing was he didn't make the soldiers fight. He made them play. Just like the kids playing outside, only more happily and better composed. 'Sometimes I think of him as that kid,' Tracy said, 'making his imaginary friends play *better* . . .'

By then Peter was up on one elbow, drawing circles around Tracy's belly button. Pale orange light fell in the window, making an orange square on the bedsheet. Next to her new red hair, it looked art-directed.

'So what happened?' he asked.

Tracy shrugged. 'What do I know? I was sixteen when he and Daddy broke up. I was like, "What?" I thought they were *married*. Even six months later, when I graduated, I was like, "Daddy, does Max know I graduated from high school? Why doesn't he call me?"'

Tracy bit the pillow, then laughed. 'So I decided to seduce him. I always felt he was sort of interested, except I was off limits . . .'

Peter felt a stab of jealousy.

'. . . and I wasn't off limits any more.'

'And?'

'What do you think? This is Hollywood – Dad started inviting me to his industry parties the day I grew *breasts*.' She spat the word out like it was a bug that had crawled into her mouth. Then she went quiet. Peter pictured Tracy at one of those parties, flaunting her nymphet body. She would have worn a halter top and stolen drinks from the bar until she was giddy. There would be torches burning in the yard and waiters in white coats.

'What about Marina?'

Tracy drifted off again. When she returned she brought back a sigh. 'We were kids, you know? We played. Her dad made boobs. Bigger boobs and smaller noses. Then we grew up, blah blah blah.'

'It's not your fault, you know,' he said.

'Don't get all shrinky on me, Peter.'

She seemed very distant. But after a moment she shrugged and rolled over, turning her back to him, then scooted over until their bodies touched. At first they just lay against each other, then she started moving her hips. He kissed her shoulder. After a few minutes she arched her back and wiggled a little to help him in.

'Am I going to get in trouble for this?' Peter said. 'Are you going to bring charges again?'

'Shut up,' Tracy said.

After ten minutes, twenty minutes, she pulled away and pushed him onto his back. She climbed on and kept up a slow, lazy rhythm, like a rower out for the long haul. Both of them were sweating, the rich dank smell of her filling the whole room. He breathed deeply and felt: This is right. This is good. He came, and eased her over on her back, then started to slide down her body, and he felt almost spiritual about it: a devotion. But she pulled at his hair. 'It's okay,' she said. He pushed her hands away and burrowed on down. 'No,' she said, tugging at his hair this time hard enough to hurt. He shook his head: He wanted to please her, didn't she understand? Maybe this would unite them. '*Goddamnit, no,*' she said, and rolled away.

'Another time, okay? I'm really tired.'

'Okay.'

'That's just really personal.'

'I was feeling personal.'

She didn't say anything for such a long time that he thought she had fallen asleep. Then she said: 'I'm sorry, okay?'

'Okay,' he said.

When they woke up it was night again. They ordered food in, got a liquor store to deliver a bottle of wine, answering the door wrapped in towels – the unspoken rule was that they had to stay naked – and spent hours talking about their pasts. Peter confessed weird little details he'd never told anyone, like how his father picked the ice cubes out of the trays with his fingernails – amazing he didn't measure them with a fucking caliper – and how his mother the cipher used to stand there saying oh dear during the ritual recitation of his sins: shoddy, imprecise, undisciplined. She told him about the good times, playing at the beach, doing shows at school, running around with Marina when flirting was a new and giddy concept. And her Dad coming home with costumes – astronaut, cowboy, belly dancer, princess . . . she'd forgotten about that . . .

But there was still something wrong. There are times when a bridge opens between people, as a crush is a bridge to true romance, and this was one of those times. The bridge was open. But they weren't quite crossing it. Something was keeping them stuck. That's why they were naked, Peter realized, as a kind of magic charm to keep the bridge open. But it wasn't enough. Finally, he blurted out the question that was still bothering him: 'So why'd you do it, Tracy?'

Tracy propped herself up on one elbow. She didn't bother to cover up, as if they were real lovers. 'You know what it really was? Max wouldn't pick me up. He refused to pick me up.'

'When?'

'After I left you.' She laughed. 'I figured, he was your boss, he was the reason you were acting like such an asshole, so the least he could do was pick me up. So I called him from a pay phone.'

'And he said no?'

'He said it was five o'clock in the fucking morning, take a fucking cab.'

Peter stared at the tattoo of the bumblebee. Was that really it? Max made her take a cab, so she tried to destroy his life? Was she just another Hollywood brat, so spoiled by the world of bigger boobs and smaller noses that she didn't quite realize other people were real? He didn't want to believe it. If that was true, then everything he was feeling was just . . . foolish. 'Let's leave this place,' he moaned.

She didn't hesitate. 'Don't be ridiculous.'

But she sounded a little sad about it, so he asked again. 'We could go to Santa Fe.'

'I hate Santa Fe. It's like a fucking theme park. Besides, everyone I know has a place there.'

There's something I'm not getting, Peter thought. Why is she still so angry? He'd given up the job, hadn't he? What did she want from him? Then he noticed that his answering machine was blinking up a storm. He'd forgotten about turning off the volume. Automatically, he hit playback.

'Where are you? Let's talk. *Call* me.'

It was Max, popping back into his life like a demented Jack-in-the-Box. Peter started to turn it off, but Tracy stopped him. 'No,' she said. 'I want to hear.'

The second message was curt: 'It's ten P.M. Call me *now*.'

The third was informative: 'I'm in a forgiving mood and you better call me soon. We have to discuss.'

After that the messages started getting less friendly. 'I *told* you to pick up your messages every hour, asshole. Just because I fired you doesn't mean you can go *out of touch*.'

'It's two. You're fired *again*.'

Tracy started laughing. Peter joined in.

'It's two twenty. Don't use me on your résumé, pal.'

'I gotta get down to the editing room. I got an *idea*. Where the fuck *are you*?'

Tracy shook her head. 'He really is insane, isn't he?' She seemed pleased, even proud.

At 3:00 A.M. Max's voice sounded woozy. 'You little shit,' he said. 'You're in a fog half the time, pretending to think. So you can feel superior. You don't care about me. You *used* me, Peter. You *used* me.'

Tracy nodded in agreement: He's got a point there.

At 6:00 A.M. the messages resumed. 'You were at Sin-a-Matic last night. You left with Tracy. Don't think you can outsmart *me*.'

At six thirty two: 'This is your last chance. I need you now. I don't want to have to call someone else.'

At seven twelve: 'You're *over*. You hear me? *Over*! Terminated, finished, *extinct*! The next time I see you, you're going to be asking me if I *want a cocktail before dinner*. Will I have *the baked potato or the rice*?'

Peter turned off the machine. 'Good-bye, Max,' he said.

'You sorry?'

He shrugged, then shook his head. 'Gotta wake up sometime.'

She should have been happy. This was what she wanted, right? For him to show backbone, to tell Max to fuck off. But she wasn't happy. She frowned and looked away. And that's when it finally came clear. It wasn't about him. It was about Max. Peter felt a hunch, took a chance: 'It wasn't you, was it? Who slept with Max back then. It was Marina.'

She rolled away again. 'Good guess, Sherlock.' She said it casually, but the words fell into the room with the density of lead, the way grave words do, creating their own cushion of silence around them. That was it, the deep dark secret, tossed off while she was rolling over – not while she was lying next to him looking deep into his eyes. Remember that, he told himself, with that prophylactic double vision that insulates people at dramatic moments in their lives – if you ever actually do make a movie, this is how the truth comes out, while they're rolling away from you, thinking it's about time to leave . . .

'He wanted me,' she said, as if it was a point of pride. 'There was never any question about that. But he was afraid of my father – afraid of losing his big chance to be in the movies. So he went for the next best thing.'

She said it with such contempt. Peter stared at her naked back and pictured a tiger there, curled up on her shoulder.

'And she was with him that night too,' Peter said.

Tracy went very still.

'That's why he told you to take a cab,' Peter said. 'She was with him.'

She didn't have to answer. Peter knew it was true. It explained everything – why Max lied to the cops and why Tracy let her father blame him. He asked his next question gently. 'You knew it too, didn't you?'

Slowly, Tracy nodded. 'I heard her voice. In the room.'

Peter stroked her hair. 'He betrayed you twice.'

She nodded again.

He kept stroking her hair, and after a few mute minutes she put her head against his shoulder and let tears flow. She cried for ten

minutes. By that time she was curled into him, thigh to thigh.
'You didn't, did you?' Peter asked.

'What?'

'Kill her?'

'If I did?'

He thought about it for just a second, hardly that. 'We'll have to get a good lawyer,' he said.

She kissed him hard, on the mouth. Then she pushed him back and started nibbling her way down his chest.

When Peter woke up she was gone. He looked at the clock: 3:30 P.M. It was Saturday afternoon already.

He found the note on his bathroom sink, under his toothbrush. Dear Peter, it said. You were so sweet. Maybe Santa Fe isn't such a bad idea . . . but . . . you made it clear to me last night, he killed the wrong one, I was the one he wanted. And I deserved it. So . . . maybe I'll see you again sometime . . . X X X all over.

Peter read the note three times, then threw it down and started putting on his clothes.

Chapter Sixteen

Back and forth and back and forth Max rolled, driven by a high-tech experimental wheelchair he cajoled out of the hospital because he was *Max Fischer*, goddamnit. When he wasn't auto-pacing, he brooded over Andy Potter's shoulder, watching every click and drag: 'Scene 93, take one. Scene 93, take two. Scene 93, take three . . .' And on up to take seventeen. Meanwhile Potter kept up a droning narrative. 'Started on the edit droid ten years ago, when Lucas first came out with it,' he said. 'That was the first nonlinear system, brilliant at the time, but now it's like an old Ford. With Avid I can click any take, access it in seconds.'

Max listened closely. The technology was important, another piece to the great puzzle. Intelligence. But Peter was going quietly insane. He wasn't sure exactly who Tracy meant by *he*, so he came here. After all, Max was the key, the problem Tracy was all twisted around. When he explained it to Max, Max glared at him, grumbled about betrayal and then – to Peter's immense surprise and gratitude – agreed to help. But first he had some work to do. That was twenty minutes ago.

'Max, we gotta *go*.'

'She's a big girl, Peter. And I'm screening this fucking thing tonight.'

Potter tucked a hippie curl behind his ears. 'If we didn't have to go back to celluloid I could snip and tuck and stitch it with a little morphing, no problem. On the computer you can morph for, like, fifty bucks a shot now.'

There were four people in the cramped room, counting the assistant running errands for Potter. On a table behind them were a dozen baskets of candy, no doubt left over from a movie set – the crafts services department always made sure there was plenty of candy around for those double-golden-time sugar blasts. Peter chewed on a piece of licorice, and felt comfort.

'I still haven't figured a way around this,' Potter said. He was looking at the final sequence in the barn, the love-death. He played it through. And it was clear that it all happened much too fast. But the reshoots they wanted were out of the question now.

'You see what he did.'

'Yeah, I see,' Max said, flipping the toggle switch that put him into reverse and grabbing a handful of jelly beans. He started hurling jelly beans into his mouth. 'It must have been one of the days I was out of town.'

'What?' Peter asked.

Potter nodded toward the screen. 'Fargo left out a couple of key shots. It's an old director's trick, so they can guarantee a few days of reshoots – tell everybody second unit is going to handle it, then don't tell the second unit.'

'I'm going to have to kill that kid,' Max said. 'Peter, put him on the death list.'

'You're an asshole,' Peter said.

Max ignored him. 'Let's see all the throat-slashing takes; maybe there's some way we can stitch 'em together. Stretch 'em out.'

Potter was back at his keyboard, typing out commands. The screen went black, and the face of Ronald Reagan appeared in the corner, the hands of a clock pivoting on his nose. Potter pushed another curl of hair behind his ears. 'Let's rock 'n' roll,' he said, clicking the icon for the first take.

It was dull work. 'I love you' over and over from every poss-ible angle, gills bubbling red over and over, the razor slicing flesh over and over . . . close-ups, medium shots, long shots, over-the-shoulder shots. With the computer Potter could snip a shot in and watch the sequence, then slap in another one and see how that looked. And so it went, over and over: 'I love you . . . I love you . . . I *love* you . . .'

Potter attacked the keyboard, murmuring under his breath: 'It's not exactly an original line.'

A new take jumped into the sequence. 'I love *you*.' Only the camera angles changed.

Max sat hunched over in a deep-thought posture: chin tucked in, eyes narrowed, lips compressed, head nodding. Every so often he jiggled the toggle switch and made the chair rock. The pane in the door glowed gold, lit by the California sun.

Then Max sat up straight. 'It needs to be more *violent*,' he said.

Potter nodded, playing through the whole sequence again. Max was right. It was a nice enough scene, but it just wasn't the end of a movie. Max zoomed back, then shot forward again. His lips worked silently, and he thrust an arm forward. Then he did the entire routine again, this time with a grunt. And again. 'That's it,' he said. 'I got it.' He acted out his idea, banging on the crafts services table until the candy jumped. 'The hayloft has a door. Who cares why, it's some kinda special *gourmet* hay, it's *movie hay*, and they don't quite escape – bad guys *chase* them! They *bang* on the door! Could do a lot with sound effects here. So the pressure is on, we cut in some chasing-the-bad-guy shots, *make it more desperate*.'

They all fell silent, contemplating the idea.

'Fargo's problem is he doesn't like *action*,' Max said. 'Thinks he's fucking Bertolucci, but he doesn't know his A-S-A from his A-S-S. I gave him my whole spiel: Artists do what they wanna do. Entertainers do what the audience *wants* them to do. When I make a film I go, This'll kill 'em. Francis Coppola, he goes, this kills *me*.' Then he wheeled around and glared at Peter as if Peter had disagreed. 'I *serve* the audience. It's the artists who are saying, "*Fuck you*, I'm gonna do exactly what I want to do, and I don't care whether you like it or not." And the critics *love* them. All I wanna do is make them happy, and they *hate* me.'

A knock on the door stopped Max in mid-monologue. Peter cracked it open to reveal a homey-looking blonde in a hippie skirt: serious eyes, wide hips and thick ankles, and straight 1960s hair. It wasn't parted in the middle but it could have been. She held the hand of a towheaded child. Max took note of them and continued: 'I can write the reviews right now: Max Fischer fucks up Shakespeare! Max Fischer pisses on literary classic!'

The woman pulled her child back and peered into the dark room. 'Andy?'

Potter crossed the room, opening the door. 'Meet the wife and kid,' he said. The little girl stepped forward and Potter crouched down, opening his arms and coming up with an armful of happy pink child.

Her mother smiled. 'Hi,' she said. 'We were just on our way back from school.'

Potter looked apologetic. 'They haven't seen me for days,' he said, nuzzling his daughter. The girl's eyes flashed with pure delight, and Peter thought how odd it was, such a young fresh thing here in this world of men and dust. It was a glimpse of another Hollywood, the hippie editor with his wrinkled shirt and jeans, his earth wife and heaven child, dropping by the studio on their way from *school*, for God's sake.

'You like candy?' Max said, zooming over to the crafts services set-up. He grabbed a handful of Tootsie Rolls and dropped them into the kid's hand.

'Oh, I don't think . . .' the hippie mom began.

But Max grabbed a fistful of lemon drops and pushed them into the girl's other hand, so many that a half-dozen fell to the floor. 'That's really enough,' the mom said, with a nervous laugh. But Max wouldn't stop: He grabbed a couple of licorice ropes and wrapped them around the girl's neck, then ripped the wrapping off a lollipop with his teeth and stuck it in her mouth. The little girl's eyes went huge.

'There ya go,' Max said. Then he patted the girl on the head and aimed the wheelchair for the door. 'We're gonna need some reshoots,' he told Potter.

Peter smiled at the child, trying to catch her attention by wiggling his eyebrows. But she was watching Max, wide-eyed – the brat hadn't even noticed him, but would probably remember Max until her dying day.

'Then we're back to square one.'

'*No*,' Max said, shaking his head furiously. 'All we need is a door – a door *closing*. Some fists banging against it. And a hand coming through a window. Three shots, no actors. Just *hands*. And I know just where to get them.'

With that Max swung the chair around again and zoomed through the door. By the time Peter caught up with him, he was already halfway down the alley. In the doorway left behind, Peter heard the little girl giggle: 'He was a *funny* man.'

Up the alley! Past Myrna Loy! Down the alley and then left, down another alley, past the generator trailers humming away, past the actors waiting nervously to be called, past the Teamsters already asleep in their trucks. Max racing along so fast Peter had to trot to keep up. He made it almost to Washington Boulevard before he marched up to a PA standing with his walkie-talkie in front of a huge stage door. 'Where's Dick?' he said.

'On the set. But—'

They pushed through the little door next to the big door and walked past the craft services tables, stepping over the giant worm ducts that carried air-conditioning to the hot sets. Beyond that was outer space – craggy rocks of a desert planet, wounded starfighters lying on their backs with huge red holes in their chests. One had half his face blown off, but he was laughing and joking with his dead mates. 'Perfect,' said the director, instantly recognizable by his casual air of authority and the long camera lens hanging from his neck.

It was Dick Donner, best known as the director of *Superman* and the *Lethal Weapon* movies. Unlike the typical film-nerd Hollywood director, Donner had the weather-beaten face of a fishing boat captain just in with a fine catch and heading off to celebrate in the rowdiest bar he could find. '*Max*,' he said. 'What happened to you?'

'Ran into a girl,' Max said.

Donner accepted the response without question, turning with a happy smile to his set. 'Look at this. Isn't this great? Like playing soldiers with real soldiers.'

For a few minutes Max and Donner enthused about the set, the lights, the costumes, the special computerized crane. Peter noticed Max wincing, and realized he was in pain. Then someone pushed into their circle, and Peter noticed the tiny tape recorder she held discreetly in her hand.

It was Kit Bradley, the *Hollywood, Inc.* reporter. Max gave a visible jerk. 'We were going to call you today,' he said.

'Too late,' she said. 'We went to page.'

Donner put an avuncular hand on Bradley's shoulder. 'My favorite journalist. Did a great piece on *Assassins* in her magazine.'

Bradley blushed. Peter remembered the piece, which had been awfully warm and cuddly for Bradley. And damned if she wasn't looking up at Donner now, blushing and giving him the Nancy-Reagan-adoring-look. 'It was one of my . . . kinder pieces,' she said.

But Max was telling Donner what he wanted.

'No sweat,' Donner said. 'Glad to help.'

'Great,' Max said. 'We'll rush 'em over to Technicolor. We'll slap them in wet this afternoon. And I'll owe you forever.'

Max started swinging toward the door. His face was coated with pain-sweat, but still he hustled along at dangerous speeds over the air-conditioning ducts and thick electrical cables. 'Come on, Peter,' he said. 'I thought you were in such a fucking hurry.'

Bradley was right behind them. 'Max? Don't you want to know what my story is going to say?'

Max stopped and turned sharply, so that Bradley had to pull up short. The sweat stained his shirt now, a sweat-delta. 'Write what you want to write, Kit,' he said.

'Yes, but . . .'

'Write what you want to write.'

They reached the stage door, open now, two stories high and padded to muffle the noises of the world. 'But I want it to be accurate,' Bradley said. 'I want it to be true. Were you sleeping with Marina Lake?'

'*Write what you want to write.*'

Max rolled into his office, which already had a little ramp installed for him. 'Sarah! Get the lab on the phone, for chrissake!' Peter followed him, almost bumping into Flip Mosely, who sat in Max's office in his own wheelchair with a copy of his script in his lap.

'See what a schmuck I am?' Max said to Mosely. 'He breaks my leg and I give him his job back.'

'I didn't break his leg,' Peter said. 'He's a fucking pathological liar. And I'm not coming back to work for him either.'

Sarah shouted from the front desk. 'Technicolor on line one!'

Max rolled to his desk and snatched up the phone, knocking over several priceless antiques. 'Phil, I gotta problem. I need a rush job, I mean like *rush rush rush*. Gotta slap it in wet in . . . three hours. Can you do it?'

While Max was talking, Peter turned to Mosely and said the first thing that came to his head. 'I got an idea for your screenplay. What if the girl who gets killed is a hooker, and the second girl, the girl the blind detective falls for, turns out to be a nice college girl, a friend of the hooker. She feels guilty for some reason, maybe the girl was hooking to pay her college tuition or something, so she takes over her dead friend's tricks to find the killer?'

Mosely frowned. 'Not bad,' he said.

Max thanked the guy from Technicolor and slammed down the phone.

'So the blind guy *follows* her,' Peter continued. He's waiting in the street in agony, not knowing what sordid thing she's doing up there.'

'A white cane tapping, red heels by the side of a bed.'

'One of those SROs in Manhattan, and he's waiting by the trash cans outside, and he lifts up his cane and starts smashing the trash cans. A rat darts out—'

'And he *spears* it,' Max said, rocketing his wheelchair forward.

'First clue of his special powers,' Mosely said.

'While she's up there screwing some dirtbag . . .'

'. . . and he doesn't know she's really doing it to *solve the crime* . . .'

They paused, nodding happily, relishing the twist.

'Max . . .'

'If she actually turns tricks, she's soiled,' Mosely said.

'Max, we should go.'

'So she dies,' Max said. He added, offhand, as if it were a given: 'Tragically. Redeemed by death.'

Mosely nodded. The redemptive-death bit never failed; in just a hundred years, Hollywood had saved more sinners than the Catholic church.

'I always thought she should die anyway,' Max said. '*Somebody's* got to die.'

Which reminded him of something. 'Let's get the fuck out of here. Peter, you coming?'

As they left, Max tossed back over his shoulder: 'I'll give you one fifty over four for the script, Flip. But start getting used to the idea that you're not going to direct.'

Flip rolled at the door. 'What? Why not?'

'Stamina, my friend,' Max said.

'Then I'm not selling the script, not in a million fucking years.'

'Fine.'

'I'll take it to Barry Rose first!'

'Go right ahead.'

* * *

Max's wheelchair wouldn't fit into the trunk of the Fiat, so they had to leave it behind. They weren't even out the gates before they started arguing.

'I'm telling you, it's Jennings West. I've been thinking about it – why's he been so friendly? Why is he so involved?'

'He's got reasons,' Max said.

'And don't forget Marina worked for him. Motives is what he's got.'

'Jennings is a pussy,' Max said. 'Don't forget – plot comes from character. Now Barry, he's a killer. Barry is the one behind all this, I promise you. So go to the baseball game. He'll be there.'

'You just want to go to the game.'

'That's what Tracy would expect. That's where she'd go.'

'Bullshit.'

'It'd be the perfect scene. Come *on*. You know she's a drama queen. If she's not there we go straight to Jennings, I swear.'

Finally Peter gave in, pointing the Fiat toward Santa Monica.

'One thing you gotta get straight,' Max said. 'Before I went to work with him,' Max continued, 'Barry Rose had never produced a movie. Don't laugh, listen to me – he had *never produced a movie*. He was a studio executive. He didn't know what making a movie *was*. All he knew was, "Sure, here's the money, go ahead and make it." He didn't even *like* movies – he liked show girls. He didn't care about movies. He didn't know anything about movies. What he knew about was hondeling – which I *learned*.'

Peter just drove and let the words wash over him. Max was doing it again, trying to suck Peter into his world, to pummel him into seeing things his way. It was his way of saying 'I forgive you.'

'Barry's idea of being a producer was setting up a bunch of shitty development deals all over town, taking a screenwriter in and pitching, and picking up fifty grand here and there in fees, hoping one of them hit. What that got you was a bunch of shitty movies – I could see that – so I bought this script, made it on my own, practically. Barry hated it, couldn't see why I was spending so much time on the set, said I was just trying to build my own relationships. And that was *Cyberkill*. After that he started leaving production to me, but he made it like an insult, like it was too plebeian for him to bother with. He had to spend all his time on those important *development deals*. There was nothing he loved more than getting one of those articles in the trades listing all your projects. It was *pathetic*.'

As he listened to Max, Peter thought about the phrase people always used to describe Hollywood: a business of relationships. What they really meant was a business of *bad* relationships, really bad relationships, where ordinary slights and insults amounted to actual battle damage; a nasty off-the-record remark to a reporter was the industry equivalent of burning a village or assassinating a rebel leader.

'You think I treated you like shit? When he fired me he scheduled an hour just to tell me all the reasons I would never work again. When I needed money Barry would make me *sign a loan*. One time we were shooting in New York and he sent me back to California for a few weeks, but he made me keep my hotel room at the Sherry just in case. But the studio won't pay your per diem if you're in L.A., so I had to pick it up myself. I tried to explain this to Barry and he says, "*Handle it*."'

They were crossing Sepulveda now, cutting up toward Brentwood. Peter glanced over at Max, who seemed to be enjoying himself. 'Even with all that, you don't really think Barry killed Marina, do you?'

Max thought about it, then shrugged. 'He's more the type to have someone do it for him.'

'A new category in the job description of the Hollywood assistant,' Peter said.

'That's an old category. You just didn't read the whole contract.'

'So why'd you and Barry stay together for ten years, if you hated him so much?'

Max didn't hesitate. 'I believe in the *traditions*,' he said. 'He was my mentor. He brought me in.'

The answer was too pat. Hyperdrive Max Fischer, sticking ten unhappy years for tradition? No, it had to go deeper. Their partnership was like a marriage, and something deep down in the heart of it had split like a fissioning atom, throwing off energy in huge and dangerous shards. Tracy was the result. And Marina . . .

'Like I brought *you* in,' Max continued. 'And then I'll be like a proud father when *you* go out and kick butt.'

'Or you'll be like Barry Rose, and do everything you can to kick *my* butt.'

'Don't be ridiculous,' Max said.

289

*　　*　　*

It was a glorious day on the softball field. The air was virginal, and the mountains stood surprisingly close, as if leaning forward to watch the game. Max leaned on Peter, hopping forward on one foot. They went straight to Barry Rose, who was sitting in the first row of the bleachers near the first base line. 'Hey, Barry,' Max said. 'You gonna play? Gonna get in there and get your hands dirty?'

Rose looked down his nose at Max, as if he'd just noticed a filthy beggar holding out his hand. 'You're the only person I ever met who fakes his injury before the game.'

'Anticipation, Barry. You taught me that.'

'Would you just stop,' Peter said to Max. Then he turned back to Rose. 'Have you seen Tracy?'

'She dropped by the house, then left again. Why?'

'I think she's in trouble.'

On the baseball field, the game continued. Max's relief pitcher threw a curveball that curved a little too much, almost hitting the batter. 'You squat when you pee,' a Thorn shouted.

Ball one.

'Did she say where she was going?' Peter asked.

Rose shook his head. He was watching the game now, trying to pretend they weren't standing there. This was stupid, Peter thought. It was Jennings. It had to be. The batter popped up the next ball and the shortstop caught it, ending the inning. The Fischer Kings started running in.

'What's the score?' Max said.

'We're ahead two runs,' Rose answered.

'*What*?' He nudged Peter. 'Take me to the bench. I gotta talk to these guys.'

'Max, we should—'

'Her own father doesn't give a damn. We can take *one* minute.'

The bench was on the way back to the car, so Peter gave in again. 'Thirty seconds,' he said. Max used every one, giving his team a pep talk on the general theme of: If you don't win this game every one of you will be hanging from a gibbet with a flock of hungry crows pecking out your eyes.

'Okay, Max, let's go,' Peter said.

Max cupped his hands and yelled to the runner up at bat, adding a carrot to the stick: 'Get a home run, and I'll make you a vice-president.'

The runner looked back. 'Production or development?'

'Whatever,' Max shouted.

The runner turned for the pitch – and hit a line drive past the first baseman into right field.

'Max, I'm going now. Are you coming?'

'Jesus, Peter,' Max said, looking longingly at his row of batters. 'You don't know what she's going to do, or when she's going to do it. Besides, my movie starts in an hour and a half. You know what that means? The first live audience. Why don't we just call the cops?' He turned and yelled at the pitcher: 'Come on, you deadbeat, throw the fucking ball.'

Peter pulled Max's arm off his neck and dumped him on the bench. Then he stood there, trying to decide whether to hit him or not.

Then the batter connected, a clean drive right past the pitcher's head, deep into center field. 'Yes!' Max shouted.

That did it. Tracy was off someplace getting herself into danger, looking for the punishment these two old bastards deserved, and all Max cared about was winning his stupid baseball game. 'All right, stay then,' Peter yelled. 'I can't believe I'm still waiting on you like a fucking servant. I can't believe I've been taking your abuse for three months! And nine days eight hours and twenty-six miserable crapulous nail-pulling thumbscrew-twisting minutes! You're such an obnoxious *thing*! You're such a *monster*!'

The game stopped, and everyone was watching. Even Barry Rose was watching. And Peter discovered that despite his concern for Tracy he was still able to enjoy the moment – he, Peter James, was yelling at Max Fischer! He could feel the eyes on him, sense the quickening of attention! 'God *damn* you Max, you gaping *hole*! You *crevice*!'

Then applause broke out – not just from the Thorns but from Max's team too. From the other side of the plate, Rose watched and grinned. He lifted his fist and gave Peter the thumb's up sign. Even Max seemed pleased.

'What? Why are you looking at me that way?'

Peter just kept staring.

'What? What?'

'Barry told me something yesterday,' Peter finally said, taking a breath to control himself. He stepped close to Max, speaking softly so that no one else heard. 'He said there were only two kinds of people in Hollywood – humans and animals.'

'Your point?'

'What are you, Max?'

'Don't be a jerk.'

'Which are you?'

'I'm about to fire you again.'

Peter ignored that. 'Tracy told me why she let her dad call the cops,' he said. 'Why all this got started.'

Max frowned, his face suspicious. 'Why?'

'Because she called you that night, and you told her to take a cab.'

Max puffed up, about to explode into Mad Max – and then he exhaled and shrank back down into normal human dimensions. Even a little smaller.

'What are you, Max?' Peter repeated. 'Human or animal?'

Max cast a longing eye at the softball game. He looked down at his leg. He looked at his watch.

Decisions, decisions . . .

Chapter Seventeen

The Fiat sped up toward the hills. 'This is ridiculous,' Max grumbled. 'We're not detectives. We don't even have guns. There's no point in being a detective if you don't have a gun. It's like being a cowboy without a horse. How're ya gonna ride into the sunset on public transportation? I can just see the Lone Ranger going "Hiyo, subway!"'

When Peter didn't respond adequately, since he wasn't really listening, Max snatched up the car phone and dialed the cutting room. 'Did it come in? How does it look? Take it over at five to seven, I'm running late.'

As they cut onto the 405, Max called Sarah and asked her to patch him through to the projection booth at the Culver Theater. It was right across from the studio lot, and Max had screened many a movie there, had even sent up a bottle of champagne to the projection booth after that first delirious screening of *Blood Hunt*. 'Hey, Santino, Max Fischer here. How's the family? Your health? . . . It's coming over at five of. Try to hold it till about ten, fifteen after, okay? I'm running late.'

Peter noted the gentle voice, the unusual personal questions: Max was acting the patrón. It couldn't have been just to buy the extra few minutes. Maybe it was a superstitious thing, propitiation of the gods; after all, the projectionist was the guy who controlled the light, and when all was said and done that was what it all came down to, light and how it bounced off things. Guys who could say 'Let there be light' and have it come true deserved a certain respect.

The skyscrapers of Westwood slid slowly past, some of them straight modernist boxes and others all odd angles, like the Big One had already hit. 'Go to Laurel Canyon,' Max said.

'I think Beverly Glen will be faster,' Peter said.

'Excuse me? Am I still the boss? Do I ever get my way anymore?'

Peter turned left, going up Beverly Glen.

'I can't believe I'm doing this,' Max whined. 'I fire you again. You're fired.'

Peter drove on.

Max looked at his watch again. 'Twenty-four minutes to curtain. If I'm not the first to see the cards, I'll kill you. I'm not kidding. I've been working on this movie for two years. I'll strangle you with an electrical wire.'

Although he'd never been to a sneak yet, Peter knew what the cards were: the all-important verdict from the only true judge, the live non-industry audience. Yes, I would recommend it to a friend. No, I would not. The minute the card results were tallied the studio accountants started charting their profit projections – the 'ultimates'.

'You've never been to a sneak,' Max said. 'You don't know how important it is – it's opening night. It's more opening night than opening night!' He was shouting now, waving his arms around the little car. 'That's the night you know, the first time an audience sees it. That's the night that everything is for!'

'Okay, okay,' Peter said. He was taking the curves so hard his tires gave off blue smoke. Every now and then Max stiff-armed the dashboard. Although it wasn't completely dark yet, Peter could already smell the night-blooming jasmine, sweet as a pretty girl on prom night. It was going to be another perfect night. God, he thought, how beautiful it is, up here in the hills. It really is paradise.

'I'm going to miss the goddamn screening,' Max said. 'It's your fault. You started all this. I blame *you*. In fact, I'm going to hire you back just so I can *fire* you again.'

They were just passing the upscale mini-mall near the top of the canyon, just before the intersection with Mulholland. Then Max suddenly slammed his hand down on the dashboard. '*STOP!*' he shouted.

'What?' Peter said, looking around half-convinced he'd hit something, or at least passed a hidden cop.

'*Stopppp!*' Max shouted again. 'Turn *around*.'

Peter did as he was told. As he straightened out the car, he figured out what Max was up to: a man hobbling along the sidewalk on a pair of crutches. The handicapped parking was all used up, evidently. Max leaned out the window.

'Hey, how're you doing?' Max said. Without waiting for an

answer, he continued: 'I'm kind of in a jam, will you help me out?
I need to borrow your crutches.'

The man stopped, looking at Max like he was crazy.

'It's a long story and we're in a hurry,' Max said, 'but basically
I broke my leg and something came up and I had to leave my
wheelchair behind and now I need some crutches.'

The man shook his head, more in amazement than refusal. He was
about forty, bearded, a crazy glint in his eye. Another Los Angeles
eccentric.

'I'll give you five hundred dollars,' Max said.

'Nope.'

A rich eccentric.

'One thousand.'

The man shook his head. 'Don't think so.'

'Five thousand.'

The man studied him. 'Who are you, anyway?' he finally said.

Max told him, and the man laughed.

'What's so funny?' Max said.

'I'm a screenwriter,' the man said.

'Of *course* you are,' Max shouted. 'You're hobbling along
Mulholland Drive on a pair of crutches. Only a fucking writer
would be that stupid.'

'You want my crutches?' the writer said. 'They'll cost you ten
grand.'

'Seven-five and I'll read one of your fucking scripts.'

The writer laughed and pointed at Peter. 'You'd just have him read
it,' he said. Peter felt insulted. 'Besides, you'd never make one of my
stories,' he said with a sneer. 'They're written for adults.'

'Okay, ten grand,' Max said. 'Hand 'em through the window.'

The man did, propping himself up with a hand on the roof of the
car.

'Call my secretary, she'll have a check cut,' Max said. Then he
looked up at the man, and in an instant his face changed from
neutral to pure contempt. 'I can tell you right now, without reading
a fucking word you've written, that you're a failure. You've always
been a failure. And you'll always be a failure. And the pathetic part
is, you'll never figure out why.'

The screenwriter leaned in the window, almost into Max's face.
'Fuck you, Fischer,' he said.

For a moment Max just looked back, expressionless. Then he grinned. 'I saw it in two minutes. And you will *never figure it out.*'

The screenwriter's knuckles turned white. 'Okay, smartass. Tell me. Why am I such a failure?'

Even across Max, Peter could smell the booze.

'You should have taken seven-five and the read,' Max said. He jabbed his finger at the road. Peter put the car in gear.

'Hey,' the screenwriter called out. 'How am I going to get to my car?'

'*Crawl,*' Max said, hitting Peter in the shoulder.

Peter pulled out, and when he straightened out of his U-turn he looked back in the rearview mirror and saw the screenwriter hopping up and down on one foot.

Max was right. He should have taken the seven-five.

They turned into West's driveway, pushed the buzzer on the metal stalk outside the gate. And again. And again.

'Shouldn't we get out and sneak around?' Max said.

Peter was about to give up when a male voice answered. 'Hello?'

'Max Fischer to see Mr West,' Peter said.

'Maaax, come in, come in.'

It was Jennings, answering his own intercom. That showed you right off that something was screwy. As they pulled the car into the driveway West came out, wearing the usual white Sansabelt pants and Pat Boone shoes, followed by a middle-aged woman who looked like she had just stepped out of a Tidy Bowl commercial. Behind the woman was a very beautiful young girl. She wore clumsy teenage makeup and a quaint plaid skirt, but the raw material was extraordinary: long legs, *Playboy* quality breasts, a fresh and perfect face . . .

West had his hand out, a big smile on his face. 'Meed Jean Amari and her lovely daughder Pamela,' he said. He sounded like his nose was packed with chewing gum. 'This is Max Fischer, dhu producer. *Blood Hund* was his movie.'

Jean seemed very impressed, and Pamela smiled as if she were posing for a picture, as if she weren't really there but had sent her face to represent her.

'We can't stay,' Max said. 'We were just looking for Tracy. Have you seen her?'

'Dhracy, lovely girl. Haven't seen her for hours. Come in come in, I was just taking Pamela to dry on some cosdumes. Jean came all the

way from Ohio to bring her to me for a screen dest. Isn'd she lovely,
Max – maybe you can use her too. In one of your movies.'

With that West started leading Pamela into the house, and Peter
thought: Better drop some breadcrumbs, kiddo.

'Let's go,' Max whispered.

'Let me take a quick look around,' Peter said.

Discreetly, Jean pretended to be interested in the jungle ferns.

Then Max gave in and threw open the car door and got the
crutches under his arms, explaining that yes, he'd broken the
damn thing walking, hit a patch of slippery pavement and just
went down, it was an amazing thing but there you were. He urged
Jean through the door, into the living room. 'So . . . you're here
from Ohio?'

'Utah, actually.'

'Ah. Utah.'

'Pamela and I just love movies. We go to the festival at Park
City every year – even see the documentaries. Last year we met
Mr West and he said if we were ever in Hollywood to just come
on down . . .'

Max took a hand off his crutch and patted Peter on the shoulder.
'Peter, why don't you go see what's keeping Jennings?' Then he
turned back to Jean. 'I'm sure Utah is much more beautiful than
anything you'll find here,' he said.

Jean looked doubtful. 'What was the movie you made?'

Peter hurried through the house, opening doors, ready to say 'Oh
there you are' or 'Sorry, just looking for Jennings,' depending on
what he saw. But the whole place was empty. The library was
empty, the thousands of old hardback books mute on the shelves.
The bathrooms were empty. The extra bedrooms were empty. The
office and the screening room were empty. West must have sent his
girls out to Disneyland or something. Finally he headed out back
past the pool, toward West's secret lair. The door was closed. His
knock got no answer. He knocked again, then tried the handle.

Unlocked. He could hear sounds, rustling, a creak.

Was that a slap?

He threw open the door . . .

. . . and saw young Pamela bent over the arm of the sofa,
her schoolgirl's skirt thrown up, her hands clutching the mink as
West drove into her from behind.

'Me boyo,' West said, not the least upset by the intrusion.

Pamela looked up at him, but she didn't seem perturbed either. She just took note of the new development as if it were another curious feature of show biz.

Frozen in the doorway, Peter felt a tingle race across his skin, arousal sending out its scouts: This child is ready for anything. 'Jesus Christ,' he said.

West grinned.

'Where's Tracy?' Peter asked. 'Where did she go?'

'She left with your little friend, Leela,' West answered. He kept right on grinning, the happiest Peter had ever seen him. All the trouble had fled his eyes, replaced with a boyish delight that made him look years younger. He stared at the mirror behind the bed, watching himself with glazed concentration. Pamela stared in the same mirror, watching West watch himself, mesmerized. Peter looked at the mirror too. The reflection bounced to the mirrors on the closet doors and then right back, multiplying West and Pamela – and Peter too – until there were enough of them to populate a world. 'Ain'd life grand?' West said.

'But Jennings,' Peter pleaded, 'her *mom* is out there.'

West's grin got wider. 'Come on, Peter,' he said. 'Don't you think she knows?'

Back in the car, Max grumbled. 'We wasted twenty minutes. It's *starting* now. Where are you going?'

Peter didn't answer. He was going to Leela's apartment in the Valley, and nothing Max said about it mattered anymore. His wheels hit sand and slid, but he caught the road again and hung a left at Laurel Canyon and roared down the hill toward Ventura. It took him just under ten minutes to find the apartment building, a fifties stucco box built around the usual courtyard, with a few palm trees and a boomerang-shaped sign outside that said LANAI COURT. Peter started to run.

'Wait for me,' Max hissed.

Impatient, but glad Max was coming along, Peter helped him out of the car and onto his crutches.

'Did you ever hear the old gag about the associate producer?' Max whispered.

'No.'

'He's the only one who will associate with the producer.'

They hurried into the courtyard, following the numbers until they got to number twelve. The curtains were pulled, and the TV was on.

'If you'd been doing your job we'd have guns,' Max hissed. 'You didn't *anticipate*.'

'Sssshh,' he said.

There was a crack of light in the center of the curtains. Max bumped Peter aside, pushed his head through the leaves and looked. 'Girl on the sofa,' he said.

'Tracy?'

'Can't tell.'

'She okay?'

'She's not moving.'

Peter pulled Max away and took a look for himself. He could see the room, lit by the flickering gray of the TV screen. A woman lay on her back, as if watching the TV, the back of her head facing the window. Her hair was black.

Then his eyes went to the video. A cartoon fire raged through a cartoon forest, squirrels and owls and deer ran: *Bambi*. It couldn't be Tracy. And come to think of it, the hair was wrong. Although with Tracy it was hard to keep track.

In the courtyard, a door opened. 'Hello?' someone said.

Quickly, Peter moved to the door and knocked. A minute later Leela looked through the eye hole and opened the door, looking sleepy. 'Peter,' she said, happily, pushing a black lock behind an ear.

'Can we come in for a sec?'

She opened the door, and Peter entered, followed by Max. They stood awkwardly.

'Great movie,' Max said.

Leela looked embarrassed. 'It's my favorite. From when I was a kid? That and *Gone With The Wind*.'

'It's awesome,' Max agreed. 'People forget. They think it's a kid's movie – but look at this! He stops! Looks around! Flames! Destruction! *Look at this*!'

They all watched Bambi hesitate at the waterfall.

'He jumps!' Max said.

And Bambi and his bride jumped, soaring out over the flames.

'What a shot,' Max said.

'You missed the fight scene, when he fights with the other deer?' Leela said. 'That always gets me so . . .' She laughed at herself. 'My heart *pounds*.'

'And the *wolves*,' Max said.

'And the wolves,' Leela repeated, nodding.

'It's an *action* movie,' Max said.

'Do you guys want to sit down?' Leela asked.

Max looked at the sofa, then at the TV again, thinking about it.

'We're looking for Tracy,' Peter said. 'Seen her?'

'She just left? Before I put on the movie?'

'Where was she going?'

Leela shook her head, slow and solemn: Can't help you there.

On the TV screen, Bambi dragged himself, half-dead, onto the island. 'It's got so much *force* in it,' Max said, almost wistfully. Then, as if *Bambi* had reminded him what was important in life, Max looked at his watch. 'Jesus Christ, do you know what time it is? We missed the whole fucking screening.'

'You have no idea? Not even a hint?'

Leela shook her head, smiling apologetically. She wanted to please, really she did.

'What did she want?'

Leela shrugged.

Max was already heading out the door, posting along on the crutches. 'I don't care who kills who,' he said. 'My ass is outta here. I gotta get those cards before Kramer does.'

'It was nice meeting you again,' Leela called after Max, meaning it. But Max was gone.

They pulled up outside the Culver Theater and Peter set the emergency brake, leaving the car running right there in front of the marquee. They got inside just in time to catch the end. To Peter's complete surprise, the whole sequence – including the new footage of hands banging on the door and breaking through the window – now took place in agonizing slow motion. So this was Max's big idea. And agonizing was definitely the right word: when Juliet took that first slice across her throat, the audience gasped, and with each cut after that they moaned like whipped dogs. Ah! Ah! Ah! Then the film was over and, in dead silence, the audience members filled out their cards. Max and Peter stood frozen in the back, while the

Columbia brass huddled on the opposite side, whispering intently.

The audience started filing out, handing their cards to ushers. They seemed dazed. When the stream became a trickle, Max ordered: 'Grab the cards.'

Peter ran up to each usher and used his most official voice to demand the cards. Only one hesitated, looking at his baseball outfit and wind-crazed hair, but Peter pointed to Max. 'That's Max Fischer. I'm his assistant.' And even though Max looked almost as bedraggled as Peter did, with his crutches and his shirttail out and the sweat heavy on his red forehead, the usher couldn't hand over the cards fast enough. When Peter had collected all the cards, he took the boxes to Max.

'Let's go,' Max said.

At that moment the Columbia executives came into the lobby to collect the cards, and Kramer caught sight of them. 'Max! Max!'

But Max started swinging away on the crutches, the Tarzan of the Trauma Ward, muttering curses every time his good foot hit the ground, and Peter ran behind him carrying the boxes. They left the car running at the curb and hustled for the studio lot across the street, leaving the puzzled executives on the sidewalk, and lurched through the brand-new studio gates, under the SONY sign.

'*Hi-yo, Peter*!' Max shouted, as they ducked past the cafeteria and then down Myrna Loy. Peter could hear Max huffing, but when he slowed down Max just snapped: '*Hurry, hurry*!' At last they made the office. Peter could feel a cold burn in his throat: out of breath. '*Lock the door*!' Max ordered.

Funny, the light was on. Peter thought he heard something scurrying. But Max was already sweeping his desk clean and waving him over.

'Dump 'em,' Max ordered. 'And get a calculator.'

Peter upturned a box, spilling the cards. Each card had a row of boxes labeled 'excellent', 'very good', 'good', 'fair', and 'poor'. Max grabbed a handful, and they both started counting. '*Yes*!' he said. 'Excellent, would recommend, young male. Here's another: excellent, would recommend, young male. Here's an excellent, would recommend, young male. You got any females? Thirty-five-and-overs?'

'I got three females eighteen to thirty-four,' Peter said, almost panting. He was punching the calculator and sorting the cards by gender and rating – a pile of 'male, excellent', another for 'female, very good', and so on. 'Very good. Excellent. Very good. And five more young males, all excellent.'

Max was reading the cards and tossing them aside, his voice as giddy and delighted as Peter had ever heard it. 'Excellent, would recommend, would recommend, would recommend.'

After another ten minutes, the only question was whether 'the number' would end up in the upper or lower nineties.

'Do you know what this *means*?' Max said. 'A picture with cards in the nineties, if it opens at ten it'll break a hundred. Guaranteed. The ultimates will be two, two fifty when you count cable and foreign and all the ancillaries.'

Peter frowned. 'Female thirty-five and over, poor.'

Max frowned, grabbing the edge of the desk and pulling himself up to his feet. He waited that way while Peter finished working the calculator. Then Peter looked up at him, keeping his face neutral. 'What? What? What?'

Peter took one last pause before answering. 'Ninety-seven,' he said.

Max smiled. It was a smile Peter had never seen before, beatific and relaxed. 'This is what it's all about,' Max said, with a satisfied sigh. 'This night. You work for years, and then the first test screening comes and you find out if you just wasted all that time and work or if you're the king. There's nothing like it.'

Peter kept stacking the cards as Max sat back down and did a little dance of triumph in his chair, swiveling around and bobbing from side to side Stevie Wonder-style. 'Isn't it *great*? Isn't it *amazing*? Come on, tell me – it's great, right?'

'It's great.'

'It's amazing, right?'

'It's amazing.'

'Did you see how they looked, coming out of the theater. They were *stunned*. They were hammered. We *nailed those fuckers to their seats*! Wasn't it awesome?'

Even in his triumph, Max was so needy it was exhausting. But tonight Peter had needs of his own. 'What about Tracy?' he asked.

Max shook his head abruptly, as if someone had just poured a bucket of water on his head. 'She'll be all right,' he said.

But the giddy moment had passed, and for a moment neither of them spoke. Max flipped through a stack of cards. When he spoke again, his voice was reflective. 'I don't understand that whole world – Angie, West, all these whores. I mean, what's the point?' He stayed reflective for another second or two, then started to warm up again. 'For me it's like the whipped-cream bikini. Did I ever tell you how that started? When I was a kid I was in this hospital, and I saw a picture in this magazine, *Playboy* or something, of this girl. She was posed like one of those Vargas girls, that old cheesecake style, with her legs drawn up a little and her ankles crossed, smiling at the camera, and all she was wearing was whipped cream. You could almost see a nipple poking through. And I just thought that was the sexiest thing in the world. For *years* I dreamed about that woman. And you know what?'

'What?'

'When I got older, and made some money, I got this girl to do it for me, put whipped cream all over her body. And I just got sick. I mean, it was nauseating. I must have gained ten pounds. The point is, sometimes things are much sexier if you *don't* see it but *think* you do, if a picture *releases* your imagination.'

Max lurched down the room, trying to pace on crutches. 'That's why Tracy hates me so much. She never understood that I had things to do. I didn't have time for her. She was a child, anyway. And her father was the same way. We had *things to do*.'

Peter looked at the stacks. The men's nineties were three times higher than the eighties, and the women's cards weren't so bad either. The wouldn't recommends were just a bump.

'But you didn't do a whipped cream bikini this time,' Peter said. 'That slo-mo was brutal. Like a medical training film.'

Max nodded, his eyes to the floor. 'Tracy inspired me,' he said.

Peter remembered his visit to the Dick Donner set, when it struck him how goofy it was to arrange all these actors and sets and lights in front of a camera. It would be an essay someday, how so much great human enterprise was given over to tombs, from the pyramids to the Taj Mahal, and how the movies marshaled all their strange iconographic power into arranging the corpse of a moment for camera and then – like Faust – saying to the moment, stop. But wasn't that why Faust got sent to hell? Wasn't there more to life than arranging people in front of cameras? 'So maybe you do love her a little bit?' Peter wondered. Max didn't answer. 'Or was it Marina?'

Max swung around, suddenly angry. 'You're not *listening to me*! I've spent my life on movie sets, eating food from Craft Services! That's my life!'

'Not much of a life,' Peter said.

'Not *for you*,' Max exploded. 'You don't love my movies. What did you call them? – adolescent fantasies? Lurid prurience? Blah blah blah? Why do you think I *hired* you? You were smart, but you didn't *see*. I thought I could help you *see* . . .'

He swept the cards off his desk, along with the lamp, pen set and the video remote controls. 'But you don't want to see what I see! You want to make art! You want respect! I say *fuck* art! *Fuck* respect! I don't want to *impress* the audience! I want them to fall in *love*!'

Peter heard the sound of truth and was startled by a sudden recognition: Max wasn't really ambitious. In his own confused way, Peter was more ambitious. He wanted life to yield some meaning.

Then they heard something banging, inside Max's private bathroom. Someone thudding against the wall.

Followed by a gunshot.

Peter moved first, grabbing the door and pulling it open. In the dark, two people struggled for a revolver. It looked like . . . Tracy.

And Marlon Spurlock.

Spurlock drove an elbow into Tracy's belly, tearing the gun loose. Peter dove for his hand but at that moment Tracy doubled over and their heads bumped together, hard. Both of them cried out. When they looked up again, Spurlock had stepped behind the desk and trained the gun at Max.

'*Move*, Max,' he said.

'You mean "Don't move", don't you Marlon?'

'He's a psycho,' Tracy cried. 'He was gonna kill me on your desk.'

'I have a gun!'

'But you still can't get your dialogue right,' Max shouted. ' "Move." What a schmuck. "*Move*."'

'I can't believe you're ridiculing me. I have a gun.'

'You *always* got things wrong,' Max ranted. 'That's why I fired you. You're a *moron*.'

'Max,' Peter said, soothingly.

Spurlock's jaw worked. Sweat popped out of his pores in beads the size of pearls, and he was albino pale. 'I think I'm going to kill you now.'

'You wouldn't dare.'

Spurlock looked hurt. 'Maybe I'll give Peter the gun, and he can shoot you.'

Peter chuckled, friendly and reassuring: Now that's a great idea, Marlon, old pal. Hand the gun right over here.

'That's *funny*?' Max said.

'We could sell tickets,' Spurlock continued, giggling. 'We could have a raffle. You want to shoot him, Tracy?'

'In the dick, maybe.'

'Very nice,' Max said.

They had to keep talking, give the security people time to react to the gunshots. Peter tried to think of something to say. 'You know, I really don't think I'm cut out for Hollywood,' he said.

Max looked outraged. 'Now he tells me.'

'I thought I was. I thought it would be the perfect place for me. The movie business. But it's not, is it? The movie business? It's the revenge business. That's the business you guys are in.'

'And I was gonna forgive you,' Max said, as if his last illusion had fallen.

An explosion ripped through the room. Chunks of plaster came down from the ceiling.

'*Excuse* me,' Spurlock said, waving the gun . . . which was, in fact, smoking. Dutifully, they all looked at him. From outside they could hear the sound of guards running around, calling out to each other.

'Marlon,' Max said. 'For the record, I want you to know – you sucked. You were a terrible assistant, and a terrible president too. I promoted you to get you out of my life. Peter was much better.'

Spurlock glared at him, aiming the gun again.

'But before you shoot me, just tell me – why'd you kill Marina?'

Spurlock nodded, as if accepting that Max deserved that much. 'She was reaching for the phone,' he said.

'What?'

'She was going to call the cops. She was going to tell them.'

His gun hand was shaking. The guards were banging on the door now. Max had locked it to keep the Columbia execs out.

'Tell them what?'

Spurlock looked like he was about to cry. 'She lied to me. She said she'd meet with Barry, talk to the cops. She said she was going to make it happen for me. But then she changed her mind. She said that I was a putz and she was going to tell them . . .'

'Tell them what?'

His face twisted, like a child about to break out in a howl of tears. 'That she was with *you*. The night of the rape. So you couldn't have done it. She was going to be your alibi.'

'So you *killed* her?'

Spurlock dropped his head. 'I didn't mean to,' he said, in a small voice.

'You hate me that much?'

THUNK! THUNK! They'd found some kind of battering ram, they were banging down the door. Spurlock whipped his head to look, then whipped it back. 'It was a *lie*,' he said. 'She was going to *lie* for you. To get you off the hook. So you'd get away with raping Tracy.' He gave Tracy a sad, affectionate look, and seemed about to cry over the injustice of it all.

'But she wasn't lying,' Max said, gently. 'She was with me that night.'

Spurlock sneered. 'You think I'm stupid? Why didn't you just tell that to the cops?'

Max looked like he could kick himself. 'I didn't want Tracy to know. It would have upset her.'

Spurlock looked from Max to Tracy.

'It wasn't like it was some big thing with Marina,' Max continued. 'She'd been calling and calling me, so much I had the phone turned off. She had this loony obsession that I was going to be overwhelmed by a sexual experience with her. Something about things she had learned in Japan, I don't know. Then Peter left, and I wasn't sleepy, and . . . I turned it back on.'

'What about after she was dead?' Tracy demanded. 'Why didn't you tell Spinks the truth then?'

Max stared at Tracy. 'I thought you did it.'

Tracy stared back at him. 'So you went through all that, the publicity, the scandal, going to jail . . . for *me*?'

Max shrugged. 'I know it doesn't fit your conception of me.'

Tracy started to laugh.

Spurlock's eyes bulged. This was too much for him. If it wasn't a lie, then . . . what had he done? He shouted – at Max, at the ceiling, at the heavens: '*Then who was the rapist?*'

Max and Tracy both turned their eyes toward Peter. Spurlock cocked his head, trying to find the answer to this mystery in Peter's face . . . he waved the gun . . .

THUNK! THUNK! THUNK!

Peter took a deep breath. Crazed as Spurlock was right now, it might be his last.

Spurlock waved the gun again. 'Well?'

Peter looked over at Tracy again. There was cynicism in her eyes, as if she was ready for one more betrayal. He realized he had never really apologized for what he did. He still didn't think of it as rape, unless there was a sex-crime equivalent to justifiable homicide . . .

THUNK! THUNK! THUNK!

But Tracy's lips were going tight, thinned by disappointment. She *felt* raped, that was clear. Or at least violated. And did it really matter how he explained it, if that was how she felt?

THUNK! THUNK!

Then it occurred to him for the first time that the phone sex routine wasn't really aimed at punishing Max, it was intended to punish *him*. To make him choose between them. To make him fight Max. 'I guess it was me,' he said.

'You *guess*?' Spurlock said.

Peter looked at Tracy again. Was that a tear?

'It was me.'

Spurlock shook his head hard, his expression stunned and unbelieving. '*BUT WHHYYY?*' he asked, less a question than a howl against the malfunctioning universe. He aimed the gun at Peter and shook it and repeated the howl, and Peter tried to think . . . he deserved an answer . . . they all did . . .

'You want to know why?'

The gun trembled.

And then the answer came. Peter shrugged, one assistant to another, at the joke of life: 'I'd just been with Max.'

A laugh cracked out of Spurlock: 'Ha!'

THUNK! THUNK!

'He was yelling at me for hours. You know what that's like.'

'Ha!'

'Trashing me.'

'Ha!'

'I was . . . wound up.'

'Ha! Ha! Ha!' The oddly mechanical laugh built up slowly, then exploded, and Peter realized he was listening to the sound of Spurlock losing his mind. He finished more for his own sake than for anything else: 'I guess I just wasn't feeling too human.'

Then the door came crashing down. Feet skittered in the hall, then stopped inside the door. 'Freeze!' someone called.

Spurlock swung the gun at Max. He straightened his elbow, and held his wrist police-style. 'Moment of truth,' he said.

Max drew himself up, striking the courageous pose . . . and then he changed his mind. 'Marlon, we can still make some chicken salad here,' he said. 'I'll option your story, you can write the script. You'll have to go to jail for a while, but the publicity will be *great* . . .'

That just started Spurlock laughing again. He squinted down the gun barrel . . .

And something big and dark crashed through the window, throwing glass shards everywhere. It was some kind of duffel bag, followed by Detective Patty Spinks, come to get her man. Startled, Spurlock wheeled upwards and his gun went off. Spinks fell to the ground. As the cops and security guards partly visible through the shredded window hesitated, Spurlock aimed the gun at Max. His finger squeezed the trigger – and Peter jumped, without a thought, pure reflex, hit Max with his shoulder, and as they went down he saw Tracy slap at the gun and heard the explosion, loud as dynamite. Immediately it started to fade and then from a very long distance off Peter heard screaming – closer and closer and then rushing right up to his ear, like a train down a tunnel. Then he realized it was Max, screaming and squirming underneath him: 'My *leg*! You're *on my fucking leg*!'

Tracy and Spurlock rolled on the floor, fighting for the gun, and bodies kept coming through the window and the door. It was just like the end of Max's movie, slow motion and all. Peter felt wet and wondered if he'd wet his pants, and since he had an infinite amount of time, he decided to send his fingers down in that direction just to check things out. They came back up red, which was strange. Blood in his urine? And there was so much noise. And people running around. Someone should take charge of things. In a minute Peter would say something.

But it was too hot. It would be much nicer outside, where it was cool.

Peter got up and stepped right through the window, which wasn't there anymore. He was right, the night was very cool. California nights were always cool. He stumbled around, glad to be alive, breathing deep for the smell of jasmine, which always made him feel like he was in the land of milk and money. Ha ha. And that was when he felt it, like someone was twisting a broken beer bottle in his gut. He touched his hand to his belly again and held it up to his nose. It smelled faintly metallic.

Time to blow this town.

He staggered down the alley, but before long he started to feel faint, so he pushed open the nearest door. Above it was the sign that read DO NOT OPEN WHILE LIGHT IS RED. It was a very heavy door. Inside it was very dark. Peter did not want to sit in the dark. That was important, not to sit in the dark. So he fumbled around until he found a switch and flipped it – and immediately the entire universe turned a brilliant electric blue.

It took him a moment to realize that he hadn't died and gone to heaven but was standing in front of a giant bluescreen. It was Donner's soundstage, where so long ago he and that nice young man named after an actor had a nice chat. But the bluescreen wasn't lit then. Now it was. It was seamless and luminescent, the high-tech kind that glowed from within, the better to light up the objects in the foreground, and it seemed almost mystical, like a chunk of moon brought down and displayed here in secret.

Peter staggered to the table, its rough wooden surface all set up with carpenter's tools. They were building spaceships here, or designing stars. He didn't want to mess them up, so he sat down on the floor, leaning against the leg of the table, and waited to die. It would be good to die here in the glowing blue light.

But something was dangling against his face, tickling him. He pushed it away.

It came back.

So he pulled on it, and a big old studio telephone came crashing down on his head. Great, he thought. Story of my life – about to die and I get brained by a fucking telephone . . .

Then he got an idea. He started to laugh but then he choked it back, because that guy with the beer bottle was at work again, rolling up Peter's guts like spaghetti on a fork.

When the pain passed Peter dragged the phone close, then stuck the receiver against his ear and dialed. Amazing that he remembered the number.

'Hello?'

'Please hold for Max Fischer,' he said.

He switched to the other line and dialed quickly. 'Max Fischer,' he said. 'It's an emergency.'

'He's . . .'

'I know. Tell him he wants to take this call. Tell him it's Barry Rose.'

Max's voice came on. 'What the fuck do you want?'

Peter pushed the conference call button. 'Hello?' Max said. 'Hello?'

'Max?'

'What do you want?'

'You called me.'

Max didn't respond right away. When he spoke again, his voice was breezy, indifferent. 'We had a little excitement here,' he said. 'Turns out Marlon Spurlock was moonlighting as a psycho killer.' He explained what had happened, his voice getting graver as he went along. 'Tracy's here,' he added, almost gently. 'She's okay.'

'Put her on,' Rose ordered.

'I didn't rape her, you know.'

Rose hesitated. 'The cops were here earlier,' he said, grudgingly. 'Looking for Marlon.'

'Your buddy Marlon,' Max said.

'Your protégé.'

It was a standoff. But then Rose gave in. 'Can I talk to Tracy now?' he asked. 'Please?'

It was as close to an apology as Max was likely to get. 'She went out looking for Peter James,' Max said. 'The idiot wandered off with a hole in his belly.' He paused for a second, so the timing was right. 'After getting blood all over me.'

They chuckled together.

'Heard the movie went well,' Rose said.

'Fantastic,' Max said.

'What's the number?'

'Ninety-seven.'

'Congratulations.'

'Thanks.'

'Well . . .'

'Yeah,' Max said.

'Max?'

'Yeah?'

Rose hesitated. 'I thought you did it,' he said.

Max hesitated just as long. 'I know,' he said

'We could have lunch . . .'

'Sure,' Max said.

'Or not.'

'No, let's.'

'Okay.'

'Okay.'

'The Palm?'

'I'll have Peter call you,' Max said.

Rose laughed, and Max laughed with him. Peter heard the affection and the relief, and put the phone down. Now I understand, he thought. At last I understand: They *love* each other. *That's* why they hate each other. And it was the same with Max and Tracy and Tracy and Marina and probably even Angie and Meursault. They each found the person who was the thing they wanted to be and opened themselves, gave themselves like a lover or an artist or a saint, but then as they learned the secrets and gained strength they started to hate the one they loved, because the love that opened them also made them weak. And they had *things to do*.

He heard a distant buzzing. 'Hey, Peter! Peter!'

It was a tiny voice coming from the phone in his lap. He hadn't hung it up. He lifted it to his ear.

'Where the fuck are you? Everybody's out looking for you.'

It was Max. You couldn't fool Max. Doubtless he'd played the telephone game himself, probably taught it to Spurlock in the first place. Peter looked up at the bluescreen, glowing like nothing on this world. He chuckled again, and it didn't hurt so bad this time. 'I'm in New York, Max – No, make that Paris. I'm in Paris.'

'Look, forget all the crap I said. I don't know what I'm blabbering about half the time. I want you to come back to work. Everything forgiven.'

'Tokyo, Max.'

You don't know who you are, Tracy said. You don't know what you want. He should go, it was the right thing to do. Go find himself.

'I'll make you vice-president,' Max said. 'Vice-president of Fischer Pictures, how does that sound? Let's make some *movies*.'

'Jeez, Max, I'm bleeding here. How about president?'

'Don't get greedy,' Max barked. 'For president you actually have to *die*.'

Peter was too tired to laugh. 'Okay, Max,' he said, putting down the phone. 'You win.'

And a thought flashed through his head, too quick to stop – too bad there isn't some film on me. If I have to actually die, that is. He frowned. A tiny buzzing hornet voice wanted to know where he was, but he ignored it as he tried to catch the fleeting thought. He pictured them shooting him, all the gaffers and soundmen and DPs and ADs and focus-pullers ringed around in a circle, staring at him, concentrated as lovers or surgeons . . . oh, shit, he was wrong, he'd been *wrong*. Movies weren't necrophilia at all, not visual fetishism or objectification, not old Faust saying to the moment, stop . . . well, they *were* . . . but they were also *love* . . . they stopped the moment because they *loved* the moment . . . and even if they killed the moment by stopping it, there was still love . . . even if it got all twisted sometimes . . . and the truth was . . . the truth was . . . he was going to *miss* it . . . all of it . . . Mad Max and Tormented Tracy and decadent old Madame Meursault and the Nurses and Cheerleaders and Schoolteachers and Co-eds and Schoolgirls and Prostitutes, and Potter bent over his digital editing machine, and that genial pervert Jennings West bent over the lovely Pamela, even shrewd old Barry Rose scheming Max's downfall . . . he was going to miss all of it . . .

It wasn't fair. Why did he have to choose one or the other? Why couldn't he have *both*?

Peter let out a weak chuckle. It was just what Max would say. His head started swimming and rolling, dizzy with ideas and images . . . Tracy in bed that first night, so white . . . the blood on her neck like a scarf . . . and she was right all along, wasn't she? He did rape her. Even if he never would have waited in the bushes with a knife, the fact was that in the moment of truth he wanted what he wanted, to hell with how she felt . . . but she was wrong about the percentage, he wasn't ever ninety-two percent good, he was closer to fifty-fifty . . . both . . . in that thin blue robe, smoking a cigarette . . . he chuckled again, even though it hurt like hell . . . he was just another fucking lunatic, that was the answer, no better than the rest, more Hollywood than he ever imagined. But why did the thought make him so happy?

He could relax now. He could rest. Leela watching *Bambi*, and he could rest . . . and the moon over Malibu, lighting a silver path along the water . . .

A path along the water . . .

He was just closing his eyes when he heard the door scrape open.

'Peter?'

'Ohhh,' he said.

Tracy was down on the floor next to him, pulling his limp body into her arms. Her other hand was grabbing at the phone, punching the numbers.

'You jerk,' she said.

Without protesting, he slumped into her body. She felt so soft, and she smelled like jasmine. Yes, it was jasmine. The night-blooming jasmine of the Hollywood Hills. It smelled so sweet. There was nothing sweeter.

Tracy finished telling Max where to find them and hung up the phone. Then she took his face in her free hand and turned it toward her own. She wasn't exactly being gentle.

Then she leaned down and kissed him.

'Ouch,' he said.

She was smiling at him, smiling down at him like nothing he had seen on this earth. Tears had washed away the mascara.

'I guess there's no way I can get you people to just leave me alone,' he said.

'Quiet, idiot,' she said, kissing him again. 'You asked for it.'

Epilogue

When Peter woke up, Max was in the bed next to him, sitting up and teasing an extra piece of cake out of the food lady. She was weakening. 'It's not very good for your heart, Mr Fischer,' she said.

'I'm a producer,' Max said. 'I don't *have* a heart – ask Peter.'

'He's not lying,' Peter croaked. His throat was beyond parched, but a glass of orange juice sat right there on the table. Was this a dream? A nightmare? Was the orange juice real? If he reached out, would his hand pass through it?

He decided to wait. If the orange juice was just an illusion, he didn't want to know.

Then Tracy came in, tossing a pile of newspapers and magazines on the side of the bed. 'Picked these up at the office. Thought you'd enjoy 'em,' she said.

Max looked at Peter, Peter looked at Max, then they both looked at Tracy. 'Your flunky is kind of incapacitated,' she said.

Max gave one businesslike nod, accepting the explanation, then turned to the media pile. Tracy or Sarah had marked the relevant pages with paper clips. 'I made *The Toronto Star*?'

'You're famous,' Tracy said. She followed Peter's eyes and walked over, picked up the orange juice and put the straw in his mouth. It was real. It was sweet.

Max read: ' "Crimes of the Heart: The Saga of a Hollywood Bad Boy." And they call *me* unoriginal. What's in the *Post*?'

'New York or Washington?'

'New York, for God's sake.'

Tracy found the right *Post* and read the headline: ' "HE RAPED HER!" '

'Not their best,' Max said. 'Ring for the nurse, will you? I need some more juice in here.'

'Me too,' Peter croaked.

'You,' Max said. 'I should put you on bread and water. You crippled me. I'm a gimp because of you.'

'Good,' Peter said. 'I hope it hurts.'

Max looked a little surprised, but he didn't say anything. And Peter started to feel a little stronger. In a minute or two, he might even try sitting up.

Then he got another flash of what happened the night before. 'Hey, what happened to Spinks?'

'Just down the hall,' Tracy said. 'When she gets a little better they'll wheel her in, the three of you can play canasta.'

'Max would cheat,' Peter said.

'Listen to how he abuses me,' Max said.

And then they knew it, both of them: Things had changed. Peter had changed. Adjustments would have to be made.

'I think I'm going to need a new assistant,' Max grumbled.

'Me too,' Peter said.

Tracy looked from one to the other, then shook her head: what a pair, what a pair. 'Don't look at me,' she said. 'I've suffered enough.'

Then Dogosta came in, carrying a package under his arm, a pillow-sized square wrapped in brown paper. He took in the sight of Tracy, then Peter . . . then grunted and tossed a fax on the bed. 'This just in,' he said. He went to sit in a chair against the wall, holding the brown-paper package on his lap.

Max picked the fax up and sounded out the title, savoring it. ' "Tracy Rose's Truth Or Dare" By Kit Bradley.'

The Dog shot a surly glance at Peter. 'At least they didn't call it "Who Dicked Tracy?" ' he said.

Max ignored them, reading in silence, grunting occasionally. As he finished the pages he tossed them in Peter's direction. It was an odd piece, beginning with a surprisingly accurate description of events and then launching into a feminist critique of Hollywood: Even though the rape charge appeared to be untrue, Bradley wrote, Max and his movies were still part of a culture that demeaned and violated women on a daily basis. It wasn't just sexism. The problem was that actual filmmakers couldn't run Hollywood. They were too undependable, and Hollywood needed dependable 'software' above all, and since movies were almost impossible to make, the town made kings out of men like Max and Barry who had enough drive to corral the artists and money men and executives and technoids and unions and government bureaucrats and get the damn things from page to screen. Was it any wonder that the movies themselves tended to reflect their image? Art is *King Lear*, love is *the Great Gatsby* but Hollywood is always *Superman*.

Max finally spoke. 'I hate the last line.'

The last line was: 'Too bad they don't have a criminal charge for failure to act like a human being.'

Max brooded. 'And this feminist crap is just ridiculous. What am I supposed to do, feel guilty? "Sorry I won, here's all the money back? I will now dedicate the rest of my life to being a *pussy*?" '

He snorted, amused at how preposterous it was, and glared at Tracy as if it were her fault.

'But you are a pig,' Tracy said.

Max didn't seem insulted. If anything, he was pleased. 'I got my human side,' he said.

Peter managed a derisive snort. 'If you prick him, he will sue.'

Tracy laughed, a real laugh, little waterfall of pleasure, then dropped her eyes on Peter like a warm hand.

Max scowled.

Without a word, Dogosta got up and handed Max the package. Max tore it open. Inside were his bedsheets, dry-cleaned and folded. Look Ma, no spots. He looked at Tracy, ducking his head like an embarrassed boy. She walked over and held out a hand. 'I'll take those.'

Max handed them over. She walked to the trash can and dropped them in.

'That reminds me,' Max said, turning his head to Peter. 'Call Rippert up and tell him to send the files *here*.' Before Peter could respond, a woman poked her head around the door. 'Max?'

She was in her forties, a weathered blonde with a wise and gentle face. Max looked puzzled.

'I'm Vicky—' she began.

'Carver,' Max said. Now he seemed happy to see her. 'How are you, Vicky?'

She crossed to the bed, then stood a foot away from it, as if afraid to approach. 'I heard the awful things,' she said. 'I felt so bad for you. I didn't want to bother you. Then I heard about your accident and, well, you visit people in the hospital.'

She stopped, smiling shyly.

Max smiled and told Peter, 'Vicky played a nurse in my first movie.'

'It was my first job,' she said.

'What have you been doing? I heard you left the business.'

She started to tell him, but then an immense black face poked around the door, a human billboard advertising a tentative expression. 'Dude!' Max cried, delighted.

The black man broke into a smile, and Peter recognized him as the man on the prison bus, the one who had borrowed Max's cellular phone: Arizona. He came up to the bed and shook Max's hand. 'Yo,' he said. 'Fucked yourself up, huh?'

'Did you call that guy?' Max said.

'I start next week.'

Another knock on the door interrupted them, followed by another and another and another: an actor grateful for a first chance, a crew member Max put on the books during an illness, a screenwriter kept afloat with a development deal, a runner who left with a glowing recommendation, even a journalist whose work he had attacked, dismissed, reviled, and ridiculed so many times the poor guy finally gave up and went into a more respectable line of work. They all teased him about running too fast, falling off the fast track, speeding on foot, but underneath there seemed to be real affection. Flip Mosely came rolling through the door in his wheelchair, and Max greeted him like an old friend. 'We're going to do his movie!' he announced to everyone. 'Made the deal with Dreamworks this morning!' (To Peter he whispered: 'I'm going to let Jennings direct. He worked hard enough for it. His fee plus fifty thou.') And the calls poured in too – Ronnie and Jeffrey and Joel and Jon and Peter, Jerry, Terry, Andy, Dawn, Mario, Arnon, Bert and Jake, as well as several major distributors from the Far East. God bless 'em all. But there was something odd about the difference between the calls and the visits. Tracy was the first to notice. 'Isn't it kind of strange,' she said, with fake innocence, 'that nobody *more* powerful than you has actually come to visit.'

Max didn't like that. A beefy gaffer broke in conveniently. 'Max is the only guy in Hollywood who pisses *up*, not down,' he said.

That did it. The adulation was getting just a little out of control. 'Funny, I don't see any former *assistants* here,' Peter said.

Max gave him another scowl. 'I *ate* them all,' he said.

And then there was another knock on the door, and Yoji the architect poked his head in the room. 'Excuse,' he said, giving Max his discreet, Americanized bow. 'Hear you having accident. Bring present.' He handed over a box, nodding profusely.

Max unwrapped a layer of rough paper. Underneath was another layer of paper. And under that another, this time a delicate lime-colored membrane that looked like the wing of a dragonfly. And another, a crinkly metallic weave. When Max finally got to the little box in the middle he found a perfect fresh fig.

'I *love* this,' Max said.

The phone rang again. Tracy picked it up. 'Alan Kramer,' she said.

'Excuse me,' Max said to Yoji, holding up a finger. 'Alan, how's it going? You saw the cards? Pretty fucking fantastic, eh?' Max was grinning now, but looking at Peter and drawing a finger across his throat. After a few more pleasantries he put the phone down. 'In Hollywood,' he said, with a smile of satisfaction, like a gourmand who'd just finished the perfect meal, 'nothing ever changes.' Then he turned to Tracy.

'By the way, that lunch with your father? *Cancel* it.'

And finally he turned back to Yoji, who bowed again. 'I bulldoze house today,' he said.

'Huh?' Max said.

'Fireplace don't make you happy, fireplace go. Walls don't make you happy, walls go. Now I think house don't make you happy, so I make house go. Bulldoze whole thing.'

Finally he smiled and they realized he was joking. Max chuckled.

Yoji grinned bigger. 'Then you be unhappy with *ground*,' he said, reaching out and patting Max's injured foot.

Max winced and smiled at the same time. 'Good,' he said. 'Knock it down.'

The laughter began in a ripple and built to whitewater: class one, class two, class three. It was cultish laughter, Peter thought. Cultish was the word. So in his new (self-appointed) capacity as antifactotum and balloon puncturer he felt compelled to proffer his shiny new needle: 'And Max,' he drawled, with a quick and mischievous glance at Tracy, 'if self don't make you happy . . . I got a suggestion.'

Max looked over, eyes pinching. 'Peter,' he snapped, 'you can take that sug—, He stopped himself. Then he too looked over at Tracy, studying the new balance of power in her face. She gave him no signs, just watched, impassive as a judge. But Max sighed and softened his tone, shaking his head with *faux* sadness. 'I guess *job* don't make you happy.'

Peter smiled back. 'Too soon to tell.'

'Pity,' said Max. 'Because you know what?'

'What?'

'You're *fired*.'